The Staycation

Michele Gorman is a *USA Today* bestselling author and has sold nearly half a million copies globally across all formats, with seven novels published by Penguin Random House and HarperCollins. She was born in the US and now makes London home, writing comedies under her own name and cosy rom coms as Lilly Bartlett.

The
Staycation

Michele Gorman

TRAPEZE

First published in Great Britain in 2020 by Trapeze
an imprint of The Orion Publishing Group Ltd
Carmelite House, 50 Victoria Embankment
London EC4Y 0DZ

An Hachette UK Company

1 3 5 7 9 10 8 6 4 2

A CIP catalogue record for this book is
available from the British Library.

ISBN (Mass Market Paperback) 978 1 4091 9010 3
ISBN (eBook) 978 1 4091 9011 0

Typeset by Born Group
Printed and bound in Great Britain by Clays Ltd, Elcograf S.p.A.

www.orionbooks.co.uk

Chapter 1

Thursday

'Do you really have to do that?' Harriet glared, first at the nose, then at her husband attached to it. It was a fine one, as noses went. She'd probably adored it when they'd been young and in love, even paid it cutesy compliments. Now she wanted to fill it with the entire pot of muesli yogurt he was eating and watch it set like the quick-dry grout she'd used on the bathroom tiles last month.

'Do what, my darling?' James's smile beamed with pure adoration. Sod that Leo DiCaprio; she'd nominate James for an Oscar any day. *The winner of this year's Best Performance by a Husband in a Dicey Marriage category is: James Cooper, for the third year in a row!*

'That. Your nose is whistling.' She could hear it wheezing over the announcement of another flight cancellation. Athens, this time. 'It's annoying.'

'My breathing annoys you?'

'You're free to breathe, James. Just do it quietly.'

He shared a look with their daughter over the mountain of hand luggage on Harriet's lap.

Billie wouldn't tear her eyes from that bloody phone if Harriet's knickers were on fire, but for her dad? She was sympathy personified.

'Oh, don't you start too,' Harriet warned her.

Billie saluted, though her eyes drifted back to her screen. 'Not breathing, sir, sorry, sir.'

'Can you at least listen for an announcement instead of obsessing over your phone? Who are you emailing anyway?'

'Pfft. Emailing. Mum, you're ancient.'

James pointed his chin at the Departures board. 'We can see what's happening. Same thing that's been happening since we got here. It's delayed. They're all delayed. Even you can't do anything about that, so why not just relax? Besides, I'm sure with your hearing you'd pick up any announcements dead easy.'

'If your breathing doesn't drown it out.' She scanned the board. The Budapest flight was still showing a gate. That would be promising, if they were going there instead of Rome. 'Bloody ash cloud. Bloody volcano,' she mumbled.

James smiled at her. 'I wish I had a quid for every time that thing erupted.'

'You'd have three quid in the last two hundred years. I wouldn't make it your retirement plan. Best stick to your goats, Bill Gates.'

'This is fun,' Billie said. 'No, really, can we go on holiday together all the time?'

Harriet crossed her arms – not easy with a lapful of luggage – closed her eyes and tried to imagine being in Rome already. Apparently being happy and content was all in the mind. What was it again? Mindfulness? No, it was the other bollocks. Positive visualisation. That was it.

Breathing deeply, Harriet imagined all the whingeing was the happy buzz of fellow travellers savouring their coffee in an ancient cobbled square near the River Tiber. The algae-tinged scent of the water tumbled over garlicky cooking smells as they wafted from the al fresco restaurants. Those weren't passenger announcements but the distant zooming of the Vespas that carried Romans, young and old, about their business in the sun-drenched city. She could almost taste the delicate almondy crumbliness of the biscotti as she lifted it, after a perfect dunk, from her steaming cappuccino. Her film star glasses shielded her eyes but she could feel the sun warming her hair, picking out the highlights she'd begrudgingly paid over a hundred quid for. The knicker-squirmingly gorgeous man who'd been giving her bedroom eyes from the next table leaned over and said—

'Mum, I'm hungry. And crampy. I need something to eat. Have you got any paracetamol?'

Was it too much to ask for two minutes of *la dolce vita* in peace?

Harriet's face flamed when she saw her own dress coming towards her in the terminal. She'd loved how gracefully slim its sleeveless silhouette had looked in the fitting room mirror but, if she was honest, it looked better on the shortish brunette. It suited curves more than Harriet's straight-up-and-downness. Her tan looked very natural, too. Unlike Harriet's, which came from Costa del Boots.

'Twinsies,' Billie called.

'Yes, thanks for pointing that out.'

A girl, her phone in hand, trailed behind the woman. Her very own delightful teen.

'Give me that.' The man loping next to the woman courteously hoisted her bag from her shoulder. 'You shouldn't have to carry anything. Isn't that better?'

Harriet could swear she knew him from somewhere, but the more she stared the more she worried that he might be someone off the telly. She'd made that mistake before, so instead she sneaked a glance at the woman's midriff. There were no obvious signs of impending birth there.

She didn't look like the type who was too good to carry her own luggage, either.

It was nice luggage, though. Unlike the outrage dangling off James's shoulder. Stained, torn and slightly smelly – which he blamed on her overdeveloped senses – that rucksack went everywhere with him. She'd wanted to accidentally-on-purpose leave it outside the house when they were packing the taxi, but it had been hard enough getting him out of his farm boots. Choose your battles.

'What about getting sandwiches from Pret?' she asked Billie. 'Though now we've lost our seats.' The terminal was heaving. Heaving; that's what James had said with his typical imprecision. There were nearly four times as many passengers as seats if, as she assumed, the chairs and people near them were a representative sample.

She knew it had been a mistake to give up those seats. Now they were three little boats cast adrift in the tumult, towing too much hand luggage.

'I want a hot breakfast.' Billie's sigh was epic. 'Like I could have had at the hotel if you hadn't rushed us. Can't we just go into a restaurant?'

But they'd twice walked past the queues snaking outside Giraffe and Wagamama. They were getting longer, not shorter. Up to 25 per cent longer, by Harriet's reckoning.

'It's not like we don't have time to wait,' Billie added. 'They're not even posting information for an hour. Look.' She pointed to a restaurant as they approached the other end of the concourse. 'No queue there.'

'That's because nobody likes Gordon Ramsay,' James pointed out.

'Their loss is our gain,' said Harriet. 'Come on.'

Even though the restaurant wasn't as full as the others, the aisles between the tables were an assault course of luggage and children. Baby-poo yellow and brown leather-and-chrome chairs were scattered with no respect for order, or for the waiting staff trying to weave their way through with big trays of cooked breakfasts. The anxious buzz of possibly stranded travellers echoed off the wall of windows looking down into the rest of the terminal.

Harriet smiled a greeting when she saw that the waiter was seating them next to her dress double. The woman smiled back uncertainly as she settled the young boy beside her. *Right, Harriet. Having stared at a total stranger for ten seconds while rating her tan doesn't make you friends.*

'Put this under your seat, will you?' She handed one of the small bags to Billie.

'They're all your bags, Mum. You said you'd carry them. That was the deal.'

Ungrateful family. They only got to travel so light because she'd thought of everything. The hats and water bottles to keep away sunstroke, the extra books, plasters (in fact the entire medical kit, because one never knew). She had packets of biscuits, raisins and nuts, plus pool towels because the hotel ones were usually too small and nobody wanted to walk around with those stripy welts across their calves from bare flesh sweating on a sun lounger. Granted, the pillows might have been a bit OTT, but one could never be sure whether the hotel paid as much attention to their bedding as she did. Besides, they squished down to nearly nothing.

'I know what the deal was, thank you, Billie. I'm not asking you to carry it, just put it under your seat. Here.' She handed another bag to James, who set it down beside his wheeled case.

'I could have done that. It's got to go under the table, James. There's not enough room with the wheelie bags.'

He looked up from his phone just as another text chimed. 'Isn't she working today?' Harriet snapped. 'I'm surprised she's getting anything done.' Even if Persephone *was* his bank manager as well as his best friend, they could not have this much to say to each other when he'd only been away from the village for less than twenty-four hours.

'She's just worried we won't get to Italy,' he said. Then he tucked away his phone.

'She can join the club.' Persephone knew how much Harriet needed this holiday. 'The bags?' she reminded her husband.

'There'd be room if we'd checked them in like everyone else,' he said.

Oh, what temptingly juicy bait. She clamped her mouth closed. James knew perfectly well that they were being extra-efficient so they could make their Vatican tour this afternoon. Though now they were so late she'd have to email the tour company to reschedule. Assuming they got to Rome at all.

Thought sabotage. *Damn it, Harriet, just what you promised not to do to yourself.*

As they scanned their menus, she overheard the woman at the next table. 'But the pancakes look delicious, Oliver.' Despite her convivial tone, Harriet heard the Mum-plea beneath. 'Mmm, look, with strawberries. Or blueberries?'

Harriet remembered those days, when every meal needed a hostage negotiator's bargaining skills. Billie ate hardly anything but tuna mayo sandwiches between the ages of four and six.

'I'll have strawberry pancakes,' their girl said. 'If the strawberries are English. If not then I'll have plain.'

Both a chivalrous husband and a reasonable teenager? That woman's cup did run over.

'I want bacon,' said Oliver. 'Dad, can't I have bacon?'

'One fried breakfast won't kill him.' He levelled a devastating smile at the woman. 'We are on holiday, sweetheart.' He turned to flag down a passing waitress to take their order.

As the woman glanced round too, Harriet caught her eye, and her eye-roll. Holiday or not, rule number one in surviving your children is not to break parental ranks.

'Nice dress,' the woman said. Her chortle made Harriet grin. 'I hope we're not having identical luck. Are you delayed?'

Her manner was too warm to be anything like a diva, which meant her husband really was just a helpful man. Harriet wanted to kick one of the bags at her feet into James's shin. 'Yes, we're on the Rome flight,' she said.

'So are we! We're all in the same sorry boat then.'

'Or plane, in this case,' the man added. Maybe he just looked like someone Harriet knew. He wasn't out of the woman's league, exactly. It would be too meowsville to say that, even if it were true. There was something about the way he carried himself, or maybe it was his perfectly put-together outfit, that let everyone know he was the successful one.

'At least we're having breakfast,' James said as the waitress brought the other family their drinks. He didn't look even mildly annoyed at their delay, despite them all being up since silly o'clock. That shouldn't surprise her. Rome might be her idea of heaven, but it was hell to someone like James. He'd be the first to say that he was about as at home in the country as cowpats.

His jiggling foot kept knocking his case into her leg, while every minute that ticked by threatened her plans. Her jaw ached from grinding her teeth.

'Oh, hell!' Oliver's dad flew out of his chair, but not before the glass of iced water had emptied into his lap.

7

'Silly bean,' he said to the woman. 'Stay there, I'll get a waitress to clean it up.'

'I didn't do it.' The woman frowned pointedly at their son.

'Sure, blame the ten year old.'

They shared a laugh. When he squeezed her shoulder and went to find someone to mop up the spill, Harriet wondered if they might be newlyweds. They both wore wedding bands. In fact, if not for the children with them, she'd have put money on this being a sneaky weekend away from their spouses. They were that charming with each other. Again, she imagined aiming the carry-on at James's shin.

She had to stop thinking like that. Hadn't she just had a word with herself? Besides, it wasn't exactly fair to compare her twenty-year relationship to a couple who probably still gushed over each other's adorable little quirks. They hadn't yet set into tedious, concrete habits. They wouldn't be so loved-up after years of stubbing their toes on those.

Ignorance might not be bliss, but it definitely took the edge off.

'What are the chances our flight will go?' the woman asked Harriet once the waitress had mopped up everything in the vicinity.

'Not great, I'm afraid. Bloody ash cloud. There've been a lot of cancellations already, and nothing has left in over an hour and . . .' She swallowed the other datapoints she'd been mentally harvesting since they'd arrived. Not everyone appreciated details as much as she did. 'But we might get a break.'

'I hope so. I'm desperate to go.' Every bit of her expression echoed her words, and Harriet's thoughts.

'I'm Harriet, by the way.' She introduced James and Billie.

'Sophie, Oliver and Katie, and my husband is Dan. He must be drying his trousers.' She squirmed in her chair. 'This delay is killing me! We've only got nine days away. We're staying at a villa in Tuscany, near Siena. With a spa! I know, it's totally la-di-da. I can't really believe we're going.'

Harriet made a quick calculation of Sophie's available sightseeing hours in Rome after subtracting for travel and meals, plus a margin of error for inevitable delays when they needed to take cash out or one of the children dithered over breakfast or they decided they just had to have tiramisu and coffee after lunch. And that didn't even include whatever days they lost to relaxation.

'Both Rome and Tuscany in nine days?' Harriet asked. 'But you could easily spend all that time just in Rome. The Coliseum, Trevi Fountain, St Peter's Basilica, the Pantheon, all those gorgeous churches.' It was exciting enough saying them. Imagine getting to actually see them!

Rome was one of those cities she'd always meant to visit while she and James were still in London. That was before Billie when, relatively speaking, they had all the time in the world. Practically speaking, though, she worked crazy hours, like all trainee solicitors. When they did get away, they always picked somewhere exotic: to see the sumptuous theatres and grand cafés of Budapest or the mosques in Istanbul. They'd once strolled through Marrakech's souks with the muezzin's call to prayer echoing around them, sipping fresh mint tea and the best orange juice Harriet had ever tasted. Rome kept sliding down their list. It might have millennia of history, but there was nothing exotic about church bells and meatballs.

At least, Harriet never used to think so. Having been stuck now in their tiny village for a dozen years, she was starting to find M&S curry kits exotic.

As they seemed to be getting on so well, she couldn't resist mentioning Sophie's tan. Looking at her own ever-so-slightly satsuma-hued hands, she had to know where she got it. 'You look like you've already been somewhere nice.'

Sophie touched her cheek. 'This, you mean? Gosh, no, it's from a bottle.'

'Oh?' Innocent as you please. 'Which brand?'

'I've got a terrible memory. It was a rainbow-y tube, if that helps.'

'I can track it down. Where'd you buy it?'

'I've no idea. Dan picked it up for me.'

Of course he did. She glanced at James, who was moving his lips as he read the menu. What was the last thing he'd bought for her? Insect repellent, on offer.

Dan returned with his halo intact and his crotch dry. They had to go through introductions again to catch him up. 'Don't I know you?' He squinted at Harriet.

'I was wondering the same thing.'

He cocked two pistol fingers at her. 'I've got it. That charity dinner last year. No, it was the year before. We sat beside each other.'

'That's right.' She'd stood in at the last minute for her boss, but only after triple-checking that she wouldn't have to work the room making small talk or, even worse, stand up and say anything. Assurances secured, she'd taken the train to London straight after work. 'Nice to see you again,' she said. 'I was just telling Sophie that next time you should take more time off to give Rome your full attention.'

Sophie shook her head. 'Actually, we won't see any of that this time.'

'What, none of it?'

'Not a thing. We're driving straight on to the villa. We live right in the middle of London, so we don't need to see another city.'

'But the museums, and the Vatican! Not to mention shopping.'

James reached for her arm. 'All right, steady on. Let the nice people do what they want on their holiday.'

Harriet felt herself blushing. 'Yes, of course, it's just a long drive from Rome, that's all.' Over three hours, depending on whether they stayed on the motorway or took the scenic route. 'Couldn't you get a closer airport? I always like to minimise the travel part as much as possible.'

James made that noise in his throat that she hated. Somewhere between laughing and clearing his post-nasal drip. 'Except last night when we stayed in London instead of coming straight here this morning.'

One extra night away from home. One! And James wasn't going to let her forget it.

She took a breath before answering. 'It was my friend Julia's fiftieth,' she explained to Sophie, 'so we came into town yesterday for the party.'

'Rome was the only airport where we could get the frequent flyer flights on the dates we wanted,' Dan said. 'We've done it all on air miles. This way we can really splash out on the holiday, and Sophie gets her pampering.'

Sophie grasped his hand.

The last time Harriet grasped James's hand was probably when she'd stumbled over the pouffe in the living room.

Billie looked up from her phone as the tide of conversation around them began to swell.

'Mum.' She stared at the Departures board on the restaurant wall.

Their flight was cancelled.

James made that noise again. 'I guess that means the Vatican's out.'

'You don't have to sound so pleased about it, James. The whole trip is probably out. Who knows when we'll get another flight?'

'I am sorry, Harriet.' Then he did reach for her hand. No stumbling necessary. 'I know you were dead keen to go.'

Chapter 2

Thursday

Sophie's tears threatened to ruin the first mascara she'd put on in weeks. And she'd had to redo it twice, too, before Dan thought it looked okay. Quick, think of something happy. Puppies. Lottery winnings. Fields of wild flowers. Puppies winning the lottery in fields of wild flowers.

Dan was waving for the waitress. 'We need the bill, now please.'

'But our food's not even here yet,' she said. That was all she needed: to blub over not getting her egg muffin, too. *Puppies, wild flowers, puppies, wild flowers, puppiespuppiespuppies.*

'Sweetheart, think. We can't risk being at the back of the queue when the airline is sorting out alternatives. You stay and eat your food, though. I'll deal with the tickets.'

'Thanks, I am starving.' She'd skipped breakfast, but at least everyone got out of the house on time.

She wasn't hangry, just hupset.

As she puckered up for Dan's kiss, one of the many carry-ons slipped from his shoulder. He shoved it back into place. 'Should I see if they can box up your food?' she asked. 'It might still be warm if we get on another flight soon.' *Please, please, please*, she prayed to the rebooking gods, let them get on another flight soon.

But then Dan started shaking his head. 'Christ, you can't stay here.' He said it like it was her idea. 'If we can get another flight right away, then you'll need to be there with the passports to check in. You'll have to come with me.'

The nice woman next to them, Harriet, was on her feet too. 'Let's go, family.' She yanked the luggage out from under their table.

Sophie caught the sharp look Dan gave Harriet. She must have seen it too, because she turned to him. 'Don't worry,' she said, 'we'll get behind you in the queue.'

Fat chance anyway of Harriet running ahead of them with all that luggage. She looked like she was moving to Rome. 'Do you want a hand with your bags?' Sophie asked as they hurried together towards Customer Services. 'Dan's got ours. Let me take one, at least.'

'It's fine,' Harriet said. 'I'm evenly balanced this way. If you took one then I'd only keel to one side.' She had the long strap of one bag slung across her body, with another one on each shoulder. They were all full duffel bags, too.

Harriet called back to her daughter. 'Billie, can you please get sandwiches in Pret for everyone? It's right there and you can meet us at Customer Services. Here's money.'

'What kind?' Billie asked, catching up to take the notes from her mother.

Harriet turned to Sophie with the question. 'Me? Oh, that's so kind, but you really don't have to.'

'We're getting them anyway,' Harriet said. 'And none of us has eaten. Any preference? Not a vegetarian?'

'No, no, we like anything. Thank you. Thanks very much,' she called to the teenager.

'Then get seven, please, Billie, one for everyone, and be quick. Customer Services is just ahead, okay? Ring me if you have trouble.'

Crikey, Sophie couldn't imagine having that kind of authority! She wouldn't mind those perfect blonde highlights or Harriet's big grey eyes, either, if the Universe was taking requests.

Up ahead of them, the Customer Services desk was already mobbed.

'I guess other people didn't have to wait to pay restaurant bills first,' Dan said.

'Sorry,' said Sophie, catching his eye. Only a miracle would get them another flight now.

'This feels pretty hopeless,' she murmured to Harriet as they inched forward in the scrum.

'Probably, but we should see it out.'

And just like that, *pop!* went Sophie's holiday dreams. Nobody ever said 'see it out' about something they had any real hope for. Seeing it out was for bad ideas and troubled relationships. They munched their ham and cheese sandwiches, shuffling politely towards the desk, while flight after flight was cancelled.

But they didn't make it to the front. One of the frazzled airline reps shouted the bad news to everyone: the authorities had just closed UK airspace, and they expected most of Europe to follow soon.

The status of all the flights on the Departures board changed to Cancelled.

'Bloody ash cloud!' Harriet and Sophie said together.

'I'm so sorry,' Sophie added as she failed to fight back her tears. 'I know it's silly to cry over a missed holiday when there are worse things in the world.'

Dan pulled her into the crook of his arm. She leaned against him.

Harriet fished around in one of her carry-ons. 'With balm or without?' She held out both tissue packets. 'This is just ridiculous. I'd still fly. Have you read the analysis? The particulate count isn't even close to the limit yet. It's still safe.'

'This is one thing you haven't got control over, darling,' Harriet's husband said.

'Too bad, because we'd all be on our way to Italy if I did.'

Wowzers, thought Sophie. If only she had a tenth of Harriet's confidence.

Dan would know what to do. 'Will we at least get our money back for the villa?'

'Don't worry, if there's a way, I'll find it.' He gave her another squeeze. 'I am a solicitor.'

Dan could do anything, Sophie thought. Well, except open international airspace.

'That's right, I remember now,' Harriet answered Dan. 'Me too, though I don't usually deal with insurance claims. Our policy has an exclusion for natural disasters, although the airlines might still give refunds. I'm sure they did when this happened in 2010. I'll need to check the cancellation policies of our hotels . . . and all the tour companies. I guess I'll have plenty of time away from the office now to look into it.' She pulled a notebook from her bag. Sophie noticed the neatly lettered coloured tabs that stuck out from its pages. 'I'll start cancelling,' Harriet said.

'Why are you so sad, Mummy?' Oliver asked when Sophie blew her nose again. His large, serious eyes peered into hers. So like Dan's: deep blue and fringed with dark lashes. She'd fallen in love with those eyes the second the midwife had put him on her chest. He'd got his dad's dark hair, too, thick and wavy, along with his athletic frame.

'Oh, I'm being silly. I really wanted to have a holiday with you and Katie and your dad, that's all. But don't worry, I'm sure we'll find something fun to do together anyway.'

'And, we'll reduce our carbon footprint,' said Katie. 'That's one good thing.'

Even the ash cloud had a silver lining, Sophie supposed. Or at least an environmentally friendly one. Leave it to Katie to find it. She only wished that her thirteen year old didn't have to fret about things like climate change and polluted oceans.

She glanced at Dan. 'You will still take the time off?'

He was already scrolling through something on his phone. 'It would be stupid to use up the days if I don't need to. What happens when we want to go away later in the year? I wouldn't be able to.'

Later in the year?! 'But what if we could find another place to go instead? Here, I mean.' The disappointment burned in her again. 'Couldn't we look for a country villa that we can get to by train?'

She hardly dared to breathe.

'Villas are abroad, Soph,' he chided. 'Do you mean a plain old house? I can look, although with it being the summer holidays, there might not be many options.'

Sophie clung for dear life to that tiny soap bubble of hope. There had to be somewhere they could go. Maybe in the Yorkshire Dales or down on the coast. The weekend supplements were always full of hotels. There must be vacancies somewhere.

But they wouldn't be free, and they'd already spent so much on the villa. 'I guess we could put it on the credit cards until we get our refund.'

She pretended not to notice the way Dan's jaw set. 'Well, I can't spend any more now. I might not even get the money back from the villa. I'm not made of cash, am I?'

'You said we'd probably get it back.'

He smirked at her. 'I could always shake the magic money tree and see if a few thousand more falls off.'

Of course. She was being selfish. It wasn't even her money. Dan was the one who worked and there she was, talking about running up their credit cards. 'No, I'm sorry,' she said.

'Maybe this is a stupid idea,' Harriet said, as she ended one of her calls. 'But if it's a country retreat you want, then why don't you spend your holiday at our cottage?'

Sophie hadn't even realised she'd been listening, let alone thinking about a solution for them.

'It wouldn't cost you anything,' she continued. 'That would be all right, wouldn't it, James?'

He took so long to answer that Sophie felt the need to apologise again. They shouldn't have to sort out her problems, though she could kiss Harriet for wanting to save their trip.

'No, no,' James said, 'I'm just thinking about it. If you're after a rural setting then our village is as beautiful as it gets.' He paused again, inspecting his shoes. 'I'm from there, so I'm biased,' he eventually went on, 'but I think it's got everything you could want. There are walking paths starting from the property itself. We've got some bikes, too. And goats. Do you like goats?'

Sophie didn't know if she had any opinion on goats.

'The village pub has good food,' he added. 'And ales, if you're an ale man, Dan?'

Dan wasn't an ale man.

'There are plenty of spare bedrooms.'

Then Sophie caught the look on Harriet's face. She knew a second thought when she saw one. 'You're being too generous,' Sophie said, feeling foolish for getting her hopes up. 'Thanks ever so much, but we couldn't stay with you.' She wished her voice wasn't wobbling. 'You don't even know us.'

But Harriet laughed. 'You've shared your tanning secrets, Sophie, and I'm assuming you wouldn't steal from us. If you did, I could always report Dan to the SRA. Only kidding! Besides, I'm not suggesting you stay with us. What if you stayed at the cottage instead of us . . . and we stayed in your house?'

'You mean, we could stay in London?' Billie asked. 'Yeah, that would be wicked! We can, can't we, Dad?'

James looked like he was facing a firing squad. 'London?'

'Yes, James, instead of Rome,' Harriet said.

'Why don't we just go home?'

'We can't!' Harriet said. 'I mean, we're already here and packed and everything. I can make London as good as Rome. We'll treat it just like a holiday. It does have loads of history, and restaurants, music and theatre, museums, walks, architecture. We could even do a Big Bus tour.'

'I'm tired just listening to you,' James said.

Harriet frowned. 'Come on, don't be a stick-in-the-mud. If you say no then none of us gets a holiday.'

James's kind eyes met Sophie's. Then he shrugged. 'I don't want to disappoint anyone.'

'I'm sure you haven't got the right insurance to cover something like this,' Dan pointed out. That torpedoed Sophie's heart.

But Harriet nodded. 'We have. With James having school groups at the farm, we need full coverage for visitors. Have *you* got insurance to cover us?'

Dan stiffened. 'Yes, as a matter of fact, we do,' he said. 'We're fully covered as well. What about rental agreements? I suppose you've thought of those, too.'

His tone was snappy, but that didn't sound like an outright no to Sophie. It might not be Tuscany, but they *could* have their holiday without running up more credit card bills. Plus, it was a proper away-holiday that Dan could justify taking time off for. If he'd go for it . . . 'Could we really do it?' She was nearly whispering. She didn't want to spook the idea and send it scampering off, never to be seen again.

'James is right, it is very nice,' Harriet added. She tapped on her phone. 'Here, see for yourself. I took these a month ago for the Scouts.'

But it was Dan who accepted her phone. 'That *is* something,' he said, scrolling through Harriet's gallery.

When Sophie leaned over for a look, Dan playfully held the phone away. 'Not so fast, sweetheart. I think you deserve a surprise. You really want this holiday, eh?'

'I do, Dan, really.'

He handed the phone back to Harriet before scooping Sophie up for a hug. 'Well then, if we can make the details work . . . How long were you thinking of doing the swap for?' he asked Harriet. When she told him two weeks, he said, 'Ah, I've only got next week booked off.'

'But you could extend it, couldn't you?' Sophie asked. 'Please?' She was too close to give up now. 'You must have the days. It's been so long since we've all been away together.'

'The alternative is for everyone to go home disappointed,' Harriet added. 'This way we can at least follow through on our plans and do something with our days off. You'll miss out on the great Italian food, but there's a woman in the village who cooks for us when I'm doing crazy hours at work. She's very good, and I'm sure she could cook for you while you're there. And there's even a spa in the village. We're in the arse end of nowhere but we've got a spa.'

Sophie couldn't wait to be in the arse end of nowhere. Imagine! Being massaged into a permanent state of drooling bliss and not even having to cook.

'Well, our house is in the middle of everything,' Sophie said, praying that Dan would see sense on this. 'There's lots of room and it's close to the Tube. Plus all the restaurants, of course, and the culture. Though we never seem to get organised to book tickets for anything.'

'Don't worry about us,' said Harriet. 'We're very organised.'

Harriet's husband made a strange noise in his throat.

'Couldn't we please do two weeks, too?' Sophie asked Dan.

'Soph, it's not that easy for me. Not all of us get to laze around every day. I've got work commitments.'

'But didn't Jeremy want you to take two weeks off? I'm sure he'd be happy for you to, and think how much fun the children would have.'

Katie and Oliver took their cue, adding their pleas to hers. She could see Dan wavering. He didn't like being the bad guy in front of other people.

Finally, he said, 'If it's what you really want, Soph, then I'll make the sacrifice.'

Sophie's mood soared as they swapped details about their homes. They were really doing this! Two whole weeks. More, actually, because today was only Thursday. Dan had been so stressed with work lately that this might actually turn out to be a blessing in disguise.

The next thing Sophie knew, they'd signed electronic lettings agreements and exchanged keys. Dan and Harriet made it all seem so easy. Bish, bash, bosh: new holidays for everyone.

Sophie couldn't keep the smug smile from her face. All the other passengers might be going home to put their clean clothes back in drawers and check the small print on their travel insurance, but they were getting their holiday after all, thanks to this angel in Terminal 5.

Harriet seemed able to make everything possible. Who was this woman who'd swooped in to save their holiday? Sophie didn't know yet, but she couldn't wait to spend the next two weeks in her house finding out. 'I just can't thank you enough for this, Harriet. And James! You're lifesavers.' Her heart flipped as she said this. They didn't know how true it was.

Then Dan hugged her. 'You are absolutely adorable when you're like this,' he murmured into her ear.

Sophie bit her bottom lip through her smile. 'Like what?'

'I don't know. Happy. Excited. Grateful, you know, pleased with me, like I'm the best thing since sliced bread.'

'You're better than sliced bread,' she said. 'You're calorie-free.'

'I've got an idea for when we get to the cottage,' he whispered. The way he held her left no doubt about what he meant by that. But they had to get there first.

'I guess we'll take the train, then?' Her eyes searched his.

'Don't worry about that, I'm hiring a car,' he told her. 'We would have needed one in Italy anyway and we don't want to faff with all the luggage on the train. Just because we can't go away doesn't mean you don't deserve the royal treatment. I'll see if I can get us a free upgrade, too.' Then his sharp glance settled on Harriet, who was watching them.

'It's the train for us,' Harriet said. 'At least there's not too far to go. We should be walking out of your Tube station in . . .' She glanced at her phone, then towards the ceiling. 'An hour and ten minutes. As long as we don't have to wait for the Heathrow Express for more than ten minutes. Give or take five minutes.'

Harriet slung a few more bags over herself as if she was a one-woman Everest support team. Was there nothing this woman couldn't handle?

Dan made a point of staring after Harriet and her family as they set off for the train. 'You don't have to carry anything, Soph. *Some* blokes are gentlemen. If you want to stay here with the luggage I can go for the car and pick you up out front. I'll text you when I'm on my way. Is your phone on? Come on, Oliver, help your dad.'

Sophie put her hand over his as he wheeled both their cases outside.

'You'll be all right here while I get the car?'

'Of course,' she answered. As if she couldn't manage to stand in front of an airport on her own.

'Good girl. You're going to get exactly the holiday you need,' said Dan. 'No stress, no drama. I'll make sure it's perfect. Don't I always?'

He always had, right from the first night they'd met.

It could not have been more perfect, the way the city lights had glistened in the warm spring air as she'd cruised up the Thames with her colleagues and about a hundred other passengers. Everyone stood out on deck with their drinks. Sophie was politely trying to listen to her boss's latest holiday plans (as if she hadn't booked most of it for him), when she noticed someone staring in her direction. She glanced over. The bloke smiled. It took a few more glances to be sure, but he seemed to be smiling at her.

Once her boss had gone off for more wine, it took about two seconds for him to come over. 'Having fun?' he asked. His long-lash-fringed eyes held hers.

'It's a work thing,' she said. 'I mean, I'm not here for fun. That was my boss, not my boyfriend.' *Smooth, Sophie. Why not just tell him about the dating dry spell, too?* Dry spell. Ha. It was a full-on drought. There'd been a hosepipe ban on her love life for months. 'Are you here for work or fun?' she asked.

23

He was wearing a summer suit, like her, but his probably came from somewhere posher than Zara. Or maybe it was the way he wore it that looked expensive. Sophie had never been good at spotting fake brands, but she was pretty sure his loafers, with the signature Gucci horsebit hardware on top, weren't from any weekend market stall. She tucked her faux-Fendi closer under her arm. 'Technically work, but hopefully fun?' It was a question. 'If I can persuade you to join me. The band isn't bad, but I think their feelings are hurt that we're all out here. We could have a dance and make them feel better.'

He introduced himself and Sophie practically floated inside on the romance of it all. The band's singer crooned a Frank Sinatra classic as Dan led her to the practically empty dance floor. She knew some of her colleagues must be watching, but any self-consciousness fell away as soon as Dan took her in his arms. He guided her easily to the music and (she hoped) into looking as if she knew what she was doing.

'You're an amazing dancer,' she said when the song ended.

'It's easy with a good partner like you. Another dance, or would you like a drink?'

'Can I be greedy and have both?'

He laughed. 'You can have whatever you want. Stay here. I'll take care of it.'

Chapter 3

Thursday

Harriet stared down the long corridor that tunnelled beneath the terminals. It would go on and on, she knew, a rat's maze leading eventually to the train. She shot another look over her shoulder, aimed at James's feet this time. 'Can you please try to hurry up! We'll miss the train.'

Instantly, she wished she hadn't snapped. Again. She'd never get things back on track like that. Her husband might be laid-back most of the time, but he could be as stubborn as his goats when she pushed him.

Must not push, she reminded herself.

But honestly, what was so hard about walking at a normal pace? That man trekked miles through the countryside every single day. It wasn't fitness slowing him down. It was sheer bloody-mindedness. She had the whole family's bags strapped over herself and was still managing to weave past people left, right and centre. The efficient tap of her sandals on the marble tiles had a pleasing rhythm.

Now that they had a new plan, she wasn't about to let any of it slip away. Tick-tock. At this rate they'd waste most of the day just getting to Sophie's house. Plus the contingency time in case they got lost. Not that Harriet usually got lost. They'd really only have sixteen days' holiday once they got settled in. That last day would be a write-off, between packing and tidying up and bickering over who had to carry what to the train.

Just thinking about the wasted hours made her sandals click faster. Her sigh carried over the echoing buzz of the other passengers shuffling towards the train. Frustration? Or maybe one of the carry-on straps was pressing too hard on her lungs. She shifted the bags around. No, it was definitely James-induced annoyance. Cold treacle moved faster than her husband. Unless one of his damn goats got loose. Then you should see him go.

Shame she wasn't one of his goats.

Shame they couldn't rewind fifteen years, either, because she was pretty sure James hadn't always made her want to set his socks on fire. What had changed?

He'd once been just the soothing balm she'd been after. True, he'd never been a fast mover, or overly proactive, but he also never got flustered or stressed. The very chilled yin to her uptight yang.

Those were carefree days, she mused. As carefree as she got, at least. She used to find it hard to get too wound up about things around James. He was the vocal equivalent of sipping hot chocolate under the duvet. Just hearing him quietened the thoughts pinging around her brain. She had enjoyed that once. She knew she had.

The trouble was, he was still carefree now while she ran around doing everything that needed doing. It was exhausting.

'Come *on*, James!'

'Sorry, darling, it must be my nose slowing me down.'

'Nice one, Dad,' Billie said. 'Mum, I'm guessing there's probably more than one train into London today. Relax.'

'Relax?' she said, calculating how many chances they'd already missed on the walk to the platform. Four an hour for the Heathrow Express alone. Plus the Underground. That was probably five more in the same space of time. Adjusted for overlapping schedules. 'Let's just try to get there before nightfall.'

But she did make herself slow down until James was alongside her.

By the time they reached Sophie's station – twenty-two minutes on the train, nine stops on the Tube, one change – Harriet had mentally unpacked her cases and recategorised all her clothes, shoes and accessories for the cooler London weather. The beach hats were a waste of space and she probably didn't have quite enough jumpers for evenings. Just knowing she was still prepared for the holiday felt better. Clothes-wise, at least.

She'd been fidgeting with the big spiky lump of Sophie's keys since they'd emerged from the station. Unnecessary things dangled from the ring: a smooth pink stone heart, a green patent leather turtle, three tiny Tesco Club Cards with different serial numbers and, by Sophie's own admission, keys she didn't recognise any more. Harriet would switch those house keys to her own neatly utilitarian ring as soon as they got to the house.

The house. Not the upscale hotel in the centre of Rome. She was doing her best to shift her expectations from the sun-baked ancient capital to north London. Still, a wave of melancholy swept over her. Sophie's house was perfectly nice, she was sure. It just wasn't in Italy.

I'm mourning for Rome, Harriet thought. All those fine plans going to waste. She'd thought of every last detail, right down to which cafés served the best coffee close to their hotel, and how many minutes' walk it was to the nearest Metro station. She'd spent weeks arranging it all for them, every fun activity, all the relaxation, each meal.

Even the surprises that no one but she would know weren't spur-of-the-moment.

She was under no illusions about herself. She knew what some people (all right, most people) thought of her. But this time she really did need to plan everything, because it was more than just a holiday.

It was the chance to reconnect with James, to remember when they'd enjoyed being in a relationship together.

She cast another backward glance at him. He was still loping along with his tatty rucksack, this time on the pavement of Sophie's road instead of the airport terminal.

The spark had fizzled in their marriage. Even the fizzle had fizzled.

Not that he was cheating, or anything like that. James wasn't the type. If someone were to draw a cartoon of a nice, stable, non-cheating bloke, it would look like her husband. There was nothing dishonest about his tall, sturdy frame either, or his hair that never looked quite tidy or his giant farmer's hands. He didn't fit the part. Not James.

Yet for months they'd been about as romantic as a pair of builders fitting someone's new kitchen. These days they were just clocking in and getting the job done. They didn't even take tea breaks together any more. She snorted at the euphemism.

'Eww, watch the poo!' Harriet warned as she stepped around the fresh pile plopped in front of Sophie's house. What was wrong with people? If you wouldn't empty your child's nappy on the pavement, you shouldn't leave your dog's poo there either. No one should have to skid through smelly leavings when they didn't even have a dog.

Although, technically, she would have one while they stayed at Sophie's. Spot, it was called, though Sophie had made a huge point of saying that their neighbour would be taking care of it.

That didn't mean she wanted to share the house with it. Dogs smelled, and they sniffed crotches and licked their bits and breathed their bitty breath into your face. She didn't actually know what kind of dog it was, but she was sure it did all of those things.

As she eased open Sophie's front door, she braced herself. 'Hello?' she called through the crack.

'Who are you talking to?' Billie asked.

'To Spot, who do you think? You have to let a dog know you mean no harm before entering its space.'

'I can't hear anything.' When Billie put her ear near the door, Harriet caught a whiff of the shampoo she'd used since she was a baby. Johnson's. It still made her pale curls soft as cashmere. Harriet wanted to plunge her face into those locks and breathe it in.

Billie would hate that.

'Maybe the neighbour took it for a walk,' Harriet mused. She pushed open the door, but it snagged on something. Hopefully not the dog!

It was only a gym bag left on the Victorian tiled floor. She glanced at the crammed hooks lining one wall, where a large swelling of coats, jumpers and carrier bags hung. 'Its lead isn't here.'

James came up behind them. 'Why don't we say he instead of it?' he whispered.

'Why he? Why not she?' Billie whispered back.

'Anything but it. Though Spot's a boy's name.'

'A dog's spots aren't gendered, Dad.'

'I s'pose not.'

Harriet turned away so Billie wouldn't see her expression. Everything with her had to be gender this and gender

29

that. '*They*'re not here, anyway.' She settled the matter in a normal voice. 'Happy?'

'Ta,' said Billie.

As Harriet picked her way along the hall, she stumbled over a muddy shoe. Dozens more, some muddy, some not, were scattered over the floor. She only righted herself by grabbing hold of a bike that leaned against the wall.

Sophie hadn't mentioned that they'd recently moved in. A few of the cardboard packing boxes lining one wall were crushed on top, some split down the side, as if one of the children had sat on them. And they weren't stacked straight. One was tipped over, its papers spilled out onto the ornate tiles.

Harriet could feel her chest constrict as she took in the mess. Clutter everywhere. Absolutely everywhere. She took a ragged breath.

Five boxes. Six, seven, eight-nine-ten-eleven. One short of a dozen. Fewer than the shoes.

She was vaguely aware of James moving closer. 'Harr—? Never mind, finish the shoes. How many?' He was smiling.

'Twenty-seven.' One missing.

'Come here.' She exhaled deeply as his arms encircled her. 'Want to tidy up?'

'Yes, please.'

'Wow, Mum,' Billie said, 'wait till you see the living room. This must be killing you.'

'It's fine.'

It wasn't fine. Her eye sought the banister spindles up the stairs. One, two, three, four-five-six-seven . . .

She counted them over and over, her mind filling with the numbers, pushing out the chaos around her. She could feel her breathing slowing as her eyes sought each spindle, ticking them off, ordering things. She tore her eyes away from the banister. That was a bit better.

This wasn't what she'd imagined, but it would be okay. She had to make it okay. She just needed a change of perspective. She was good at that. Not being in Rome simply meant that their London calendar was an opportunity. A chance to replan everything with her usual efficiency. She worked best with a sense of purpose, a problem to solve. She loved that challenge as much as she loathed looking down the long, long corridor of unplanned days. All those minutes and hours to fill.

But first, she had some tidying to do. 'Take the bags into the bedrooms, will you, James? I just want to put a few things away.' Her hands clenched with the thought of the task ahead.

It didn't take that long, really, once Harriet got started.

She could feel the calm begin to blanket her most soothingly by the time she'd cleared off the table beside the sofa in the big living room. All the papers and pens, crayons, coins and small plastic figures fitted into the drawer. Maybe if she had time later, she'd find out where those figures went. With each item straightened – the lampshade, a picture frame, the scatter cushion – her mind straightened as well. She plucked odd socks, a hairbrush and two eyeliners from crevices between the cushions. More shoes needed pairing and putting out of sight. The coffee table was inches-deep in higgledy-piggledy newspapers, magazines and schoolwork. Much as she'd love to, she couldn't just chuck it all into the recycling. One of the sideboard cabinets made a good temporary home. Just while they were staying.

She hummed as she worked her way through the room, then the whole of the downstairs. The secret to any good tidy-up was economy of motion. Why carry one item to its proper place when she could sweep up five or six things along her path? She had no time for all those extra trips back and forth.

Toast plates and teacups went into one pile for the kitchen. Nail clippers, bath towels and beauty products went into another. Little piles. Nothing pleased her more than those purposeful little piles waiting to be whisked away.

'You're making judgements about her?' James asked when she finally threw herself down on the bare sofa. She knew she'd taken hours to finish, but already the details of her frenzy were fading. That's what happened when she got focused.

The room was bright with the afternoon sunlight streaming through the tall front windows. It bathed the cheery pale-yellow walls. Specks of dust still floated in the beams of light from all Harriet's activity.

She bristled at James's question. 'Who, Sophie? Why blame her when it's all of their responsibility to keep a house tidy? Honestly, James.'

Billie gave her father The Stare from the overstuffed armchair she'd claimed. 'Yeah, really, Dad.'

Then she raised her eyebrows at Harriet's smile. 'What? I don't disagree with everything you say.'

It only felt like it. Billie had her legs thrown over the side of the chair. Harriet wanted to tell her to sit like a lady, but that would only spoil this rare moment of solidarity. 'Let's do something,' she said instead. 'Here, I've downloaded a top ten list for London.'

'Oh God, Mum, please don't schedule everything. Can't we just do whatever?'

'What's whatever?' Harriet's colleagues sometimes tried that on her, too, with their free-form brainstorming meetings. Solicitors should have more sense than to waste time like that.

32

Billie was back on her phone. 'I don't know. Whatever we want. That's the whole point of a holiday.'

'Okay. What do you want to do?'

'Whatever I feel like.'

'Which is?' *Sitting there staring at your phone.*

'I don't know right now.'

'God, you're infuriating,' Harriet snapped.

'Me?! Hello pot, this is kettle.' Then she got a strange look. 'I found Spot, by the way. Upstairs in the far bedroom. Go on, Mum. Go and look.'

'Billie.' James's voice held a warning. 'Darling, don't freak out.'

She was halfway up the stairs before James had even stood up. 'Of course I'm going to freak out when you tell me not to,' she muttered. She might not like dogs but they shouldn't be locked up in a bedroom. That didn't seem like Sophie, but then she'd already been wrong about them once. There'd been no clue at the airport about what slobs they were. How could people with such nice luggage hide toast plates under their sofa, and possibly dogs in their back bedroom?

Personal feelings aside, she was not about to keep the poor thing in there. 'Spot? Don't worry, darling, you can come out.'

At first when she opened the door, she thought her eyes were playing tricks. The bedroom was suffused with dim red light. Her hand searched for a light switch. It wasn't even dark outside. They must have blackout curtains on the windows or something. And a room lit like an Amsterdam brothel. What kind of people kept a dog like this?

'It's okay, Spot, darling, come out and meet us. It's all right, don't be frightened.'

Spot didn't make a sound. The poor thing must be terrified, maybe hiding under the bed.

Then her fingers found a switch. She flicked it on.

A huge python was coiled around a log in the middle of the bedroom. Not six feet from where she was standing. Six easily slitherable feet.

Her throat tightened as she drew in a sharp breath. Tingles flooded her body and her muscles tensed. Fight or flight. Well, for God's sake, that was no contest. Her shriek was proper horror film. Long, piercing waves of I'm-being-murdered-here screams. If the snake was bothered, he (she? they?) didn't let on. Not that Harriet was about to wait around to find out. She dashed back through the door and slammed it shut.

'What the *fuck*, James!' she shouted as he ambled up the stairs.

'I'm sorry.' He might look sheepish, but the bastard had the cheek to laugh. The actual cheek.

'I cannot believe you let me walk in there like that. Anything could have happened.'

'Don't be so dramatic,' he said. 'He's in a sturdy enclosure.'

'I don't care if he's in a nuclear bunker, James. You did that on purpose. And you would be bloody sorry if I'd had a heart attack.' At least, she hoped that was true.

'Oh, please. You? With all that carry-on, the snake probably needs CPR right now.'

They both jumped when someone started pounding on the door downstairs. A man's deep voice reverberated through the solid front door. 'Sophie? Sophie! What's going on? What's happened?'

'You probably woke the dead with that scream of yours,' James said, starting back down the stairs.

'I doubt the dead knock, James.'

Billie hovered with them in the hall as they listened to the lock clicking back, then watched as the doorknob turned. The man was coming into the house!

'Excuse me, what the hell do you think you're doing?' Harriet glanced around for something to protect the family. But she'd tidied too well. Only a neat row of shoes remained.

She could use that plimsoll with malice if she had to.

'Who are you?' the man demanded.

She had to admit he didn't look like a dangerous felon. His button-down shirt was too well-pressed, for one thing. But he was nearly as big as James, and younger-looking. His hair was jet black, not greying at the temples like James's. His fists were clenched and one couldn't take chances. 'No, who the hell are you?'

'I'm Sophie and Dan's neighbour,' said Sophie and Dan's neighbour. 'Carlos.'

Deadly intruders didn't usually introduce themselves, either. Or wear thick-framed tortoiseshell glasses or dark stubble that made them look like the barista in the coffee shop next to her office.

She felt a bit silly with the shoe in her hand. 'Oh, well, we're their house guests.' She looked pointedly at her husband. 'Jump in any time, James.'

Carlos's hands unclenched. 'I heard screaming. I thought it was Sophie.'

'She's on holiday,' James said. 'We've swapped houses, actually. They're staying up in ours. In Gloucestershire. Moreton-in-Marsh. Do you know it? Lovely little village.'

'Of course he doesn't,' said Harriet. 'I'm so sorry.' She gave Carlos what she hoped was a disarming smile. 'I'm afraid it was me who screamed. I found Spot.'

35

'You didn't scream in front of her?' Carlos looked worried again.

'Well, where else?'

He pulled a face. 'Can I go and check on her? Make sure she's all right?'

'Make sure *she*'s all right?' Harriet said. 'Oh, yes, by all means, make sure the snake wasn't frightened by me.'

James started for the stairs with Carlos when Billie suddenly said, 'Dad! You're not seriously about to let some stranger into the house just because he says he's the neighbour?' She marched straight up to Carlos. 'Excuse me. Can I see some identification before you go wandering around the house?'

Even Billie adulted better than James, Harriet thought. She wasn't a little girl any more. Harriet proudly watched her daughter, the way she carried herself with confidence. Their Billie definitely knew her own mind. Her gaze was hewn from steel. Not a bit of her childish clumsiness was left. She was lithe and graceful. She was beautiful.

'Of course, sorry, what am I thinking!' Carlos took his bank cards and driving licence from his wallet. 'I didn't mean to make you uncomfortable. Sophie and Dan asked me to look after Spot when they're away. My son had a python, too. I'm afraid that's why Katie got one, so it's my fault, in a way.'

Once Billie was happy that Carlos wasn't a serial killer, she let him go upstairs. She trailed behind him though. 'Come on,' she taunted Harriet. 'You're not scared, are you?'

'I was just surprised.'

'Right.'

Together the Cooper family went to meet their housemate.

Harriet crept closer to the glass for a better look at the snake. When Spot shifted position, she could see the muscles

36

move beneath its smooth scales. Its body was twisted around the heavy tree limb, so she could only count the spots she could see. As frustrating as it was, that was the rule.

'You said your son had one. Did it escape?' she asked Carlos.

'No. My wife made him get rid of it when they moved out. My wife – ex-wife – hated it. She was against having it in the first place.'

Harriet stared at Carlos. 'I hope that wasn't the reason for the divorce.'

Billie sighed. 'Mum.'

'Well, it's a possibility, isn't it?'

But Carlos shook his head. 'It wasn't the reason. Though she wouldn't go anywhere near the enclosure.' Carlos glanced at Spot. 'People think she's scary just because of the things they've heard.'

'People say the same thing about my wife,' said James.

'Piss off, James.'

Billie rolled her eyes. 'Carlos, I'm not sure my parents properly introduced themselves before. They're the Snarkersons.'

'You piss off, too, Billie,' Harriet snapped. 'I'm going downstairs now. Enjoy your love-in with the snake.'

Chapter 4

Thursday

'Ohmygodohmygodohmygod! Just look at that!' The narrow lane had widened after Sophie and her family drove through another tunnel of trees. The steep banks that hugged the road were carpeted with ferns, moss and little white flowers, and the sunshine filtered through the deep-green foliage overhead. 'This is incredible!' She reached over to cover Dan's gear hand with hers as she turned to the children in the back. 'What do you think of this? It looks like we're travelling to The Shire!'

'We are,' Dan reminded her. 'This is Gloucester*shire*.'

'I mean with the Hobbits. Bilbo and such.'

'Silly bean, everyone knows what you meant.'

Oliver and Katie had their noses pressed against the car windows. 'Cool!' they said together. 'Mum, do you think there'll be horses?' Katie asked. 'Maybe somewhere we can ride?'

'There must be stables. We'll ask.' Sophie patted herself on the back for finding Katie those lessons in Hyde Park for her birthday. Her heart was in her throat as she'd watched her precious girl climb aboard the huge animal, but Katie came away in one piece, with more confidence than Sophie had at her age, not to mention her now signature long fishtail plait that she'd learned to do on her own (though Sophie liked to do it for her when she was allowed).

Sophie shifted back round when the satnav told them to turn. 'This is – this can't be it.' They stopped in front of an imposing black metal gate flanked by towering, immaculately clipped box hedges. 'Are you sure? How will we get in?'

Dan patted her knee. 'It's all taken care of, sweetheart, Harriet emailed me the code.' He rolled down the window, but no matter how far he stretched, he couldn't reach the keypad. 'Damn it!'

The door dinged the post as he flung it open to punch in the code. Sophie felt a shiver. She watched Dan carefully as he took a deep breath. Then the gate swung open and they were on their way up the drive.

She gasped when the house came into view around the last stand of fir trees. 'This is their idea of a cottage?' She'd been in smaller Tescos. And not the Tesco Metros, either. She felt another guilty twinge about their swap with Harriet and James because this, well . . . this was something else.

The cottage was more like a stately home, if a thatched one. The main building had two storeys, with single-storey extensions off both ends. She took it all in in an instant, but knew she'd remember it for the rest of her life: the attic windows cocooned in the weathered grey thatch along the roofline, and the warm yellow Cotswold stone front; all the small-paned windows that didn't completely line up, and the eight chimneys that did. Not to mention the tumbling profusion of cottage garden flowers and neatly trimmed shrubs that could have been a gold medal display at the Chelsea Flower Show.

The children's seat belts were off before Dan had put the car into park. But Sophie hesitated.

'Soph?'

'This is too high-end for us,' she murmured. 'Dan, this looks like a film set!' She thought of the house she'd grown up in. They'd been bungalow people, not stately home people. Her family had eaten dinner on their laps in front of the telly, and fought over the single bathroom when they all had to get ready for school and work in the mornings. Her mum would have had a lot to say about a place like this. A little sadly, she imagined her running commentary. It would have started as soon as they'd left the motorway.

These moments ambushed her, even years after her mum's death, when she'd give almost anything for her mum to answer the phone one more time. To hear her voice instead of having to imagine it.

She would ring her dad in a bit to let him know about the change of plan, and she was ever so grateful that she could still do that. But it wasn't the same. She wondered if anything could ever be quite the same after losing her mum.

Dan shook his head, then walked around the car to take Sophie's hand through the open door. 'Silly bean, nothing's too good for us. Don't you know that by now?'

He'd rung her the day after the river cruise. 'I loved meeting you last night,' he'd said, 'and I know I'm supposed to wait three days, but I've got tickets to the opera tonight. If you're interested?'

He could have asked if she was interested in watching surgery being performed and she'd have said yes. As soon as they'd agreed where to meet and had hung up, she'd phoned her mum.

'Well, that's posh,' she'd said. 'Do you have to wear a gown or anything?'

'Gosh, I don't know. Do you think so?' She didn't own a gown.

She was glad she asked her boss, who'd definitely been to the opera before. Otherwise she might have turned up in some over-the-top frock while everyone else wore their normal work clothes.

Dan met her outside the Royal Opera House, looking at least as handsome as he had the night before. His suit fitted him perfectly, but then he had the ideal tall, slim, strong-shouldered physique for it. 'I'm so glad you could make it,' he said. When he leaned in to kiss both her cheeks, she smelled the most delicious earthy scent.

She couldn't hide her amazement as they stepped inside the atrium. 'It looks like a giant greenhouse!' she said, staring at all the wrought-iron-and-glass Victorian splendour. The round bar in the middle was flanked by elegantly tall floral arrangements. People milled about holding champagne glasses. She wished she had a camera to take a photo for her mum.

Dan laughed. 'I'm glad you like it. Have you seen *Arabella* before?'

She hadn't even heard of it before his call. 'I guess this is where I confess I don't know a thing about opera. I'm sorry, I feel like I'm here under false pretences.'

'Don't be sorry,' he said. 'I'm happy that you wanted to come. And I'm glad you haven't seen it. It means you've got a lot to look forward to. Sometimes it's nice being . . .'

'Naive?'

'I was going to say unspoilt. So many women I meet are jaded. You're such a breath of fresh air, Sophie.'

As Sophie wondered how many women were 'so many', Dan went to get the champagne.

★

41

'Didn't I promise to give you the holiday of your dreams?' Dan said now. 'I can't import the handsome Italian masseurs – you'll have to make do with the spa in the village – but you're going to have the perfect holiday. Starting with this.' He swept his arm across their view.

Sophie smiled as Dan helped her from her seat. *Let yourself enjoy this*, a little voice warned. Dan was right. She'd jumped at the chance to go to a spa hotel in Italy, so why not here instead? Nobody needed to know that she was an impostor who'd picked up her sparkly new sandals a few aisles over from their breakfast cereal. They didn't *say* ASDA on them. She shoved those pinchy thoughts from her mind and followed Dan to the ancient-looking front door.

It was ridiculously perfect, right down to the scent of jasmine on the warm breeze and the sound of birdsong all around them. She half-expected Snow White to turn up with Bambi and Thumper and all their forest friends. But she was mixing up her Disney classics. Snow White and the Seven Dwarves, then.

She coughed.

'All right?' Dan asked. 'Your heart?'

She nodded. It was worst at night. Lying in bed, trying not to obsess over that miraculous little pump keeping each of them alive, she swore she could feel every heartbeat. Once she started noticing, she felt the skips constantly. Every one made her sure she'd end up like her mum. She tried convincing herself that it was too much coffee, or the cheeky bottles of wine she'd sunk with Dan for their anniversary, or her imagination, or about a hundred other things that had nothing to do with a dicky heart that could stop at any time.

But her heart wasn't trying to kill her. At least, not in the way she'd feared. The GP promised her that those skips were common, and not dangerous. Some people felt the urge to cough when they felt them. Nothing to worry about, really.

She wanted to kiss that man, until he gave her the real bad news. She did have dangerously high blood pressure. She'd need medication to control it. And she needed to avoid stress.

How exactly was that supposed to happen when she spent nearly every waking moment running around? If she wasn't chauffeuring the children to school or ballet, or chess club, science club, art club, ping-pong (thankfully only a fleeting interest), football practice, piano, violin and saxophone lessons, or that sodding art appreciation course that had just started at the Tate, then she was up to her elbows in the charity work Dan kept finding for her.

He'd thought she was joking when she told him that the GP said she should avoid stress. Well, why wouldn't he? On the surface she was the most relaxed person either of them knew. 'What have you got to be stressed about?' Dan had scoffed. 'You don't even have to go to work. Fridge-freezers aren't as chilled as you.'

He honestly seemed to believe that it took no time or effort to run the children everywhere and generally be the family's dogsbody.

Besides, no matter what he thought, her blood pressure begged to differ. That's what had her so scared. Maybe she was like her mum after all. She just hadn't reached the same unfunny punchline yet. A stroke at fifty-two with no warning at all. Mum never even left the hospital.

'Coming inside?' she called to the children. Katie had her arm hooked around Oliver's neck as they peered behind the house. Sisterly love sometimes looked a lot like assault, but her gentle son never seemed to mind.

'Mum, look, the goats, there they are!' Oliver couldn't have been more excited if he'd spotted a unicorn. 'There really are goats!'

She smiled at her animal-mad son. 'Don't go there yet, okay? Either come in or stay out in front where we can see you. We'll all go together in a minute.' What kind of parent would she be if she let her city children fall victim to some barn-related horror? Being a child of the suburbs herself, she wasn't sure what that might be.

She jumped at Dan's exclamation as he opened Harriet's front door. It wasn't anger this time, though.

'It *is* a film set!' Sophie said. The front hall wasn't huge but it felt spacious. It took Sophie a second to realise why. It was completely clear of clutter. A few tastefully framed paintings dotted the walls at regular intervals, and the only piece of furniture was a highly polished church pew against one wall. But there was nothing under the bench: not so much as an umbrella (or the water stains that were always under the umbrellas in Sophie's house). No dust bunnies, spare bits of paper, lost homework, sweet wrappers, discarded socks, schoolbooks or old newspapers. Not so much as a shoe.

Homes & Gardens could walk in and start photographing.

She was going to be living here for the next two weeks!

Sophie's pace picked up as she roamed through the ground floor. She wasn't exactly sure what she'd expected when Harriet had talked about the cottage, but it wasn't this. The ceilings were beamed but they weren't low. The whole house had a serene feeling of air and space despite not having big windows. She thought of their town house with its tall sash windows. This felt lighter.

She raced through the interconnected rooms until she reached the back of the house. 'Crikey! Dan, you're going to love this!' The enormous Aga gleamed against one wall and there seemed to be miles of warm stone flooring between the worktops. The pristine farm table could seat a dozen people.

There wasn't a single item on the table or on any of the worktops that wasn't a kitchen accessory. A beautiful bowl stood in the exact middle of the table, without a spare key, button, USB stick, screwdriver or other cast-off in it. Sophie just knew that when Harriet was home it would hold a selection of seasonal fruit that never went off. They probably didn't even get fruit flies. She thought about the veg drawer that she'd forgotten to empty before they left their house.

'Do they actually live here?' she asked Dan as he came up behind her to put his arms around her waist. She leaned against his chest.

'It would be a pretty big scam otherwise. Unless they're really burglars who wait at the airport for gullible families to swap houses with. Maybe that's how they get their kicks. What do you think? Should we call the police?'

'Don't you dare, I never want to leave here.'

His arms tightened. 'Let's go upstairs.'

She knew by the way he said it that he wasn't talking about inspecting the bathrooms. 'I should check on the children.'

'After,' he whispered into her ear. 'Come on.' Strands of hair tickled her neck from his breath.

The children probably wouldn't *die* in half an hour. But then again, they might. She couldn't leave them to fend for themselves in the countryside. They hadn't even been inside the house yet. 'Let's just check on them quickly. First.'

They found Katie and Oliver in one of the airy barns, exactly where they were told not to go, but Sophie's annoyance disappeared when she saw the goats. They were pure white, and they had babies.

'They're kids,' Katie told her. 'Saanen kids.'

Oliver pointed at one mother, whose greedy offspring were butting her udder. Every so often their tiny tails wagged madly as they drank. 'That's Ophelia,' he said. 'And that one over there is Pandora. Is that right?' he asked the young woman in wellies who stood inside the pen.

'Other way round, but well remembered. Hi, I'm Marion.' She held out her hand, first to Sophie, then to Dan, as they made their introductions over the pen's wooden barrier. She worked with James, she told them. She was in charge of the goats while he was away.

'It's a shame you didn't get the time off, too,' Sophie said. Her mum's office used to close when the owners went on holiday, so everyone got the same weeks off. And the week between Christmas and New Year. They'd closed, too, the day of her mum's funeral.

'Silly bean,' Dan said. 'They can't exactly turn off the goats whenever it suits them.'

'Right, of course, they still need milking every day,' Sophie said. 'I hadn't thought.' The goats were clustered at the edge of their pens, staring at her with their pale hazel eyes. One stood on her back legs with her front ones on the rail.

'What's your capacity here?' Dan asked Marion. He was all business now.

'Production-wise?' Marion asked. 'Forty-one now, plus six bucks and the kids.'

'And your yield?'

'Just over eight pounds per day.' Marion put her hands into the pockets of her dungarees.

'You make the cheese, too? I'd love to see that. If you wouldn't mind.'

'You're welcome any time,' she said. 'I make it every day.'

'No rest for the farmer, eh?' Dan grinned. 'Well, we don't want to get in your way.' He turned towards Katie and Oliver. 'Let's leave Marion to do her job . . . unless you want to stay?'

Marion jumped in, just as Dan must have known she would. 'I don't mind having them here. If you're happy then I can even put them to work.'

'As long as you're sure it's no bother,' Dan said. 'We'll just be in the house if you need us. C'mon, Soph.'

Sophie checked over the children's clothes. Nothing that couldn't be washed. Besides, she didn't have the heart to tear Oliver away. 'I'll unpack, okay?' she told Katie. But Katie wasn't listening.

Dan grabbed her hand as they made their way from the barns. 'That was easy.'

He was kissing her before they'd even closed the front door. 'Time to see what's upstairs.'

'Let me ring Dad first,' she said.

'We don't need his permission.'

'Ha ha. Just to tell him we're here.'

'I've got a better idea.' He held his hand out for her phone.

'What are you doing?'

'Texting. It's quicker. If you ring, you know you won't be able to get off quickly . . . and you deserve to get off – quickly.'

There was no mistaking what he meant by that. The GP *had* recommended more exercise, and she wasn't one to go against sound medical advice. She gave him her phone.

She'd always found Dan so sexy, the way he told her exactly what he wanted in bed. Something about his voice then, low and urgent, never failed to make her quiver. She was one lucky woman, she thought. Soon, though, she wasn't thinking anything because their lovemaking whisked her off into another world.

Her heartbeat finally slowed again as they lay together on the huge bed. Dan drew slow circles on her bare tummy, sending more shivers through her.

'How many blokes can still perform like that after sixteen years?' His chest was puffed up to chocolate soufflé proportions.

'It's because I still turn you on,' she said, glancing side-ways to see his reaction.

'Even after two children, you've still got it, Soph.'

She play-slapped his hand away. Then she started to get up.

'Stay here,' he said. 'You need to relax.' He kissed her deeply, then grabbed his jeans.

'I can't. What will the children think if they come back?'

'They'll think you're resting. And you are. Now's the time to indulge yourself, Soph.' He reached beneath her to pull out the pillow that she'd crushed. He fluffed it before adjusting it behind her back. 'Where's your book?'

Sophie stretched. She could get used to this. 'In my little bag, there.'

He put on her glasses for her, poking the arms behind her ears. They were crooked but she didn't adjust them. 'Have a read. Or a nap,' he said.

'Nice idea, but we need to get food. You saw the fridge.' Completely empty and cleaned to within an inch of its life. Again, she thought of her vegetable drawer.

'Why don't I go into town?' Dan offered. 'I'll take the kids with me. Marion will probably be sick of them by now.'

She probably *could* manage a little nap. They'd been up at dawn to get to the airport. Had all this really happened since this morning?

Dan buttoned his shirt. Then he brushed the front to smooth it. 'I can do the cooking, so just leave everything to me.'

'Or we could make it easy and get takeaway tonight,' she suggested. 'And Harriet said there's a cook in the village. I bet she could come to us from tomorrow if we ring her now.'

'I don't need some stranger cooking when I'm taking care of you now, Soph. I'll cook.'

'That's not much of a holiday for you.' It wasn't much of holiday for her, either, if she was honest. Dan cooking was better than her having to do it, like she did most days, but she'd looked forward to tasting some new dishes.

'I don't mind,' Dan said. 'I want to.'

That seemed to settle that. Sophie wasn't about to look a gift chef in the mouth. She stretched again and snuggled further down under the duvet.

She'd barely started to drift off when Dan's voice floated through the window from below. He must have gone outside to ring the office. Typically thoughtful.

'We're in the fucking English countryside,' she heard him say. Her skin began to prickle. *Fucking English countryside?* He'd seemed as excited to be here as she was.

'But the good news is, we've landed on our feet,' he went on. 'And then some. Sophie loves this place. It's straight out of a film. Now that I'll be in the UK you can ring any time something comes up, okay? How's everything?'

Sophie wished he'd at least waited a little while before talking to Laxmi. She ran his entire office, and that made her worth her weight in the artisan chocolate that he bought by the caseload for her every Christmas. But she was as much a workaholic as Dan.

'What do you mean, carry on for me?' Dan's voice was tense now. Sophie wondered if that made Laxmi as anxious as it did her. 'I told you, Laxmi, nobody is to touch my cases. It doesn't matter. If anyone needs anything, *anything*, you ring me, okay? I'm handling my cases. It makes no difference that I'm not in the office. All right. I will. I'll talk to you later.'

So much for Dan getting a break from work, thought Sophie.

Chapter 5
Thursday

If only Harriet had packed her labelmaker! How annoying that she hadn't predicted needing it, even though she couldn't think of a single scenario in Rome where it would have been handy.

It wasn't just handy in Sophie's house, it was necessary. By Harriet's yardstick, anyway.

She didn't need anyone to point out that her love of orderliness was a bit OTT. She'd always been like that. She recalled being surprised that her friends didn't have an inventory for their toys like she had. She could still clearly remember the sturdy little journal with her neat lettering on the front. *Signing Out Book for Toys (and Games)*. How else could they be sure they never lost anything?

She'd tidied up Sophie's house a lot, but she could still see too much clutter. Every extra kitchen appliance that didn't fit into the overfull cabinets, each pair of shoes that had to live in the hall (neatly arranged, but still), made her teeth clench.

Harriet needed a little sit-down when she opened the linen cupboard.

She assumed it was the linen cupboard, though t-shirts and kitchen cleaning products were also stuffed onto the shelves along with a pair of wellies and, as she excavated further, an array of winter coats. The sheets that were folded – and that wasn't a given, either – didn't even lie flat. They'd just been pushed up against the already teetering piles.

The labelmaker that Harriet ordered online was just what Sophie needed. She'd found an identical one to hers, the original and best, with the spinny alphabet embossing wheel. It would be one of tomorrow's projects. And how happy would Sophie be when she saw everything neatly labelled! Though much of the fun came from making them: the satisfaction of aligning each letter on the wheel. Feeling the faint click as the letter lined up. Working her thumbnail under the back to peel off the stiff label and then running her finger over the raised letters on shiny red tape and, finally, seeing it stuck perfectly centred and level on the edge of its shelf.

When she went downstairs, her family were in the same places she'd left them in the living room.

'Ready for dinner?' They didn't usually eat this late. James was up with the goats, so he had an excuse for eating like a farmer. Harriet and Billie had fallen into the same early habits.

Well, now they were out of their routines.

Billie glanced up from her phone but said nothing.

'Good idea,' James said.

'Good, let's go.'

'Where?' Billie wanted to know.

'We'll find something. Close.' Harriet added this last bit especially for Billie. She was so like James, and it was a blessing, she supposed, that she hadn't inherited Harriet's pinging mind. Billie seemed happy sitting for hours doing nothing. 'Just being', she claimed. Harriet wasn't interested in *just being* when she could be *just doing*. 'Come on, let's go.'

'Why can't we order in?' Billie looked at James, not Harriet.

'Mm, yeah, let's order in. We could get anything we want,' James said. He'd been *just being*, too, reading a book about trees.

'We're in London! We can get anything we want by walking out the front door. Honestly. Get up. We're going out for dinner like civilised humans do.'

Massive inconvenience was written all over Billie's face as she unfolded herself from the armchair. 'You win.'

'We all win,' Harriet reminded her.

Sophie had been right: they were in the middle of everything, which made it doubly annoying when Billie wanted to stop at the very first restaurant they passed. Harriet didn't break her stride as she said no. The second? No. Third, fourth and fifth? 'It's not like home,' she snapped. 'We actually have choices here.'

'And you're making us walk past every single one before you decide,' Billie grumbled back.

'Fine, have it your way.' Harriet yanked open the door to a passable-looking Italian. 'Just don't complain to me if it's not good.'

Inside, Harriet considered her family across the small table. They loved to think they were so flexible, but they were creatures of habit, too. Who didn't enjoy the comfort of sameness? Eating the same breakfast, stopping at the same café, standing in the same spot waiting for the train, listening to the same radio stations, checking the same websites and apps online. Harriet was just aware enough to admit that she preferred living in an orderly world.

Billie happily tucked into the bread basket like she always did. James was running his finger down the menu. Harriet knew what he was doing. James was an includer when it came to ordering. He gathered together all of the options he thought he'd like, then chose the most appealing. That way, if the waiter said they'd run out of his first choice, he'd still be happy with his next one.

Harriet, on the other hand, was an excluder. Whenever a menu choice had an ingredient that she didn't fancy, she knocked it out of the running. Then she picked from what was left over.

They both got what they wanted in the end, but from opposite positions.

Story of their lives, really.

If only her family would be the tiniest bit grateful for the effort she was making. No matter what activities she offered over dinner: the Natural History Museum and London Zoo for James, a West End show that Billie had mentioned wanting to see, guided walks by the river or through some of London's historic areas, their reaction was only slightly warmer than a proposed trip to the supermarket on a Saturday morning.

It didn't seem too much to ask that her family try to enjoy themselves in one of the greatest cities in the world, when she'd spent the last three years' holidays bumping her head on the low beams of the most remote cottages she could find, because she knew how much James loved being in the middle of nowhere. She'd even gone walking every day with him and Billie, slogging up mountainsides laden with packed sandwiches and extra plasters, maps, trail mix, mosquito repellent, sunscreen, the wireless phone charger, emergency water bottles and half a dozen extra layers for when everyone got cold or wet or the wind picked up.

'Listen,' she said, poking her tiramisu spoon across the table at them, 'we're going to treat London as a holiday whether you like it or not. Otherwise why did we come here?'

'Because you wanted to,' James said.

She shot a dirty look first at her husband in general, then at the chocolate powder in one corner of his mouth. 'So did Billie, if I remember correctly.' Harriet always remembered correctly. 'I believe she thought the idea was wicked. There's nothing wicked about sitting in someone else's house doing nothing, so I suggest you both get on board with this, because it's happening. You can either be happy or unhappy about it. Your choice.'

'Our choice?' said James. 'Since when is anything our choice?'

'Come on, James, please. Can't you even appreciate that I'm trying to make it a nice holiday for everyone?' She knew she pushed them sometimes, but they wouldn't do anything otherwise. And she really was doing her very best to accommodate them.

'I know you are.' James started to reach for her non-tiramisu hand, but stopped. 'Only you could manoeuvre your way around a continent-wide natural disaster and get a holiday out of it. We can do a museum tomorrow if you want.' He searched her face. 'And a walk,' he added. 'What do you say, Billie? For Mum's sake.' He pushed his chair back. ''Scuse me, I'll just pop to the loo.'

'We're nearly finished. Why not go at the house?'

But he was already out of his chair. 'Won't take a minute. Grab the waiter for the bill if you see him.'

She knew exactly why he didn't wait till they got back. It would be harder to use his phone with her around. She couldn't very well burst in on him here like she sometimes did at home. Not all the time, obviously. A person does need their privacy in toilet habits. She only did it when she knew he was in there faffing with his phone. Perusing *Goat Monthly* or *Farmer's Bazaar* or some such ridiculous website. That man couldn't stop thinking about his animals for one minute. It drove her mad.

Not to mention the questionable hygiene of handling phones in loos.

Her eyes drifted to the huge wall of wine bottles behind the narrow bar at the back of the restaurant. There was room for three bottles by four in each square, eight squares across by six squares high was forty-eight, times twelve was 576, minus . . . she counted the few empty spaces until James returned to the table.

'Get your fix?' she asked.

His eyes darted to the loo and back. 'What do you mean?'

Then his phone chimed. Harriet saw Persephone's name flash on his screen. James put the phone back in his pocket.

'Never mind,' she said.

Harriet waited until after breakfast the next morning to ring Sophie. 'Your house is so beautiful!' Sophie gushed when she answered. 'It's perfect, the whole area, the village and everything, it's just stunning. You are so lucky.'

Try living there, Harriet thought. But instead she said, 'Your house is . . . very central. We went to the Italian place near you for dinner last night. It was tasty. I'm afraid you won't find any Italian in our village except for ASK Pizza.'

'That's okay, we want to eat locally. Dan did a little shop yesterday at the butcher's. Does everyone here know each other?'

Harriet sighed. 'Yes.'

'That's lovely. We've lived in our house for ten years and I still don't know all my neighbours.'

What a heavenly thought.

'It was such an inspired idea to swap houses,' Sophie went on. 'Although I'm afraid we left ours in a bit of a tip in our rush to catch the flight. I'm sorry about that. Especially since yours is so tidy. Feel free to shove anything out of the way while you're there, of course.'

Harriet was glad for the retrospective permission. 'I've moved a few things,' she said, 'but we can put everything back before we leave.'

'Oh, don't bother with that. We're used to not knowing where anything is.'

Yet another reason for her labelmaker. 'There's a lot of food in the fridge,' said Harriet. 'Would you like me to check the dates?'

'The dates? Crikey, no, don't make more work for yourself. I just throw it away when it smells.'

'It smells.'

Sophie laughed. 'Then throw it away. Are you finding everything okay?'

'Yes, including the snake.'

There was a pause on the line. 'Oh? Yes, I hope that's not a problem. I guess I think of her like I would a fish. Well, not exactly a fish. Just that she stays in her enclosure most of the time.'

'What do you mean, most of the time?'

'You can leave her in the whole time you're there. Carlos will be in and out to look after her anyway. He knows we're away an extra week.'

Harriet laughed. 'Yes, I'll do that.'

She found herself still smiling after she'd hung up. Other than officially for work, she didn't usually talk to people on the phone. James arranged periodic nights out with Persephone in the village. She had a standing dinner date with Julia and her London friends, always at the same restaurant at the same time on the last Thursday of the quarter. She booked the table on a rolling twelve-month basis. That way nobody wasted time wondering where to go or whether they'd like the menu. Her only other social engagements were the post-work drinks with her colleagues that she said yes to every third time they asked her.

Harriet was studying the online map when James shuffled into the kitchen with the newspaper under his arm. He'd been up at his usual time, even though there probably wasn't a goat to milk within twenty miles. Harriet woke to find him showered and dressed, with breakfast bought and coffee brewed. 'Would you rather go to Harrods or the Fortnum & Mason food hall after the museum?' she asked. 'Harrods is thirteen minutes' walk, but there's a forty per cent chance of rain this afternoon. Fortnum's is fifteen minutes by Tube. No changes.'

He scanned every headline on the front page before he answered. 'That sounds like a maths problem from school.'

'Can you solve it?'

The pages rustled as he folded them to just the article he wanted. For some reason he always did that instead of laying it out on the table. 'Answer C? I was just at Waitrose. It's five minutes round the corner.'

Harriet was tempted to remind him how nice that kind of convenience was. 'I want to get some special treats while we can,' she said. 'So, will it be Harrods or Fortnum's?'

He sauntered to the coffee-maker and took an age to fill his mug. Then he opened the lid on the milk for a sniff. Harriet could count on one hand the number of times in all their years together that the milk had gone off, yet he'd never lost that habit.

Leaning against the worktop, James slurped his coffee. Eventually he said, 'Why do we have to schedule our schedule to keep to a schedule?'

'We could spend two weeks staring at each other in the house. Would that be better?'

He sighed. 'What do you need to get? Waitrose has a lot, you know.'

'You're talking to me like I don't order from Waitrose every single week. I want delicacies, terrines and fresh pasta and delicious cakes. And those crumbly biscuits for cheese.'

'Maybe some goat's cheese?' James ventured.

She stared at him. He must know what a red rag that was to her. 'You could get some of your own cheese if you'd bothered to take my advice. In fact, you could have picked some up when you got breakfast this morning.'

James closed his eyes. 'If I'd taken your advice then my cheese would be right next to the Babybel at ASDA. Why can't you drop it? Haven't we been over this enough?' He shook his head.

'Your crown is crooked, drama queen,' she said.

'That award goes to you in this case, dear heart. I didn't make a big deal of it, remember?'

She wished she could forget. If only she'd never heard of the International Cheese Awards, then this thorn of resentment wouldn't still be digging into their relationship.

Actually, she shouldn't wish away the awards, because James took the bronze medal there. She'd been so proud of him for that. And when the Waitrose rep had emailed him, Harriet was sure he'd been talent-spotted. 'I'm the Spice Girl of the cheese world,' he'd joked.

His business was on its way, Harriet just knew it. The mail orders were doing well, but Waitrose was huge. James was about to hit the big time.

She'd kept her mobile on her desk at work the day of his meeting (something she never did), waiting for his call after he'd finished.

He rang just after lunchtime. There was a tasting, as she predicted. Everyone said the right things, naturally. Then they broke it to him, right after they'd tucked into two of his favourite cheeses. They loved it. It just needed to be a bit less *goaty*. James might have won an award for it, and it was delicious. But goaty. Many of their customers preferred a less strong flavour. Could he do that?

'What did you say?' Harriet kept her voice measured. She knew her husband. She feared the answer.

'I asked why not make it a bit less cheesy, too, while I'm at it? I could talk to my goats, maybe, and get them to be less goaty. Then I could spend four months – feeding and keeping the goats, milking, pasteurising, cutting, draining, moulding, ageing and turning the cheeses – to make goat's cheese that didn't taste goaty or cheesy. No problem. I'll call it butter.'

James had burned his butter with Waitrose.

They'd been bickering over it ever since.

'You know something?' James said now. 'I hope I don't die before you do. You'll probably etch it on my headstone.'

'*Could have been in Waitrose*,' she said. '*Instead of Only in Our Hearts*.'

'*Never did What was Asked of Him*,' he added. '*Finally Resting in Peace*.'

They smiled at each other.

Chapter 6
Friday

Sophie floated from the massage room in exactly the gelatinous state she'd hoped for when her Italian holiday was still on the cards. Who needed Italy when she had the New You Spa? She hadn't felt so relaxed in ages, though she was now heartily sorry for all the times she'd made fun of the pampered women in her neighbourhood who swanned around in yoga pants and bragged about their treatments. That's what people in the know call them: treatments.

Now she was one of those women, using words like treatments. Though she didn't see herself in yoga pants. She preferred dresses. So did Dan. She hardly ever wore jeans any more. Not like when they'd first met. She cringed to remember her fashion non-sense then.

She didn't have the right wardrobe to go out with Dan, and there seemed to be no end to the invitations to glamorous events. With each one, she fell deeper in love, and deeper in debt as she tried not to embarrass him at Wimbledon and Royal Ascot (Ladies Day, no less!) and even the famous polo tournaments, where she definitely channelled Julia Roberts in *Pretty Woman*. There was more opera at the giant greenhouse, and even a catered picnic with proper cutlery and real glasses at Glyndebourne. She did need a gown for that. Mum met her in Oxford Street to help her find something.

'Though I don't know what's in style, ballgown-wise,' Mum said as they made their way to Selfridges. 'They don't wear them much down at the pub, but we'll find something nice. Maybe something you can shorten later if you don't need it again.' She must have noticed Sophie's expression. 'I just mean that I've only worn a long gown once in my life, when I married Dad. How many operas are you going to go to? It's not really your thing.'

Sophie pulled up short. 'It is Dan's thing, though,' she said, 'and if we're going to be together then it's mine, too. Mum? Do you think I'm being silly, trying so hard?'

'What? No, love, why would you say that?'

She watched the shoppers streaming past them. 'Because I love him so much,' she murmured. 'I can hardly believe we're together, that he wants to do so much for me . . . That he loves me, too.'

Her mum spun her around on the pavement. 'Sophie Marie, you listen to me. You're just as good as him, and of course he loves you because you're my wonderful girl. I want you to ring me up whenever you need a reminder. Got it?'

'Got it, Mum. Thanks.'

But Sophie didn't need reminding when Dan told her constantly. He only wanted what was best for her.

Now, she wondered why she'd never done regular spa sessions before like he'd suggested. She hadn't minded the pan pipe music or the incense that reminded her of Camden Market or Molly the masseuse's constant questions, whispered while she thumbed the knots out of Sophie's back.

She didn't even care about wearing paper pants in front of Molly. She was paying the young woman to handle her wobbly bits. Well, Dan was paying her.

Not that Sophie minded her figure. She never had, though all of her school friends seemed to be squeezing themselves into skinny jeans (never in a million years would Sophie be caught dead in those) or surviving on cabbage soup and grapefruit juice. She couldn't be bothered when everything about her was soft and ample and, she thought, quite nice.

Even now, beyond the tautness of youth, she hardly ever looked over her shoulder into the wall mirror at home. Not because she wouldn't like what she saw. Only because there was no need. She knew exactly how much orange peel was back there. Enough for a citrus and sultana scone, maybe. Definitely not enough for a whole cake.

People often described her as cuddly, just like her mum and gran had been. She'd take that any day over skinny and grumpy. If it meant her thighs stopped moving slightly after she did, then so be it.

'Shall we book you in for another treatment?' Molly whispered as they made their way back to the reception desk. Whispering was required here. Molly looked like she whispered outside of work anyway. She was tiny, from her narrow shoulders to her handspan waist to her delicate feet. Her dark eyes were huge in her heart-shaped face. That, and the wisps of pale hair that floated around her head like she'd rubbed it with a balloon, gave her a very otherworldly look.

'Yes please, for tomorrow. Could I do three o'clock again?' She hoped Molly would be free. She had amazingly strong hands for such a little woman.

'I'm sorry, but that time is already taken.'

The teenage receptionist leaned over Molly's shoulder to check the appointment book. 'You're Sophie, right? I've already booked you in for tomorrow at three.'

'Wow, psychic, too!' Sophie said. 'Thank you.'

'I wish. I'd play the lottery. Your husband rang and booked everything ahead.'

How typically thoughtful. 'Great, a massage a day keeps the doctor away.'

'Exactly, though it's not for a massage tomorrow. It's a lymphatic drainage.'

'Do my lymphatics need draining?' That sounded painful.

The receptionist shrugged. 'I s'pose so.' She looked at the book again. 'Then on Monday you've got the age defy facial, Tuesday it's the toning tightener, that's the seaweed wrap—'

'It'll take inches off, you'll love it!' Molly said.

Sophie didn't mention that that wasn't a priority. It might make Molly think she wasn't grateful for all this effort.

'Then Wednesday morning . . .' the receptionist went on. 'I can write them all down if you like.'

'No, it's okay, actually,' said Sophie, 'surprises will be more fun.'

The sun warmed her face as she walked along the footpath back to the house. Birds chirped and darted around the hedge that ran between the path and the vivid green fields. What were they growing? Not lettuce, but something leafy. If ASDA didn't label it then she didn't usually know what it was.

Everyone around here probably knew their apples from their elbows. All this nature was so soothing! She could hear traffic on the other side of the trees, but it was only background noise. All the little birds nearly drowned it out.

She stopped to watch a tractor chugging up and down the rows in a distant field.

Nobody passed her on the path, but she wished they would – a dog walker or child on a pony or even a Lycra-clad runner. She was brimming with the urge to wish someone a cheery afternoon.

Molly must have rubbed loose some extra happy hormones.

But a little of her happy bubble deflated when she reached the house. Katie and Oliver were bickering in the front garden. 'What's wrong?'

'Dad won't let us go to the barns.' Oliver was close to tears. Sophie's heart squeezed for him as she glanced around. Dan didn't like it when he got emotional. 'He's banned us. It's not fair!' He was trying very hard not to let his lip quiver.

Katie balled her fists on her hips. 'We weren't bothering Marion. I hate Dad.' Wisps of hair had come loose from her plait. They quivered in her anger.

'If you hate Dad, then why are you arguing with each other instead of him?'

Katie stared at her.

'Dunno.' Oliver sniffed.

Sophie felt a prick of annoyance at Dan. 'Where's your father?'

'He's down there making cheese with Marion. It's not fair.'

'You've mentioned that,' she said. 'Let's go and talk to him.'

She knew that the cheesemaking kitchen was in the barn, but she didn't know why she was creeping there. She couldn't hear any voices inside. 'Hello?' she called through the closed door.

'Hang on,' Marion called back. Then the door opened. Marion was dressed all in white, from her hat to her coat to her shoe coverings. 'Hi! Do you want to come in? I'll get you kitted out.'

'Oh, well, no, that's okay, we were just . . .' Now that she was there, she wasn't sure what she was doing.

'Really, it's fine,' Marion said. 'I'm happy to show you.' She was already pulling more coats off the shelf by the door. She rolled up the sleeves for Oliver, but the hat kept slipping over his eyes. 'Sorry – we're out of small ones,' Marion said, leading them all back into the cheese kitchen. 'I need to order more. We let the children take them home. For some reason they love the hats.'

Dan grinned at her as she tucked her hair into the hat Marion gave her. He, too, was all in white. 'You're gorgeous,' he told her as she shuffled beside him with the children.

She was pretty sure he was teasing but she thanked him anyway. She felt like a great white lump, but Marion managed to look perfectly comfortable despite being dressed like a nuclear scientist. Some people suited uniforms better than others.

'It's just about ready for me to add the bacteria culture,' Marion told everyone as she slowly stirred an oar through the pale-yellow liquid in the big tub.

'Wow, it's a very physical process,' Sophie said. How had she got herself into this cheesemaking lesson? All she wanted to do was go into the house and read her book.

''Tis, all the cheeses are made by hand. Saves me going to the gym.'

'You're adding good bacteria, aren't you?' Katie asked. 'Not the kind that Dad uses the antibacterial wipes on. He's not supposed to use them because they end up in the ocean. Plus, they kill the weak bugs, which lets the strong ones get stronger.' She levelled a look at her father. 'It's only our entire future, Dad, but don't mind us kids.'

Marion buried a smile. 'Those wipes don't make any distinction between good and bad bacteria, but no, this isn't harmful. It's what helps give the cheese its nice flavour.'

It was almost an hour later before Sophie found a way to politely extract herself with the children.

Katie threw herself into the reading chair in the conservatory. The long summer day bathed them all in sunlight. 'That was cool,' Katie said. 'I don't know why Dad didn't want us there. Mum, did you know that's how cheese was made?' But instead of waiting for her mother's answer (which was no, but still), she said, 'I bet Dad knew already.'

'Dad knows everything,' Oliver added with absolute certainty.

Well, he certainly thinks he does, Sophie thought. 'I do know some things too, you know.'

'Like what?' Katie sounded genuinely surprised by the notion.

'I know when a thirteen year old is skating on very thin ice.'

But Oliver jumped to Sophie's defence. 'Mum knows lots of things. She can bake a cake without looking at the recipe, and make pancakes and . . . eggs. And she always knows where my book bag is. And she only shrank the clothes that one time when Dad's new jumper was in it.'

'I am a bit of a scrambled egg expert.' Sophie laughed. High praise indeed.

Dan came in not long after them.

'I should start dinner,' he said as he reached for her hand. 'How was your treatment? Though your hand is like jelly, so I can guess.'

'It was beyond wonderful! So relaxing.' She hesitated. 'Thanks for booking more treatments, though I don't know what half of them are.'

Dan smiled. 'You're welcome. Don't worry, they're all exactly what you need.'

'I need a fat wrap?'

Dan looked at her. 'I thought you'd like that one. You mentioned that you felt a bit puffy.'

Had she? That didn't sound like her. 'They'll all be lovely, thank you.'

As she watched Dan busy himself around the kitchen, pulling out pots, chopping fresh herbs and generally being the perfect partner, Sophie counted her blessings. Dan did know what she needed. He reminded her of that all the time.

'I've got to make a few calls,' he said. 'I'll be quick. Don't bother with any of this. I'll put dinner together when I'm finished. You just relax.' He was staring at his phone as he left for James's office.

She was glad to leave it. He'd only get cross if she tried to help, anyway. Dan liked to make everything perfect for them. Sophie sank down onto the plush sofa, sighed deeply and closed her eyes. Yes, she counted her blessings.

The next morning, she pressed her fingers into the tops of her shoulders as she listened to Harriet's mobile start ringing. She was a bit tender from Molly's magic massage fingers. 'Did you have fun yesterday?' she asked when Harriet picked up.

'It was everything I hoped for! We saw two exhibitions at the Natural History Museum and then popped into the V&A, though we'll go back there, I'm sure. We made it to Harrods food hall and then had a late lunch in Soho. Then mussels for dinner at Belgo.'

That was more than Sophie usually did in a week. Maybe she'd take the children to explore a new footpath today. Before her treatment, though, in case she needed all the lymphs she could get for the walk. 'You're definitely making the most of London.'

'I always loved living here,' Harriet explained. 'I feel like a Londoner even though I wasn't born here.'

'Oh? Where were you born?'

'Not far away. In Epping. Essex.'

'You don't have the Essex accent,' Sophie said. 'Though is that really Essex?'

'Yes.'

'Anyway, the forest is pretty there. I'm from West Ruislip,' Sophie went on. 'We're at opposite ends of—'

'The Central line,' said Harriet.

'Maybe we've stood next to each other at the same station and didn't know it.'

'That's not likely, statistically, given the number of people who use the Tube. At best we've breathed the same nano-dust particles. Twelve million per minute according to TFL's data. By the way, I meant to tell you to turn on the air purifiers. They're very quiet. You won't even know they're running.'

'But this is the countryside,' Sophie said. 'What are you purifying?'

Harriet laughed. 'The countryside. How can you stand the smell? Dung. Haven't you noticed?'

'I suppose you've got special purifiers that blow nano-dust particles around the house, just to get that authentic London feel, eh?'

'I'd take particulate matter over dung any day,' said Harriet.

When she'd hung up with Harriet, she said to Dan, 'I hope they weren't too surprised by Spot.'

He had his feet propped up on one of the chairs at the enormous farm table. Katie and Oliver were on the sofas

69

in the conservatory. The TV in there was on but the volume was low. She didn't know where Harriet's family spent most of their time, but this was already the heart of the house for them.

At first Sophie wasn't sure he'd heard her. That happened a lot, but then Dan looked up from his phone. 'You didn't tell them about Spot?'

'Of course I bloody didn't! They might not have swapped.'

Dan chuckled. 'Good thinking.'

Sophie revelled in the compliment.

'Mum,' Katie called from the sofa, 'could we ring Carlos to see how Spot is doing?'

Sophie's glance darted to Dan. He wasn't crazy about the snake. But his eyes stayed on his phone.

'It's only been a day, Katie. Let's give her a chance to miss you.'

'But I miss her!'

'It's not like she's going to talk on the phone, is she? Leave it.'

'But Mum!' Katie whined. 'Why can't you just ring Carlos?'

'I said leave it, Katie.' Her glance darted again towards Dan. 'We'll ring tomorrow and ask Carlos to text you some photos. Now, enough.'

She never liked disciplining the children, but it usually fell to her. Not that Dan wasn't a hands-on father, but his long hours at the office meant that she was the one who was with them most.

That's why this holiday was going to be such bliss. It had been ages since they'd spent so much time all together with no distractions.

Sophie was pouring a second bowl of cereal for herself when Oliver said, 'Someone's in the garden.'

'He's probably a neighbour who's lost his cow or something,' said Dan. He ambled into the conservatory. Sophie followed. Soon they were all peering through the French doors.

'He looks like a soldier with that uniform,' Katie said.

Dan flung open the doors. 'Hey, hello!'

The man gave a cheery wave.

Dan and Sophie made their way towards the man. The dewy grass felt good on Sophie's bare feet. 'Can I help you?' Dan called.

'Sorry if I disturbed you! I'm just looking things over for the fundraiser.'

'The what?' Dan asked.

'The fundraiser. For the Scouts. I've been dealing with Harriet about it?' His eyes darted to Sophie. 'She did say it was all right to come today.'

Now Sophie saw that his uniform wasn't armed forces at all. That's right. Harriet had mentioned the Boy Scouts event.

'Sorry,' she told him. 'They're away. We're just staying in their house. Would you like a cup of tea? Coffee? We've just made some. Have you had breakfast?'

'Soph, let the man do his job.'

'Oh, sorry, yes of course.'

The man answered with a kindly smile. 'No, thank you. I'll be out of your way in no time. Just seeing where everything's going to go. You know, be prepared and all that. Don't mind me.' He waved to the children, who were watching him from the doorway.

'Should I ring Harriet?' Sophie wondered when they'd returned to the conservatory.

'No need, it's taken care of,' said Dan. 'We don't want her to think we can't handle things here. It sounds like

71

she's got it all organised. Don't worry yourself, okay? Now, I need to make a few phone calls. Call me if he needs anything, though.'

'I'll let you know if he decides he wants a cup of tea.' She smirked, but Dan was already on his way down the hall towards James's office.

Sophie didn't mean to eavesdrop, she really didn't, but Dan wasn't making any effort to keep his phone call private. He could have at least closed the door.

'I don't want Jeremy covering my clients,' she heard him say. 'I told you, Laxmi, I can do whatever's needed. You were to ring me as soon as anything came in.'

In the kitchen, Sophie busied herself with a few dirty dishes, but she soon lost interest in the washing-up. Something about the way he was speaking – level, almost robotic – made her nervous for Laxmi.

'I'm always on my mobile,' Dan said. 'Are you trying to tell me what's best for *my* clients? I'm sorry, I mistook you for the assistant and me for the solicitor. Do you think I don't know what's best? Well, do you? Am I some trainee, Laxmi, who needs his boss looking over his shoulder, dotting all his Is and crossing his Ts?' His voice rose. 'Don't you dare let Jeremy near my files, or I swear to God you won't have a job when I get back. Do you understand me? You work for *me*. Tell me you understand me, Laxmi!'

Sophie had never heard Dan shout like that at anyone other than her before. It sounded so nasty. Nasty and disrespectful. It shot such dread into her heart that she found it hard to breathe.

She crept to the office to knock on the door frame. 'Dan, is everything all right?'

He put his hand over his mobile. 'It's fine, darling. Laxmi's out getting coffee. I think the entire police force might be driving by with their sirens on. Just making sure she can hear me. I'm sorry I disturbed you.'

Then, more quietly to Laxmi, he said, 'Did you get that, Laxmi? Are we all clear? Good girl.'

Chapter 7

Saturday

Although there was no rule, it seemed like Harriet's turn to ring Sophie. Maybe she should establish that formally, just so there were no misunderstandings. Harriet didn't want any misunderstandings with Sophie. She felt very warm towards the woman, and wondered if they were becoming friends. Then she wondered if she should establish that formally, too.

Sophie made her laugh, and didn't seem to take herself too seriously. Harriet took everything seriously, but she admired informality in others.

It had been quite a while since she'd had a new friend. Eleven years and seven months. That's when she'd started at her law firm. New friend-making options narrowed outside of work. They'd squeezed to a pinpoint when she moved to the village. With an hour and a half return commute to Oxford, there wasn't time for extracurricular relationship-building. A few people in the village had been civil, like Bea from the tea shop, and the butcher, but they weren't falling over themselves to be her bestie. Only Persephone made the effort, but they were already friendly thanks to James, so she wasn't a new datapoint.

'Some of your spices are out of date,' she told Sophie. 'I could replace them for you.'

'Hello to you, too,' Sophie answered.

'Yes, hello. How are you?'

'Good, thanks. I had a lymphatic drainage massage yesterday at the spa.'

'How are they today? Your lymphatics?'

'Well-drained, I think. I was definitely a puddle after. Do you go to that spa a lot?'

'Six times a year,' Harriet said. 'Does that qualify as a lot?'

'I've been to a spa about three times in my life, so yes, compared to me.'

'Why haven't you gone more often if you enjoy it? Can you afford it?'

When Sophie hesitated, Harriet figured she must be tallying up the annual cost.

'Disposable income-wise, I mean,' Harriet clarified, to help Sophie with her calculation.

'Well, um, yes, we've got plenty. Although it's Dan's, really. I don't work, so I shouldn't be wasting it.'

Harriet paused to slot her answers into the right order. 'But Sophie, just because he gets the pay cheque doesn't mean you don't work. You've got a full-time job looking after your children. A live-in nanny averages two thousand pounds or more a month in London. Plus room and board. You do that job.'

'Not as much now that they're older,' said Sophie. 'Although I seem to be carting them around to more activities all the time. I can handle that, since I don't have a job. I just do some volunteer work in the Salvation Army kitchen. It's nothing special, peeling hard-boiled eggs or chopping onions, whatever the cooks need on the day. Do you have any idea how much chopped onion goes into their lunches?'

Harriet admitted that she'd never thought about it.

'I also stuff envelopes for a few of the charity appeals.'

'Right,' said Harriet. 'That's . . .'

'That's Mondays and Wednesdays,' Sophie went on. 'Then on Tuesdays and Thursdays I'm a stockroom assistant for the cancer charity shop, you know, just getting donated clothes ready for sale. Fridays there's the food bank.'

'Sophie, then you are working,' Harriet said.

'Oh no, it's only volunteering.' She laughed. 'I haven't got any real responsibility. I'd be hopeless at a proper job. I didn't even get the volunteer work myself, Dan did. He's always finding worthwhile things for me to do. Except in summer, obviously, and term breaks when the children are off. But that doesn't count as a job because I love it.'

What silliness. 'Just because I love being a solicitor doesn't mean it's not a job. If you work then you should get paid. That's the deal. If an employer tried paying you in enjoyment he'd be taken to a tribunal.'

Harriet didn't like hearing stay-at-home parents talking like this. Couldn't they see that they simply enjoyed an alternative method of accounting? 'Your pay is an internal transfer, that's all, for looking after the children, the house, Dan. And you don't get time off. Dan couldn't have the life he does without you. He's lucky he's got you to mind the children. You're more reliable than anyone he could hire. And as for wasting money, what's wasteful about looking after your health? Or at least your drainage.'

Sophie laughed. 'You're right. I'm going to book more massages when I get back to London. Maybe I'll ask for a course of treatments for my birthday.'

'When is that? How old are you?' She'd guess mid-thirties.

'Forty-one, and not till October. When's yours?'

'That's too long to wait. You should book a course as soon as you get back.'

'When's your birthday?' Sophie repeated.

Harriet hadn't forgotten the question. 'Two weeks from tomorrow.'

'Are you going to celebrate?'

'Absolutely not,' said Harriet. She hadn't celebrated her birthday since she was twenty-five. Then it was only because her parents threw a surprise party for her. She gave strict orders, before they'd even cut the cake, that *that* wasn't ever to happen again.

People made too much of birthdays, especially the 'big' ones. The date of one's birth was no more momentous than the date before or after it. A birthday was simply the point at which one person was born within one of earth's twenty-four-hour rotations (out of something like 350,000, as it happened). In other words, not worth the breath it took to blow up the balloons.

'I love my birthday,' said Sophie. 'You might change your mind.'

Harriet doubted that, when she got the sweats at the very idea of talking to any more people than could fit comfortably in the back of a taxi.

'The Scout leader was here to look at the garden, by the way,' Sophie added.

'Good. He was scheduled to.' She was glad to move away from birthdays.

'Is there anything I should do for that?'

'No, I've arranged it all,' Harriet told her. Her mind raced over the plan. 'The organiser will be there on Monday for the initial assessment, although the Scout leader should have fed back. He won't need access to the house, and I've sent him a schematic for the outside. The vendors have all got their deadlines for delivery. I'm sorry about that, but everything should be taken care of with no disruption for you.'

'No problem. So how are you enjoying London?'

'I love being here, though James doesn't.'

'Oh no, I'm sorry! Do make everything comfortable for yourselves in the house. If there's anything you need, just say.'

'It's not the house. It's him. He hates the city, which is problematic because he needs to love this holiday.'

'I guess he needs the break. I know how you feel. Dan hasn't had a holiday in three years.'

Sophie was missing the point, but that wasn't her fault when Harriet hadn't told her the point. The urge to share this information surprised her. On the one hand, she barely knew Sophie. She wasn't in the habit of bringing strangers into her confidence, especially about something so personal. But it would feel really good to have someone to talk to. Usually that was James. There were advantages in talking to an outside party. Should she?

But then Sophie added, 'I really hope Dan can relax, too. So far he's been on his phone a lot.'

The moment was gone. 'That's understandable when he's away from his clients. The work doesn't stop, much as we'd like it to.' She thought of her own office. She'd promised she would only ring once, next Friday, to check in. In her opinion, Dan should have made the same commitment to his family. 'Are you sure I can't replace your out-of-date spices?'

'What do you mean by out of date?' Sophie asked. 'It's oregano, not chicken. I'm sure they're fine, but knock yourself out if you want. You must be sure to give me your bank details though, for anything you buy.'

Harriet promised before they said goodbye. Then she turned to James and said, 'We're winning. In the house swap.'

'It's not a competition, dear heart.'

Pssh, as if. 'We're still winning.'

Carlos rang the doorbell just after breakfast. At least he didn't let himself in with his keys this time.

'Do you want a drink?' James prompted from the kitchen when she'd answered the door.

'Oh, yes. Do you want a drink?' Harriet repeated.

'Sure, thank you, a tea would be nice.' He followed her back to the kitchen. 'Have you heard from Sophie and Dan?'

'I've just been on the phone to Sophie.' Harriet flicked on the kettle.

'Is she having fun?'

'Yes.' She added a teabag to one of the mugs from the cabinet. At least they were all together in one place now. Sophie had had them scattered everywhere: mixed in with glasses, piled on top of dishes, even in the drawers where most of the pots and pans had been.

Harriet didn't say anything else, so Carlos didn't take long to drink his tea. Then he disappeared upstairs to do whatever one did to amuse a python.

She had to bite down a sigh when Billie came into the kitchen. 'You are not wearing that today.'

James gave her a look but didn't say anything.

'Quite obviously, Mum, I am.' Once she'd poured herself some coffee, she hitched up the back of her faded cut-off denim shorts. 'You're the one who's always saying I should get my legs out more. See? They're out.'

'I meant in something pretty. How long have you had those tatty old things?' She could almost forgive the shorts, which were too long for Billie's slim legs, if she'd wear a nice top instead of that stretched-out old rainbow t-shirt (also faded). 'You're such a lovely girl. I just wish you'd put in some effort. You will change before we go into town, won't you?'

'No, Mum, I won't, actually. I'm sorry, for the millionth time, that I'm not the fashion model you want me to be, but this is what I like to wear. I don't criticise your clothes.'

'What's wrong with my clothes?' Harriet knew they were perfectly fine. Better than fine. Stylish, even. She'd set out every single outfit, from the shoes to the top, before she'd packed. And repacked.

Billie didn't even give her the courtesy of an answer. Instead she started flicking around on her blasted phone.

Their daughter could creep under her skin and lodge herself there like nobody else. Even James didn't unsettle her the way Billie could.

Harriet's heart slivered a little more every time she thought about the way they'd been getting on lately. Which she couldn't help but do whenever they were in the same room.

Billie's independent streak was nothing new. She was Harriet's daughter, after all. Her smart, funny, proud, kind, engaging and beautiful daughter. The daughter who wouldn't let Harriet close now no matter what she did. That was the constantly heartbreaking part: to be so near such a wonderful girl, yet not be allowed to reach her.

Other mothers had good relationships with their daughters. Harriet envied those women. Sometimes she hated them.

She'd tried everything she could think of, but she hadn't a clue how to fix what she was sure she'd somehow broken. She'd spent a fortune on courses and books promising answers. Amazon would deliver another one this week while they were away, but she didn't hold out much hope. She already knew all about how teenage brains were wired.

She'd studied all the advice about talking so they'd listen, listening so they'd talk, being firm, being easy, being their friend, not being their friend, setting boundaries, not setting boundaries. She'd tried love, logic and leaving Billie alone.

They may as well have been from different countries for all they understood each other.

'Are you coming with us today or not?' she asked Billie. She heard the exhaustion in her own voice.

James folded the paper into another article-sized square.

'Will I have to change clothes?'

'I'd like that,' Harriet told her.

'Then I'll stay here, thanks. I'll hang out with the snake.'

'Billie . . .'

'We'll text you where we are in case you change your mind.' James had cut her off.

'Thanks, Dad.'

He smiled at his daughter while Harriet imagined popping his eye out with his cereal spoon. She stamped on the thought almost as soon as it came into her head, though. What was wrong with her? She was supposed to be rekindling her relationship with the man she loved. She shouldn't be thinking about maiming him.

Instead, she hunted through Sophie's cabinets and plucked out all the herb and spice jars. Twenty-six. She lined them up on the worktop, smallest to biggest. Then she reordered them, herbs on one end, spices on the other. Then she sorted them by expiry date.

She texted an update to Sophie.

I'm binning your cloves.

That's fine. I can't remember ever using them. S

You haven't. They're unopened. Your parsley is still in date, but it's supposed to be green, not grey. I'm making the call.

Parsley doesn't taste like anything anyway.

Not when it's grey. Cinnamon is out too. And 5-spice. Are there spices anywhere else I should know about?

Check above the washing machine.

We need to talk about your filing system. Is it better to give you a summary when I'm done?

No, I like the play-by-play.

Despite the calming effect of sorting through Sophie's kitchen, something was still nipping at Harriet later, while she and James were in town. Try as hard as she might, she couldn't ignore it. 'Why do you always have to do that?' she asked him as they were on their way to dinner. Billie hadn't turned up to meet them, despite her carrying on a near-constant stream of texts with James. She treated him like one of her friends. Harriet, on the other hand, was apparently worse company than a reptile.

'Do what? Is my nose whistling again?' James asked. He pinched his nostrils.

'Be the good guy. With Billie. You always do it.' It definitely felt like them against her most of the time. It used to be her and James against the world. She missed her partner.

'I'm not trying to,' he said. 'I'm just being me.'

As usual, James was a man of few words, but the ones he chose prodded her sore spot. That was the real problem.

Billie didn't object to her parents. She just didn't like Harriet. She was old enough now to decide who she valued and wanted in her life. Harriet was not that person. She'd been tried and found wanting, maybe not as a parent but as a person.

She breathed away the familiar tears that stung the backs of her eyes. That was a snivel for another day.

Inside the half-empty restaurant, James glanced around with a little smile playing on his lips. White tablecloths, spotless wine glasses and proper silver gleamed in the candle-light. The clientele was as well-polished as the cutlery. 'We're out of our league here,' he said.

'Speak for yourself.'

'I am.'

Harriet considered her husband, trying to see him as an outsider would. He wasn't a head-turner – despite his hulking presence, he was too low-key for that – but he was still good-looking beneath the dishevelled hair and love of faded tartan. Handsome even, once one took the time to notice.

Harriet hadn't noticed at first. The night they met, they'd stood nearly back-to-back at the pub for hours. She hadn't been on the lookout for prospects. That wasn't her style, and besides, she was out with colleagues and she didn't like mixing business with pleasure. She was too busy being a trainee solicitor in those early days to mix very much pleasure with pleasure, either.

So James was a surprise. He was out with colleagues, too. That was back when his colleagues had only two feet and didn't need milking. They were celebrating a big deal they'd just won, and James was the man of the hour. It was his worst nightmare, being the centre of attention like that. He was much happier alone in a field, knee-deep in manure.

Farmer James. That's how all of her friends knew him nearly the entire time they were dating. Not that he was a farmer then. He was a marketing exec, biding his time until he could get back home.

She'd known that about him from the start, yet it was easy to ignore the *goat threat*, as she'd thought of it. James wasn't thinking practically. Gloucestershire was his past, not his future. It was full of farm animals and roofs that needed thatching. She had no inkling the night they met that one day they would become *her* farm animals and thatched roof.

She wished they had a cute story about meeting. A spilled drink, maybe, or clumsily trodden-on foot or some clever comment that had drawn them together. The mundane truth was that neither of them could remember why they first spoke. They just found themselves face to face at the bar.

His direct gaze got her attention. 'Hello,' he'd said.

Normally she would have stayed focused on the bartender so she wouldn't miss her chance to order. 'Hello.'

'Enjoying your night?'

'No, it's very average.'

'That's an honest answer. Me neither.' He raised his full pint. 'I reckon I can sneak off after this.'

But he didn't sneak off. He stayed talking to Harriet.

She did remember the frothy happiness she felt when he asked to see her again. She'd fancied the pants off James. She didn't know she'd fall in love with him, too.

Now James rubbed his nose again with his fingers. 'Have I got something . . .?'

'What? No, no, sorry. I was just thinking about the night we met.'

James smiled. 'You mean the way I swept you off your feet?'

'Get over yourself. I was definitely still on my feet.'

'Not later that night you weren't.'

They both laughed and Harriet was able to breathe for the first time in what seemed like for ever. Maybe this would work.

'It was a fun night,' she said.

James smiled. 'I couldn't believe my luck, meeting someone like you.' He was obviously in the mood to reminisce, too. 'The way your mind flew between ideas. You even made connections between whatever bollocks I was spouting. That's saying something. You were the most exciting woman I'd ever met.'

Harriet smiled. This was starting to feel like old times. She *knew* this holiday was a good idea. 'Now I'm just the most annoying,' she teased.

'Only most of the time, but I'm used to you.'

They both heard his mobile ringing.

'Are you going to get that?'

'That's okay,' he said.

'What if it's Billie?' She almost always rang him instead of her.

James took his phone out to look. 'Hi, what's up?' *Persephone*, he mouthed. 'We just walked around, really,' he told her. 'We're having dinner now. Yeah, it's posh. I know. Listen, I don't think we're supposed to use phones in here. I'd better go. Still two weeks . . . you know I do. Okay. No, better not. Okay, text then. Bye.'

'That was Persephone,' he said, putting his phone away.

'You said. What's she texting?'

'Hmm? Oh, just some business stuff about the loan. She thinks we can restructure it somehow to save some interest. Then I can borrow more for the new equipment.' He laughed. 'You know I leave the details to other people. She just tells me where to sign.'

'She knows you do what?'

He stared at her.

'You said, "you know I do".'

'I don't remember,' he said. 'So, what are you going to have?'

'You don't remember from thirty seconds ago?'

He shrugged. 'The lamb looks good,' he said.

Clearly, he wasn't going to tell her what Persephone had said.

They didn't talk any more about when they first met.

Chapter 8

Sunday

Sophie had been in less formal museums, so how the bloomin' blazes was she meant to relax in Harriet's house? When she was little, she loved imagining she lived somewhere really grand. She might have set her fantasy in a stately home, if she'd ever been inside one.

John Lewis on Oxford Street was as close as she got. She and her mum used to go there every Christmas, while her dad happily stayed home with a stack of his favourite takeaway menus and free reign to watch all the football he could on telly.

Sophie had walked arm in arm with her mum from one end of the long road to the other. The Christmas lights had twinkled above them as they popped in and out of the shops, gathering inexpensive gifts. John Lewis's merchandise was mostly out of reach ('too dear', her mum would whisper), but they'd spend hours wandering through every department anyway, fantasising about what they'd buy if they were the type of family who had 500-thread-count sheets and real crystal.

It may have been under an hour on the Tube, but the shop felt a million miles away from their little suburban bungalow. So that became Sophie's ideal. Sleeping in one of the huge ornate beds upstairs, wearing the coolest new pyjamas, finding the perfect slippers to pad down to the kitchen shop for breakfast on pretty plates.

She wiped her eyes with the tips of her fingers. It wasn't normal to still feel this sad about losing her mum. She hardly ever let Dan see her upset about it any more. His patience had worn out years ago. She just wished the feelings didn't creep up on her every time she had a nice memory, that tears weren't the price she had to pay for the happy thoughts.

Now that she was here in a real-life stately home (nearly), the reality wasn't as fun as her childhood imagination had pictured it anyway. Harriet's house might be gorgeous, but Sophie was terrified of ruining it. Absolutely everything was perfectly presented or tidied away. Just seeing all the lists neatly taped up in the kitchen gave her the shakes. To constantly be reminded of so much to do, on top of not breaking anything? Nightmare.

There were To Dos inside the cabinets, too. All the herbs and spices were inventoried. No wonder Harriet had gone after her oregano. Each tin of beans and every different kind of rice was recorded. What was Camargue? She didn't even know how to pronounce it, let alone what it tasted like.

Even the bed linen was labelled. *In her own house*, as if Harriet would forget where her pillowslips went. Or care that they were in the wrong place.

That must be the kind of planning it took to be a successful career woman *and* the perfect homemaker. Obviously, Sophie didn't have what it took to be either. She managed to get a meal on the table for her family each night and make sure they had clean underpants, even if they weren't quite dry when they were needed. But they sometimes had to use washing-up liquid in the bath and, as often as not, a roll of kitchen towel sat beside the toilet.

She stared again at the closed office door. What was it that Dan had asked her to check for? Fennel and something. *Think, Sophie, think.* It was for a stew. Stock cubes? No, something from Harriet's herb cabinet. That must be why she'd opened it in the first place.

Whatever it was, Harriet probably had some – in date, of course. Someone like Harriet would have every ingredient known to humankind. Even the weird ones, like star anise, and what was that Moroccan mix Dan liked to use (though she suspected he also just liked to say it)? Ras-el-hanout, that was it.

But what if she was wrong, and Harriet didn't normally cook with cumin or coriander or . . . what *was* it that Dan needed?

Then he'd be cross. He usually was when she messed up the shopping. It was always something: low-fat coconut milk instead of regular, or bread with the wrong kind of seeds. It wasn't as bad when she was the one cooking. That just earned a lengthy critique of the meal. But when he was about to do the cooking, like now . . .

She racked her brain some more.

Why couldn't she even remember a simple thing like that? It wasn't too much to ask, when he'd already done the shopping and the thinking about the recipe in the first place and he was about to do the cooking.

One little thing.

She couldn't disturb him when he was working. He was on another very important call with his boss, he'd said, so she'd just have to remember on her own.

As she scanned the packets again, hoping to jog her memory, a tiny niggle worked away at her. She was grateful for everything Dan did for them. She was. It was just that sometimes he was a smidge of a diva about it. His meals were tasty, but it would be nice if he could cook them without messing up every single pot, pan and utensil to do it. She always had a mountain of cleaning up to do. Or chopping at the start, or peeling the potatoes or getting the skin off the peppers or some other tedious prep so that Dan had everything he needed to channel his inner Ramsay.

Dan had always been the big picture man. Details were for other people. How many times had she heard that? Even though that couldn't really be true, or he wouldn't be such a good solicitor. He could handle details. He just didn't like to. That's why he had Laxmi, she supposed.

Sometimes he forgot that Sophie wasn't his at-home Laxmi.

It hadn't taken the children long to claim their favourite spots in the conservatory: Oliver was propped up against the arm of the sofa and Katie in one of the roomy reading chairs. 'Do you remember what Dad wanted to make for dinner tonight?' she asked them.

Katie didn't answer until she'd finished tapping on her phone. 'Pork stew. Why?'

'Bavarian pork stew,' Oliver clarified. He was watching one of those David Attenborough documentaries. Between the goats and the Discovery Channel, this holiday was heaven for him.

'I just want to check that we have everything he'll need.' She could find the recipe on the BBC website.

Chopped tomatoes! That was it. She checked the cabinets for the other ingredients, but a careful examination – twice – didn't turn up the thyme that the recipe called for. Was it possible that perfect Harriet had run out of something as basic as thyme? Even Sophie had that at home. Out of date, no doubt, and probably spattered with who-knew-what, but there nevertheless.

Dan definitely hadn't asked for it, either. She smiled to herself as she glanced at the wall clock. It was nice to know that he wasn't always perfect. Much as he liked to think it. 'Let's pop into the village,' she told the children. 'We need some things for later.'

They glanced up. 'Can we see the goats first?' Oliver asked.

'I'll stay here,' said Katie.

Fat chance. 'Dad's working.'

'I am old enough to stay in by myself,' she said.

'Maybe, but I'd still like you to come with us. It's a family outing.'

'It's not a family outing if Dad's not coming.'

'Then it's three quarters of a family outing. Come on. We can go to the barns first. Just for a few minutes, though. Marion will be busy.'

Oliver jumped to his feet but Katie took her time. Sophie was grateful that her daughter still (mostly) listened to her and Dan. She knew some of her classmates were giving their parents sleepless nights. Luckily not any of Katie's close friends, though. That would probably change when boys started getting involved. At thirteen, so far Katie wasn't interested. Dan always said he hoped that would be true for another decade or two.

Dashing off a note for him, Sophie grabbed a few reusable bags from the wall hook.

They strolled towards the village along the wide gravel path that ran beside a stand of bright white birch. Leaves whispered in the warm breeze. Sophie filled her lungs with the fresh air, though Harriet had been right. There was definitely a tinge of dung.

'Poor Artemis!' Oliver said. He'd been worrying since they left the barn. 'How does a goat get pink-eye, Mum?'

'I haven't a clue, darling. That's a question for Marion. We can ask her later. Then you'll know and you'll be ahead of the game for when you're a vet.'

Oliver nodded gravely. 'Maybe I'll take notes. I might not remember when I'm an actual vet. How many years of uni is it?'

He knew the answer. They'd looked it up enough times. He just liked to hear it. 'Five years, six if you go to Cambridge.'

'But I'm not going to Cambridge, remember? It's too far. I'm living with you at our house.'

Sophie hoped he'd always be such a homebody. 'That's right. But really, darling, you don't need to worry about that right now. It's years away.'

'Mum. I'll need to prepare.'

Sophie matched his serious face. 'Of course. Sorry.'

'But what if he doesn't get better? Artemis, I mean.' His bottom lip quivered. 'If he goes blind . . . or dies? James will be sad.'

Artemis was James's prize billy. Sophie was pretty sure that a weepy eye wouldn't kill him, although until it cleared up, he was being kept away from the lady goats. For a randy billy, that probably was a fate worse than death. *Poor Artemis*, Sophie agreed. 'I wouldn't worry about it too much, darling, Marion knows how to cure him. She's an expert.'

She stared off into the meandering green fields that rolled on for miles. She was glad there weren't big hills. After years of walking on city pavements – and being completely allergic to the gym – her heart might not take too much incline.

The children were quiet as they walked a little bit behind her. Sophie was tempted to talk to them, but then she thought, *why shouldn't they get their own space to enjoy all this, too?* She'd been thinking more and more lately that she'd have to start facing the fact that her babies had become their own people.

The village looked picture-postcard perfect. The summer sun brightened the buttery-yellow stone of the old buildings, and she couldn't spot a single drooping bloom in any of the riotous hanging baskets that lined the pavement. It was breathtakingly pretty.

At least, she hoped it was the view taking her breath away. 'Let's sit for a minute and soak all this up.' They crossed to the narrow village green where an iron bench sat in the shade of a huge tree. She slumped onto the seat.

'Are you okay, Mum?' Katie asked. 'Oliver, wait for Mum.'

'I'm fine. Perfectly fine. I just wanted to look at the view.' She tried not to sound as puffy as she felt. When Sophie breathed in, she started to cough. 'Whew, all this fresh air,' she joked. 'I'm not used to it.'

It was nothing to worry about. Her GP and cardiologist agreed on that. Just a skippy heart that definitely didn't mean her imminent demise. Definitely not.

That was easy for them to say. It wasn't their heart going like the clappers. They should try living with it. Or not, as the case may be. 'Isn't this nice?' She gestured to the bench. 'Let me just see if Harriet needs us to pick anything up while we're here.' That might buy her a few more minutes to catch her breath.

Hi, she texted, *we're shopping in the village. Do you need me to get anything for you?*

I get everything delivered from Waitrose, thanks. Where are you going? I can send you directions. H

That's okay, we'll just wander. S

Or a map?

Sophie smiled. *Sure, that would be useful, thanks. Sx*

Her phone pinged a few seconds later. Harriet didn't waste time.

Ignoring her still-pounding heart, Sophie got up and followed the children up the high street. *Move along, nothing to see here, just a woman hopefully not about to have a stroke.*

Her breathing eased after a few more steps. By the time Oliver waved at one of the windows, Sophie felt okay again. 'It's the butcher.' He waved again. 'We met him here with Dad yesterday!'

A bell jingled as they pushed open the old-fashioned shop door. The meaty aroma that hit them made Sophie's mouth water. Those sausage rolls looked like lunch to her.

The spectacled young butcher stood behind a long scarred wooden table with all the meats behind him or laid out in the big bay window beside him. Wooden crates stacked with vegetables and interesting-looking packets lined the opposite wall.

A severe-looking woman with a distinctly Thatcheresque hairstyle was just paying.

'How be?' said the butcher.

'Very well, thank you,' Oliver answered. 'This is my mum.'

'How be?' he repeated to Sophie.

She could feel the severe-looking woman staring at her. 'You're the lady needing the rest.' Now she was staring at Sophie like she was terminal. 'For your nerves,' the woman added.

Her nerves! That made her sound like a nineteenth-century lady. Where did she put those smelling salts? 'Actually, it's my heart. Well, not my heart, exactly, but my blood pressure. My mum had a stroke when she was only young.'

Now why had she told that to a perfect stranger?

The woman nodded. 'Bea told me.'

'Who?' asked Sophie. She didn't remember meeting any Bea. The masseuse was called Molly.

'You mean the lady with the tea shop?' Oliver asked the woman. 'We talked to her yesterday, when we were here with Dad.'

The woman nodded. 'That's right. 'Ow are you feeling?' she asked Sophie. The woman's hair might be severe, but her voice was kind.

'Fine, thank you. I'm having massages at the spa. They're wonderful, although I've never heard of most of the techniques.'

Sophie couldn't tear her eyes away from that hair. Not a strand moved out of place when the lady shook her head. 'Molly loves 'er Eastern ways. Not me. Sticks and stones will break my bones.' But Sophie was too busy wondering how much hairspray the woman used to pay attention to what she was saying.

'You're off today,' she added.

'I beg your pardon?'

'You have today off. No massage.'

'Erm, that's right.' How did she know so much about Sophie's schedule?

"Ow were the kebabs?' the butcher asked.

'Great,' said Oliver.

'You should get a pie from Hazel while you're here.' The butcher pointed out of his bay window. 'Hazel's Pies. She's got cherry now.'

'No, out of the cherry,' said the lady. 'There's still a plum one, though.'

'Well, thank you, maybe we'll get one,' said Sophie. 'Do you know where I can get some thyme?' These people clearly had their fingers on the pulse of the village if they could inventory Hazel's pies.

'Delia's,' said the butcher, pointing again out of the window.

Delia's Deli was nearly next door. The walls of the small shop were lined to the ceiling with pale-green shelves full of colourful tins and jars of pickle, pots of jam, biscuits, fancy pasta and oils. Everywhere Sophie looked made her mouth water. A big basket filled with crusty bread sat on top of a glass case full of cheeses, meats, olives and pesto.

The woman behind the till wore a red apron that said *No, not that Delia*.

'I take it you're Delia?' Sophie asked.

'But not that Delia,' Delia answered. 'How can I help?' Her lipstick was bright red and perfectly applied. Sophie had always envied women who could pull that off.

'I'm just after some thyme. Oh, and chopped tomatoes.' Sophie squinted at the pâtés in the case. 'But that looks delicious. Is it made locally?'

'Everything is,' Delia said. 'Would you like to taste a sample?' She was already lifting one of the pâtés out of the case. 'Here, try the Brussels. I prefer it to the Ardennes.'

Sophie took the biscuit Delia offered. The smooth pâté melted in her mouth. 'Mmm, I could eat that for dinner!

I'll take some, about this much, please.' She held her thumb and finger apart. 'Does anyone not love this?'

Delia shook her head. 'Hardly anyone.' She neatly sliced a good portion and wrapped it in some deli paper. 'Are you visiting?'

'Hey, Mum, look, that's our farm's cheese!' Katie pointed to a small, neatly lettered sign stuck into a soft round cheese. 'And there.'

'Do you know James?' Delia asked.

'Not really. We've done a house swap with Harriet for two weeks.' She was sure she saw Delia's expression change.

'I see. You're friends with her, then?'

The sudden chill in the shop definitely wasn't coming from the cheese case. 'We've only just met,' she said. 'My husband is a solicitor, too. They know each other professionally. That's all.'

Delia smiled again. 'James is a top bloke, but that wife of his is another story.'

In the entire history of gossip, nothing flattering ever followed the phrase *that wife of his*. 'Oh?' It was absolutely none of Sophie's business what the village thought of Harriet. But that bait was possibly even more tempting than the pâté Delia had just fed her.

On the other hand, Sophie wasn't sure she wanted to draw out any criticism. Short as their acquaintance had been, she already knew she liked Harriet. She was perhaps a bit . . . regimented, but she had saved their holiday. She felt some loyalty to the woman.

Delia clearly didn't. 'We have tried to welcome her, but, well, she's a bit peculiar, don't you think? Some of the things she's come out with. It's like she doesn't want to be friendly. It's only right to expect a person to make a bit of an effort if they want to fit in. But we don't judge.'

Sophie begged to differ about that point.

'I've heard from Susan,' she went on, 'she's the woman who cooks sometimes for them, that she's got everyone under her thumb at home.'

'She's got lists!' Oliver said. 'Everywhere, even in the bathroom.'

Delia pulled a face of mock-shock.

'Well, with working full-time I guess she needs everything organised,' Sophie murmured.

'But you said she was anal,' Oliver added.

Sophie felt her cheeks burning. 'We'll just take these things, thanks.' She hurried them out to continue their shopping.

'Everyone here is so nice!' Oliver said as they made their way back to the farm.

Sophie wouldn't say that. 'Careful you don't tip the box, darling, or the pie will squash.'

Oliver righted the bag.

'Hungry?' she asked the children as they crunched up the gravel drive. She could hear the bees buzzing in the lavender. Katie would be happy that Harriet's garden was doing its bit to save them. 'We could take lunch into the garden. They've got that nice table out the back.' *That might even lure Dan away from his work*, she thought as she turned the key in the lock.

Dan flung open the door. 'Where've you been, Soph?'

'You frightened the life out of me!' She laughed. 'Have you been waiting there for us? I'm flattered. We went to the shops. I told you.'

'You didn't.'

'I mean, I left you a note. I didn't want to disturb you while you were working.'

'There's no note.' There was that edge to his voice again.

She frowned. 'I'm sure I did.' He followed her into the kitchen where she searched on, around and under the kitchen table. 'I left it just here, I know I did.'

'If you'd left it, then I would have seen it. That's how notes work. I was worried. Anything could have happened to you.'

'But we only went to the village. I wanted to help you.' She held up her canvas bag. 'I picked up a few extra things for meals.'

'I only asked for chopped tomatoes. Soph, was that really so hard?' He held up the tins she'd got. 'Wrong, wrong, wrong again. I didn't want them with herbs.'

'I didn't notice. Will that ruin the taste?'

'Let's hope not,' he said. 'What extra things did you get? Show me.' With every little pot and packet, his expression grew more thundery. 'We probably won't eat all this. Did you get biscuits?' He held up the pâté, then shook his head. 'What makes you think I need help, anyway? I asked you for one simple thing and you come back with all this.'

'You forgot thyme,' she said. He could point out her errors all he wanted. The fact was, he hadn't done the whole shop when he had the chance, which was why she had to go out in the first place. His mistake, not hers.

She kept these thoughts to herself.

'Come with me,' he said, taking her hand. She followed him out the front door. He pointed to one of the borders. Unlike the others that ringed the garden, this was filled with shrubs instead of flowers. 'What do you think that is?' He pointed to a scrubby-looking bush.

Sophie hated quizzes like this, but she was used to playing the game.

'I'm guessing thyme,' she said. She should have known that, first, Harriet would grow her own herbs and, second, that Dan would find them. She mentally subtracted the point she thought she'd scored. 'Of course, there's fresh thyme. Sorry.'

'Don't I always take care of it? Silly bean, you're hopeless.' Then he folded her into his arms. 'You did one thing right, though. That plum pie.'

She leaned into his chest. She was always so grateful for these moments, after, when everything was okay again.

There was no trace of his aggravation any more. 'Want to eat it now?'

'What, before our meal? Yes, please!'

'Do we have to tell the children?' he asked.

'Let's wait till they're distracted and I'll meet you in the kitchen with a fork.'

Their arms tightened around each other. How she loved their world-of-two conspiracies.

'Oh,' Sophie whispered as she twisted in his arms to take something from her pocket. She held up two scraps of paper.

Thyme, read one.

The other was her note.

'Silly bean,' he said again.

Chapter 9

Monday

Harriet couldn't believe her eyes, even after she'd rubbed the sleep from them. She wasn't seeing things. There was a man in their kitchen! A giant, hulking man dressed all in black, like a deadly ninja, with his hood pulled up over his head to hide his felonious face.

Harriet froze in the corridor as he ransacked another cabinet. The hairs stood up on her neck. Billie and James were upstairs, unaware that they were about to have their throats cut.

Well, not if Harriet had anything to say about it. She retraced her steps a little back into the hallway. Even though she was facing mortal danger, she congratulated herself on tidying away the shoes. That was just the kind of thing that would have tripped her up and let the murderer pounce.

This was exactly why she'd had the security wall built around the Gloucestershire house before they moved in. With cameras. James said it was a stupid waste of money, not to mention insulting to the neighbours, who were nothing but honest. Besides, they'd never been broken into in all the years that Coopers Farm had existed.

Well, who was stupid now, eh, James?

Harriet crept to the tall box where she'd stored all the sports equipment she'd found scattered throughout the house. She'd never been a cricket fan – *until now*, she thought as she hefted the sturdy bat.

She just wished she had a bra on. She was about to swing more than the cricket bat.

Harriet peered round the corner. The man had moved to the fridge. Clever. She'd read an article saying that a surprising percentage of old people kept their pension money in the fridge. Or was it the freezer?

Even in her socked feet, the man heard her as she ran into the kitchen.

'Aaaaarrrggghhhhhhhh!' she screamed, swinging the bat as hard as she could.

'What the *fuck*?!' He threw himself backward, landing hard on the edge of the kitchen island worktop. 'Oof!' He slumped to the floor, the breath knocked out of him. 'Yo, don't hit me!' he said.

He was shielding his head, but Harriet glimpsed it anyway: pudgy, bright-red cheeks, bare of beard, and floppy boy band hair.

This wasn't a man. 'Who are you?'

'Owen.' His wide, frightened eyes peeped out from between his raised arms.

She'd never been on first-name terms with a burglar before.

Her grip on the bat loosened. 'What are you doing in our kitchen, Owen?'

'It's Sophie's kitchen.' Now he looked confused.

'Oh, right. Technically, yes.'

'You're not gonna hit me?'

They both glanced at the bat. 'Sorry, no, but you frightened me.'

'You?' he answered, still glaring at the bat.

Harriet put it behind her back. To think, she could have

brained this child! He was probably no older than Billie. She felt her hands start to tremble. 'I'm sorry.'

Owen lowered his arms. 'I didn't know anyone was here. I would have knocked.' He took her extended hand and pulled himself upright. 'Thanks.'

'How did you get in?' She glanced at the wall clock. It was barely 8 a.m.

Owen held up his key fob. 'I crash here sometimes. Sophie doesn't mind.'

Beneath the teen's surprisingly deep voice, Harriet heard his vulnerability. 'But you don't want to stay here, not now?' That was inconvenient. 'We're staying here.'

'Sorry, but I didn't know that, did I?'

'Well, let me ring Sophie. In a little while. It's early yet . . . why *are* you here so early?' Billie was never out of bed before ten these days. That was one of the reasons she'd brought them all to London the night before their flight. She had been thinking of her family, not just herself, like James did.

'Mum and I had a row,' Owen said. He hunched further into his sweatshirt. Even so, he towered over Harriet.

She had to wonder what there was to fight about at such an hour, but she didn't ask. It wasn't her business. 'Do you want a cup of tea?'

Owen went straight to the cabinet to get a mug. He looked uncertainly at the neat stacks of dishes. 'Where're the mugs?'

There had been a few in that cabinet, and the one next to it, and the two below, before she'd reorganised. 'They're all above the coffee-maker.' She'd moved that, too, to a more sensible place. Sophie had seemed to store everything in proximity to the dishwasher: mugs, glasses, dishes, bowls, even some tins of beans and an open packet of salted nuts. 'I've tidied up a bit,' she told Owen.

'Are you alone here?' he asked.

That raised alarm bells, even though, now that she'd had a good look at him, Owen was about as intimidating as those giant stuffed bears they sold in Hamleys.

'My husband is upstairs.' Come to think of it, where was he? James must have heard her screaming, yet he didn't bother to see what was wrong. She could be dead down here.

That said something about the state of their relationship.

'Ohhh. Owen,' said Sophie when Harriet rang her later. 'Yes, he sometimes stays with us. I hope that's not a problem. He's a very nice boy. He usually just comes and goes with his key.'

'But *why* does he stay?' Harriet knew lots of nice people. None of them had a key to her house. She couldn't get her head around giving a strange teenager free rein.

'He has a difficult relationship with his mother,' Sophie said.

Owen had already admitted as much, but that still didn't answer Harriet's question. 'No, I mean why does he stay with *you*?' She kept her voice down so it didn't carry through the house to the kitchen, where Owen was eating breakfast.

'Ah, of course, I should have said. We fostered him for about a year when he was ten. He became part of the family and I guess he still is, even though he's back with his mum now. It's not always easy for him, but they do try as best they can to get on. Well, you know what it's like living with a teenager.'

'Actually, Sophie, now that you bring it up. I don't want to sound paranoid, but will he be okay here with Billie? It's just that, well, two teens under the same roof. A boy and a girl . . .'

'Gosh, it hadn't occurred to me,' Sophie admitted. 'But Owen is such a nice boy that I can't imagine there'd be any, um, impropriety. Katie's thirteen, and I've never worried about him being in the house with her. They're like brother and sister.'

'Well, yes, they would be if they'd lived together for a year,' said Harriet. 'That's the point of fostering, I believe, to give a child a stable family environment. It was a lot for you to take on another child, though.'

'It was Dan's idea to do it,' Sophie explained. 'He thought it would be good for me after I got broody again. He was right. I loved having Owen with us.' Sophie sounded wistful. 'He stays in Spot's room, so he wouldn't be in the way,' she added. 'Hopefully he and his mum will work out whatever's going on. They usually do after a few days and then he'll go home again. As long as it's okay for him to stay. I'll tell him no if you're not comfortable with it.'

How could she be comfortable having a random teenage boy staying with them? Random. Teenage. Boy. Three reasons right there to object. This was meant to be a family holiday, too, and as nice as this Owen person might be, he was not family. 'I'm not sure it's a good idea,' she told Sophie. Not that he looked dangerous, now that Harriet had had a good look at him. His haircut and thick eyebrows were a bit too Paul McCartney circa 1964 to be threatening.

'Of course, that's fine,' said Sophie. 'I'll ring him and let him know. I'm really so sorry, Harriet, I didn't mean to put you in an awkward position. I honestly did forget he might turn up. We never know when he will, you see. It's only when things get really bad at home.'

Guilt nipped at Harriet's heels. 'He's having breakfast now,' she said. 'Wait a bit to ring him. I don't want to chase him out of the house.'

'That's very kind,' said Sophie.

Funnily enough, Harriet didn't feel very kind at all.

She was finishing her own late breakfast when James came into the kitchen. Owen was still at the table, and seemed willing to chat to her. What unusual teen behaviour. Billie approached every one of Harriet's questions like she was demanding a tooth extraction without novocaine.

James said hello in such a kindly way that Owen's worried face immediately melted into a smile. Harriet winced to remember her own reception. She might never forget the poor boy cowering beneath her cricket bat.

'This is Owen, one of Sophie and Dan's friends.' She wasn't about to mention the fostering. She'd tell James later, away from the boy. Not that there was anything wrong with being fostered. She'd admired Sophie when she'd told her. She could never do it. Too much of a wild card. Harriet did not do wild cards.

'You might have heard me scream when he came in?' she added.

'Nah, I was dead to the world.'

Said the man who woke with his goats every day. He'd probably been too absorbed in one of his nature books to hear her.

She realised as James shook Owen's hand that they were nearly the same height.

James, oblivious that she'd just saved his life – in theory – poured himself a cup of coffee from the now properly located machine. Without hesitating, he opened the cabinet to the right of it for the sugar. That's exactly where Harriet had put it. 'Do you live close by?' he asked Owen.

'No,' said Owen. 'I'm in south London.'

'Oh, crikey, did you know they were on holiday?'

Owen nodded. 'Yeah, Sophie told me.' Then his glance darted to Harriet. 'I thought the place would be empty.'

James scrunched his eyebrows together. They weren't miles apart when he wasn't confused. When he was, they looked like two voles holding hands on his forehead.

'I crash here sometimes,' Owen explained. 'When Mum and I fight.'

'I know how that feels,' he said. 'You're welcome here.'

'James,' she said. This was exactly the kind of thing he was always doing, being kind and accommodating – everyone's best mate – and leaving Harriet to consider the consequences. Which made her the killjoy.

Billie shuffled into the kitchen in her usual uniform: sweatpants and a stretched-out sweatshirt. She and Owen glanced at each other. 'S'up,' Owen said.

Billie nodded back.

'This is Sophie's friend, Owen,' Harriet said. 'He sometimes stays, but he doesn't have to while we're here, if you're uncomfortable with that.' Surely Billie would give Harriet the perfect excuse to object.

Billie shrugged. 'S'okay.'

Well, that was perfect. Now she couldn't very well chuck Owen out without looking like the arse. They'd be stuck with the boy until he made up with his mum. She wasn't thrilled with the temporary addition to their holiday, but if he'd lived with Sophie and her family, then she supposed he probably was a very nice person, like she'd said. 'Do you want to ring your mum and let her know where you are?' Harriet asked.

'She knows where I am,' said Owen. He hauled himself from the chair. 'I'll go and have a shower. If that's okay.'

James was already nodding. 'Of course, of course. We're probably going to do some sightseeing later, if you want to join us?'

Harriet glared at James. 'You don't have to, Owen.' She needed to nip this in the bud. 'I'm sure you've got better things to do than hang out with strangers.' How could James not see any problem with inviting a boy they'd known for about two minutes along on what was supposed to be their perfect family holiday?

James's ringing phone interrupted her train of thought. He laughed at whatever the caller was saying. 'She is.' He covered the phone with his big hand. 'I'll just take it out—' He nodded towards the front of the house. 'Well, that's nice to hear,' she heard him say as he left the kitchen. It must be Persephone again.

Harriet wondered why she'd never noticed before that they talked every day.

Chapter 10

Tuesday

Dan was holed up in his office on the morning the first delivery truck crunched its way up the pebble drive. *I mean James's office*, thought Sophie. *Not Dan's*. It just seemed like that now that he was spending every day in there.

Sophie had jumped when the front gate intercom buzzed, slopping a bit of coffee on Harriet's leather sofa. 'Oh, bollocks!' She'd scrambled to the kitchen to get a cloth. Hopefully leather was waterproof. Cows didn't soak up rain, right?

The intercom had buzzed again. Two impatient blasts this time. She'd lunged for the handset before it disturbed Dan. Waterproof or not, the leather would have to wait.

Now Sophie stood beside the back of the open truck. 'Sign 'ere.' The spotty youth shoved a clipboard into her hands. Then he climbed into the back where he manhandled the first large square table to the electronic lift. The lift delivered him and the table to the drive, where he lugged it onto the grass.

Sophie said, 'Can I please see the order form again?' It had Harriet's name in the customer box, but the date was wrong. 'It's only the fourteenth,' she told the driver.

He paused. 'We're early.'

'Is this for the Scouts' thingy?'

'Dunno.'

'Because that's not for another week and a bit. What am I supposed to do with these until then?'

'Dunno.' He lowered another table and dragged it across the drive towards the grass. The corner carved a deep rut through the pebbles.

'You're not going to leave all those here?' There looked to be about a dozen tables still in the truck.

'It's delivery to the door.' The boy pointed to the house. 'That's the door.'

Sophie watched the darkening clouds skittering across the sky. 'Can you at least help me move them round the back to the barn?'

To give him credit, he did look sorry as he shook his head. 'Health an' safety. This is how it's done.'

He started piling three tables onto the lift at a time. It was precarious, and they clattered to the drive when they reached the bottom, but he didn't take long to get them all into a heap on the grass. Then he was off, the wheels of his truck crunching back down the drive.

Her dad was a delivery driver and she knew for a fact that he'd never dump his cargo off the back of his lorry like that. But that's probably why he'd kept his job for Sophie's entire life. She bet that boy would have an appointment at the Jobcentre within the month.

She rang her dad then, even though she knew it would go to voicemail. He rarely answered while he was working. 'Hi Dad,' she said. 'It's just me checking in. I've got another spa treatment later. I know, la-di-da, hey?' She laughed. 'I love it so much here that I don't even miss being in Italy now. Anyway, hope your day is going well. I'll have my phone off between three and four when I'm at the spa, but I'll ring you after. Love you!'

Just as she ended the call, a raindrop plopped into her eye. What was she supposed to do now? The tabletops were wooden and she was starting to think her cow absorbability theory wasn't true after all. Trees didn't absorb rain either, yet she knew what water did to wooden tabletops.

At least the delivery hadn't disturbed Dan. The office door was still closed when she got back inside.

'Hey, Katie, Oliver.' She was nearly whispering. 'I need some help, please.' A few tiny drops had already streaked the windows. 'Let's hurry.'

But the tables were surprisingly heavy, and the barn seemed miles away. Sophie's biceps were screaming by the time they finished.

Katie laughed as Sophie collapsed on the sofa, rubbing her arms. 'Mum, if you think that was hard, you'd die at my football practice. Maybe you should try the gym once in a while.'

'All right, Sporty Spice, thanks for the advice.' She was incredibly proud of her daughter, though. One entire bedroom wall at home was hung with running medals.

'I might go for a run later if Dad goes,' Katie said, as if reading her mind. 'I need to stretch my legs.'

She definitely took after Dan like that. They were both part greyhound. 'Are you getting bored without all your usual activities?'

'Are you mad?' she said. 'It's great not having to do anything.'

'But you like football and art, and your piano?'

Katie shrugged. 'Yeah.'

'Just nice to get out of the old routine,' Sophie said. 'I get it.' She winced, prodding her bicep. She might even have built a muscle or two. More importantly, she'd taken care of those tables and let Dan keep working.

To her surprise, a sensation welled up. It tickled her insides till she smiled. She couldn't be sure, but it felt like it might be pride. When was the last time she'd felt *that*? Probably back when she'd been working. She must have been a problem-solver once upon a time. That's what admin assistants did, and she always had good reviews, so she guessed she'd done it well. Objectively, she knew this. So why was she so surprised to find that, when faced with the unexpected delivery, she'd assessed the situation and managed a solution?

She could do it.

She *did* do it.

She'd done it for years, actually, before Dan started riding to her rescue. She'd forgotten that. Maybe confidence was like a muscle: use it or lose it. She probably needed more exercise.

She rubbed her arms again and went to make herself a cup of tea.

As she was filling the kettle, she gazed out of the kitchen window and over the back garden to the barns. Marion seemed to be having a conversation with the goats. They said that plants liked being talked to, so why wouldn't goats? It probably made the cheese taste better.

She threw a teabag into a second cup.

'I've made an extra cup if you want it,' she called, carefully carrying the steaming drinks towards the barns. 'You probably have your own tea and kettle, but it's always nice when someone else makes it for you.'

'You read my mind,' Marion said. 'I was just about to make one. Thank you. Mmm, perfect. James and I usually share making the drinks. It's been weird this week, doing them all myself.' Inside the barn, they sat on the plastic chairs that stood between the pens. 'Time for a break.'

Sophie loved the smell of the clean hay that cushioned the goats' pens. She could smell the animals, too, even though most of them were outside on the grass. It wasn't an unpleasant smell. Sharp and earthy. Inside the barn it was cooler than outside. The rain had freshened the air. A nice breeze channelled between the open doors at either end, lifting the ends of Sophie's hair. She took a deep breath. It was easy to see why James loved his goat business.

'Have you worked with James for long?' she asked Marion. She was clearly younger than Sophie but seemed mature. Capable. That's how she'd describe her.

'Going on five years,' she said. 'I did an internship with him and he took me on after. These goats are like his family. It's exactly the kind of place I wanted to work.'

'He'll be missing them then,' Sophie said.

Marion laughed. 'He's rung every day to check on them. He'll probably ask to talk to them at some point.'

'You're lucky to have such good employers.'

'Employer,' Marion corrected. 'Just James. Harriet hasn't got anything to do with the goats.'

'She's a solicitor, so I guess not,' said Sophie.

Marion shook her head. 'That's not why. James grew up with the goats. His father started this herd. It's in his blood, even though his dad did everything he could to keep James from following in his footsteps.'

'That's weird. Why would he do that?'

'I know, I never got it, especially when most farmers would love to have someone to take over. I could understand if he didn't want to tie James to a loss-making business, but this was already doing well even before James took over and expanded.' She shrugged. 'They didn't even let him do the animal husbandry course he wanted

113

at university. They made him study something else. Then they made him work in London. He still talks about how much he hated it. He only got the farm when his parents finally moved to Spain.'

Poor James, thought Sophie. That must have been so frustrating for him. 'At least he met Harriet in London.'

Marion grimaced. 'Opinions are split around here on how lucky that was. I've got no problem with her, but lots of people think she's stuck-up. She can be very . . .'

'Direct,' Sophie finished. 'I've noticed. I think she's just really smart. Maybe that makes her words sound abrupt. It must be hard for her living here if she hasn't got many friends.'

Her own friendship circle had shrunk to, well, a dot in the past few years, despite the children's ever-expanding activities and all the volunteering. She mentally ticked off the women she knew, from the school run, her charities, university and old work colleagues. She always made sure she liked their posts on Facebook, yet that wasn't the same thing as seeing them in person, or even talking on the phone. She was embarrassed to admit that she'd talked to Harriet more in the past few days than she had her friends in ages.

Marion finished her tea. 'People would accept Harriet because they like James so much, but she barely goes into the village. Except for Zumba on Saturdays, and it sounds like she doesn't talk to anyone then.'

Sophie jumped to her new friend's defence. 'Who can talk during Zumba? I'd be too busy trying to breathe.'

Marion laughed. 'I know, but after. I guess she's just not a natural people person. Anyway, I'd better get back to work. Thanks ever so much for the tea.'

On her way back to the house, Sophie texted Harriet.

Just talked to Marion. She's nice! She hesitated, then added, *She likes you. She might make a nice friend. Sx*

Ha, that sounded as awkward as the time her mum had tried to set Sophie up with her hairstylist's son. His main selling point seemed to be that he had his own car. Sophie passed on the offer and kept taking the bus.

She's a solid employee. I have no reservations about recommending her as a friend if you want. H

Not me, you! Sx

I'll bear it in mind. Thanks. H

Dan emerged from the office at exactly one o'clock. 'Just like I promised,' he told Sophie with a smile. 'Now, did you have a nice morning?'

But instead of waiting for her answer, he went to the leaded window at the front of the house. She trailed behind him and, as he gazed out, Sophie opened her mouth to tell him about the delivery. He was looking at the very spot on the lawn where all the tables had lain. Now only raindrops covered the grass there, a sparkling blanket in the bright sun that beamed between fast-moving clouds.

Now you see them, now you don't. Maybe he'd congratulate her on her resourcefulness, kiss her on the nose and tell her he loved her. No, probably he'd kiss her on the nose, tell her he loved her and then say something that rubbished all her efforts.

She didn't want to hear that. She closed her mouth just as her phone dinged with a text.

On reflection, I think
that Marion could be a
friend, temperamentally,
but practically there's the
employer/employee issue.
Even though she technically
works for James, any future
difficulties between us could
compromise that working
relationship so, on balance,
I think she could be an
acquaintance at best. H

Then a few seconds later came the next message.

x

'Who's that?' Dan asked.

'Only Harriet.'

'Why are you texting each other?'

'Oh, you know, house stuff.' She tucked her phone away. 'Did you see the rainbow earlier, over the barns?'

She followed him back into the kitchen where the children were finishing their sandwiches. 'I was working, wasn't I?' he said. 'I can drive you to the spa. If you'll let me have a sandwich first.' He snatched a crisp from Oliver's plate, but instead of complaining, Oliver reached for the bag to offer more to his father.

'That's okay,' Sophie said, 'it looks like the rain clouds have passed. Anyway, I don't want to put you out.'

'You always put me out, silly bean, I'm used to it, but you don't have to lift a finger while you're here.'

'Or a foot,' she said.

'Or a foot. You're to be a complete slacker for the next two weeks. I mean officially. Doctor's orders.'

Katie spoke up. 'But Mum—'

'But Mum nothing, Katie,' said Dan. 'Mum isn't doing anything while we're here. We'll all just have to pick up the slack for her.'

Sophie caught her daughter's eye. She winked. Katie smiled back. That was enough.

Sophie sort of liked having no idea what treatment she was about to have. She just turned up and assumed the position. She was about to take her top off this time when Molly whispered, 'Keep your bra on today, and your jeans are okay. Unless you're more comfortable with them off?'

She thought about the paper pants. 'No, I'm fine with them on, if you are.'

She handed Sophie one of the spa's fluffy white robes. 'When you're ready, lie on your back, please.' She gestured like a game show presenter at the massage table. 'And close your eyes.'

Already this was fun! She could feel her breathing ease as she lay down on the table, tucked up in her cosy robe. What a transformation in just a few days! She'd been as rigid as one of the ceiling beams in Harriet's house during her first massage.

Now everything about the spa felt familiar: the gentle glow given off by all the candles and the spicy incense that tickled her nose. She'd get some of that before she went home to London. The scent would bring her back to this wonderful place. Her fingers found the edge of her robe. So soft. She'd see about buying one of those, too.

Molly crept back into the room. 'Now, just relax, Sophie. You're going to love this.'

Sophie got ready for the bliss.

She could hear a jar being opened. With her eyes closed she liked trying to guess what was coming next. It must be a delicious cream of some kind to clean her face.

She was right! Molly's fingers slid over her cheeks, her nose, her chin and forehead, spreading the soft, herby scent all around. Then came the warm cloth to wash it off. It was rough, like a cat's tongue.

A sigh squeezed out. She might even have a nap. She was already that relaxed. Idly, she wondered where the closest spa was to their house in London. Walking distance, she hoped.

Then she felt something small, soft and damp pressed to her cheek. Molly held it there. After a few seconds she felt the same thing on her other cheek.

Stones, maybe? No, those were cool, not warm. Some kind of fruit, she'd bet, although her nose gave her no clues. Kiwi didn't always have a strong aroma. And they were about the right size. Kiwi, then.

Molly began moving the kiwi slices oh so slowly towards her nose. What patience she must have, because she was moving them just millimetres at a time. At that rate it would take the whole hour to go once round her face.

Sophie didn't mind. She sighed again. It was such heaven being pampered. She'd been right to book this holiday. Well, not this holiday, but the Italian one that turned into this.

This time her sigh wasn't because of the facial. The only thing missing, aside from Italian sunsets, was the food. She'd been so looking forward to that. Maybe she'd suggest that Dan try a few pastas later in the week if he still insisted on cooking. Perhaps an oozy cheesy risotto, too.

She could feel her mouth starting to water. 'There's no Italian restaurant in the village, is there?' she asked Molly.

'No talking, please. Only till the treatment is finished. There's an ASK.'

A pizza chain. She had one of those five minutes from their house. 'Mmm.' She hoped that didn't count as talking.

Molly now had one kiwi slice moving slowly up the side of Sophie's nose, but the other one was moving down her cheek. She wondered if she was doing something with pressure points. Otherwise why not just put the slices in the same place on either side of her face?

Was it kiwi? The way Molly was moving the slices made them feel like they were sticking to her skin. The shower squeegee at home suddenly popped into her mind. Not the blade. The suction cup holding it.

She peeked one eye open.

Something horrific was slithering towards her eyeball.

'Aaarrrgggghhhhhh!'

Snakes. There were *snakes* on her face! She swiped at them. 'What the *FUCK*, Molly?!'

She clamped her hand to her mouth. 'I'm so sorry,' she mumbled through her fingers. She hardly ever swore.

Molly sprang from her stool and rushed to one corner of the room. She crouched down. 'Oh, nooo.'

'Molly, seriously, you could have given me a heart attack.'

She shook her head. 'You said you didn't want to know what the massage was beforehand.' Carefully she plucked something from the stone floor.

Sophie leaned over the edge of the table to see what Molly had picked up. 'Is that . . .?'

'It was.' Gingerly, she held up the crushed snail shell.

'Oh. Is it definitely . . .?'

'Dead.' Then Molly's head shot up. She stood. 'Where's the other one?'

'Um. I think it went that way.' She pointed to the opposite wall. God, this was embarrassing. 'I didn't mean to kill it.' Well, okay, she probably had, given that she'd thought there were snakes on her face. But only for a split second.

A split second was all it took for a snail.

'Found 'er.' Molly cradled the other snail in her palm. Then, to Sophie's surprise, she started crooning something into her hands. Her voice was gravelly, soulful and reminded Sophie of the blues albums her mum used to play whenever she did the housework. The soundtrack to Sophie's childhood was Eric Clapton, Bonnie Raitt and Henry Hoover.

Her therapist was singing to the snail. 'Er, are you singing about salad?' Sophie asked.

Molly glanced up from her palm. 'She likes it.'

She shouldn't laugh. She really shouldn't laugh. She'd just killed a living thing.

Molly went through one more chorus of 'Polk Salad Annie' before the snail's head emerged.

Sophie studied it as Molly held out her palm. Not close enough for Sophie to touch, she noticed. 'It's huge.' She was sure she'd never slid on one that big in the garden at home. Not that she ever trod on snails on purpose. Another wave of guilt washed over her. 'How do you know it's a her?'

'They're all 'ers. And 'ims. Hermaphrodites.'

Sophie had to admit that it didn't look nearly as scary as when its tentacles had been about to blind her. After a few exploratory wriggles of the stalky bits on its head, it began to stretch along Molly's palm. Sophie felt slightly sick.

'Snails. Who'd have thought?' That explained why they hadn't felt like snakes when she'd dashed the beasts off. And why she'd thought of her bath squeegee.

'These were specially trained.'

'What, like from a circus?'

At least Molly smiled at that. She must not hate Sophie too much for killing half of her facial product. 'I am really so sorry. I'll pay for a replacement, of course.'

She was glad the receptionist wasn't at the front desk when she slunk from the spa. The fewer witnesses to this, the better.

Sophie was just about to start for home when she noticed the pub across the road. Like the other old buildings on the high street, its yellow stone frontage glowed warmly. Well, why not? If they'd made it to Italy, she'd have been liver-deep in Prosecco by now. Besides, she didn't feel like going back just yet.

Smiling into the sunshine, she made her way to the pub.

Inside it looked even older than Harriet's house. The ceiling wasn't especially low, but the dark beams overhead made her want to duck. It was probably cosier at night, or in winter, when the huge fireplaces would be lit. At four in the afternoon the swirly stain-hiding carpets and bashed-up wooden tables looked a bit tatty.

She hesitated near the door, unsure when she'd last been on her own in a pub, but the barmaid's friendly smile encouraged her. 'Have you got any Prosecco?' she asked. An old man sitting at the bar tore his gaze from his nearly empty pint long enough to stare at her.

'I'm afraid not. Oh, wait, you know what? I think there's . . .' She pulled several wine bottles from the fridge. 'Yep, there's a bottle of champagne. Celebrating something?'

'I guess so,' Sophie said. 'We're here on holiday this week. And next. It's the first time we've been away in three years. Our original holiday got cancelled because of the ash cloud, you see. We were supposed to fly to Italy, so I thought, when in Rome . . . or not, in this case, drink Prosecco. Champagne is close enough. May I please have a glass?'

'It's by the bottle only. Otherwise I'd never sell the rest. The best I could do by the glass is a fizzy cider,' she said. 'It's a nice one. Local. Will that do?'

'Yes, thank you.'

While she poured Sophie's half-pint, she asked where they were staying. Sophie's answer prodded the old man to perk up.

'I knew Jimmy Cooper,' he said. His pale-blue eyes were rimmed with pink and his hands a bit shaky, but his shave was as fresh as his three-piece suit. Though it looked uncomfortably hot for the summer weather. 'The young un's father.'

Sophie wanted to hear more, after what Marion had said. 'He was quite successful, I understand. With the farm.'

'Aye, he was better than his father-in-law, but 'e never took to it.'

'Oh, I thought James's father started the herd.'

'He did, but the farm was his mother's family. Old Jimmy only took it on after the father died.'

'Then he wasn't always a farmer.'

The man finished his pint. ''E did something in banking in Cheltenham. The Gentleman Farmer, 'e was known as. 'E hated that.'

She wondered why Marion hadn't mentioned that. Though this would have been before James was even born. Maybe she didn't know.

'The parents are in Spain now, I understand,' she said. 'Malaga,' said the barmaid.

'And to you, madam!' the old man answered and they both laughed. Then the door opened and the man beamed. 'Ah, young lady, how glorious it is to see you.'

The way the woman's grey hair was braided around her head gave her an Alpine look and, like him, she was dapperly dressed. But Sophie felt warm just seeing the flowery scarf looped round and round her neck and tucked into her buttoned-up cardigan.

He stood when she reached him and, very formally, kissed her lips.

'See you tomorrow,' he told the barmaid. Then he put his finger to his lips, and said, 'Don't tell my wife.' He held out his arm to the woman.

'He's kidding, isn't he, about his wife?' Sophie asked when they'd gone.

'He's serious. That's his girlfriend. He meets her here every day. His wife is at home.'

'Every day? But she must know something is going on.'

'She knows,' said the barmaid, 'but she'd murder us if we told him she did. This way she gets him out of the house for a few hours. Sometimes she and Alison, that's his girlfriend, come in here together in the evening. He's probably asleep at home in his chair, none the wiser. Another half?' She pointed at Sophie's nearly empty glass.

This village was full of surprises. 'Sure, thanks, why not?'

On the walk home from the pub, Sophie rang her dad again. 'You'd love it here,' she told him when he answered. 'I've just been to the pub and met some of the locals.'

Her dad laughed. 'That's my Sophie, already making yourself at home. You were always good at that.'

Sophie smiled at her Dad's compliment. 'The children are loving the goats. I'm afraid they're going to want one when we get back to London.'

'How will Spot feel about that? Don't pythons eat goats?'

'I'll use that as my excuse, thanks, Dad.'

'That's what dads are for,' he said.

When Sophie told Dan later about her treatment, he thought it was the funniest thing in the world. 'But I squashed the poor thing!' she said again. 'I'm sure that wasn't a good death.'

Dan wiped his eyes. 'I suppose the other one is a widow now.'

Ha ha-bloody-ha. 'Don't make me feel any worse than I already do. You'd have been shocked, too.' What person in their right mind thinks: I know a great facial cleanser! Live snail juice.

It couldn't be good for those snails, either. She had half a mind to ring the RSPCA. Except then she'd have to confess to snailicide.

He shook his head. 'It wouldn't have shocked me.'

'Only because you booked it.'

'Uh-uh. Because I already know about snail facials. They're huge in Japan. Aw, Soph, don't be hard on yourself just because you didn't know. You've not been around as much as I have. We'll make a worldly wife of you yet.'

He went to hug her but she ducked his arms. 'I didn't know you were so knowledgeable about molluscs.' She saw his raised eyebrows. 'Yes, I know the word.'

'They're gastropods, actually, and how about a thank you for booking your facial?' His voice had turned hard. No more joking.

'Thank you.'

Sophie looked it up later. Snails were also molluscs. She didn't bother telling Dan. She wasn't in the mood for that gamble. Sometimes he loved it when she was clever.

Sometimes he didn't.

Chapter 11

Wednesday / Thursday

When life gives you lemons, forget the lemonade. Make margaritas. Harriet smiled at James over her salted rim. Was he remembering their nights here, too? That might have been over a decade ago but it hadn't changed at all. The cramped restaurant was still overlit, overcrowded and overpriced. It smelled strongly of frying cumin and onions from the sizzling grill plates on the tables beside them. She loved it.

She could hardly believe that it was the middle of their first holiday week already. She swallowed another gulp of tequila along with her slight panic. That left only ten more nights for her plan to work. Nine days. Even worse, because it was much harder to be a temptress in daylight.

'Want to share some guacamole?' James asked. She smiled at his pronunciation. *Gawkermoll*. She'd never been sure whether he'd done that on purpose when they'd first met. She'd made a joke out of it anyway.

James filled her glass again from the sweating pitcher of slush on their table. Delicious slush. 'What are you having?' she asked.

He glanced at the menu. 'Fageetas.'

'Then definitely yes to the gawkermoll. And another pitcher?' Those frozen things were mostly ice anyway.

'I love being here with you,' she told him as she took another sip. 'It reminds me of when we first lived together in London. Remember?'

'I remember almost *not* living together because I completely botched asking you.'

'Don't be so hard on yourself,' she said. 'I definitely came off worse that time.'

'No, I shouldn't have used Ikea as an excuse, but then you were so keen to go . . .'

In fairness to Harriet, if someone says they want help picking a sofa big enough for two at Ikea, why would she think that was code for *I love you, let's live together*? Going over the equation now, she should have calculated that they had, in fact, both fitted on his current sofa several times (in various configurations). They'd moved successfully beyond casual dates to the assumed weekends, and most weeknights, together. Add the number of I love yous exchanged, and she should have arrived at the right answer.

Instead, they'd travelled all the way to the huge shop, shuffled through for hours with the rest of humanity, and it wasn't until after James had spent five hundred quid on a sofa he didn't need that he plucked up the courage to ask her outright to move in.

'We did eventually get there,' she said.

'After you'd put the sofa together. You impressed me with your toolbox.' He was watching her laugh. He used to do that all the time. He hadn't lately. Seeing it again, like this when they were remembering, made her sad for what they'd missed.

'One never knows whether an Allen key will be enough,' she joked. It was better than dwelling on all those lost laughs.

They clinked their nearly empty glasses as the waitress brought more margaritas.

Those pitchers had in fact probably contained quite a lot more alcohol than ice, based on their walk back from the Tube after dinner. Harriet stumbled up the front step. 'Whoops!' The key in her hand missed the lock by inches.

'Shh, you'll wake the kid,' James said. She leaned into him when he looped a steadying arm around her waist. 'And then she'll ground us.'

Harriet giggled as she opened the door into the dark house.

James's hands had moved to more interesting places than her waist. 'To steady myself,' he claimed.

'Those aren't grab rails, you know.'

'Come here.' He pulled her down with him as he sat on the staircase. When he tucked her hair back, his massive hand nearly covered her face. His gentleness always surprised her. 'What do you say we do it here?'

Thank God for margaritas! Or maybe those qwaysadillas were aphrodisiacs. Either way, she was definitely putting Mexican on the menu more often.

She thought she heard a noise upstairs. 'Shh!'

'Shshing is just more noise, you know.'

'We can't here.' Now she was whispering. She had very clear feelings about traumatising children with their parents' sexual antics. 'What if Billie is up? Or Owen?'

James moved her hand to his trousers. 'I'm up.'

'Come on then.' She led him upstairs to their bedroom. Luckily she was holding James's hand. Otherwise she might have hurt herself when she tripped on the step.

She was so pleasantly drunk! Why didn't she do this more often? Probably because there was no Mexican in their village. There was nothing fun in their village. Stupid village.

'Let me brush my teeth first,' she whispered.

But the toothpaste tube was slippery as a seal. Slippery as a seal! That was a tongue twister. She knocked the tumbler full of toothbrushes into the sink. *Shh!* She giggled.

She put her finger through her tights trying to yank them off to go to the loo. 'Aw, damn.' Stupid tights.

The toilet lid slammed down when she flushed. Shh!

'Jesus, could you be any louder?' Billie called out from her room.

Harriet froze. She should have closed the bedroom door, or at least the en-suite door. She made a face at James on the bed. 'Sorry!' she called to her daughter. 'She's awake,' she warned James.

'We'll be quiet,' he said.

They both cringed as Harriet sat on the bed. Sophie's bed frame was one of those old-fashioned brass ones. It sounded like an angry duck.

That was only half the problem. 'You're never quiet,' she reminded him. It wasn't until she'd seen that programme about mating tortoises that she realised her husband could have done the sound effects. She liked the sound of mating tortoises, as it happened, but Billie would never nod off if she heard that. 'We'll have to wait till she's sleeping.' His hands went straight for her pants. The mattress quacked. She slapped him away. 'James, I mean it. Wait.'

They both lay down on their backs. James's hand found hers.

Billie's light hadn't been on, Harriet remembered. She'd go back to sleep soon. Harriet was sleepy herself. She closed her eyes. Too much food. It had been a good night. Like the old days when they still liked each other. That seemed such a long time ago, she thought as she drifted into sleep.

★

The next morning, Harriet picked up her mobile again, but she couldn't cancel the appointment. She'd chosen all the right treatments for an absolutely perfect spa day. Besides, she was not the kind of woman who changed her plans for a man. Even when last night was *such* a good start – until she fell into a margarita slumber – and she was clearly on a roll now and they should probably do something equally fun with their clothes on today. Just to cement things.

But that was a slippery slope. It might start with a single cancelled appointment. The next thing you know, you're going to lectures on obscure Russian philosophers to improve yourself. All for him.

She was fine the way she was, thank you very much. 'What are you doing today?' she asked James when he came into the kitchen for breakfast, wearing stretched-out jogging bottoms and a t-shirt. His thick hair was all squashed on one side and sticking up on the other. 'I packed more than one thing to sleep in, you know.'

He leaned down to kiss her as if he hadn't heard. 'I thought maybe the Transport Museum.'

'I didn't know you were fond of buses. I thought tractors were your thing.'

The sticking-up part of his hair waved around when he shook his head. 'I guess I'll have to expand my horizons.'

'Your hair's all . . .' She pointed.

'Good thing I didn't accept that invite to the Oscars, then.'

'Hilarious. Will Billie join you?'

He was opening and closing all the kitchen cabinets. 'What's that? Probably not. She didn't sound interested. Have you seen any painkillers? It's fine, I don't mind going on my own.'

She pointed to the open bottle of paracetamol. They'd already started working on her hangover.

'I couldn't get her to come to the spa with me either,' she told him. It would have been such a nice thing for them to do together – just the girls – that Harriet felt sure she'd at least be tempted. 'What's Billie going to do then?'

He shrugged. 'Ask her.'

She hated it when he got practical like that. 'She always says *dunno*.'

'Maybe she does dunno.'

'Maybe she's wasting her life on that damn phone. She needs to be with real people, James, not looking at a screen.'

He circled his arms around her as she sat on one of Sophie's stools. She leaned her head back against his chest. She stayed like that even though his t-shirt needed a wash. 'She is usually with real people,' he said. 'Who do you think she's on her phone to? That's what kids do now. We talked on the phone at that age, too, remember, way back when?'

'They're not talking, though. They're Instagramming pictures of their breakfasts. How do we even know who's at the other end? It could be some forty-year-old perv and we'd have no idea. His Facebook picture is probably a unicorn.'

'Nobody's on Facebook any more,' James said.

'Oh, so you know all about social media now?' He didn't even Instagram his own goats. He got Marion to do it. Probably their breakfasts, too.

'Want some coffee?' he asked.

'No. I want to know who our daughter is talking to.'

'Ask her.'

Like it was that easy.

Chapter 12
Thursday

Sophie did a double take. It was James, right there on the high street! She was sure she recognised his big frame and wild hair, even all the way across the road. She glanced at her phone. Only twenty-five minutes till her treatment. She wouldn't have enough time to go with him to the house and then back. Then there'd be a chat and tea, and she'd definitely miss her appointment.

Why hadn't he rung first? Dan was locked up in his office. James's office. Would he mind Dan using it? She should ring to warn him. But he'd be cross at being disturbed.

She had a better idea. She could have a chat with him in the village and save him a trip to the farm. Then Dan wouldn't need to be interrupted. *Good plan, Soph.*

She waved to catch James's attention, but he was staring down the road. She'd just started to cross over to see him when his face broke into a grin. He still wasn't looking at her, though. His smile was for the woman hurrying his way. She was tall, trouser-suited and very, very sleek. She could have come fresh from a spa treatment herself. She was that kind of glowy.

Sophie's greeting died on her lips when the woman wrapped her arms around James. She crept back onto the pavement, turning her face away. The village green might

131

be between them, but still. Not that they'd probably notice her. They were too absorbed in each other as they walked together to a little convertible parked further along. James folded himself into the front seat and they sped off.

How odd, she thought as she looked for the shop that she'd noticed the other day. Harriet hadn't mentioned anything about James coming to visit. But then she, Sophie, hadn't told Harriet anything about Dan's activities, either.

She gazed into another shop window. Books, this time. Nice, but not what she was after.

Harriet and Sophie had hardly talked about Dan or the children. Or James or Billie for that matter. Harriet's questions, she realised, were always about her, not her as a mum or a wife. In real life, whenever she did manage to snatch conversations, usually with other mums on the chauffeuring circuit, talk swirled around the school-children-partner vortex. It was even worse when Oliver and Katie had been babies. Then, she did meet up with others from her NCT group, playgroup and nursery, yet she had felt like one more formula debate or cracked nipple description might tip her over the edge.

Talking to Harriet was different. Dan didn't get any of Harriet's time. Neither did the children. Sophie liked not having to share. Harriet felt almost like a proper friend, the kind she used to have.

Glancing into another window, she caught herself smiling.

Then, towards the top of the high street, Sophie found the shop she wanted. Its front window was festooned with bunting and sparkling crockery, interesting-looking books, pretty ceramic egg cups and homely jams. It was the needlepoint cushion that had first caught her eye. *Stressed Spelled Backwards is Desserts*. She'd buy it for Harriet as a thank you present.

'Hello again!' called out the woman sitting behind the till.

It took Sophie a moment to place her. It was Delia from the deli. 'Oh, hello, I didn't recognise you without the apron.'

Her smooth dark hair might be swept into the same up-do and the flick of her liquid liner as bold and perfect as the other day but here, surrounded by etched martini glasses, funky butter dishes and shiny silk robes, she looked more like a 1960s party hostess than a celebrity chef. Context was all.

Delia stood, pulling at the bustline of her very fitted jumper. 'I'm a woman of many talents.'

Delia's many talents were clearly on display but, glancing around the shop, Sophie didn't see any more of the cushions. That figured. She didn't want Delia going to the bother of getting it out of the window before she knew the price. There was probably only so much demand in a village this size for dust mop slippers and ceramic ducks. Maybe she charged a fortune for everything. Or what if it was some kind of rare Cotswold needlepoint technique that was too dear? Then she'd have to buy it anyway.

The front door slammed open just as Delia was reaching into the display for the cushion. 'Mum! I need change.' The young woman's eyes widened when she saw Sophie. 'Sorry.' With the same eyeliner flick as her mother, her giant eyes looked like they'd been filtered through Katie's Snapchat account.

'Mind, Becca!' Delia handed Sophie the cushion. Luckily there was a faded sticker on the back. It wouldn't cost the earth.

'How much do you need?' Delia asked her daughter. 'Because I haven't got a lot of change.' She looked at Sophie. 'Will that be card?'

Sophie slipped the twenty-pound note back into her pocket. 'I can pay by card if it helps.'

The card machine wasn't as interested in making Delia's life as easy as Sophie was. 'Let me just try it in another minute,' Delia said, holding the little machine in the air. 'The network gets fiddly.'

'It's just that I need to be at the spa soon.' She glanced at the loudly ticking wall clock.

'Another treatment?' Delia squinted through her acid-green reading glasses at the tiny screen. 'It's connecting now. That's progress. It was a snail facial you had, wasn't it?'

'Killed one, did you?' Becca said. 'Creamed 'im, I heard.'

'Becca, manners.'

Word got around fast. Sophie felt her face bloom red. 'By accident!'

'She threw 'im at the wall.' Becca's stare wasn't rude, though it was direct. 'Slime everywhere. Molly slipped in it.'

'I didn't throw him!' Sophie protested. 'It was just a natural reaction. It wasn't that messy.'

'Tell that to the snails.'

Delia ignored her daughter. 'Too right, love,' Delia consoled Sophie. 'Letting garden pests on your face. Don't blame you. Ah, it's gone through now. Wait and I'll give you a receipt.'

'No need!' Sophie thanked her and fled the shop.

She was flustered and puffing when she turned up at the spa. 'I'm sorry I'm late! The card machine over the road wasn't working.'

'That's okay.' When Molly whispered, Sophie could feel herself calming down. It *was* okay. It would be okay.

'Do you want to know about the treatment today?' Molly asked. She didn't seem to be holding a grudge about yesterday.

'As long as no live animals are involved, I don't need to know.' They probably wouldn't let her within ten feet of so much as a pot plant.

Molly led her to their usual massage room. 'You'll want to be completely undressed today,' Molly murmured, holding out the paper pants. 'But keep your robe on. I'll be back when you've changed.'

Sophie was in position on the massage table with her face in the hole when Molly came back in. It was a bit uncomfortable with the double knot of her robe digging into her tummy. 'Come with me, please,' said Molly. 'We're changing rooms.'

Awkwardly, trying to keep her robe closed, she climbed off the table and followed Molly.

When Molly opened the door at the end of the corridor, Sophie walked into a wall of heat. The sauna was lit only by a single red light in the ceiling, but she could just make out that everything was panelled in pale wood. And it was about seven hundred degrees. Sophie could feel her actual hair sweating.

'Aren't you going to boil in that?' she asked Molly. Then she worried that that sounded like the start of a porn film. Especially in a sauna. *Bom-chicka-wow-wow.*

Molly glanced down at her tunic. 'I'm fine,' she whispered. 'If you want to take off your robe?'

Sophie was already pulling at the belt. Nudity-schmoodity. She could die in here.

Lying on the wooden bench and trying not to think of all the sweaty bodies who'd been there before her, she positioned the (too small in her opinion) towel over her behind as best she could.

It took about ten seconds for her boobs to start sweating. That bench would look like the Shroud of Turin with nipples by the time she got up.

She'd heard of sweaty yoga – which sounded like a circle of hell beyond exercise – but never sweaty massage.

She waited for Molly to drip the oil on her back, but all she heard was rustling. Then the wet hiss of water being poured on hot coals. *Oh great, more heat.*

She waited. Molly rustled. Sweet wrappers? Probably too good to be true. Something paper, then. Maybe it was an origami massage. That was Japanese, too, she thought, like the snails.

She was about to be rubbed with paper cranes.

Thwack!

What the . . .?

Molly took aim again. *Thwack!* Something decidedly twiggy poked her arm on that round. She twisted her head around for a look.

Molly shook handfuls of thick green foliage at her. 'Relax,' she cooed.

Fat chance of that when someone was swinging garden clippings at her naked body. 'What is this?'

'It's a banya massage from Russia. It stimulates the circulatory system.'

Not to mention that she'd leave smelling like she'd just strimmed the lawn. Suddenly the comment from the village's own Mrs Thatcher made sense. 'Sticks and stones will break my bones,' she'd told her at the butcher's shop. Sophie hoped not.

Thwack! For such a gentle-sounding girl, Molly must have a lot of pent-up anger. Sophie wasn't sure her masseuse had read the whole instruction booklet on this technique. Maybe it was in Russian. Surely it wasn't supposed to hurt.

She stifled a giggle. She was paying for this! Well, Dan was paying for this.

No, Soph, she thought as another thwack made her jump. *You're paying for this.* That would take time to get used to, but Harriet had been perfectly right. She'd earned this. For better or worse.

By the time Molly had exhausted her branches, Sophie was feeling something close to relaxed. Light-headed, anyway, from the heat.

'Maybe something a little gentler next time,' she told Molly.

Back outside, Molly scanned the appointment book. 'Tomorrow will be perfect for you. Do you want me to tell you?'

Even with the garden theme that was emerging at the spa, she was still enjoying the adventure of not knowing what came next. That just showed how little adventure she'd had lately, she supposed. Oh, Dan sometimes sprang a night out on her, and she did love those, but she had to face facts. She got excited when the café round the corner put a new cake on the menu.

This week had been different. For once, the journey seemed like hers.

Take the walks back from the village. She didn't have to pick anyone up from practice or lessons or do the shopping or cooking that was inevitably wrong anyway. Nobody was depending on her. The laundry mountain was back in London.

She hadn't felt this light in years. She hoped it wouldn't be years before she did so again.

Sophie went home, crawled into bed and had a nap.

Before this week, she hadn't done that in years, either.

She had no idea what time it was when Oliver stuck his face inches from hers. 'Mum? Mum! Someone's here.'

The light streaming through the bedroom windows was still bright. She mustn't have been asleep for long. 'Who is it?'

'A lady with flowers. Dad's not here.'

'Where is he?' Flowers for her? Dan could be sweet sometimes. He was probably sorry about having to work so much. That was the kind of gesture he loved.

'He's gone for a run,' said Oliver. 'He wouldn't let me go, even though I can keep up.'

Sophie hated hearing the hurt in Oliver's voice. He idolised his dad. 'Of course you could, darling. Dad just wants some time alone.'

Didn't they all? She could have slept for hours more. 'Tell the lady I'll be down.'

Checking in the mirror, her face was a little creased from the pillow, but at least it wasn't beetroot red from the sauna any more. She smoothed her hair and straightened her dress.

It wasn't a thoughtful bouquet from Dan, though. It wasn't a bouquet from anyone, but a middle-aged woman pulling boxes from the back of a van painted all over with brightly coloured daisies. Her thin arms, sticking out from her faded sleeveless cotton blouse, flexed as she carefully lifted each box.

'Hello? Can I help you?' Though it looked like more arm exercises.

The woman hesitated when she looked up. 'Thank you. Is Mrs Cooper not in?'

'No, she's on holiday. We're staying in the house while they're away.' This woman must not be from the village, because everyone there already knew that, and a lot more besides.

'These are all the jars,' the woman explained. 'Where would you like them?'

Ah, the fundraiser. At least she wasn't going to dump them on the grass like the other delivery person had done with the tables. 'In the barn, please, but I'll help you. Those, too?' They both looked at the paper-wrapped bunches of flowers sticking out of wooden frames on the floor.

'Isn't it a bit early for the flowers?' Sophie asked as she held out her arms for the first batch.

The woman shook her head, explaining that they always delivered at least forty-eight hours before an event so they'd have a chance to open.

'But the event isn't till next weekend.' In other words, after they'd gone back to London.

'Mmm, no.' The woman pulled the order sheet from her jeans pocket. 'This Sunday. Look, the note says right here.'

'But that's three days away!' Sophie cried.

'You don't have to worry. They'll open in time. They'll be perfect.'

That was not what Sophie was worried about. She didn't give a toss about whether they'd be perfect, or even if they'd open, frankly. She cared that hordes of Boy Scouts were about to overrun her holiday.

But that wouldn't be this woman's problem.

It would be Sophie's.

She felt her pulse racing. All Molly's twig-beating for nothing.

She rang Harriet the minute the woman left, after detonating her flower bomb all over Sophie's weekend. 'Just to let you know,' she told Harriet's voicemail, 'that the flowers have turned up for the event. The event this weekend? I thought it wasn't till Sunday week, after we'd gone. If you could please give me a ring, that would be great. Thanks, bye!'

She had no idea how to get hold of the planner. Or the Scout leader, for that matter. She tried to remember what he looked like. *Pssh*. What did she plan to do with that information, exactly? Tack posters up in the village as if he were a missing cat?

Silly bean.

Dan came inside, panting and sweaty and happy. She'd never understood the runner's high. The loafer's lie-down, yes.

When he dropped his trainers on the floor, smudges of mud and clumps of grass streaked the tiles. She wasn't cross, though, as it only added to the streaks that were already there from the rest of their shoes. It didn't make sense to go through the effort of cleaning it all up when he was only going to go out into the fields again tomorrow.

Sophie would never have put such light-coloured tiling on a kitchen floor. 'Get off me!' she shouted when he hugged her. 'You stink.'

'It's clean sweat,' he said.

'Sweat is sweat. Speaking of which, I had my special Russian massage today.'

'Did I do well or what?' He couldn't be prouder of himself.

'You ordered a stranger to beat me with sticks.' She couldn't keep a straight face, though.

'C'mon, lighten up.' He wrestled her off her chair, clamped her in his arms and danced her around the kitchen.

Oliver was watching them from his spot on the sofa. Katie rolled her eyes. Parental affection was beyond yuck to her. 'You loved the massage. Admit it.'

'I'll go so far as to say it was interesting.'

'First Japan, now Russia. My Soph is getting a tour of the world without having to leave England. We might even get you speaking another language one day.'

Just as she wondered how to say *arrogant bollocks* in Russian, Dan fished his phone from the little zipped pocket at the back of his shorts. After a glance, he set it on the table and announced, 'I'm having a shower.'

As soon as he'd said it, Sophie wished she'd got in there first. She really felt like a bath. What a perfect way to keep the luxurious spa feeling going. Now she'd have to wait till he was finished. Not that Harriet's house had the water pressure issues, she was betting, that theirs did, or the lack of bathrooms, but she didn't want to deal with a dripping wet, angry Dan.

She'd just made herself a cup of tea when Dan's phone lit up with his boss's name.

'Hi there, Jeremy,' she answered. 'This is Sophie.'

'Sophie, how are you?' Jeremy asked warmly. He'd always been very kind to her when they had spouse events together. 'I hope your holiday is everything you hoped for. Sorry you didn't make it to Italy.'

'That's okay, this is a wonderful alternative!' she said. 'Has Dan told you about it? It's practically a mansion, with a darling village that we can walk to, and I've been having spa treatments every day. I'm being spoilt rotten.'

'Well, you deserve it. Actually, I'm glad I got you. I'm sure Dan passed it on, but I wanted to say sorry if you were disappointed with the lack of bonus last year. It was a lean year for everyone.'

'Not at all, Jeremy, please don't worry.' *What lack of bonus?* Dan had been pleased with it. He'd bought champagne to celebrate and everything.

'I don't suppose your husband is around?' Jeremy went on. 'I've been chasing him all week.'

'Hang on, I'll just see if he's out of the shower. I think he is.' She hurried upstairs to the bedroom with Dan's phone in her hand.

He had his towel wrapped low around his waist. His hair stood up at all angles. Sophie always loved seeing him like that. It reminded her of sexy weekends when they first got together. 'It's Jeremy,' she said, handing him the phone.

The look he gave her for her delivery service wasn't exactly thankful. He waved her out of the bedroom.

He didn't stay long on the call, though, because it seemed to Sophie that he practically followed her downstairs.

'Please don't answer my phone when it's work,' he said.

'Sorry, I thought it might be urgent.'

'It wasn't.'

'But Jeremy said he'd been trying to get hold of you.' Which was odd, because Dan had definitely said they'd been talking every day.

'I said it wasn't urgent, so drop it, Soph. I'll decide when to answer my calls from now on.'

Just then, her own mobile started ringing. It wasn't Harriet, though, like she'd hoped. She snatched up the handset and waved it at her daughter. 'Katie? It's Carlos. Want to talk to him?'

Katie was being maddeningly slow about getting up, so Sophie had no choice but to answer. 'Hi, Carlos. All okay?'

'It'll be better when you're back,' Carlos said.

She turned to her husband. 'Dan? Maybe Oliver can give you a hand with dinner. He missed out on your run.' Oliver sprang from the sofa to help his dad. 'Sorry, Carlos. Does Spot miss us?'

'Sounds like one big happy family there,' Carlos said.

'Yep. Here's Katie. Talk to you later.' Gratefully, Sophie handed over her phone. 'I'm going to have a bath,' she told Dan. 'You okay to hold the fort for half an hour?'

'Aren't I always?' he said, tying one of the aprons around Oliver's waist. 'Come on, Katie, I need you to help me, too.'

Katie's sigh was monumental. 'I have to go, Carlos, but text pictures, okay?' Just as Sophie started to climb the stairs, she heard her daughter say, 'She's gone for a bath.'

Chapter 13

Thursday / Friday

Harriet got straight on the phone to the Scout leader after she listened to Sophie's message. 'You've got the wrong weekend for the fundraiser,' she said when he answered. He must not have earned his badge in calendar-reading yet. 'This is Harriet.'

He acted like he didn't understand. 'The. Wrong. Weekend,' she said. 'It's next weekend, not this one, but the flowers turned up today. They'll be dead by next weekend.' Not that that was her problem. 'Can I please have the planner's mobile number? I need the florist to take the flowers back till next week.'

The leader had the nerve (the nerve!) to claim that Harriet had agreed to this weekend. She had not. It was the organiser's mistake, and she was very sorry that all the posters were up and the Scouts had been selling raffle tickets for weeks. No, of course she hadn't seen the notices. 'I agreed to next weekend, not this one. I can prove it. I sent you a text. Just a minute. I'm sending it to you again.' That would settle things.

They'd only agreed to host the event because, let's be honest, Harriet needed all the brownie points she could get in the village. James was always running goat-petting days, or whatever they were, for the local school groups. Everyone knew they had plenty of room on the farm for the fundraiser.

When they'd first moved into James's parents' house, Harriet had wondered if people didn't warm to her because she'd married James. You know, well-loved local boy snatched by outsider city woman. She had tried. She'd even followed the advice she found on how to make friends. Yet people seemed put off when she showed interest by asking questions about them. They didn't laugh when she demonstrated her lighter side by making a joke, and got uneasy when she listened intently to them. No matter how hard she'd tried to fit in, for whatever reason the villagers didn't get her.

She tapped through to her texts, scrolling down till she found the Scout leader's mobile. Quickly she read through the trail of messages. 'Oh.'

He was right. The delivery people were right. Everyone was right except her. The fundraiser was this weekend. How could she have messed that up? Harriet was the least messing-things-up person she knew. She just didn't make mistakes like that.

It was the damn holiday. She'd been distracted. Not to mention that she'd been planning the revival of her marriage, too. It was a lot to deal with.

'Given that it's this weekend, I'll need to make sure the planner is on top of his game so that it doesn't disturb my friends too much,' she told the leader. 'I'm disappointed about this.' This mistake that she'd made, she didn't say. 'I'm very sorry, and goodbye.'

Sophie rang again just as she was about to ring the planner. 'I'm sorry,' Harriet said as soon as she picked up. 'I messed up the dates. I feel terrible about it, but I've got the planner's number and I'm ringing him now to put everything right. Don't worry, I'll make sure you won't even know they're there on Sunday.'

'Crikey, then they really are coming this weekend?' Sophie asked.

'Yes, but like I said, you won't even know. They'll come in the morning, set up, run their events and be cleaned up and gone by five. That was the agreement. I'll ring the planner now.'

Sophie laughed. 'I guess it's cosmic payback for not telling you that Spot was a snake. No, why don't you give me the number and I'll ring? I'm on the ground, as it were, and . . . honestly, it's felt good to have something to do here.'

'Are you bored? Because I could send you an itinerary of things to do in the area.'

It wouldn't take more than a few minutes to knock something up. Maybe one of the local attractions followed by a walk. Her finger itched to end the call and check the weather. She could rank a top ten list of touristy things for Sophie based on the number and average star rating on TripAdvisor. Though she'd have to control for the obviously wrong reviews, and distance from the house, because that had to be taken into account. Very few people wanted to drive a hundred miles for a pencil museum. It wouldn't take more than half an hour to put something together. An hour, tops. With driving directions; they'd need those too. Two hours, max. She had time after breakfast and before their 11 a.m. museum visit.

'No thanks! I'm fine,' Sophie said. 'Maybe we'll have a walk into the village later. Speaking of which, I saw James yesterday.' She laughed. 'He can't stay away from his goats for very long, can he?'

Harriet froze. 'Was he at the house?' Because the London Transport Museum definitely didn't have a branch in their village.

If Sophie noticed Harriet's hesitation, she had the good grace not to let on. He was in the village, she explained, yesterday afternoon.

Harriet felt ill as everything started falling into place. The worry that something was wrong and the distance that she'd definitely felt between them. The fact that their duvet cover got more action in the spin cycle than Harriet had in months. While she was at the spa, assuming he was swotting up on the history of the steam engine, he could have been enjoying another kind of steamy exhibition. 'Was he on his own?' She knew the question sounded suspicious. Sod it. She was suspicious now. Could James really be carrying on with someone from the village?

'Yesss. Oh, then he saw a friend.' Sophie made that sound like an afterthought but Harriet knew better. 'Should I not have said anything?'

'No, no, it's fine.' It made no sense to ignore facts when they came to light. She may as well know the truth, much as she might not want to hear it. Much as she couldn't wrap her head around James doing something like this. For nineteen years he'd been nothing but steadfast and devoted to his family and friends. James was the one everyone knew they could depend on.

'Okay, good,' said Sophie. 'They seemed like great mates.'

Great mates. For a split second, the relief that flooded through Harriet made her giddy. 'Then I'm sure it was his best friend. Tall, brunette?'

'That's her.'

It was only Persephone, not some man-stealing temptress. Why had her mind gone there so quickly? She was a solicitor. It was her job not to jump to conclusions, but to establish the truth based on the careful examination of evidence.

But then Harriet's memory did disclose more evidence. At Persephone's birthday party, months ago, when she'd stumbled upon them whispering together. That wasn't unusual. They were best friends, after all. It was the way they froze, like two children playing Statues, when they saw her. Persephone had claimed they were talking boring goat stuff, and Harriet might have thought no more about it – she was James's bank adviser, after all – if they hadn't both looked so uncomfortable. She realised with horror just how many interrupted phone calls and furtive conversations she'd heard over the past few months. Hadn't they been texting and ringing every day while he was in London? And now James had run back to see the woman the first chance he got.

Was it possible? She'd seemed so harmless – pretty, but nowhere near fall-in-love-and-leave-your-wife territory. Not to mention that she'd been James's mate all through childhood and puberty and they'd had absolutely no interest in each other even when their hormones were at their most raging. So why should they now? They'd passed their expiry date on romance.

It was like suddenly expecting to travel on an old train ticket. It might have been perfectly valid once upon a time, but now someone else held the ticket for that journey. Rules were rules for a reason. Otherwise they were no better than James's goats, and Harriet was pretty sure she'd feel the same way even if this was happening to someone else.

'Hmm, yes, great mates,' she said to Sophie.

'Harriet? What's wrong?'

She wasn't ready for the concern in Sophie's voice. It threatened to undo her. 'Things haven't been great between us lately,' she admitted. 'That's why I wanted this holiday, to give me the chance to, I don't know, make things better.'

She found herself outlining to Sophie her entire plan to get back the relationship with James she'd once had. One that was nice and even and not off kilter and sagging with emotional atrophy, and now . . . Persephone. Of all people.

They had been happy once. She wasn't imagining that. Of course, day-to-day life wore the edges off the passion they'd felt at the beginning, but that had only been hormones anyway.

She still loved him even though, God, he could drive her mad. She was so tired of feeling like the not-well-liked headmistress all the time.

'It's a good plan,' said Sophie, 'though do be sure you're not blaming yourself, because it takes two to make a relationship.'

'I'm not blaming myself,' Harriet said.

'That's what you just said.'

'You're very imprecise with language, Sophie. I didn't. I said I'm trying to make things better. And I will. It's all planned.'

'Do you have different plans, depending on the weather?' Sophie asked.

Harriet thought she heard laughter in her tone. 'Doesn't everyone?'

'Er, not really.'

'Have you even checked the forecast for today?' asked Harriet.

'No, why, is it going to rain here?'

'I don't know, that's the point of having forecasts.'

Sophie did laugh that time. 'I love how literal you are. It's fine, I'm sure. We can take our chances with a walk anyway.'

Harriet searched the Met Office site as soon as she hung up. *Less than 20% chance of rain*, she texted Sophie.

Her phone buzzed back immediately. *Told you it was fine.*

If only the same could be said for her marriage. Even faced with an eyewitness to his sneaking around, she didn't want to believe it. James and Persephone?

There seemed an easy resolution, of course. She could go in right now and ask him. As tempting as that was, she couldn't let her emotions overrule common sense. The key to a successful prosecution was always solid preparation. She'd only known about him sneaking off to Persephone for about two minutes. There might not even be sufficient evidence to charge him. What if she was wrong? That wouldn't give him the warm fuzzies about their marriage.

No, she had to stick to her plan and keep her eyes open. If there was any truth to her suspicion, she was sure she'd see it now.

Without an itinerary to prepare for Sophie, and their own plans for the day nailed firmly down, and definitely not thinking about what James might or might not have been up to with his best friend, Harriet found herself at a loose end after breakfast. Billie was still asleep, of course. Owen must be as well, because Spot's bedroom door was firmly closed when she crept by.

She had her eye on the towel cupboard in the bathroom. Or, to be more literal, it *would* be the towel cupboard by the time she was finished. A shiver ran down her spine when the sliding door got snagged on something. Peering in, she saw the problem. Some of the towels had fallen off the shelf and were wedged between the door and whatever was on the floor behind them. It took a few contortions to reach in and clear it, but the towels were a red herring. It was the shoes mixed in there that stopped the door.

It was a relief to finally get it open. Harriet liked things sliding smoothly, in life and in household hardware. But what a landslide inside! All the shelves but the bottom one, which had emptied itself onto the floor, were stuffed full. She couldn't make head nor tail of the contents.

Plunging her arm right into the heaped depths of the shelf, she swept everything to the floor.

A thrill ran through her. To instantly sweep clear such chaos! This was creative destruction playing out in Sophie's cupboard, except that it wasn't products and services but facecloths and those silly loofahs that women only got as gifts. As if the giver thinks: *I know what she'd love for Christmas . . . a strong hint to exfoliate more.*

Along with the loofahs, Harriet excavated a trove of informational items from the pile. For instance, she now knew that someone suffered from earwax build-up (three open kits) and thrush (hopefully only Sophie). Sophie's favourite colour was probably aqua. Most of the towels were that colour even though the bathroom accessories were dark blue and clashed a bit. There were enough scented candles to light a Roman Catholic Mass, but not one had been lit anywhere in the house. Someone was either romantically optimistic or had a friend who thought their house could use the extra fragrance. There was a secret midnight chocolate eater in residence, because otherwise the half-crushed boxes of Celebrations with only the Bounties left would have been kept downstairs in the kitchen. And Dan's willy was probably big. This last titbit came courtesy of the open box of extra-roomy condoms hidden at the back of the shelf.

It wasn't a complete picture, but Harriet did think she was getting to know Sophie better. So far Sophie was a guilty work-at-home mum with confidence, thrush and possible earwax issues who enjoyed aqua, bedtime chocolate and big penises, but not coconut, candles or loofahs.

★

When Harriet went out into the garden the next morning, goosebumps popped up on her bare arms. The sun hadn't yet reached over the tall fence that ran down one side, and most of the patio was still in shade. Harriet nudged her notebook so that it lined up with the bottom edge of Sophie's glass-topped garden table. The two pens, one black and one blue, she set together beside the notebook. With her thumb she wiped a tiny coffee drip from the side of her mug. Then she rotated it so the handle lined up with the edge of the notebook, and rang her office at exactly 9 a.m. as arranged.

It was the only call she'd make to work. Otherwise there was no point in physically being away if mentally she was still going to be in the office. A short sharp shock of work to the system, and then she'd repack her notebook and pens and be off again for a week.

But first she had to go through all the pleasantries with her colleague, Sam, who saw no irony in telling her that she should get back to her holiday, which only delayed Harriet getting back to her holiday. 'This is a scheduled call,' she said, to pre-empt any more time-wasting. 'As agreed, I'm ringing for an update on my cases and to see if there are any questions to answer.'

'That's me told then,' said Sam. But Harriet knew she wasn't offended. Sam was one of her eleven-years-and-seven-months friends. 'But first you have to tell me: how is Rome? Is it sunny? Are you surrounded by gorgeous men?'

'You'd have to check the forecast to see, but I imagine it's a little hotter than here. I'm in London.'

'What happened to Rome?'

'The ash cloud happened. Sam, don't you ever watch the news?'

'You know I get my news off Twitter. Come to think of it, I did see a hashtag. How did you end up in London?'

Harriet wasted more time explaining about the house swap with Sophie.

'That's risky. How do you know you can trust them? I wouldn't give my house keys to strangers.'

'No kidding, Sam, nor would I. I know the husband already from a charity dinner. It was just a coincidence they were booked on the same flight. He's a solicitor. Dan Mitchell? The name didn't ring a bell till he reminded me that we'd met.'

'Dan Mitchell? Why does that . . .? Hang on.'

Harriet could hear the handset being put down. 'Sam? Sam! I haven't got time for this.'

She heard Sam's distant voice. 'Just hang on a sec!'

More scraping. 'Right, I thought the name sounded familiar. That guy is well dodgy. He was accused of perverting the course of justice a few years ago. Don't you remember? They said he destroyed some of the evidential statements his client made. I think there were witness-tampering rumours as well. It went to court. It's all right here on Twitter.'

Rumours and Twitter. 'Oh, then it must be true.'

'It is true! Come on, you must remember. They unearthed it all while he was on holiday, when the client told his colleague about the documents. That's why they make bankers take two weeks straight, you know. It's hard to hide fraud for two weeks in a row.'

'He's not a banker, Sam, he's a solicitor.'

'You're splitting hairs, as usual. It's the same *idea*, Harriet, that's all I mean. Hang on, I'm putting you on speaker.'

'Don't do that.' She'd never get off this call.

'Just so I can read the article. Here. He claimed he'd taken the documents home to work on them. Even though they happened to be only the witness statements and, let's see . . .' She made vague noises, presumably as she read. 'Yes, here. They happened to be all the ones that would have weakened his client's defence. He hadn't logged them into the system, so the prosecution didn't have access. It was only because he was able to produce them again that he got off. Looks like he got a slap on the wrist, when everyone knows that's well shady. I'm surprised the firm didn't fire him after. He must bring in too many fees for them.'

Come to think of it, Harriet did recall reading something. 'Are you sure it's the same person? It's not exactly an uncommon name.'

Sam mentioned Dan's law firm. 'It is the same bloke then. I guess he probably won't be a risk to your house, but everyone still thinks he's hiding something. Where there's smoke there's usually fire.'

As Sam went on to brief Harriet on her cases, Harriet wondered how much about Dan Sophie already knew.

'I found some shoes,' she told Sophie when she rang her later. She didn't mention the other things she'd discovered. 'In the bathroom cupboard. I put them all in your wardrobe.'

'Oh those! I'd forgotten. They're my old work shoes. I should donate them. They just take up space and I'll never use them.'

Harriet would never question a person's decision to work outside the home or in it. That was a personal choice that didn't have a right or wrong answer and wasn't anyone else's business anyway. But since Sophie had brought it up, Harriet *had* wondered. 'You might go back into an office one day. When the children are older.'

'They're ten and thirteen! They're old enough now. That's not why I'm not working.'

'You are working,' she reminded Sophie. 'Running the house and volunteering are still work.'

'In an office I mean, for pay. I found it very stressful.' Sophie laughed. 'Now I press clothes and peel eggs and stuff envelopes instead. What's the worst that can happen? I get a paper cut?'

'Well, I guess if it was too stressful then I'm not surprised you gave it up.'

Sophie took a moment to reply. 'Do you know what? It was so long ago now that I'm not sure. I didn't really notice the strain for the first few years at my job. I was an administrator, so I was crazy busy, and there were always fires to fight. Especially with my boss. But I don't remember the stress now. I remember liking it.'

'But you just said that's why you quit.'

'I have always said that, so I must have felt it then. Dan noticed it, that's for sure. He said it made me a different person. Interesting, isn't it, how one's point of view changes with time.'

Harriet thought about James. Her view of him had definitely changed lately. 'Interesting.'

Chapter 14
Friday

As Sophie shoved aside Dan's sweatshirt and Katie's pyjamas and two pot lids from Dan's cooking the other night to clear a little space on the farm table, one of the glasses of water there tipped over. Of course the kitchen roll holder was empty. She mopped it up with Dan's sweatshirt.

She looked again at the number she'd scrawled on the back of a receipt. *Ka-thunk!* went her heart. *Come on, Soph, it's only a phone call. Just do it, like those adverts said.* She looked at her phone, rehearsing what she was going to say, then tapped in the number.

It kept ringing. She was just about to hang up when a man answered. 'Oh, hello,' she said, 'this is Sophie Mitchell. Well, that wouldn't mean anything to you. I'm staying at Harriet Cooper's house? I think you're organising their event?'

'Oh, yes, yes.' The man sounded vague. 'Right.'

'Well, I just wanted to let you know that some of the things have arrived, the tables and the flowers, and I wondered if you'd like me to do anything special with them. I've just put them in the barn for now.' She was keeping an ear out for more delivery vans. It was already Friday. She remembered back to her and Dan's wedding, those last few days before – ready or not – all her nearest and dearest turned up expecting a party. There'd been about a million moving parts to think of. Tables and chairs and flowers were only the tip of the iceberg, she knew, even though the fundraiser would probably be a little less complicated than a wedding. No fighting relatives to keep apart on the seating plan, for one thing.

'That's fine, cheers . . .' he said. Sophie had to strain to hear him. The man was nearly whispering. 'Ta-ra now.'

'Wait! Will you be, er, coming by to—' Do your job? she wanted to say. 'Organise things? Because isn't it in two days?'

'That's right. I'm not sure I can make it, though.'

He made it sound like she was asking for an RSVP. This wasn't a Regrets Only type situation. 'Okayyy. Then who is coming?'

'My mum is in hospital,' the man said. That explained the whispering. 'I can't leave her now.'

Oh dear, she knew that feeling. When her mum had suffered the stroke, Sophie barely left the critical care ward. She was sure the minute she did, her mother would die. She couldn't let her be alone when that happened. She had to schedule her wees around when Dan or her dad came. Mum couldn't speak but she knew Sophie was there.

Tears welled in her eyes. What that poor man must be going through. 'Please don't worry,' she said. 'You've got enough on your plate right now. Can you get some of your guys here to take care of things?'

'Honestly, this is my first event. I was going to do it all myself. There's a lot more to it than I thought. Maybe I'm not cut out for it.'

Was he *crying*? 'Well, you got everything ordered at least, didn't you? Well done, because that's a big part of it.' She was desperate to make him feel better. 'So, all the major stuff is taken care of, I guess. You've got food? A caterer or something?' She prayed he wouldn't say he'd planned on throwing together a few cheese and tomato sandwiches. 'And drinks? Not a bar, probably, since they are Scouts. Unless it's for adults too?'

''Tis.' The man sniffed. 'It's a fundraiser. The caterer is taking care of the bar.'

'Well, you see? That's not so bad, then. All that's left is setting up, right?'

'S'pose. I don't know what to do.' The anguish in the man's voice pulled at Sophie. She wanted so much to ask what was wrong with his mother, but he'd only just stopped crying. 'I'm sorry,' he said.

'Don't be sorry, *I* can help! It's just setting up the tables and decorations, and . . . will there be tablecloths or anything?' The man said those were being delivered with the chairs. 'It'll be easy! No problem at all.' What was she saying? There were who-knew-how-many people turning up in the garden in two days. Since when was she in the event management business? 'Don't worry. I can be there to make sure it all goes smoothly.'

It would only be one day out of their holiday. It was the least she could do for someone who might be losing his mother.

'Thank you, you're a lifesaver,' he answered before hanging up.

Right, she could do this. Assuming the planner had really arranged all the deliveries, she could handle each thing as it turned up. And if he'd forgotten something, well, then they'd have to make do.

But first, the flowers. They weren't going to bouquet themselves.

The sun warmed her face when she stepped outside. Most of the goats were on the grass, bright white against the green. Their bleating conversations mixed with the sound of birdsong. She waved to Oliver and Katie. Marion had let them do a bit of the milking this morning.

The flowers had survived the night, and a few were starting to open. Sophie prised open one of the cardboard boxes and took out a few of the glass jars. That made her smile.

Her best friend growing up had one of those mums who used Kilner jars in real life, not just to keep spare change in like most people. She'd made pickles, chutneys and jams and even lemon curd that she gave away at Christmas. Sophie would have loved having her very own jam-maker in the family, but that kind of homeliness took time that Sophie's mum didn't have. Not with the long hours she and Sophie's dad worked just to make ends meet. Ready meals were called home-made in their house because they needed heating up.

No wonder she'd never learned to cook till she'd had to feed herself at uni.

The flowers hadn't started releasing their scent yet, but they looked pretty in a mix of gentle colours: dusty rose, yellows and whites, snapdragons, something with loads of petals that she always forgot the name of, miniature bottle-brush fronds and delicate Queen Anne's Lace. They all looked like they could have come from the nearby fields.

Sophie counted sixty jars. She found a pair of rusting secateurs hanging on the wall inside the barn and worked methodically till each jar was tumbling with blooms. They looked lovely all sitting together on the barn floor.

Standing and stretching, she felt a few vertebrae crack. She had no idea what time it was, but her tummy told her it might be getting close to lunch.

Then she went inside to tell Dan what she was doing. He'd be proud of her.

But the office door was still closed. The kitchen was exactly as she'd left it. He'd been in there for hours.

She crept to the door. She could hear Dan talking to someone on speakerphone. Judging by the soothing tone her husband was using, it must be a client. 'If you're not comfortable doing it then that's fine,' he was saying, 'although there's nothing illegal about *talking* to him. Gently, I mean, nothing intimidating. It's up to you, obviously, but it would be useful.'

Another voice said, 'As long as you're sure it's a good idea.'

'I'm sure,' Dan confirmed, 'but I want you to be comfortable. That's the most important thing. Why don't you think about it and ring me back? Any time. You know I'm always available.'

Sophie waited a moment before calling to Dan through the door. 'Sorry, it's just me. Will you be finishing work soon?'

There was some shuffling before the door opened. 'Do you miss me?' He was smiling.

Sophie relaxed. 'Of course I do,' she said. 'Come out and be on holiday with me.'

She folded herself into his open arms. The smell of Harriet's shower gel was unfamiliar, but she really liked it: it reminded her of Christmas and lemons. She'd look for the same kind when they got home. 'I wish you didn't have to work.' She was starting to hate that office of James's.

'I'm not working.'

'Well, you're in there for hours every day. You must be doing something.'

Dan kissed the top of her head. 'We don't all have someone taking care of us, Soph. Besides, this holiday is for you, not me. You're the one who's meant to be relaxing.'

'I like having you with me while I'm relaxing.' Dan was her favourite person to be around when he was in a good mood.

'That's sweet,' he said. 'Tell you what. Give me another thirty minutes and then we'll all do something after lunch. I can look up some options and you pick anything you want. I'll leave it to you to coax the children out of that barn.'

'Great, give me the hard job. Thank you,' she said.

He did appear in the kitchen half an hour later, just as he promised. He reached for his sweatshirt on the table. 'This is sopping wet.'

'Is it?' She was the picture of innocence. 'Hmm.'

As Sophie started pulling things out of the fridge for lunch, a lorry pulled up in front of the house. 'Chairs,' shouted the driver as he hopped down from his cab. She waited for him to give her the order sheet to sign.

At least the main things were there now, she thought. The planner hadn't done such a bad job. Aside from not turning up, that is. He'd even ordered the Portaloos – something that Sophie wouldn't have remembered till the first child needed to take unsteady aim at their downstairs loo. The delivery person had driven over the lawn to deposit the tiny cabins, hopefully downwind, near the treeline.

Sophie had her own mini-Glastonbury!

As long as the caterer turned up. She should have asked the planner for those details while she had him on the phone. If his mum took a turn for the worse, he probably wouldn't answer her call.

She could see stacks of metal chairs inside the cavernous trailer, and rows of folding wooden chairs, which he began to unload. 'I don't suppose you'll take them into the barn for me?'

'Health and—'

'Safety, I know. It's fine. I'll take them down.'

She didn't like the look the driver was giving her. 'Isn't there a bloke around who could do it?' he asked.

'You mean aside from you?' He didn't catch the sarcasm. 'My husband is in the house, but actually, I don't need a bloke to do it.' Like she was some weak little woman. She hooked one arm through the backs of three chairs and did the same on the other side. They weighed a ton, but she'd break her back before she'd put any down while he was watching.

Sophie grumbled as she staggered towards the barn. Women could run everything from households to countries, inventing and creating, all while juggling childbirth and careers, partners and finances, yet people like that driver still thought they were the weaker sex. Weak? Hah! Give men one menstrual cycle and they'd change the employment laws to give paid leave for PMS.

Her mind flitted to Dan, but as she dropped the chairs inside the barn, she was already arguing with herself. That was different. Dan wasn't sexist. He did everything he could for her because he was generous. He might go over the top when she didn't really need the help, but she wasn't putting up a fight, either. She was sure she could do more for herself whenever she wanted to. It was just that he'd always wanted to take care of her because he loved doing it. He'd told her that a million times. People like Dan were natural carers. Why wouldn't she love that?

Wait. Who said she didn't love it? Maybe she didn't love that he could be so critical sometimes. Okay, much of the time. And his joking about her unworldliness had worn thin over the years. But it wasn't worth fighting about.

Now who'd said anything about fighting?

This country air was doing strange things to her thoughts.

She went out front for more chairs.

'Want a hand?' Marion called from behind her. Through the sweaty hair that fell across her face, Sophie saw the young woman over the goat fence. 'Oh, thank you, that's really kind but you shouldn't have to do any more work.'

Marion swung herself over the top rail. 'Don't be silly. You shouldn't have to carry them all by yourself. Here, let me take those. We'll relay, how's that?'

Together they quickly shifted all the chairs. 'You look like you could use a cup of tea,' Marion said when they stood in the barn. 'I was about to take a break anyway.'

Sophie smoothed her hair as best she could. 'I must look a fright.'

Marion pointed at her dungarees. 'Whereas I'm ready for the catwalk. Come on, I'll put the kettle on.'

The office was framed out in one corner of the biggest barn, with plasterboard walls that ended well below the roofline. Above them, Sophie could see bits of hay and other barn debris floating in the criss-crossing beams of sunlight. The office itself, though, could have been used for any business, with its utilitarian desks, chairs, computers, printer and an overflow of paperwork stuffed into shelves. A battered radio was playing a chill-out soundtrack.

'The goats like music?' she asked.

'We fight over the station all the time,' said Marion. 'I mean James and I, not the goats. Milk? Sugar?' She got the carton from the mini-fridge in the corner.

'Yes, and one, please.' Then she noticed the ribbons tacked to the wall beside one of the filing cabinets. 'All these for the cheese?' One went back nine years. 'You've been busy.'

Marion handed her a mug. 'James has. He's won all kinds of awards. He's really quite well known. Around here, at least.'

Sophie sipped her tea. 'I saw some of his cheeses at the deli in the village. Delia's.'

'Yeah, well, she'd stock the goat's dung if he asked her to.'

'Really? It sounds like there's a story there.'

Marion shrugged. 'Oh, just the usual. She had a thing for him at school. I get the feeling he was quite the catch.'

'Then Harriet caught him.' That explained Delia's comments about her. 'I should have guessed. She had a lot to say about Harriet.'

'Everyone is into everyone's business around here. They're convinced she's out to turn James into some corporate type.'

'You mean like her.'

'Exactly. It didn't help when they heard about the Waitrose meeting.' Marion relayed the whole story, goaty comments and all. 'Even though he stood up for himself and didn't do what Harriet wanted, they still think she's pulling his strings. But I don't think they actually dislike her. Well, aside from Delia. They just don't understand her.'

'She is unusual,' Sophie admitted. 'But I really like her.'

Companionably, they finished their tea.

Sophie went back to the house floating on the warmth she felt towards Marion and Harriet. Or maybe it wasn't the feeling, exactly, that made her so happy, but its rediscovery. Like tasting a favourite childhood treat she hadn't realised she'd missed. She wanted to gobble up these women.

Dan was waiting for her when she got back to the house. 'Been out playing with the goats?' he asked. Then he gently wiped her cheek with his finger.

'Talking to Marion,' she said. 'She helped me carry the chairs into the barn.'

'What chairs?'

'For Harriet's fundraiser. It's not a problem. I've done it now.'

'I would have helped if I'd known, but I can't read your mind, Soph.'

'I'm not saying you should have helped. I'm just saying I did it. I didn't want to disturb you if you were still working.'

He levelled her with a look. Sophie braced herself. She should know better than to give him any excuse to remind her how hard he worked for them. 'Where else is the money supposed to come from?' he asked. 'Huh? For this holiday? Or your spa appointments? Those aren't free, you know.'

'I know! I wasn't criticising, really I wasn't. You know how much I appreciate everything you do. I was only answering your question.'

'By implying that you had to ask Marion.'

He wasn't in the mood to let this go. Sophie sighed. It really shouldn't be a big deal. 'She offered, Dan, that was all.' She ducked her head under his arm for a hug. That usually worked better than more talking.

As his arms tightened, he murmured, 'Fine, whatever.' She relaxed against him. 'What do you want to do today? I looked up some options for us. Caving or the falconry centre or the model village?'

'Shall we go to the model village?' she wondered.

'Why not the falconry?'

'Because I'm not sure I want the children handling birds. They're so big and dangerous.'

'They don't have to handle them. We can look at them, can't we? Look, Soph, you asked me to find something to do, so I did.'

'You offered,' she pointed out. They were no longer hugging. 'And you know they're going to want to fly them once we get there. I think the model village will be fun, too.'

'You want to see a scale model of a village that's *in the village*? Why wouldn't you just look at the real village when it's all around you? Or look at this village? It's right down the road. Saves me driving.'

'Fine, let's go to the falconry centre,' she said. 'But you're going to tell the children no when they ask to handle the birds.'

'No, we'll go to the model village, since you're so keen on it. I wouldn't want to disappoint you.'

'Dan, come on, don't be like that.'

'I'm not like anything. I just said you get what you want. Come on. Get the kids.'

Sophie faltered. 'We can go to the falconry centre.'

'Now I don't want to,' he told her. 'I want to go to the model village. Tell the kids the good news. Today's going to be thrilling, thanks to you.'

Chapter 15

Saturday

'It was such a stupid thing to fight over,' Sophie confided to Harriet the next morning. Harriet's shoulder held her phone to her ear as she slid the hot iron across another pillowslip. Ironing was almost as relaxing as counting. She'd thought about not taking Sophie's call so she could luxuriate in it, but she also enjoyed talking to Sophie. 'I mean, the children weren't exactly going to be carried off by a falcon, were they?' Sophie went on. 'I should have just gone along with Dan's idea.'

A burst of steam hissed from the iron. 'Sophie, have you ever actually used your iron?'

'That's a random question. Are you ironing?'

'Obviously. I don't ask random questions.' Sophie was very nice but she wasn't always logical. A question wouldn't be asked unless it had a purpose. Even if the purpose was to make idle conversation. Which this wasn't.

'You really don't have to do the ironing for me,' she said. 'I've lived in wrinkles just fine all these years. It's bad enough when I have to iron at the donations place. Anyway, what was I saying? Right, instead we ended up at that model village and Dan was totally right. We stood in the village looking at a replica of the village. I was being ridiculous.'

'What's ridiculous about saying what you do and don't want?' Harriet asked.

'Well, if we'd gone to the falconry centre then everyone would have been happy.'

'Is that important to you?' She folded the material, trapping the warmth between the layers. It would leave creases, but deliberate creases were fine. 'Because *everyone* can't be happy if you're unhappy, so you wouldn't have achieved your goal anyway. Are you happy, Sophie?'

'Of course I am.'

'Why of course? You've just said that Dan shouted at you. Does he do that a lot?'

'No, I mean, not more than usual. It's not usually serious. It's just when I'm being silly.'

'Which is how often?'

'Oh, I do something wrong most days.'

'You know that's not normal,' Harriet said. 'Look at your friends' relationships. Are their partners shouting at them most days?'

Sophie hesitated. 'I haven't really . . . I'm not in touch with my friends as much as I used to be. You know how it is, with family obligations it gets harder to find the time.'

Warning bells were ringing all around this conversation. Could Sophie really not see? 'When was the last time you saw your friends?'

'I don't know, Harriet, I don't keep records. Let me think. Maybe a year or two ago? Dan and the children are my priority. That's what being a good wife and mother is, making them happy.'

'But why is that more important than making yourself happy?' Harriet pulled another pillowslip from the dwindling pile. Only three to go. The flat and fitted sheets were already cooling on their labelled shelves in the cupboard. She'd saved these as a treat for last.

Sophie hesitated. 'It's not more important, but it's *as* important. That's what I'm saying.'

'Then you still wouldn't have achieved your goal for everyone to be happy. *You* wouldn't be happy.'

Harriet worried that might sound harsh. Yes, it was nice for everyone to get their way, but it wasn't always possible. Then one had to weigh the feelings of others against one's own. That was the point. Sometimes James or Billie got what they wanted, but sometimes Harriet did, too. Sophie didn't seem to get her turn very often.

Harriet was about to clarify her position – she didn't want Sophie thinking she was being judged – when Sophie moved on.

'I've been meeting some of your neighbours. Well, not neighbours exactly, but people in the village. The butcher, and the barmaid at the pub across from the spa. And Delia.'

'Hmph, Delia. She's not my biggest fan.'

'No, I got that impression,' said Sophie.

'Delia thinks I'm autistic. Most of them probably do.'

Sophie paused. 'You don't, though? Think you are? I don't mean to offend you by asking. It's just that you brought it up and there's a lot of talk about it now, you know, documentaries and things, and people are recognising it more.'

'I'm not autistic,' said Harriet.

'Are you offended?'

She truly wasn't. She'd had the word thrown at her many times, by classmates and colleagues who didn't know her very well. People loved easy labels almost as much as they did their own judgements. It wasn't usually malicious, just ill-informed. Harriet never minded correcting them. 'Why would I be offended? You only asked a question. I know how I am, and I can see why you'd ask. So no, I'm not offended.' Harriet paused. 'The opposite, actually. It's only because I'm so organised that I can do everything I do. I'm a good solicitor because of it, and I can run a house and keep the family happy and do everything I want because of it.'

'It just seems exhausting,' Sophie said. 'Don't you get tired?'

'Of course. Don't you?'

'I mean inside your head. I'd need a lie-down if I had to think about everything you do.'

'That's why I count,' said Harriet. She didn't tell everyone this. It must mean that Sophie was her friend. She smiled. 'Patterns. I see them all the time, so I count them. And outlines of things. Geometric shapes. They're everywhere.' She glanced around the living room. 'Windowpanes and the wooden bits in between, the sash, sides, top. The architrave is in three pieces . . . the walls, the pictures, each side of the matt, each side of the frame.' Her eyes travelled into the hall. 'Then the spindles on the stairs, the bottom square parts and the rounded top parts and the empty spaces in between, then the handrail, the one at the bottom, the newel, that round part at the top. And the stairs, of course. It's very relaxing.'

'Blimey, Harriet, that sounds like a nightmare.'

'It's not. I like it.'

'And you see these patterns everywhere?'

'Everywhere.'

'No wonder everything is so neat.'

'Right.' Harriet felt like Sophie understood her.

'You're in the right profession,' Sophie said. 'You and Dan. Even if it is really frustrating living with one of you.'

'One of us?'

'Solicitors,' Sophie said. 'You can be so infuriating. Not you-you, you solicitors, I mean. You haven't been working as much as Dan this week, have you? I'm afraid you'll have to throw him out of the office when you get back. I'm living with a workaholic.'

Harriet laughed. Right now she'd swap her potentially (but hopefully not) straying husband for Sophie's workaholic one in a heartbeat. 'You can't blame Dan for keeping a close eye on things after what happened,' she mused. 'I wouldn't be away from my desk for two weeks either if I were him. It's better to be safe than sorry. In fact, I did ring in, and I'm not even dodgy.' She jumped into the yawning silence at Sophie's end. 'I'm not saying he's definitely dodgy this time.'

'There is nothing dodgy about Dan.'

She might have heard the warning in Sophie's voice if she hadn't been so distracted by the flaw in her logic. 'I don't want to split hairs, but un-dodgy solicitors don't end up in court over missing evidence unless they're wrongly charged, and Dan was, in point of fact, responsible for missing evidence. He took witness statements home in the client files when they should have been logged in and kept where the prosecutor could access them. That's not my opinion. It's a matter of public record,' she added, just to clarify things. 'But I'll concede that he might not be dodgy any more.' Although that wasn't what her colleague had intimated, and leopards and spots and smoke and fire came to mind, but she was willing to give her friend the benefit of the doubt.

'I don't know what the hell you're talking about,' Sophie said, 'but stop calling my husband dodgy!'

'I'm talking about his last offence. Over the missing evidence.' Surely Sophie wasn't claiming not to know about this. 'And I said he might not still be dodgy.' Honestly, Sophie should listen more carefully.

'The only offence is what you're giving me right now,' Sophie said. 'How can you say something like that? I thought we were friends.'

'But we are friends!'

'Not when you start throwing accusations around, we're not. Really, that's so mean.'

Harriet wasn't trying to be mean. She never imagined that Dan would go through all that and not tell his wife. She'd assumed Sophie knew.

Even if she hadn't assumed that, though, she still wouldn't have kept it from her, precisely because she *was* Sophie's friend. And Sophie should want to know. She should be grateful to have a friend looking out for her best interests. Just like Harriet was grateful for Sophie telling her about seeing James in the village. Was that easy to hear? No, of course not. That's what made friends so valuable. They sometimes said the hard things.

But Sophie wasn't sounding at all grateful. 'I think I'd like to go now.' Harriet could feel the chill all the way from the Cotswolds. 'I'll thank you to keep your rumour-mongering to yourself from now on.' With that, she hung up on Harriet.

Harriet had no trouble seeing that Sophie was cross. She just couldn't understand why, when she was doing her friend a favour by telling her. Where was the sense in shooting the messenger when the facts were still the facts?

Nobody seemed keen to talk to Harriet. Billie sloped into the kitchen, phone in hand as usual. Harriet's perfectly amenable attempts to engage her daughter were met with grunts. Until she started outlining the plan for the day.

'Mum, I really don't want to go on another forced tour today.'

James looked up from his paper. 'I second that. I think even prisoners of war got rest time under the Geneva Convention. Let's just relax today.'

'We are relaxing,' said Harriet. 'And I cannot believe you've just compared yourself to a POW. We'll take a picnic onto Hampstead Heath. What's not relaxing about that? We've got the whole afternoon until we go to the zoo. It's only a forty-minute walk from the bottom of the heath, or thirty minutes if we catch the Overground and walk.'

Harriet had loved the heath since even before she'd met James. Not normally one for willy-nilly nature, she was surprised by how calm she felt there. No matter how often she tried to explain the difference, James never understood how she could love it so much and yet hate the countryside. But it was rural open-endedness that she objected to. The heath was huge. It felt wild and natural, but it had borders, and distinct areas inside it, with the ponds and Kenwood House at the top. Countryside was okay when it was contained.

'You're ridiculous.' Billie poured herself a bowl of cereal as Harriet tried to remember what that insult was for. Oh yes, today's plan.

'You're coming with us, so you may as well get used to the idea. We're leaving at eleven thirty.' Harriet glanced at the ticking clock on Sophie's wall. Billie looked at her phone. 'And why don't you leave that thing at home today? I'm sure there's nothing so urgent that you can't give it a rest for a few hours.'

'Yeah, right, good one, Mum.'

They both glanced up when Owen came in. He might not have been part of the plan but Harriet found that she was glad to have him in the house, even if he had nearly given her a heart attack when he'd first turned up. Sophie had been right. The boy really wasn't any bother at all. If anything, he gave Billie something to focus on aside from Harriet's faults.

He was a lot more pleasant than Billie about the offer to come with them. The poor lamb, he probably didn't get much quality family time. Each morning when he emerged from Spot's room with his shaggy hair sticking out in all directions, Harriet asked whether he'd talked to his mum. Not that she wasn't firmly on Owen's side. He wasn't at fault for whatever had gone wrong between them. He was too nice a boy. Besides, as much as she hated admitting it, because she was pointing the finger at herself, too, parents had to take responsibility for breakdowns with their children. They're older and supposed to be smarter.

'You coming too?' Billie asked Owen when she'd emerged from her shower with her hair twisted up in a towel. 'Cool.'

Owen barely nodded. Harriet assumed that meant they were both looking forward to the day and were excited by the idea of spending time together. In teen-speak.

But you wouldn't know it, because they barely spoke again all the way to the heath.

Even with the picnic bags bouncing against her bare legs, Harriet was glad she'd worn a dress. It was definitely summer. Her sun hat kept the worst of the heat off her head but sweat dribbled down the sides of her sleeveless dress.

She glanced up ahead. The dark patch on the back of Billie's black band t-shirt was getting steadily bigger. Stretched out and faded, it was hardly better than the checked shirt she'd changed out of. She had to be baking in those jeans but, as usual, she'd completely ignored Harriet's suggestions about a dress, or shorts at least. She seemed to want to look like a dock worker. Harriet used to wonder if that was what passed for fashion these days, but no, most of Billie's school friends dressed normally.

She shifted her daughter's fashion choices from her mind. At least James was enjoying himself, despite that POW dig. Sometimes she swore he took sides against her on purpose.

He seemed to tense, though, as much as she did when his phone rang. 'Hi, Persephone, Harriet and I are on the heath,' he said. Was she imagining that he sounded very rehearsed? 'Yes, it's really nice. Sunny today. I don't think it's going to rain.'

Since when did he discuss the weather with her? Harriet watched him carefully as they continued up the hill.

'Okay, have fun, talk to you later.' He hung up.

'What's she doing?' Harriet asked.

'Oh, just going for a run.'

'She rang to tell you that?'

'No, she rang to see what we were doing. This is nice, isn't it?' He made a big show of looking around. He reached for the bag with their lunch. 'Good choice. Though I did get some countryside yesterday, too.' He met her gaze. 'I had a quick trip back to the village. I rang you, but your phone was off.'

'I was in the spa.' She felt her legs weaken. So, he was going to admit to his secret scarpering.

'Billie wasn't interested in the museum and I thought you and I could go another day,' he said. 'I wanted to check in with Marion.'

'You could do that on the phone.' He'd rung her every day, morning and night.

He sighed. 'I know, it was just an excuse. I'm sorry, Harriet, I really am. S'pose I didn't think I'd miss the goats this much.'

174

'You miss the goats?'

He pulled that sad frown face that pushed out his lip and made his chin wrinkle up like a peach stone. 'You think it's daft, but they are family to me, just like your cats were to you.'

It was not the same thing. She didn't milk her childhood pets or make them sleep in a barn.

'I think about them when I'm away,' he said. 'I worry about them, and with Artemis not being well . . . I wanted to see them. I ran into Persephone while I was there.'

He couldn't have sounded more bright and breezy saying that last bit. 'You just ran into her?'

'Yep. She's jealous we went to our old Mexican.'

Join the jealous club, Harriet thought. Though this wasn't definitive proof, was it? James *was* daft enough to travel two hours to see his goats. He didn't usually do things without telling her, as far as she knew, but her phone had been off all morning. And in a village as small as theirs, he could have run into Persephone.

Or was she being naive? One thing was for sure: she wouldn't get to the bottom of it during a family picnic. She just wished that uncertainty didn't always force her off balance like this. 'Step on it,' she called as they closed the gap on Billie and Owen. She shoved the uncomfortable thoughts from her mind. 'We've only got two hours and forty-five minutes till we need to start for the zoo.'

'I'm not going,' Billie said over her shoulder. 'I'll just head back when Owen does.'

'Yeah, if that's all right,' Owen added.

'Thank you for asking, Owen.' Billie could learn some manners from that boy. It was no use trying to get Billie to stay with them. She watched her daughter talking to Owen as they continued speeding up the hill. They were probably comparing music or courses they hated or how ghastly their parents were, but Harriet hoped against hope that Owen might suggest maybe she wasn't the complete ogre Billie thought she was.

She'd take any support she could get. Lord knew, James didn't do it. He was too afraid of tarnishing his Favourite Parent status.

She shot him a dirty look.

He blew her a kiss.

'Should we worry about them being alone together?' she asked. 'Back at the house, I mean?'

'I trust Billie.' Implying that she didn't.

'It's not about trust, James, it's about being a responsible parent and not just her mate.'

'She's almost seventeen.' He squinted into the sun, where a small flock of birds caught his attention. He twisted round to watch them fly off while Harriet waited for him to tell her why that made one tiny bit of difference. If anything, that's why they should be more careful. 'Owen lived with Sophie,' he said eventually. 'She vouches for him. Besides, do you really think there's any attraction there?'

They both looked towards the teenagers. Owen was slouched into his hoodie. The hood covered most of his face. Harriet wondered whether he was self-conscious about his acne. She had been at his age. Her skin hadn't cleared up until she was well into her twenties. It would have been nice then to have had a trendy hood to hide under.

Billie had her hands shoved into her jeans pockets and they walked with about five feet between them.

She had to admit she saw no signs of romance. Billie didn't seem to be interested in boys yet. She had a few friends who were boys, who they trusted, but no boyfriends, who they definitely wouldn't.

Harriet supposed she should be grateful that Billie was a late bloomer in that respect. Still, she didn't want to risk her daughter blooming in Sophie's house.

James gently reached for her arm a split second before she started towards Billie to say she had to stay with them. *How did he know?* 'They'll be fine back at the house. Carlos will be coming in anyway. They'll probably just stare at their phones and ignore each other.'

Fighting every instinct, Harriet didn't even tell Billie to be good when they left.

She and James made excellent time to the zoo after the picnic, and zipped straight through the just-opened ticket queue, which put them eighteen minutes ahead of schedule.

James wasn't nearly as tickled by the time saved as Harriet, but then she wasn't as charged up about the animals, so they were even in the excitement stakes. By the time she had ticked off all the enclosures on her map, a tiny part of her dared to believe that James really hadn't had anything to hide when he'd gone back to the village. He hadn't needed to tell her about it. He didn't know that Sophie had spotted him, or that she'd told Harriet. Logically then, on this occasion at least, it wasn't a case of confession before accusation.

Back at Sophie's, the lights were on but the house was silent. They caught each other's eye. Harriet wasn't about to say *I told you so* when it meant gloating over her daughter having sex. James's voice was firm when he called up the stairs. 'Hello?'

'Hi, Dad! Come and see this!'

James's shoulders dropped as he exhaled. Nice to know she wasn't the only one whose mind had raced ahead to becoming young grandparents.

'Make them come downstairs,' she told James. She knew she should be modern and cool about this but, acne or not, she didn't like Owen upstairs in a bedroom with her sixteen year old.

For once James did what she asked, calling them into the kitchen. 'What are we doing for dinner?' he asked her. 'I'd be happy staying in.'

Harriet rifled through the cabinets for options. Then she checked Sophie's freezer. She unearthed some prawns and peas from the ice-bound tundra that lay within. She'd defrost that for her tomorrow.

She added the foraged ingredients to the list that sat, neatly expanding day by day, on the worktop beside the fridge. Then she added defrosting to the list on the kitchen table.

'Nice fashion accessory,' James said while Harriet's head was in the fridge searching for parmesan cheese. He obviously wasn't talking about her. Maybe Owen was a good influence on Billie, she thought, reaching for the Cheddar that would have to do.

Harriet turned round, hoping to see her daughter in something pretty. It didn't even have to be a dress.

The smile froze on her face when she saw the flickering tongue inches from Billie's delicate face. That snake was coiled around her baby's neck! Slithering and squeezing and wrapping its malicious tail around her arm.

'GET THAT SNAKE OFF YOUR NECK!'

'Jesus, Mum, relax.' Billie's voice was perfectly calm. 'Don't scare her again.'

Harriet's heart pounded in her ears. The need to protect her daughter reared up so suddenly that it knocked the breath out of her. She wanted to rip the reptile off and stomp it into the tiles. 'Billie, take it off! It's dangerous!'

'Nah, fam,' Owen objected. 'Carlos lets me carry her round my neck all the time.' Gently he unwound the snake from Billie and plopped it over his own shoulders. Spot took the move well. Its tongue flicked at Owen's cheek.

'Jesus, that's disgusting,' said Harriet. 'It shouldn't be out of its enclosure.'

'She's out all the time when Sophie's home,' he said.

'Sophie's not home, so put it back, please. And wash your hands before you set foot in this kitchen again,' she called after them.

Harriet would rather be a young grandparent than have that thing in the house. At least she wouldn't be afraid of a grandchild.

The next morning, James and Harriet both stared at Billie when she came downstairs. She hadn't been up that early for as long as they could remember. Harriet hadn't even finished her second coffee.

'This is unprecedented,' Harriet said with a smile. Maybe her daughter was starting to enjoy their holiday.

Billie didn't smile back. 'Mum? I don't want you to flip out, but Spot might be somewhere in the house.'

Harriet's face blanched. 'You'd better mean *in its cage* in the house, Billie, or I swear—'

'I'm sure we'll find her, Mum. She's got to be here. A snake can't just disappear.'

'What the hell, Billie,' said James. 'Your mother told you to put her back in her enclosure last night.'

'We did, I swear! I'm sorry, Mum.' She looked exactly as young as her sixteen years just then. 'I'm sure she's here somewhere.'

'That is not comforting.' The thought of it slithering around her neck as she slept made her feel ill. She shuddered.

'Ring Carlos. Seriously, I want him over here now to find that snake.'

'It's not even nine yet,' James said. 'We can have a look for her.'

'Are you mad?' Harriet noticed that her hand was on her own neck. 'I'm not going near any cabinets where it can jump out at me.'

'It's not a cobra, dear heart,' James noted. 'Come on, Billie, I'll help you look.'

But they wouldn't find it, would they, because 'I can't see it' was the most often uttered phrase in their house, in spite of Harriet having just pointed out exactly where their keys, phones, extra washing-up liquid, new coffee filters or about a million other things were. Half the time she could actually see what they were looking for. She was sure she'd even used the phrase *if it was a snake it would have bitten you.*

Harriet sighed. 'I'm coming. First thing is to wake up Owen. We're going through that room properly. I'm not about to turn the house upside down when it might be in there after all.'

'Don't worry,' said James. 'If anyone can find her, you can.'

'*I'd* better not find it,' she snapped back.

Chapter 16

Sunday

Sophie was up with the birds on the morning of the Scouts event, her tummy fizzing with excitement. She listened to Dan breathing deeply beside her in the big bed. She admired his ability to sleep. And when she said 'admired', she meant resented. He did it so bloody easily while she tossed and turned, flipped and flopped and made hopeless bargains with her brain to let her get off before dawn. Frustration sometimes made her do unattractive things, like poking him just enough to make him stir but not enough to rouse him. He never remembered the next morning why his sleep was dodgy.

She'd become a light sleeper when Katie was born – chalked up to motherhood along with sneeze-wees – but the insomnia was new. Well, newish. It wasn't helped by her GP's diagnosis. He'd offered her sleeping tablets, but she wasn't keen on that idea. It felt weak to give in to medication when you couldn't open a magazine without reading about how everyone was curing diabetes and preventing cancer by eating superfoods and decluttering their wardrobes. The holiday was meant to be the start of her own major changes – without having to declutter her wardrobes – but now she feared it wouldn't be enough. The treatments were terrific, yes, and she was a happy bowlful of jelly every time Molly whispered for her to get dressed again. The walks to and from the village filled her with the joys of spring, summer, autumn *and* winter. She'd already resolved to do more ambling through their local parks when she was back home.

But here, in the house, she wasn't any calmer. She was starting to wonder whether part of the problem had just parped under the duvet beside her.

She'd supposed her stress was part and parcel of being a mother and wife in London. She knew women who were just as frazzled as her. Most of the other mums on the school run, for a start; though none of them was at risk of a stroke, as far as she knew. When the GP had broken the news to her, he'd explained that the stress itself didn't cause long-term high blood pressure, but that the hormone surge from stress raised your blood pressure, which damaged your blood vessels, which caused long-term high blood pressure. That was splitting hairs when the result was the same. If she didn't calm down, she'd stress herself into the same fate as her mum.

She had to ask herself now, as she lay there listening to a blackbird singing in the tree beside the window: was she looking in the wrong place?

Dan had been livid when he found out she'd be filling in for the event planner today. He'd have rung that poor man at his mother's bedside if Sophie hadn't refused to tell him her phone password.

She was surprised by how good she'd felt. Not at knowing that she'd upset him, but that she hadn't given in to him. *That* was new.

'Just don't expect my help when it all goes wrong,' he'd said, shaking his head like he did when she'd massively disappointed him. 'You've brought this on yourself. It's your health, so knock yourself out.' Then he gave her the silent treatment.

Of course, the silent treatment. How could she have forgotten about that? Those days and nights when Sophie felt so desperate to please Dan that she'd do just about anything. There was such deafening disappointment in those silences. Sophie had always caved in.

But not this time. She glanced at her sleeping husband. Then she poked him again and bounced out of bed.

When she turned on her phone, there was a text from Harriet.

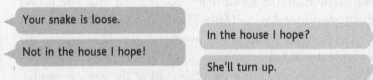

Your snake is loose.

In the house I hope?

Not in the house I hope!

She'll turn up.

Sophie put her phone away. She was in no mood for banter with Harriet. She, Sophie, might have every right to rubbish Dan in her small ways, but she was not about to let someone else do it. Dan might be many things – didn't Sophie know that – but he wasn't the fraudster that Harriet claimed. He was an excellent solicitor who used his skills to help his clients. His career meant everything to him. He would never risk that, and Harriet had absolutely no right to be spreading rumours about him. She barely knew him! They'd met, what, once at a charity dinner. Sophie probably knew more about Molly at the spa than Harriet did about Dan.

Well, she *did* know Dan, thank you very much. This was the bloke who always told assistants in shops when they accidentally gave back too much change. Always. He'd never even had a speeding fine. The idea that he'd tamper with evidence, or whatever it was Harriet was accusing him of. Harriet had actually sounded surprised by Sophie's reaction. What did she expect, that she'd automatically take the side of a woman she'd known less than two weeks over her husband? Even if she had felt like they were becoming real friends. That was the sad part.

Harriet needed to stop gossiping about Sophie's family and start paying more attention to her own. Sophie had a good mind to ring her back to say that. Dan wasn't the one she should be worried about, not when James was sneaking back to meet that woman. And yet, was Sophie spreading rumours about that? No, she was not. She hadn't even mentioned it to Dan. That's how discreet she was.

She brewed a cup of tea, wrapped herself in one of the oversized padded coats that hung on the hook beside the door and let herself out into the chill of the early morning.

Just what she needed to clear her head.

She loved this quiet before the family stirred. When Katie was a baby, she used to creep into the dark kitchen with her just to sit and stare at nothing.

Even though all hell was probably about to break loose, Sophie's mind was perfectly calm. It was exactly what she'd hoped for from this holiday. She'd assumed it would happen in the middle of an especially good treatment, or maybe forking up a mouthful of delicious home-made pasta or savouring a Tuscan sunset. Not sitting on a creaky old bench with a bog-standard cup of tea in familiar-as-you-like England.

It was true what they said: happiness is a state of mind.

She sounded like a greetings card. Where had that come from? She'd better watch out or the next thing she knew she'd be stencilling slogans on driftwood to hang all over the house.

She breathed in the fresh air. The goats were awake, too. She could hear them bleating in the barns. Maybe Marion was about to milk them. She had an ingenious assembly line that the goats actually queued up for. Every morning they clip-clopped up a ramp to present their udders at eye level for Marion to hook up to the milking machine. Aside from the odd stomp or kick, they hardly seemed to notice the suckling contraption. They were too busy snaffling their favourite treats from the back of the ramp.

By the time Sophie finished her shower, butterflies had started fluttering in her tummy. It wasn't the usual about-to-mess-up-the-event nervousness, though. It was excitement. There were a million things to do, but she could do it.

She gave her reflection a no-nonsense stare in the steamed-up bathroom mirror. She'd put out all the tables and chairs, and if the Scout leader needed them in a different place then he could bloody well move them himself. Otherwise he'd have to work around her set-up.

Sophie's back would probably ache by the end of the day, but it wouldn't be bending. She smiled again through the steam.

Dan was up when she went back to the kitchen, dressed and make-up on, but with a towel still turbaned round her wet hair. 'Ready for your big day?'

She wanted to wipe that smirk off his face. 'Perfectly ready, thanks.'

'Need any help?'

It was a trap that he'd spring either way. She could say no. Then he'd lord it over her if anything went wrong. If she accepted his help then it would become his day, not hers.

She ignored him.

'Soph. Did you hear me?'

'Sorry? My mind's on other things. Help yourself to breakfast if you want. I've got a lot to get on with.' She dropped the damp towel on the worktop and headed for the barn.

Let him chew on that with his slurpy spoonful of Weetabix. She wasn't about to pass up this chance to do something for herself. If she thought about it, that's what was bothering her so much.

Now she remembered that somewhere in the dim and distant past, she'd been a capable woman. Yet according to Dan, she couldn't do anything right. No, that wasn't quite it. She couldn't do anything at all, wouldn't be anything at all, without him.

When had she given away all of her power?

The caterer was a bubbly Spanish woman with an English boyfriend who took care of the cooking. Sophie expected the food to be made ahead of time and plopped into those metal warming trays, like they'd done for their wedding, but Marta and Joe turned up towing an enormous barbecue. 'We cook fresh,' she said, donning her Smokin' Marta apron. 'It adds to the theatre.' Smokin' Joe tied on his apron, too.

'Where do you want us to set up?'

Sophie scanned the huge garden. She could see why the Scouts wanted to use it. It was completely flat, with trees ringing the edge furthest from the house and the barns making a gorgeously rural backdrop. 'Away from the Portaloos, I guess. How about there?'

'Can we help, Mum?' Oliver called as her children tracked footprints from the house across the still-dewy grass.

'Of course you can! Thank you.' Just to show that it wasn't the help she resented, not at all. It was Dan's intention behind it.

They got to work topping the tables with the gaily red-checked oilcloths and Sophie's jam jar flower arrangements. By the time they were set up, her arms ached from all the carrying. It looked so countryside-perfect. Joe had hoisted colourful flags and poles for bunting all around the cart (half barbecue, half bar – Joe had many talents). The flags fluttered gently against the bright-green foliage, and several of the goats were curiously watching them with wide, pale eyes from behind their fence.

She was sorry when the Scout leader turned up, even though she hadn't the faintest clue what had been organised for the day and loads of people were probably expecting fundraising things.

'Everyone ready?' he said. His uniform – from his crisply ironed, badge-laden khaki shirt to his navy walking shorts – looked like it had been bought for a slenderer man. His Scout belt squeezed him in the middle like the twist between two sausage links.

'Mr Simmons.' He held his hand out for Katie and Oliver to shake. Then he shook her hand. 'Jim. You've done a proper good job there.'

'Did the planner let you know that I'd be helping today?' Sophie asked him.

Jim nodded. 'I expect his mum'll be feeling better once the swelling goes down.'

'Oh, I hope so! Do you know what was wrong with her?'

''Er nose,' he said.

'Oh.' Skin cancer, maybe? Or even worse, some horrible flesh-eating bacteria that made people look like apple crumble.

'And her neck, I think, for the chicken skin,' Jim went on. 'That's what Bea says, anyway, and she's usually spot on. I expect we'll know when we see 'er.' He swiped his fingers across each side of his nose. 'If she looks like she's done ten rounds in the ring.'

Ten rounds? Chicken skin? The penny dropped. This was no deadly, apple-crumble-looking bacteria that the planner was nursing his mum through. The only deadly bacteria she'd got was probably Botox.

His mum was having plastic surgery. And to think Sophie had felt sorry for the man! He hadn't corrected the misunderstanding, either. She'd actually thought about getting a card for his mum. Ha. She might still. *So sorry for your wrinkles. Hope you have lots of supportive bandages around you at this difficult time.*

Sophie smiled. She couldn't be too angry when it meant she got to be the planner for the day. He probably wasn't cut out for the stress of event management, anyway, if his mother's facelift could throw him into such a flap. One overdone spare rib and he'd probably walk off the job. It was definitely better for her to handle things.

'I'll go and set up the show ring,' Jim told her. 'Is there somewhere out of the sun to put the cupcakes, till later?' He waved to the woman who'd just parked up the Bumblebee Bakery van.

Sophie jogged over to the drive to show the baker the way to the barn. Jogged! When had she last done that? Probably not since she'd locked sleeping baby Oliver in the car in the ASDA car park. In fairness (Your Honour), he was only a few weeks old, so she wasn't yet used to having to fetch two children from the back seat, and Katie was screaming her head off, and Sophie was so focused on getting the wriggling child out of her car seat that by the time she did, in her sleep-deprived state she didn't even notice Oliver also peacefully asleep there. She only realised she was missing something when she got to the stack of baskets inside the supermarket doors. She usually had a pram to hook the basket on.

That was when she remembered that the pram was in the car.

With the baby!

She could have beaten Usain Bolt's 100 metres record. With Katie in her arms.

She wasn't quite as out of breath when she reached the Bumblebee Bakery van as she'd been at ASDA, probably because nobody prosecuted you for leaving a cupcake in the car.

'You must be the most popular person everywhere you go,' Sophie told the baker as they each carried a large cellophane-windowed box. With such squishable cargo inside, they didn't dare stack them.

The young woman smiled. 'It's a dream job. Except for the four a.m. starts and always smelling of butter.'

'Sounds like being a new parent, though I usually smelled of worse things than butter.'

Together they carpeted the barn floor with dozens of cupcakes. They looked gorgeous, all laid out in their pristine white boxes: neat rows of blue-iced vanilla cakes with the Scout logo on top. Those were going to fetch a pretty penny for the fundraiser.

As she helped Jim set up the highlight of the day — the dog show judging ring — Sophie's glance kept stealing back to the house. But with the sun angled the way it was, she couldn't see whether Dan was spying from any of the windows. Part of her hoped so. Then he'd see that she could stand on her own two feet. Another part of her hoped he'd leave her alone, though, because the very idea that he might take over made her angry.

Sophie liked having responsibility like this. Dan didn't need to take it all on himself.

She didn't want him to.

He'd probably be relieved to hear that. He was the one who loved to complain about how hard he worked, yet he always took over for her. Even this holiday, as she thought about it. As soon as she'd mentioned Italy, Dan got Laxmi to find out where the best spa hotels were, and he signed up to those websites for airfare price alerts. Suddenly it went from her holiday to his. He was such a natural leader that it hadn't occurred to Sophie not to follow.

By the time the lawn was bustling with dozens of people, Sophie was ready for them. Everyone seemed to bring a dog. Before they'd turned up, though, she and Marion had moved the goats into the barns so that they weren't frightened. With the stone wall encircling the entire property, the dogs were free to roam while their owners tucked into barbecue and beer.

'Mum, can we get a puppy?' Oliver was cuddling a Yorkshire terrier who kept licking his face. 'Please?'

'That's not a puppy,' Sophie pointed out. 'It's a tiny dog.'

'Then can we get a tiny dog?'

'We'll see.' In other words: not in a million aeons. 'You're having fun, aren't you?' She smoothed his dark hair. 'I'm glad.'

'This is the best holiday ever, and you're the best Mum in the world for letting us have it. I love you.'

'I love you, too,' she said through her smile, 'but that doesn't mean you're getting a dog.'

Katie had overheard them. 'You'd get us one if you really loved us.'

'You'd clean your room if you really loved me,' said Sophie. 'Why don't you work on that before you worry about cleaning up after a dog?'

A few of the adults had started rounding up their pets for the judging, but others were calling in vain. The dogs couldn't have escaped over the wall. 'They must be here somewhere,' she told their anxious owners. 'Jim has walked the whole perimeter and there's no way out.' Anyway, James would have had to make sure about that when he got the goats, or he'd end up chasing them all over the county.

'They're here!' cried a Scout. 'Bad dog!' He was standing in the doorway to the barn where she'd stored all the party supplies.

For the second time in a day, Sophie ran.

Half a dozen dogs had their snouts shoved into the torn-open bakery boxes. They'd managed to savage every single box.

A black spotted standard poodle looked like the ring-leader. His mouth was a vivid blue from the icing.

One Jack Russell had given up on the feast. He was lying on his side, panting, his blue tongue darting in and out.

Everyone rushed towards their pets as the air filled with questions.

'Are cakes toxic to dogs?'

'They are! I read it.'

'Only if they're chocolate.'

'Is there any sugar substitute in these?'

'That's bad!'

'Nuts? What about nuts?'

'Who puts nuts in cupcakes?'

'Who leaves cupcakes on the floor??'

'We need to ring the baker.'

Sophie agreed with that. 'Should we also ring a vet?'

'My sister-in-law's a vet,' said one woman, pulling out her phone.

It was a tense few minutes while Sophie relayed all the cupcake ingredients to the vet via her sister-in-law, but there was nothing toxic in them. The dogs' poo, on the other hand, would probably require a hazmat suit to clear up tomorrow.

The cake sale was off, but the rest of the afternoon was a success.

Sophie was still full of barbecue when she threw herself down on the sofa that Oliver usually claimed as his. She ached from the ends of her fingers to the tips of her toes. 'Sorry, mate, Mum's in a coma,' she told Oliver.

'That's okay.' He sat on her.

'Oi!' But she drew her arms around her boy. Thank goodness he was still young enough to enjoy it. He might think now that he wanted to live at home until he collected his pension, but Sophie was pretty sure that one day she'd long to have her organs crushed like that. 'Good day, wasn't it?'

Oliver's lids were heavy as he nodded. They'd all go to bed early tonight. 'It was the best.'

Katie glanced up from her phone. 'I wish we'd had the cupcakes.'

'My God, you can't still be hungry.'

'I'm a growing girl. Will we do something fun tomorrow, too?'

Ha, she'd raised the holiday bar now. 'Let's see if Dad fancies anything special. I've got my treatment at ten, so I'll be finished by lunchtime.'

'Should I ask Dad?' Oliver asked.

'Nah, leave him alone in there. He'll come out when he wants to.' She knew he could hear them. What a baby, ignoring her now just because she hadn't gone running to him for help. Well, sod it, why should she? She'd done fine on her own.

She had to be honest with herself. She wasn't having as much fun with Dan on holiday as she'd thought she would. She'd been desperate to go away with him, imagining all the perfect days they'd have together as a family. Yet now, she remembered, the last holiday they took wasn't as much fun as she'd thought it would be, either. They'd had a villa in Majorca then, that even had its own pool. The children loved it but Dan had been annoyed with her most of the time. If she wasn't wearing the wrong shoes for walking, she picked the wrong restaurant for dinner.

She'd been relieved when they returned to London and he'd gone back to working long hours. Being lonely didn't seem as bad as walking on eggshells all the time.

Dan still hadn't come out of the office by the time Harriet rang her. They'd have to knock before dinner time.

She was tempted not to answer Harriet's call, but then she wanted someone to brag to. It was at times like this that she really missed her mum.

'Any idea where your snake might like to hide?' Harriet asked the second Sophie picked up.

'She'll be around somewhere. So you did let her out.'

'I didn't let it out. It got out and we can't find it.'

'Don't worry, she can't leave the house. She'll turn up when she's hungry. She always does.'

'I'm not worried about it leaving the house, Sophie, or not turning up. I'm worried about where it'll turn up when it does.'

'You sound stressed.' That pleased Sophie. How did Harriet think she'd felt hearing her accusations about Dan?

'Of course I'm stressed when there's a python loose in the house.'

'She'll go back into her enclosure eventually, so just leave the door open for her.'

'I don't feel like you're grasping the seriousness of this situation,' said Harriet.

'Well, I can't make her come out now, can I? We don't know where she goes, either. I'm sorry, but she will go back into her cage. Ask Owen to have a look. He's usually pretty good at finding her.'

'I did. He can't. He and his mum haven't made up yet. Is that normal?'

'Sometimes.' Owen's mother wasn't the most reliable person. Sometimes she disappeared for days. That was why he'd gone into care in the first place. 'He usually comes and goes.'

'And Dan doesn't mind that?' Harriet asked. 'I mean, having a teenage boy in the house?'

Sophie thought back to when Owen first came. Dan knew how much she'd love having another child to look after, and he was right. Oliver was a few years out of nappies by then, and that feeling was overwhelming her again. The same one she'd had when Katie got to that age. If she couldn't have another baby, then at least she could look after Owen. That little boy had needed her so badly. Dan called him her little project.

'He knows how much I love Owen,' Sophie said. 'So he doesn't mind.'

'He's welcome to stay as long as he needs to. He really is no trouble. How was today?'

'Fine.'

'Only fine? You sound like my teenager.'

Sophie could hear herself. Just because she was cross didn't mean she couldn't be a civil adult. 'There was a dog show,' she added. 'Put it this way: Crufts doesn't need to

194

worry about the competition. They got at the cupcakes, though. The ones for the cake sale.'

'That would have put a dent in their takings,' said Harriet.

'It did, but they sold more barbecue and drinks than they planned, so that helped make up for it. And we scrambled together a baking auction at the last minute. Some of the parents offered cake prizes as IOUs.' That was her idea, and it had worked! That had earned the Scouts nearly £100, thanks to her quick thinking.

'Did you take pics?' Harriet asked.

She should have! Not that one event made her a party planner, so get over yourself, Sophie Mitchell. Although the original planner hadn't even done one event, and he'd set up his own business.

Why was she thinking about party planning anyway? It wasn't like she didn't have enough to do with looking after the children. 'I was too busy running around, but it looked gorgeous. I'm surprised you don't know all the details. Weren't you in on the planning?'

Harriet laughed. 'Definitely not. Why would I want to know details that don't affect me? There's enough on my plate as it is. When the leader asked to use the garden, all I needed to do was check with James that the goats wouldn't be stressed and make sure there weren't any liability issues. It was up to the planner to make it work. That's poor business to back out at the last minute. You did well to step in. I hope you're proud of yourself. You should be.'

'Do you know, I really am.' When was the last time she could have said that?

She hung up still angry with Harriet, but happy with herself.

Dan hadn't come out of the office yet. 'Oliver, go and see what Dad's doing,' she told him. This was getting ridiculous.

But he didn't answer Oliver's knock. Rude. When Sophie opened the office door, she found the room empty. Dan wasn't upstairs, either. Then she noticed that the car wasn't out front.

He answered his mobile on the first ring. 'Where are you?' She could hear people talking.

'At the pub. Is that a problem?'

'No, but you didn't tell anyone.'

'You were too busy with your fundraiser.'

Hearing the peevishness in his voice did nothing to make her soften. 'A note would have been good,' she said. 'Are you okay driving?'

'Don't worry about me. I'll be home in an hour. There's leftover cottage pie for dinner. Can you put some carrots on?'

'I think I can handle that.' After today, she felt like she could handle quite a lot of things. 'See you in a bit.'

She was glad he'd be gone for a little longer.

Chapter 17

Monday

Harriet had instructed Owen to leave his bedroom door open last night. Just to be sure there were no misunderstandings, after he went to bed she propped the door open with a sturdy boot. Nothing should keep that snake from slinking back into its enclosure.

But Spot was still on the loose in their holiday home this morning.

Just thinking about that thing slithering around the house was enough to put Harriet off her breakfast. She added another text to the string she'd sent since last night.

Carlos, Spot still missing. Best you find it before I do.

It wasn't only the snake, though, making Harriet want to count to a million until the kitchen patterns – cabinet fronts and borders and handles and all the little screws attaching them and ooh, those wall tiles! – steadied her pitching mind. They only had six full days left. When she was planning this spouse-salvaging operation, two weeks had seemed like enough time. Barely, but enough.

What had she actually achieved so far, aside from a

margarita hangover and a quick fumble on a squeaky bed? If this was a performance review, Harriet would be close to a verbal warning.

She'd never failed an evaluation in her life. She couldn't start now in what was possibly her most crucial role.

What she needed was a stern talking-to. And a performance improvement plan. Just thinking about it made her feel a bit better. Besides, she hadn't the energy to waste worrying about something she couldn't control, and as good as she was, she couldn't control time. She set about controlling her angst instead.

This wasn't an end, she told herself. As long as Persephone really wasn't the reason for their troubles. She wanted so badly to believe that that was true. Otherwise this was all for nothing.

She and James had both let their priorities slip, she supposed. What with her daily commute and her cases and despising every bloody thing about that village, Harriet didn't make enough time or energy for James. Ditto with James's early mornings, and most evenings when he climbed into bed before it was dark. Even good marriages take work. Harriet and James weren't working hard enough. One wouldn't spend all the time and effort finding and planting a favourite tree in the garden and then not make sure it had enough water, or that its branches weren't overgrowing or under threat from fungus.

Harriet and James had been under threat from fungus for a while.

She might loathe her husband when his nose whistled or he refused to speak more than six words at a time, but she still couldn't let herself believe that he was the cheating kind. Not deep down. Some people treated their love life like a smoking habit, always lighting a new cigarette with the butt of the old. That wasn't James.

She went to the kitchen after her shower. James was at the table with his tree book propped against the milk jug. Billie didn't even look up from her phone.

'We're having breakfast at eleven,' she reminded him.

James froze with the cereal spoon halfway to his lips. 'But I'm hungry now.'

'That's because you get up at the crack of dawn even though you don't have to.'

He shrugged and kept eating.

'Sweetheart?' She gave Billie her most patient smile. 'Why don't you put on something else? That's not really appropriate for The Wolseley.' Masterful understatement, if she said so herself.

Billie glanced down at her oversized checked shirt, which Harriet was pretty sure had once been James's. It wasn't even tucked into her shapeless jeans. 'I'm fine.'

'How about your sundress? I packed it. It's going to be nice later.' Although she'd probably wear those stupid high-top Converse with it. 'You'd look so much prettier if you made an effort.'

'Thanks for that, Mum.' Billie went back to whatever was so fascinating on her bloody phone.

Harriet started unloading the dishwasher. 'I just mean that it wouldn't hurt to look like a girl sometimes,' she said over the sound of clattering plates.

When Billie set her phone down, for the briefest second Harriet believed she was getting through to her daughter.

She was, but not in the way she'd hoped.

'Do you have any idea how bored I am of listening to you trash me? I'm my own person, Mum, and I know what I like, so you can't control me any more, no matter how much you want to. Whether you like it or not, you can't tell me what to do. I'm an adult now.'

Harriet stared at her daughter. So like herself, from her mind to her maddening bloody-mindedness. 'You are not an adult, not while you're living under our roof and expecting me to sort out your lifts and laundry and all the care and feeding I've been giving you since you were born.' Harriet's voice was barely above a whisper. 'Yes, you've got the right to make your own decisions, but you've still got some growing up to do. And if I make suggestions about how you dress or ask you not to have that phone fused to you all the time, it's because I care. This is about respecting what I say. You could do a lot worse than me, you know.' She thought of Owen's mother.

James watched this exchange from the table. Of course, he wasn't bloody saying anything to help. She was *so* sick and tired of him being a passenger in their marriage, leaving her to do all the driving and maintenance and the tricky reverse parking.

'That's all such bollocks, Mum,' said Billie, 'because you don't respect me. You just want to turn me into a carbon copy of you. Can't you see how stupid that is?'

'I'll respect you when you've earned it, not when you do exactly as you please and sod the consequences to you or anyone else. Billie, what is so hard about doing as I ask every once in a while? And I'm sorry that you find it so horrible to be like me. All I'm asking is that you look nice sometimes and not embarrass me and be the tiniest bit appreciative of what I'm trying to do for you. I don't understand what's wrong with you.'

Enough was enough. If Billie couldn't even change her clothes, or James save his appetite after she'd been the one to find the restaurant, check the menu, make the reservation and then rearrange the rest of the day around it, well then they could feed themselves from the bins from now on for all she cared.

'Jesus, Mum, there's nothing wrong with me because I don't want to be like you.' The sneer in Billie's voice cut Harriet to the bone. 'And I'm sorry if I embarrass you so much just because I don't want to wear a stupid dress, but seriously, get over it because if *that* embarrasses you . . .' Her eyes darted from Harriet to James. 'Never mind.'

'Oh, no, don't stop now you're on a roll. What were you going to say? Come on, since we're being so honest.'

'You don't want honesty, Mum, that's the last thing you want. You've got this crazy idea of perfection that doesn't even exist. You make us go through all this la-di-da bullshit that nobody likes. You expect me to live up to your perfect ideal, or don't you let me know it. I am so tired of it, and I'm sorry I'm not your ideal daughter and I won't ever be, but just get over it and leave me alone.'

Harriet was stunned. 'I only want what's best for you. If I seem harsh sometimes it's only because I know what it's like—'

'You don't, though. You don't even know me.'

'I know you as well as I know myself,' Harriet said.

'Do you really? If you think so then you're deluded. You know what you want me to be. That's all. Well, take that and think the opposite, because that's what I am, Mum, the opposite of what you want me to be.'

'You're the one who's deluded, Billie. You hate me now, and I understand that. It's cool to hate your parents when you're a teenager. I was sixteen once, too, remember. So don't think I don't know exactly what you're thinking. Despite what you want to believe, you are like me.' Then she went over to her daughter. She didn't dare touch her, though. The rage in the girl's face warned her not

201

to. 'Billie, I know how hard it is to be your age. I know what that pressure feels like, with school and exams and your friends and boys.'

'Girls,' Billie said. 'Not boys, Mum, girls.' She widened her eyes. 'Since you know me so well, you know I'm gay, yeah?'

'Pshh, gay.' Billie wasn't gay. She was trying to get a rise out of her. Like every teenager on the planet did with their parents.

Billie crossed her arms over her horrible shirt. 'That honest enough for you?'

'Don't be ridiculous, you're not gay,' Harriet said. She looked to James for support, but he was too busy staring at Billie with his mouth open.

'I promise you, Mum, I am. One hundred per cent totally gay.'

'But you don't seem gay.'

'What, just because I'm not wearing my Women Turn Me On t-shirt?'

Harriet said nothing for a moment. 'You don't . . .?'

'Christ, Mum, I can't even *talk* to you!'

Harriet's eyes sought the windowpanes in the doors that led to the garden. Five rows, ten panes on each French door plus fifteen on each window either side. Then the casements (four) made up of four sides each, sixteen, plus the wooden strips between the panes. Twenty-one plus twenty-one plus thirteen plus thirteen.

'Is it true?' she murmured.

'Why would I lie about it? It's no big deal, so get over it. And by the way, I'm going to Pride in Brighton on Saturday, and I'm meeting friends there. You don't know them.'

'I know your friends, Billie.' Harriet's mind raced through them, but none of them seemed gay, either.

'Not those ones. I'm taking the train down to meet them.' Her expression challenged Harriet to try stopping her.

By 'meet them', she'd better not mean she was meeting them for the first time, that these people were online friends, because that could be anyone posing as a teenager: weird man (or woman!), murderous psychopath, anyone.

They all watched Owen stroll into the kitchen in his sweatshirt and tracksuit bottoms. He shuffled to the fridge, filled a glass with orange juice and downed it while he leaned against the worktop. Then he must have noticed the yawning silence in the room. 'What's up?'

Harriet looked between Billie and James. She was not about to be the one to out her daughter. Finally, Billie spoke up. 'I've just told them I'm gay.'

'Cool,' he said. 'Anybody wanna finish this?' When they didn't answer, he drank the rest of the juice from the carton and wandered back upstairs.

A thought occurred to Harriet. 'Did he already know?'

'Yeah, so?'

'I can't believe you'd tell a complete stranger before your own parents.'

'Oh, because you're taking it so well. Mum, it's not a big deal.'

Now James spoke up. He covered the distance between them in a few long strides. 'That can't have been easy to tell us, sweetheart, so thank you. You're dead right, it's no big deal, and we love you.'

'Thanks, Dad,' she said as she accepted his hug. A willing hug!

Billie went upstairs then, without looking at Harriet.

Much as that hurt, it was probably better, because Harriet could form no words. She hadn't seen this coming. She had no plan for it.

'Do you think she cares about going to The Wolseley?' she asked James.

'I don't think any of us cares about The Wolseley, dear heart.'

She cancelled their reservation. Her heart wasn't in it any more, either. James got another cereal bowl from the cabinet for Harriet, but her appetite had gone.

When her support would have really mattered to Billie, she'd won first prize in the world's worst parent contest. James had been sensible and encouraging, but not her. She had to go and say the first thing that came to mind. Now Billie would probably remember that for the rest of her life whenever she thought about coming out to her parents.

Harriet had fucked up. That was textbook: how not to react when your child tells you she's gay.

When she thought about it, though, Billie had been right about one thing. She *was* disappointing Harriet. What a horrible, judgemental thing to think, but there it was. She'd never admit it out loud – it just added to her Crap Parent status – but Harriet could think of loads of times when Billie had fallen short of her expectations.

That wasn't Billie's fault. Never her fault. The fault was all Harriet's. She'd been lying to herself since before her daughter was even born. *We just want a healthy child*, she'd tell anyone who asked whether she preferred a boy or a girl.

Since everyone was so keen for honesty today, Harriet had to admit that she'd wanted much more than that. A healthy baby, of course, obviously. Billie hadn't even finished her first cry when Harriet thanked their biology for a girl. That was the first lie – that she hadn't cared what sex she was. She'd know how to raise a girl. By the time the midwife had counted the baby's fingers and toes and pronounced her healthy, Harriet was already hoping for more. She saw the wisps of Billie's soft blonde hair and wanted it to be immune to the frizz that she had to pay good money to have smoothed at the salon. She looked into the baby's deep-blue eyes and wanted them to stay as bright (they'd turned grey like hers).

That was just the tip of the iceberg. Sleek hair and blue eyes were superficial wishes, but it didn't take long for Harriet to get greedy for achievements, too.

She wanted a good sleeper, a non-fussy eater, a child like her who walked and talked and read early. Billie wasn't any of those things, and Harriet was disappointed. No matter that Billie reached all the amazing milestones that children do, Harriet wanted more.

When Billie started doing well at school, Harriet wondered if she might end up going to University College London like she had. When she joined the school hockey team, Harriet gave her the old captain's armband she'd worn.

On and on, Harriet had mapped out Billie's life. It looked a lot like Harriet's.

So, what was her daughter now doing, marching at Pride? Harriet had never marched at anything in her life, let alone anything to be proud of.

Billie was right. All this time she hadn't known her own daughter.

Chapter 18

Monday

Dan didn't give Sophie the bitter pill till he got out of the shower on Monday morning. He was going into the office. That was the London office, not the one he'd been squatting in, down the corridor from the kitchen. He'd be gone the whole day.

She watched him putting on his tie. 'You packed your suit?' She was sure she hadn't seen him do that.

He came round to her side of the bed, kissed her on the nose and took her hands in his. 'Always prepared, just like the Scouts.' He inspected the backs of her hands. 'Did you bring your tanning cream?'

'Hmm? No, I forgot.' She let out a big sigh.

'Come on, Soph, it's only one day. You won't even miss me.'

She hadn't been worried about that. 'This is a family holiday, Dan.' He should be there, too, whether it was comfortable for her or not.

'Don't be cross. I'll make it up to you tonight.' His kiss left no doubt about what he meant.

'Then promise me something. Promise me that after you get back tonight, you aren't going to lock yourself in that office for the rest of the week.'

She'd meant to sound playful, but something in Dan's expression shifted and she knew she was off the mark.

'Sophie. You don't understand what it's like to work like I do. I've got obligations, people depending on me. I don't want to go to the office, but I have to. You were the one who extended this holiday to two weeks, remember? I've taken extra days off for you, so I'd appreciate it if you didn't put any more pressure on me than I've already got.'

'I'm sorry, I didn't mean to. We'll be fine. If I drive you to the station then we could use the car today.'

'I'll drive myself,' he said.

'Then we haven't got the car.'

'No change there, when you haven't driven it since we've been here.'

'But it would be nice to do something later. You'd mentioned that we would, remember?'

'I can't help going into work, Soph, I told you that! Please, now, don't make it harder.'

She wasn't ready to give up the point. 'I'm not. I'm making it easier. If I keep the car then you won't have to worry about us being stuck here all day. I can get something for dinner, too, if you want.'

Dan shook his head. 'I'll get something for us on the way back. Where will you go?'

Sophie shrugged. 'We can decide after my treatment. Is it an hour again today?' She knew it sounded incredibly spoilt, but she was starting to tire of going to the spa. Much as Dan wanted her to be, she wasn't a luxury kind of woman.

'They're all an hour long, but you'll need to skip it today,' he said. 'The children, remember? Who's supposed to look after them? I can't be in two places.' He mock-knocked on her head. Silly bean.

Of course. She wasn't thinking straight this morning.

Dan looked satisfied. 'Fine, take the car. I'll be back by dinner time. Will you be okay driving, then?'

'I'll use the GPS.'

'I'll show you.'

'I know how to use the GPS, Dan.' It couldn't be any harder than Google Maps, and she managed to use that all over London without ending up in the Thames.

'Soph, I'm just trying to help you.' He sounded weary. 'Now, tell me where you'll go today and I'll type it in for you.'

But she'd just said she didn't want him to do that, not when the idea of taking the children in the car excited her so much. It would be an adventure! 'That's okay. We'll sort it out later.'

'Why won't you tell me?' Dan snapped.

'I'm not *not* telling you, I'm just waiting to talk to the children. I don't know what they'll want to do. That's all.' Dan watched her. 'Maybe the aviation museum.'

'Fine, then I'll put the coordinates in for you.'

Whatever. She could do as she pleased as soon as he was on his way to London. She stretched again.

But she wasn't to get any peace and quiet yet, because Dan made a call as he finished getting ready. 'Hope you're enjoying yourself, wherever you are, *not* picking up your phone. As soon as you get to the office, I want you to pull out the Mason file, the Khan file and the Cipriani file. Sign them out. That's Mason, Khan and Cipriani. Do this, Laxmi, okay? No excuses. You didn't manage to follow my simple instructions last time, so now you'll do this. I want you to ring me back and tell me it's done.'

The dread made itself at home in Sophie's ribcage again, but now she wasn't just upset on Laxmi's behalf. As uncomfortable as the thought was, she was starting to wonder if

Harriet's accusation might be closer to home than she'd let herself believe.

Dan got straight back on his phone. 'Hi, this is Dan Mitchell ringing for Sophie Mitchell. I need to cancel Sophie's treatment today. She'll be there tomorrow as scheduled. Also, do you do spray tans?'

'Where're we going?' Katie asked.

'It's a surprise.' Sophie smiled as the car reached the end of the drive. 'Now, left or right?'

'To go where?' Katie asked again.

'Depends on whether we go left or right, doesn't it?'

'Right,' Oliver said.

Sophie eased the car out onto the road. 'We're off!' To where, she had no idea. She only knew that it was up to her. 'Let's see what we find.' When they reached the next intersection, she said, 'Left or right?'

'Left,' said Katie.

'Right,' Oliver said again.

'Tie break.' Sophie laughed. 'I'm the deciding vote.' She put her left indicator on. They drove to the next intersection.

'Right!' both children said.

They drove like that for miles.

It was hours later when Sophie found a parking spot back in the village.

'Can we do that when we get back to London?' Oliver wondered.

Sophie smiled at him in the rear-view mirror. 'You mean drive around? We'd be stuck in traffic the whole time.'

'Nuh-uh, I mean be allowed to go anywhere we want.'

'I guess so,' she said, 'as long as you don't mind me being with you.'

'I don't mind.'

The children had so many activities and lessons, not to mention the birthday parties that seemed to take up every weekend. Her own childhood outside of school had felt like nothing but free time to play and explore. She realised that if it were only up to her, Katie and Oliver wouldn't be half as busy as they were. So maybe that *should* be up to her more.

The little bell tinkled over the butcher's shop door as they entered. Only a few people were waiting. The butcher kept up a conversation while he weighed each customer's selections, so that by the time Sophie's turn came, she knew a lot about the village residents. She knew that the middle-aged lady with the whippet tied up outside was soon to leave for her sister's in Penrith for two weeks to cheer her up after Gareth, her husband of eleven years, left the poor woman to find himself in India and, of course, there must be another woman involved. She learned all about Mr Clifton's most recent hospital visit but, luckily, they caught it early so he should be fine after the chemo. Speaking of hospitals, the party planner's mum was healing nicely and already looked twenty years younger even with the swelling. And that Eleanor Davies was going after the children again when she knew very well they had every right to be on that footpath and just because it ran across her property didn't mean she owned it. Besides, she wasn't local. She'd only married into the family. Granted, it was over fifty years ago.

No wonder they viewed Harriet with suspicion if Mrs Davies's fifty years didn't count for anything.

The butcher smiled at Sophie when her turn came. 'May I please have a pork loin?'

'And could you please put it in that paper instead of plastic?' Katie added, though Sophie was about to ask the same thing. Katie's influence had rubbed off, though it still came more naturally to the kids.

'Aye. How'll you cook it?' the butcher asked, reaching into the large window at the front.

'Oh. I'm not sure, actually. I'll look up a recipe, I guess.'

'Excuse me, sir?' Katie said. 'Can I ask where your pork comes from? Is it local?'

'Right up the road, young lady,' he said. 'From a farm that's reintroducing rare breeds.'

His answer satisfied Katie's air mile criteria. Luckily she hadn't yet objected to them driving.

'And I bet they're delicious!' Sophie added.

'Aye, what you want to do is wrap it in foil with some herbs and butter,' said the stout grey-haired lady beside her. Despite the summer weather she wore two or maybe three cardigans over her blouse.

'Don't forget salt,' the butcher added. The other customers nodded. 'And throw in a few cut-up apples.'

'Thank you,' Sophie said. 'My mouth is watering already.'

'Ta-raa, see you again!' said the stout lady when they left.

Dan rang her from the train. 'I'll be thirty minutes,' he said.

'Not a problem, we only got back an hour ago.'

'Did you have fun?'

'We did! We just explored some of the countryside, all the way over into Herefordshire. It's so gorgeous here. Did you get a lot done at the office?'

'Yes, it was productive. I shouldn't have to go in again. I'm glad you got out.'

'Me too,' Sophie said. 'We stopped at the butcher on the way back and I got pork loin. It won't be ready for at least an hour, though.'

At first, she thought his silence meant he'd gone into a tunnel. 'I picked up Nando's for dinner.'

'Can't we have that for lunch tomorrow? The butcher gave me the recipe. I think it'll be delicious.'

How quickly things turned bitter between them. 'So will the chicken I bought. Come on, Soph, can't you see I'm trying to make your life easy? Why do you have to make mine harder?'

'I doubt your life is harder because of a pork loin, Dan.' When she hung up, she realised that she never talked back like that. The ceiling hadn't fallen in or anything.

Chapter 19

Monday

Billie wanted to watch something on her phone rather than see London by night with them. Harriet was relieved to leave her at home. Then she felt guilty that she was relieved. Then she was afraid that she was relieved because Billie was gay.

She used to love coming to the South Bank when she'd worked in London. Not actually *when* she worked, naturally, although her office was only a twenty-one-minute walk away if most of the crossing lights were green.

Once a quarter, Harriet would spend a Saturday morning booking her events for the following three months. There was always something on at the South Bank: a play at the National Theatre, or music at Queen Elizabeth Hall or one of the big photo prize exhibitions at the Hayward Gallery. It always topped her up, culturally speaking.

Lots of people hated its concrete brutalist architecture, but it was perfection in Harriet's greedy eyes. All those bold geometric patterns. The windows alone on the Royal Festival Hall could occupy her for many happy minutes.

She started counting them now as they meandered past, even though she could already see that the trees obscuring some of them would frustrate her.

Throngs of people strolled along the wide walk, taking selfies, stopping to peer over the parapet at the river current.

The notes of a busker's rousing cello concerto floated over them. Bach's Cello Suite No. 1 in G Major, an obvious choice, but always a goodie.

'Smell that. It's making me hungry,' said James. 'Want to grab something after the wheel?'

'Yes, we've got dinner after, in Soho,' she said.

'I mean here, at one of the stalls. Why wouldn't we stay?'

'Because there's a table waiting for us in Soho.'

He laughed. 'Can't you at least try to see that it's easier to walk ten steps to one of these stalls rather than travel somewhere else?'

'I've already booked somewhere else.'

'Oh, for God's sake, Harriet!'

Why was he getting so vexed, when she was the one who'd gone to the trouble of booking the perfect restaurant for them? And now he wanted to change that.

She took a deep breath. She was supposed to be trying to make things better. 'I guess we could eat here,' she conceded. 'Where?'

James glanced down the long row of kiosks.

'Right,' she said. 'We can walk up and down and see what looks good.' While that was definitely not the most efficient method, she could see it was what James wanted. 'We'll just play it by ear.'

The words tasted funny on her tongue.

Their fast-track tickets let them board the London Eye quickly. There were twenty other people in the pod with them, Harriet noted, though nobody looked like they expected a conversation from her, so she wasn't too anxious. Besides, everyone was busy staring out of the windows. The clear evening was perfect for a skyline view.

The wheel started its gradual revolution. Thanks to the long summer day, the sun was still in the sky. Sightseeing boats and ferries shuttled passengers up and down the brown Thames below, past the Houses of Parliament and Big Ben, which gleamed warmly on the opposite side of the river. Further downriver, the Shard's sleek glass tower cut high into the sky. It had opened just after they left London.

From this high up, the city leaked over the horizon all around them.

'You're not really okay with all this, are you?' she asked James when they got near the top.

'The wheel? It's safe.'

'Not this, James. I'm guessing the architects and builders who took six years to erect it made sure of that. I mean Billie.' Harriet kept her voice low. 'About what she said. I was thinking. She might not even be gay, you know. I read that fifty per cent of young people say they're not straight. If everybody's doing it, then it could just be a phase.'

'Then she'll snap out of it,' he said, 'and you won't have to worry.'

'What do you mean, *I* won't have to worry? This concerns you too, you know.'

'Well,' James said, with his eyes trained on Big Ben, 'it does and it doesn't. Obviously I want her to be okay. That's the most important thing. But I don't care who she falls in love with, as long as they treat her the way she wants to be treated.'

'Come off it, James, this has got to bother you just like it does me. Have you even thought about it, what it means for her life, or are you automatically saying it's all fine because that's what cool parents do? She's going to have problems because of this. Prejudice. Job discrimination.'

'I'm worried about that, too,' he said, finally looking at her. 'But we have to hope that it'll be okay for her. Believe me, I'm thinking exactly what you are.'

Harriet doubted that. What she was thinking was *what about my grandchildren? Will I have any now?*

'She might not even have children,' she told James. 'What about that?'

'Lots of people don't have children,' James said. 'It wouldn't be the end of the world, would it? As long as she's happy.'

'Will you stop acting so bloody reasonable? It just makes me look like the arse again.'

Harriet knew exactly what his shrug meant. *If the arse fits . . .*

James let out a sigh so loud the couple beside them looked over. 'Has it ever occurred to you that you can't anticipate everything in this world? You can't control this. Not this. Not when it's so important to get it right for Billie. I mean, Jesus, Harriet, our daughter has probably just told us the most important thing in her life, and you're worried about whether she'll have children? Please, get some perspective. There's no script for this one.'

Harriet was stung. 'I know we need to get it right. That's what I'm saying. James, I've done everything wrong and I don't know how to make it better. Now our daughter hates me and I don't know what to do.' If she ever needed James to be the partner she married, it was now.

'She doesn't hate you,' he said. 'She's a teenager. They say mean things to their parents. And vice versa.' His look was pointed. Harriet couldn't deny his judgement. But then he said, 'Come here,' and gathered her into his arms.

'She doesn't ever say mean things to you, though, does she?' Harriet hated her jealousy over that.

'Daughters fight with their mothers,' he said.

'How does she actually know she's gay anyway?' She grasped again at that slender straw. 'I mean, what if this is just theoretical?'

James shook his head. 'I knew I liked girls before I ever had any working knowledge of one. Do you want to ask her?'

Harried sighed. 'Maybe she's doing it to get back at me.'

'I wouldn't say that to her if I were you. It sounds . . . dismissive.'

'You don't think she is, then? Getting back at me?'

'It would be a pretty serious thing to fake just to piss you off.'

'Well, if it's true then I fear for her out there in the real world. I don't want her to have to go through that. It's hard enough being normal.'

'You mean straight,' James said.

'That's what I mean.' But she hadn't said that, had she?

Now she'd disappointed James, too. She couldn't make anyone happy.

If Harriet didn't do much better, and sharpish, she was going to lose her daughter. They hadn't exactly been rock solid to begin with. Harriet stared at the horizon. Suddenly everything – making sure the holiday was perfect and the worry over James and their marriage – took a back seat to her and Billie.

James was watching her. 'What?' she asked.

'We'll all be fine,' he said.

But he couldn't promise that any more than she could.

When they got back to the house, Harriet wasn't in the mood to carry on with her plan – a post-sightseeing glass of wine in the garden followed by a romantic interlude upstairs. She didn't even want to take her make-up off, which she did every night. That's how bad it was. She stripped off and crawled under the duvet, even before James.

Later, James came to bed in his usual manner, with the grace of a hippo on land. Just when she'd drifted off, too. The old bedsprings creaked their protest under the moonlight filtering through the flimsy curtains. When he lifted the duvet, a blast of cool air rushed across her naked body. Then he said what he always said when she yanked the bedclothes back around her. 'Sorry, did I wake you?'

She ignored him, but James wasn't ready for sleep yet. It wasn't long before his fingers started up the side of her thigh as she lay with her back to him. At first, she barely felt it, just a tickle that raised goosebumps despite the heat under the blanket. He'd always had a feather-light touch. Surprising for such an oaf. She held her breath as he caressed her across her hip. His touch travelled up her back.

'Mmm, that feels good.' They needed this, she realised, this reconnection after today. She scooted herself back towards her husband as long-forgotten memories bubbled up. She used to love falling asleep with her back spooned against James's chest. It was also a very handy position for when they didn't want to sleep. Like now.

But instead of pulling her to him, James kept tracing his fingers up her back, so slowly, until he reached her hairline. Another shiver ran down her. She adored having her hair played with. 'That's almost better than foreplay,' she murmured. She wanted both, though.

'Hmm?' James said from what sounded like the other side of the mattress.

She turned to look over her shoulder in the murky darkness. 'I said that's almost better than foreplay.'

Just then, something blurry with a flickering tongue drifted into her peripheral vision.

Her heart leapt into her mouth as the delicious tickling turned sinister.

'GET IT OFF ME!' she screamed. 'JAMES, THE SNAKE, GET IT OFF!'

'Jesus Christ, is it around you? I can't see. Don't move!' He flipped on the light.

Harriet froze. The snake's mouth was inches from her neck. What if it bit her? And then started strangling her?

But Spot was more interested in tickling Harriet's neck. She could feel its tongue darting in and out. *Pthlthlop pthlthlop* went that horrid tongue. 'It's getting a taste for me, James. Get it OFF!' What the hell was the man waiting for?

Gently, James picked up the snake, leaving Harriet free to scramble from the bed. 'Careful!' She didn't want James to be suffocated either.

Spot's tongue flicked at James's arm. Slowly, her body coiled around it. 'It's okay, Harriet. It's all right. She's calm.'

'*She's* calm?!' That bloody snake.

Billie knocked at the door. 'Mum, what are you screaming about?'

'We found Spot,' James called.

Harriet dove for the duvet as the bedroom door opened. It was a good thing she did, because Owen was right behind Billie.

'That's all?' Billie said. 'I thought something was really wrong. You don't need to scream the house down.'

'That's all? THAT'S ALL? I've just had a deadly snake about to squeeze the life out of me, so no, that is not all.' She glared at Billie's smirk.

'She's not exactly deadly, is she?'

'You wouldn't say that if it was your neck.'

Owen took the snake from James. 'Good one, Mr Cooper.'

'Be sure that door is locked when it's inside,' Harriet said. 'And close the bedroom door, too.'

'Your mum is mental,' she heard Owen say as they went to put Spot back in its enclosure.

'Tell me about it.'

What was *mental*, thought Harriet, was having a bloody python in the house in the first place.

Chapter 20

Tuesday

Sophie was awake before anyone else the next morning. She snuggled deeper under the ultra-soft duvet – Harriet's sheets must have a thread count of over a million – listening to a bird singing in the tree beside the window, like he had every morning since they'd arrived. When she stretched, Dan stirred on his side. She peered at him, listening for his regular breathing to start up again. She waited, waited, then bucked her shoulders and her legs, bouncing on the mattress. Disturbed once more, he turned onto his tummy with a sigh. More waiting, then she did it again.

He squinted at her. 'Soph?'

Oops. A bounce too far. 'Ssh, it's still early,' she whispered, carefully peeling back the covers on her side. 'Go back to sleep.'

Downstairs, she surveyed the kitchen while she waited for the kettle to boil. Harriet wouldn't like what they'd done to her house. Shoes littered the floor where they'd been kicked off. One of Oliver's trainers was on the breakfast table without any laces. She'd never get round to buying new ones for it. He had half a dozen strays in the same state at home. She was down to around three laces to share between them all, like that Greek myth where the witches pass a single eye between them.

She could at least wipe up the tea rings and toast crumbs, she supposed. Maybe empty the overflowing bin and put a few of the cereal boxes back in the cabinet that Harriet had so neatly labelled. Half an effort was better than no effort at all, as her dad liked to say. But she hadn't the motivation to collect up all the dishes – how did one little family use so many – or all the cast-off clothes that had piled up on the sofa and chairs. They'd have all Sunday morning to tidy up before they left.

As her family woke and migrated to the kitchen, the peace seeped from Sophie. The minute she stepped outside, though, leaving Dan muttering over some outrage in the paper, she felt that lightness again. The same way she'd felt walking between here and the village each day. It was almost a tipsy sensation – not unpleasant at all – as if the edge had been taken off her life.

But that couldn't be right, because Sophie didn't have any edges on her life to speak of. Dan made sure those were all sanded away.

She couldn't deny the feeling, though. Free-floating. No, not free-floating. Free *and* floating. Sophie was starting to feel free. But from what, exactly? What was happening to her?

Her phone rang on the walk to the village for her treatment. Tempting as it was to let it go to voicemail, it could be Katie or Oliver needing something.

She shouldn't have looked. 'Hi, Carlos.' She'd already ignored one call from him.

'Morning. Is it too early?'

'I'm on my way to the village. Are you well?'

'Well enough.' He matched her formality. 'They found Spot last night. You know how she likes warm places.'

Of course! The hot-water pipe ran close to the floorboards

under the sink in the downstairs loo. 'I should have thought of the loo,' she said.

'They'd have been lucky if she was there. No, she got into bed with the woman.' Carlos chuckled. 'She screamed blue murder. I heard her through the wall.'

That would have put a serious dampener on Harriet's night.

'She asked me if I could take Spot to my house till you got back,' Carlos added. 'When *are* you coming back? Still Saturday?'

'No, Sunday.' She'd told him that already. 'It was only because of the flights that we had to come back a day early before.'

'It seems like a long time away.'

'Mmm-hmm, two whole weeks. And then some.' What bliss.

'That's not—'

'Sorry to rush you off, but I should ring Harriet and I'm nearly at the spa.' She stared over the green fields at the village church spire, still in the distance. 'Talk to you later. Thanks for dealing with Spot!'

She switched her phone off and tried to settle back into the peaceful walk, but mentioning Harriet conjured up bad feelings again. Fat chance that Sophie would be ringing her to apologise for Spot. Harriet should be the one apologising.

Great. Now she was thinking about Harriet instead of being serene and at one with the universe like she was supposed to be. Damn you, Harriet!

Peace . . . love . . . happiness, she chanted to herself. Peace, love, happiness. The mechanical rumble of the tractor in the next field was a perfectly fitting backing track to her chant.

Her GP had told her it was all about mindfulness these days. What was the technique he said to try? Something about water and leaves. Imagine standing in a stream where leaves are flowing past on the current. Then plonk all your negative thoughts on the leaves and watch them float away.

Bye-bye Harriet.

That was better. Yes, much better. Sophie was pushed along by the brisk wind rustling the leaves and flinging bits of hair into her face. She loved that rustling and didn't mind the hair in her mouth too much, either. Then she imagined Harriet carried off by the wind, too. Why not? It was her mindfulness. She could aim it where she liked.

The sound of traffic rumbled along the lane, but it didn't disrupt the atmosphere. The bucolic atmosphere. Her face flamed, remembering the time she accidentally said the bucolic plague. Dan hadn't let her forget that quickly.

Now why had that popped into her head when she was just starting to have a perfectly nice time out here? She chucked Dan on the next leaf to pass.

Honestly, she did sabotage herself sometimes. And just when she was feeling so good, too. Floaty and good.

If they'd gone abroad like they'd planned, she'd probably assume it was an odd kind of jet lag or maybe brought on by too much pasta. Yet she hadn't travelled and she wasn't carb-loading.

It wasn't the clean country air, either, or the oxygen rush disorientating her. The answer wasn't coming from inside. Her body wasn't letting her down.

Dan was. She didn't like to think it, but there it was. All this time she'd congratulated herself on her fairy-tale life. She'd gloated, knowing that she'd found her very own knight in shining armour. Dan was always riding to the rescue.

But it wasn't just his wing that she'd been safely tucked up under, was it? Often it was his thumb, too.

The house was her remit, he liked to say, yet he never let her do things her way. Or when he did, then she could be sure that the meal, task, food shop or errand would prompt his opinion about how she should be doing it better. She was the only person she knew who broke out in a cold sweat when Tesco was out of stock of something her partner wanted.

Why hadn't she noticed before that she dangled from the strings her husband pulled? The answer popped into her head with the memory of the way he'd spoken to Laxmi when they'd first arrived at Harriet's house.

He could blame the traffic noise all he wanted. *Traffic noise, my arse*, she thought. That was a bollocking. He'd done it again just yesterday, leaving Laxmi that rude voicemail. Sophie had assumed her discomfort was for the poor woman, but it wasn't only that. For the first time, it seemed, she also heard the way Dan spoke to her.

Sophie didn't always live in a fairy tale, did she?

So maybe she was chaotic. She always had been. She wasn't sophisticated or well travelled and she used words like bucolic when she meant bubonic. She'd never particularly seen those as faults, but maybe she had benefited from a guiding hand. Dan would be the first to say how much he loved taking care of her. For years he made Sophie feel special like no one else she'd ever met. He couldn't do enough for her, and she loved that about him.

Bad habits must have crept in somewhere along the way. She couldn't remember when Dan started being so critical. Maybe she'd become lazy, too, letting him make all the decisions when she was capable of doing things for herself. This holiday had reminded her of that. More importantly, she wanted to. She wasn't keen to go back to the way her life had been. This new feeling was addictive.

She would talk to Dan about it. He'd probably be over the moon to have some of the pressure taken off. He was always saying how hard he worked for them.

By the time she reached the village, Sophie looked forward to seeing Dan later. It could be the start of a new phase for them. Those women's magazines were always talking about letting changes spice up one's relationship. After sixteen years together, this was going to be just the seasoning they needed.

Molly was ready for her when she got to the spa. 'Today you can keep your trousers on,' she whispered when they reached the treatment room, 'but please take off your top and bra. Sit on the table, and you can tuck this around your front.' She handed Sophie a fluffy white towel. 'It's a sitting-up massage.'

She'd never heard of a sitting-up massage. Maybe it needed gravity to work on her lymphatic drains again. Her plugholes must really be blocked. She stripped off and waited for Molly's gentle knock.

The masseuse busied herself behind Sophie's bare back while Sophie tried to figure out what she was doing. She could have turned to watch her, but that would spoil the game.

Molly's touch flickered across her shoulders, playing Sophie like she might a harp's strings. She thrummed across the middle of her back, then the bottom. 'Mmm, that feels nice.'

She was just getting into the routine when it stopped. Then she felt the whisper of something up her side.

'*Bwaa ha ha ha ha ha ha!*' She squirmed away. 'I'm sorry, sorry. Please continue.'

Molly stroked again. Sophie's arms stiffened with trying not to laugh. It was no good. '*Bwaa ha ha ha ha ha ha!*'

'Let's try something else,' Molly whispered.

When Sophie glanced over her shoulder, Molly was wearing a red feather boa around her neck. 'That's very glamorous,' she said.

Molly smiled and reached for one of the paintbrushes laid out on the small table beside her. 'It's a tickle massage.'

Sophie nearly fell off the table in stitches for most of the next hour, as Molly worked her way through more brushes, cheerleader pom-poms and (surprisingly tickle-making) dusting cloths. By the time Sophie left, she knew she'd never look at an electric toothbrush in quite the same way again.

She stopped again at the tea shop where she'd gone with the children yesterday. It looked exactly like a village tea shop should: whitewashed and strung with bunting, with vintage teacups and cake stands everywhere and flowers spilling out of milk jugs. There was a friendly buzz from the men and women who chatted around a few of the tables. The vibe was cosy and inviting, and Sophie didn't mind sitting on her own.

She poured more peppermint tea from the second pot that she'd needed to wash down the extra wodge of cake she'd just finished. Given how much tiramisu she'd factored into her holiday, she was still behind on her pudding quota. *Must try harder, Sophie.*

She fibbed when the tea shop owner, Bea, asked how she'd liked her treatment. Not an outright lie; more of a glossing over of all the squirming she'd done through most of it.

Bea seemed to know Sophie's entire spa schedule. Not to mention what Dan had been making for dinner, and exactly how much the Scouts event had raised on Sunday. The villagers must keep a bulletin board tucked out of sight where they posted about all the comings and goings of visitors like Sophie.

On a sliding scale, the tickle massage hadn't been as bad as, say, teeth-cleaning or karaoke, but she wouldn't rush back for another one. In fact, a thought drifted in with the minty aroma in her cup: why was she still following Dan's schedule? It had been very thoughtful of him to get the ball rolling for her, but she should make the most of the treatments she had left. Now she knew that snails and sticks weren't her thing. She'd ring the spa later and book the treatments she knew she'd like.

That was the kind of support she wanted; normal relationship stuff like lending a hand or an ear or a shoulder to cry on when one of them faltered, and cheerleading every success. She didn't need him booking her massages or buying her clothes or advising her on haircuts or – she glanced at her bare forearm – getting the shade of fake tan he thought would look best.

When was the last time she'd been clothes shopping for herself? Dan did it all online. The delivery bloke turned up a few times a month with more things to try on. She used to do that as soon as she got the package, but it was a waste of time, since Dan would only make her put everything on again for him when he got home from work. He always sent back the ones he didn't like.

Bea was glancing with pride at Sophie's empty plate. 'Something else?'

'I'll explode if I have anything else, but thanks, just the bill, please. Though it's so nice here I could stay all afternoon.' She tipped her face towards the sun streaming through the front window.

''Spect so.' She picked up the plates. 'We're not your in-and-out job like you get in London.'

Sophie nodded. Of course Bea knew where they came from, too. 'I'll be sad to go back. It's so lovely here.'

''Tis that,' said Bea. 'But James'll be itching to get home. It's hard for him being away. He was raised here, not like her.' Bea's feelings about Harriet were written all over her face, and that seemed to be the end of the conversation.

Sophie pulled her purse from her handbag to pay the bill. Her phone! It had been off since the morning.

She rang Dan straight away.

'Where have you been?' he demanded.

'I'm sorry, Dan, I turned the phone off for my treatment and forgot. Sorry. I'm just leaving the tea shop now.' She mouthed a thank you to Bea for the change. 'Do you need me to pick anything up while I'm here?'

'No, Sophie, I've got everything we need. The children have been waiting for you and they're bored. I'll come and pick you up.'

She hated that angry edge to his voice. But she hated more that she felt herself folding into the perfectly accommodating wifey-sized woman she always tried to be in the face of it. The folds pinched. That was new. 'No, don't worry, I can walk back. It won't take long. The massage was interesting, by the way. It tickled!' *Distract distract distract.* It worked on children and pets and sometimes husbands.

'I'm glad you were having so much fun while I was here holding the fort for you.'

She wasn't in the mood to pander to him. 'Sorry, but you knew I had a treatment. And I wouldn't say it was fun. It was weird.'

'Then I'm sorry I bothered to book it for you if it was so weird.'

'I mean I'm grateful you did, thank you. It was just surprising, that's all.' He didn't respond and she felt herself folding again. 'Do you want me to bring you a slice of cake? The chocolate is delicious.'

He ignored her offer. 'There are a lot of different kinds of treatments in the world, Sophie. I'm trying to give you a wider experience, but if you can't appreciate that . . . And you should have been home over an hour ago. You're not the only one with things to do other than sitting in some tea shop. Why are you there anyway?'

To drink tea, she wanted to say. But he was cross enough as it was. 'It's really pretty. We stopped by yesterday on the way home.'

'How nice for you.'

'I'll be home as soon as I can,' she said. It was definitely not the time to talk to Dan about their relationship.

Chapter 21

Tuesday

Nineteen years. For nineteen years Harriet had watched James eat breakfast. Even though he was up way before her at home to deal with the goats, he always came inside to join her when she had her morning toast (with butter and a generous slathering of Marmite that went right to the very edges). Nineteen years. She could predict every single movement and each facial expression of his, from the way he overfilled his cereal bowl to how he unscrewed the cap on the milk – for some reason turning the bottle instead of the cap – to the number of seconds he poured and the way he cupped his giant hand around the rim of the bowl to keep the cereal from spilling over when the milk displaced it. She knew he'd take the first mouthful with a slurp and smack his lips in satisfaction. She hated the sound of that smacking.

The milk dribble on his chin was a wild card, though. Sometimes he managed an accurate approach. Usually a slick of wet white glistened amid his stubble till she told him to wipe his chin.

She watched him scratch a spot on his back with his breakfast fork. 'James, that's disgusting.' And new. He was full of surprises these days.

'What? I'm not using it.' He held up his spoon, dripping with cereal milk.

'That's not the point. It's for eating, not scratching.' Honestly.

James raised his bushy eyebrows. 'Eating what? When was the last time I used a fork at breakfast?'

That wasn't the point, either. Harriet set the breakfast table the same way she set every other table.

'Why do you always do that?' he went on. She could see bits of masticated muesli in his mouth. 'Is it in case the queen decides to eat her Weetabix here?'

'I wouldn't subject Her Majesty to your dining habits.'

'It's a waste of washing-up,' he said.

'Only if you scratch yourself with the fork so that I have to wash it.'

He just smiled over his overfull bowl.

Something felt different this morning. Not just the breakfast ritual, but something. Harriet wasn't always attuned to other people's feelings – she'd been told that often enough to believe it was true – but she could feel this. And Billie wasn't up yet, so the change was in James.

He was too willing to do what she asked. He hadn't put up a fight when she'd told him they were going shopping today. Something was up. 'I thought we might go for afternoon tea, too.' That would get a rise out of him. It wasn't the tiny portions of cake or even the crustless sandwiches with fancy fillings that he objected to. It was having to sit in opulence. You'd think she was asking him to bathe in pig shit. Afternoon tea was that loathsome to her husband.

'Whatever you like,' he said.

'You're not going to object to my scheduling a schedule to keep to a schedule? Did you get a terminal diagnosis you're not telling me about? Trying to make amends before you meet your maker?'

'It's called compromise. Most people would call that marriage,' he said with a smirk.

'Most people don't have our marriage.'

He kissed her forehead as he went to rinse out his bowl. 'I'll give the fork a wash, shall I?'

What, no prison guard comments? Something was definitely up.

She'd carried on with her afternoon plans anyway, but now she felt bad as she watched James sitting with his knees squeezed close together under the small table. His farmer fingers barely fitted into the delicate teacup handle. He could have crushed it in his palm, but he was doing his best. He popped another egg and cress sandwich into his mouth. Down in one. Harriet pointedly nibbled her ham and cheese as the pianist began another tune.

James whispered something. He'd been doing that since the frock-coated waiter had shown them to their table.

'Pardon?'

He raised his voice about two decibels. 'The scones are good.'

'Evidently.' At least he'd enjoyed those. She surveyed the bits of cake strewn across his side of the table. He slid his plate over, trying to hide the smear of mustard, but that only exposed the smear of jam. The waiter had been around twice already with his tiny silver crumb duster.

So much to talk about, yet they'd been commenting on sandwich fillings for an hour. She realised she'd just heaved a colossal sigh when James said, 'What's wrong?'

'Thinking about Billie, that's all. I'm trying to work out when we should have known. A child shouldn't have to come out to her parents. That's something we should have picked up on. We were clueless. I was clueless. You too, I'm guessing.'

James nodded. Thank God it wasn't only her. 'Don't be so hard on yourself.'

'She doesn't look gay,' Harriet mused. She knew how utterly ridiculous it was to even think such a thing. Just because a girl didn't love pink or wear dresses or play with dolls didn't mean she was gay. She knew that, and yet she couldn't help thinking it.

'I'm not sure there's always a gay look,' he said.

'Yes, I know that.' She wasn't thinking logically. James didn't need to point it out. 'I don't understand why she waited so long to tell us when she must have known for ages.' Harriet didn't dare try on the answer to that question. It didn't look good on her. Maybe James would give her something that was a better fit.

'At least she feels comfortable telling us now,' said James.

'Only out of spite, though. It came out in a row, remember?' A row with Harriet, not James. Billie hadn't told them willingly. She'd been goaded by her mother.

James fitted another mini scone into his mouth, but at least he swallowed it before speaking. 'Well, we know now, so we can give her all the support she needs. We can do that, can't we?'

'Of course I'll support her.' He wasn't questioning himself.

They both glanced at a table where the waiters and waitresses had gathered to sing a discreet 'Happy Birthday'. The girl looked about Billie's age. Harriet tried not to be jealous as she hugged her beaming mother.

'She didn't let on that time you talked to her about sex?' James asked.

'You don't think that put her off?' Harriet had been accurate and anatomically correct in that lecture. It was simply a biological process, after all. Though the illustrations might have been a step too far. 'I mean, it is a weird business when you actually describe it. Not that it's weird with you. Or that I described sex with you.' Maybe she had messed that up.

But James didn't think so, and that did make her feel a little better. She still should have known before Billie told them.

She pushed her plate away. 'I couldn't eat another bite.' He just stared at her. 'What are you looking at?'

'You,' said James. 'It's been nice seeing you happy here. In London, I mean, not right now. Now you look a little sick.' He leaned over the table, pointing to the leftover sandwiches, whose edges had started to curl. 'I can get these into my pockets.'

She shuddered to think of all the farm germs in those pockets. 'We're fine leaving them here. I never knew you liked them so much.'

'I'm partial to anything someone else makes for me.'

That was true. Harriet couldn't recall James ever complaining about a meal. 'Bea does an afternoon tea, you know. Scones and sandwiches and everything. I go there sometimes after Zumba. Not for all that, just for a coffee. But we could do tea there some time. If you want.' In all the years they'd lived in the village, they'd never been for tea together. James didn't immediately strike one as the pinkie-finger-in-the-air type. Maybe she'd underestimated him.

'Whatever makes you happy. It's nice to see you like this.'

'I'm always happy in the city,' she told him.

'But I don't see you in the city.'

'That's because you never want to come here.'

'I'm sorry. I'll do it more.'

'But you're just doing it for me, not because you want to.'

'Exactly.' He squeezed her hand.

That felt good.

Chapter 22

Wednesday

Sophie jerked open the fridge door but there was nothing obvious to have for lunch. Only the remnants of PorkLoinGate.

Yet she wasn't keen on eating cereal like yesterday, and they were low on milk anyway. The car keys were on the worktop. Why shouldn't they go out? Dan would probably be in that office all morning.

She knocked. 'Dan?'

'Not now, Sophie!'

She could only just hear him beyond the solid oak door. 'But—'

'I said not fucking now. Jesus, what part of busy do you not understand?'

Sophie crept from the door. Why the *hell* didn't she know by now what would set him off? At least the children hadn't heard him.

Her hands trembled as she grabbed her handbag and went to fetch them from the barns.

There wasn't a leaf big enough to carry these feelings away downstream. She hadn't even done anything wrong; only knocked on the door to tell him where she was going. The fault was his.

She couldn't let Dan be hazardous to her health any more. She wouldn't.

Her hands had steadied by the time she reached the barn door. She listened to the children inside, chattering away to the goats – Artemis and a few others who were in quarantine. Then Katie began laughing. When Oliver joined her, it began to forge something in Sophie. She didn't want them to have parents who weren't kind and respectful to each other.

She might not be able to change the way Dan behaved – that would be up to him – but she could change how she reacted.

Sophie's rolling-over days were numbered.

Marion truly didn't seem to mind having Oliver and Katie underfoot every day, but that might be because she'd put them to work mucking out the enclosures. Sophie couldn't get them to pick up their socks off the floor, but for the goats they'd shovel dung. She'd have another go at the socks when they got back to London.

'Who wants to go to the falconry centre?' she called.

'Me!' Marion said along with the children.

'You're welcome to come,' Sophie said. 'That would be really nice, actually.'

'Thanks, but I've got work to do. You have fun, though.'

That was exactly what Sophie planned to do.

A warm wind from the open car windows blew everyone's hair all over the place while they sang along to 'Bohemian Rhapsody'. She'd managed to put Dan's outburst miles behind them. Even in spite of him, she'd felt better these past two weeks than she had in years. When was the last time? Maybe back during her first years working in London, when the world seemed open, fresh and all hers. Or at uni, surrounded by loads of friends, learning so many new things that she could almost feel her brain sparking with the activity.

She squirmed to realise that none of that happened with Dan. He would say their wedding day should be on her list. It would have been, if it hadn't been such a stressful time. Dan might have left the organising to her, but it wasn't like he didn't have a lot to say about every one of her ideas. Sophie saw pretty quickly that she didn't fit in very well with his vision, between her unsophisticated family and the wedding dress she chose (he overruled that for something more tasteful) to the terrifying idea of spending their honeymoon at an exclusive resort in the Seychelles where she'd have to dress up for every meal and probably wouldn't know what half the things on the menu were anyway. She had let him down so constantly that by the time their wedding day dawned, she couldn't wait to get it over with.

'Will we see bald eagles?' Oliver pointed towards the illustration on the falconry centre sign.

'I don't know, maybe. It's false advertising if not, promising birds that aren't even here. The picture should at least be accurate.' That kind of detail orientation would warm Harriet's heart. If Sophie cared a bit about Harriet's heart.

She shoved those thoughts from her mind.

They had to walk up a steep slope to reach the ancient-looking yellow stone building where the tickets were sold. 'One adult and two children,' she told the boy at the till. Despite it being summer, he wore a grey knitted beanie with his long blond fringe sticking out from it just so.

'You could book the experience, and then the admission price would be included,' he told them. 'Then you'd get to fly the birds, too. We haven't usually got tickets on the day but there's been a cancellation.'

Oliver gasped. 'Yes, please, can we, Mum, please?'

Look at that absolutely innocent face. Crafty upselling.

As they wandered around the enclosures looking at the birds, which she had to admit were impressive, she glanced at her phone. No missed calls. Not that she really expected Harriet to ring her back.

The sun shone on the semicircle of rustic wooden benches where people had started to gather at the back of the property. The murmur of conversation died down as a middle-aged man strode to the centre of the semicircle. He looked perfectly at home in his blue tartan shirt and flat cap. Perched on his gloved forearm was a breathtakingly beautiful bird. His deep-brown feathers glinted in the sunlight as he gripped the man's rough leather glove. Sophie stared into his unflinching gaze. He seemed to frown at her. No, it was probably just a case of resting bird face.

'Are you sure you want to have that bird land on you?' Her children acted like she was mad for even asking. What could be more fun than being clung onto by a deadly animal while their mother had a heart attack from worry? Nothing, clearly.

Katie gloved up first, then Oliver. Despite Sophie's worry about her children being carried off into a faraway nest to become breakfast for eagle chicks, they loved it.

Then it was Sophie's turn. 'Actually, I'm fine, thank you,' she told the flat-capped man. Her heart was already in her throat from watching her children. Perspiration started beading on her forehead. Pretending to sweep her hair back, she dashed it away. 'I'll just watch.' She should probably try to get a refund since she wasn't getting within ten feet of that bird. She'd seen enough David Attenborough programmes with Oliver to know what those deadly beaks and razor-sharp talons could do.

'He won't harm you.'

That was patently not true, when he'd just explained how these birds might live at the centre but they were still very much wild animals.

Yet she lived with a python, and no one could argue that those weren't wild animals, even if Spot did mostly lie curled up on her lap when she watched *Loose Women*.

Besides, this holiday felt like the place to try new things. Hadn't she run an entire charity event? A few dog-slob-bered cupcakes didn't change the fact that it had been a success. She'd had snails on her face. Surely a bird on her arm wouldn't be as bad. She just had to remember not to fling it off.

She sidled up to the man, who shimmied the bird from his glove to hers. 'It's not very heavy,' she said.

'He's full-grown,' he assured her. She gazed at the bird's glossy feathers. She was actually doing this! When Dan had suggested the falconry centre, she never imagined wanting to get anywhere near one of the big birds. Yet there she was, staring wild nature in the eye. Well, side-eyeing nature anyway, in case it got cross.

When the man blew his whistle, the bird pushed off from Sophie's arm. Everyone squinted into the sky to watch it gracefully circle the property. *How wonderful to be a bird*, she thought. Except for catching live rodents and tearing them up into little pieces for dinner and living on top of the whole family in a cramped nest. Still, the flying would be nice.

Later, as they finished looking at the enclosures, she glanced again at her phone. If she was honest with herself, she did miss talking to Harriet. This would be the exact kind of thing they'd text about. Harriet would probably send back a dossier on the subject. She smiled. Then she remembered that she was cross.

It was lunchtime when they got back to the house. 'We're home!' Sophie called as she unlocked the front door. 'Drop the bags in the kitchen,' she told the kids. 'I'll put them away.'

Oliver and Katie did exactly as they were told. Sophie heard the distinctive pop of a glass jar breaking as the shopping bags hit the tiled floor. Katie's hand flew to her mouth. 'Sorry, Mum!'

'It's all right, it was my fault. I didn't mean you should literally drop them.'

Sighing, she wet a sponge. Beetroot juice was already leaking from the bag.

'Who was murdered?' Dan asked as he stepped around the widening puddle.

So, he was in a good mood now. 'Professor Beetroot in the kitchen with a glass jar. Did you have to work all morning?'

'Yep. Just taking a break now.' He glanced over when her phone lit up. 'Text from Owen,' he said, as if she wasn't perfectly capable of reading.

She scrolled through the full message. 'He wants to have some people over for his birthday. That's okay, isn't it? I'll let Harriet know.'

'You two are talking a lot. What are you, best friends now?'

Not lately, she thought. She carefully lifted the sodden loaf of crusty bread from the bag. 'We picked up some lunch. As long as you like beetroot juice with your sandwich. I got ham and cheese. And some nice steaks for tonight.'

'I'm making pasta later.'

'Oh, well, I didn't know. I didn't see anything in the fridge. It'll keep till tomorrow, won't it? The children saw the gas grill outside, so I thought we could do a barbecue.'

Something funny passed over Dan's face. 'Anything else you'd like me to change for tonight?'

'Don't be like that, Dan, it's just a suggestion, because the weather's gorgeous. Make your pasta if you want to.'

'It's not *my* pasta, it's *our* pasta. I'll barbecue.' He made it sound like he was having to repaint the house.

'Never mind, I can do it,' she snapped.

'You cannot. When have you ever barbecued in your life?'

He was definitely in a funny mood. 'It's not rocket science. I think I can manage to turn on the grill and cook the meat. I'm familiar with how cooking works.'

'What are you doing shopping, anyway? I was supposed to do that.'

'Well, you didn't do it, did you? You've been in that office all week. I only picked up a few things.'

'That's pretty ungrateful, Soph.'

'I'm grateful. I just mean that you don't have to do everything for me. I can do things myself, too.'

'Pssh, no you can't, silly bean, but it's sweet that you want to try.'

Sophie's mouth dropped open. 'Don't patronise me, Dan.'

He shrugged. 'I just said I'll take care of it, but if you want to try then I'm not going to stop you.' She wanted to wipe the condescending look off his face. 'I'll be here to pick up the pieces. You didn't need to, that's all.'

'Why are we fighting when it's no big deal? It was on our way back.'

'What did the kids do while you had your treatment?'

The treatment! She'd completely forgotten. 'I cancelled it.' She'd have to use her credit card tomorrow to pay for it. She didn't need Dan being any tetchier than he was.

'Where were you, then?'

'I took the children to the falconry centre. You were right, it was fantastic.' She held her breath. He wouldn't be placated by the praise, but sod it. If he hadn't barked at her earlier, then he could have come with them.

'How could you do it without me when you know I wanted to go? I was the one who suggested it.'

'What am I supposed to do, sit around all day hoping you'll come out of that office so we can do something together? I did try to tell you but you shouted at me. It's our holiday, too, mine and the kids', and we do want to do things with you, but we can't when you're working all the time. We've only got a few days left here. I'm sorry, but if you're not going to participate in this holiday with us, then we'll have to do it on our own. I don't want to, but I will.'

'No, I'm sorry,' Dan said, taking Sophie's hands and pulling her to him. 'You're right, and I apologise. I shouldn't have shouted.' She could feel his body against hers. 'I haven't wanted to spend this much time with work. It's just all the emails that I've got to stay on top of. I don't want Jeremy to have to take on my work. He's got enough going on already. I'm trying to do two things at once, and clearly I'm not doing either one well enough. I'll barbecue tonight. We'll open a nice bottle of wine, sit in the garden and relax.'

Sophie *did* relax then. Dan had apologised. Maybe things would be all right.

Chapter 23

Wednesday

This time when Harriet stumbled over Owen in the kitchen, she didn't try to thrash him with a cricket bat. But she was surprised, given that he'd finally gone home yesterday. She hadn't even noticed him missing. Billie acted like Harriet had forgotten her own child, not a near stranger who was dossing in their holiday home. 'Back again?' she asked, watching him reach around the healthy cereals she'd bought to get Sophie's Frosties from the back of the cabinet. 'Those are pure sugar, you know.'

'It's why they taste so good.' He overfilled the bowl and slopped milk on the worktop. Then he sat opposite James, who was still in his sweatpants, reading his book.

Owen had barely snatched his bowl out of the way before Harriet was there with her soapy sponge. 'I didn't know you were coming back. It's all right,' she added, seeing his face fall. 'It's fine to be here. I didn't know, that's all. Do you want me to wash that for you?' She hadn't seen him out of the hoodie since they'd met. It made her glad they'd had a girl. From everything she'd heard from parents of boys, they needed to be prised out of clothing that could stand up on its own. Billie might not wear what Harriet wanted, but at least she was clean.

But clean or not, she'd barely spoken to Harriet, which thwarted all her plans to be forgiven by her daughter. She couldn't very well mime her apology. Sad face, tears dripping.

'What are you going to do today?' she asked Owen. Not that it was really her business. It just felt nice to have at least one teenager talking to her.

'Dunno. Just chill, I guess. What's Billie doing?'

The million-dollar question. 'I wish I knew, Owen.' Then, when he looked at her oddly, she added, 'She probably wants to chill, too. Chill is her middle name.' It wasn't. It was Charlotte. 'You can chill together, if you want.' She wished she could stop saying chill.

That's what she had scheduled for today, too, though. To chill with James. First, the London Transport Museum. James had suggested it, which gave her hope that he might enjoy this trip yet. As long as the pace was (don't say chill) slow enough for him. Then a two-hour session at one of the original 1930s public baths, followed by an early dinner and home to chill some more with the bottle of wine that she'd just put in the fridge to (do *not* say chill) cool.

Harriet was looking forward to relaxing, but James would need to hurry. 'Can you be ready in thirty minutes?' she asked him.

'Why, are they timed tickets or something?'

'Well, no, but we've got a lot to do today.'

'So much for chilling,' Owen muttered. James nodded, then shrugged when Harriet caught his eye.

'Why don't we just wander around today?' James asked. 'We don't always have to have a plan.'

Wander, thought Harriet. He'd forgotten who he was talking to. 'Where do you want to wander?'

'I don't know. It doesn't matter.'

'The recycling centre, then? How about Tesco's, or the car park behind B&Q? I think it does matter, James. Clearly it does matter.'

'Somewhere nice, then,' he conceded.

'Good. That's exactly what we'll do at the museum.' They were only going because he wanted to. 'Look lively, now, or we'll be late.'

Owen raised his eyebrow at James. 'Look lively,' he mimicked. 'Have fun chilling.'

Harriet wasn't sure what she'd expected of the London Transport Museum – more of a dingy depot, she supposed – but the old Covent Garden flower market building, with its ornate Victorian ironwork pillars and supports and soaring ceiling, was beautiful. As if the huge fan-shaped windows at one end weren't enough, the entire top storey was walled with glass, which let the sunshine flood in over the brightly painted vehicles below.

The old taxis, buses, trams and trolleys might not be her cup of tea, but at least James had made the suggestion. Even if he did try to get out of it. 'I'm glad you wanted to do this,' she told him. 'You know, you can plan just as well as I can. It doesn't always have to be me.' She had told him that a million times, but maybe, she conceded, in more of an exasperated grumble than a helpful tone. If this holiday had taught her anything, it was that she wasn't perfect, either. Ha, understatement of the year. 'I just mean that you can decide what we do any time you like.'

'As long as it fits with your schedule,' he said. 'How often does that happen?'

'How often do you bother trying?' she snapped. 'I only do a schedule because nobody else lifts a finger.' So much for helpful tones.

'Maybe we don't want our fingers bitten off,' he said.

This was going downhill fast. 'Maybe I'm pretty sick and flipping tired of being the only one you all rely on to do every single thing.'

James stopped them in front of a vintage trolleybus. 'Are you being serious? That's how you *like* it. And you're so good at it.'

'Of course I'm good at it. I've had years of practice.' She honestly couldn't pinpoint when James had started taking a back seat. She sighed. 'I know it's not all your fault.'

'Well, thanks for that,' he said.

'And you're not completely useless.'

'You flatterer.'

'I mean you *do* do things.'

He thought for a second. 'You mean spiders. And pancakes.'

Harriet nodded. 'And the barbecue, and the cars.' She could feel herself softening. 'You and Billie act like I'm Stalin most of the time, and I understand that it's easy to snipe about all the planning, but I only do it because nobody else does.'

A smile played around James's lips. 'You only do it because nobody else does? Are you sure it's not because you want to have complete control over everything?'

'Well, I'm not going to throw away my diary, am I? But yes, I'm saying it would be nice to share some of the planning.'

'I can do that,' he said. 'Even if I won't be as good at it as you.'

'I'd appreciate the effort, anyway,' she said.

'Do you want to catch spiders, too? I'm willing to share.'

Harriet gave a shudder.

Just then, James's mobile rang. He smiled as he answered. 'What's up, sweetheart? Yeah, great, of course. Mum can text you the address.' He covered his phone with his hand. 'What time is the spa? Billie wants to come.'

'It's booked from one thirty to three thirty, but I'll have to ring to see if I can add another person. She said she didn't want to come.'

'She does now,' he said.

'It's fine, James, I'm not saying she can't come, only that I need to add her to the booking.' This might mean a thaw in their relations. Billie wasn't usually keen on spending time with them any more than she liked being in a swimsuit. Which was silly because she had such a nice figure, but that was beside the point. The point was, Billie must not be too angry with her.

'I can ring the spa to add her if you give me the number,' said James when he'd hung up.

Harriet smiled. 'It's just as quick for me to do it. This time. But James, it's not just spas or museums or restaurant bookings. I need you to share the responsibility. Really share it, like we used to. Remember? I feel like I've lost my partner. Especially with Billie. Especially now, and I really need it.'

He was doing his peach stone frown. 'This has really got to you.'

'It hasn't got to me.'

'It has. You're never unsure about things.'

She was the least unsure person she knew, but this was more important than doing her job or planning holidays or calculating the fastest commute or telling James how to run his business. This was their daughter. 'You're right, I am. I've got ground to make up. This is bigger than The Bra Incident.'

That's what they all called it, always in implied capital letters.

It marked the exact time and place that Harriet became such an embarrassment to her daughter that she was banned from ever shopping in public with her again. Not that she wasn't an embarrassment before, just not an unforgivable one.

It was two days after Billie's fourteenth birthday and they'd gone to Cheltenham shopping. Harriet wouldn't have needed to rush them to get back in time for Zumba if they hadn't got such a late start because Billie refused to get out of bed. But she never admitted to her part in their little drama. If they'd had more time then Harriet wouldn't have been so impatient for Billie to try things on instead of talking with the group of friends she'd run into. Friends she saw every day at school, and who surely could have done the oh-my-god-what-are-you-doing-here-no-what-are-you-doing-here script a little quicker.

She still didn't see what the big problem had been. Her friends knew she wore a bra – they'd been changing with her for PE all year – so what was so horrible about bringing a few choices over to where they stood talking? Billie seemed to have no appreciation that they were in a rush. Just because it had been in the shop's café, and she may have been a bit far away when she held them up for Billie to see, she didn't need to act like Harriet had turned up modelling the lingerie over her jumper.

Billie still made Harriet buy all her bras online.

The spa was all that Harriet hoped it would be – retro and hot – but before they'd even started sweating properly, she had annoyed Billie.

'Jesus, Mum.' Billie shifted her towel further along the tiled bench where she, Harriet and James sat.

'What? All I said was that she's pretty.' Even whispering, Harriet's words echoed around the walls of the hammam.

Billie's already flushed face went redder. 'Keep your voice down. Jesus.' She scooted further away from Harriet.

Harriet followed. 'Stop Jesusing me, I'm taking an interest.'

'In women?' Billie hissed. 'Thanks, but you don't need to pimp for me.'

She couldn't win. When she'd shown her surprise about Billie being gay, she got cross. Now she was telling her how cool she was with it, yet Billie was still cross. 'I'm confused. Do you not want me to bring it up?'

'Do you want me to bring up your sex life?' Billie snapped.

'That's different. I didn't announce it to you.'

'Thank God. I'm going in the steam room.' She threw her towel over her shoulder. 'Don't follow me.' She left the hammam.

'I was only trying to show my support,' Harriet murmured as she stared after her daughter.

When James carried his towel to where she'd scooted in pursuit of their daughter, Harriet realised she'd covered quite a bit of ground. 'Don't fret, love,' he said, 'just give her time.'

But Harriet didn't think she had time. She could feel her daughter pulling away.

She ran her fingers under her eyes. Hopefully anyone looking at her would assume it was only perspiration she was wiping.

'But James, now she thinks I want to pimp her out to some sweaty woman.' When the sweaty woman frowned at her, she said, 'Sorry, no offence. I think there are extra towels in reception, though.'

James patted her thigh. 'Going after her right now won't help.'

She knew that, but she had to make things better before they got any worse. 'I'll just see that she's okay,' she said, taking her towel with her.

Harriet hated steam rooms, with their drippy walls, lung-stifling air and chewing gum reek. Billie probably knew that, she realised, as she opened the heavy glass door.

The steam was so thick that it took her a few seconds before she could even make out vague figures inside. 'Billie? I just want to make sure you're okay. Are you okay? Do you need anything?'

'Close the door,' came a manly whisper, 'you're letting the steam out.'

'I'm looking for my daughter,' Harriet explained.

More hisses. 'Close the door!'

Reluctantly, she stepped into the wall of steam. It was as bad as she remembered. 'Billie?' Sweat rivulets started trickling down her scalp. 'I can't see. Are you in here?' Gingerly she stepped further into the room, but it was so dim that she could barely see her own feet, let alone anyone else's. 'Billie?'

'For God's sake,' said someone, 'Billie, answer the woman if you're in here.'

Harriet caught a swift movement from the corner of the room. 'Way to go, Mum,' Billie snapped as she stormed out of the steam room.

'Excuse me for wanting to be sure you're okay.' Harriet trailed after her to the changing room. 'You're not leaving?'

'It's not exactly relaxing, is it? You should stay.' She found her locker.

'Tell me how to make this right. Please.'

Billie sat on one of the benches with her clothes balled up in her hands. 'I don't know, Mum. Be normal. Why can't you just be normal instead of trying to make this about how you react instead of about how I'm living? I'd prefer it if you'd shouted or, I don't know, told me God disapproves.'

'I'd never do those things.'

'Some of my friends' parents have. Look, all you have to do is accept it. That's all. Not follow me around trying to fix . . . I don't even know what you're trying to fix. Hopefully not me.'

'No! Not you. Me.'

'Then that's your deal to work on. This is me. Just accept that it's my life. Can you do that?'

'I'm so sorry.'

'Go back to Dad,' Billie said when Harriet tried to hug her. 'I'll see you later.'

Harriet went home with wide open pores, a headache from the heat and an idea forming in her mind.

'Sophie rang, and I missed it!' she said when she turned her phone back on. She'd left her a voicemail before heading off to the museum. She must not be angry any more. But as she listened to the message, her smile faded. Owen had texted, Sophie relayed, asking if he could have a few friends over for his birthday. Sophie had told him it was fine with her but that Harriet might find it too messy, so he needed to check.

She ended the call with nothing more than a curt thank you.

Of course a teenager's party would be too messy, but that wasn't the point. Owen could stage the ultimate cage fight in their kitchen and Harriet wouldn't object, if it meant getting back into Sophie's good books.

Chapter 24
Thursday

Sophie peered again through the front window to be doubly sure that Dan was still out on his run. Then she crept into the office and eased the door closed behind her. Like the rest of the house, the room was countrified chic, kitted out with expensive-looking rugs and a few tasteful paintings. The muted shades of green of the curtains and reading chairs gave it a sense of calm, and there wasn't so much as a stray paper in sight. The few items on the dark old oak desk – a pen, stapler, in-tray – were perfectly lined up.

It wasn't James's office after all. Of course it wasn't. She'd been in James's office in the barn. This was Harriet's. It hadn't occurred to her because . . . because she'd assumed the office would be the man's domain. She was ashamed of herself.

At first, she didn't see Dan's briefcase. She had to open nearly every cabinet and drawer until she found it. She glanced again at the door. She shouldn't be doing this. She wasn't even sure what she was looking for.

She hoisted the heavy leather case over to the desk and opened it. The Khan file was right at the front. The one he'd told Laxmi to sign out. And behind it were Mason and Cipriani.

Dan had taken the files from his office. That's exactly what had landed him in court, according to Harriet.

She didn't know what he was doing, but he definitely shouldn't be doing it.

She could make all the excuses she wanted. She could mentally float Harriet down every stream between here and London. She couldn't avoid the truth any more.

Her hands shook as she tapped Dan's name into her phone's Google search. At first, only links to Dan's firm and a few articles about notable trials he'd (mostly) won came up. She added a few more search terms. Awful-sounding ones like *intimidation. Accused. Destroying evidence.*

It was all there. The names matched. The firm matched. Her husband matched. Her heart sank further with every result she clicked on: Dan being investigated over missing witness statements. Dan being cleared – reluctantly from the sound of the quotes from the magistrate. Most importantly, Dan not telling her a word about it.

Carefully replacing the case, she made sure nothing else was disturbed and left the office.

Because she didn't know what else to do, she grabbed the car keys from the kitchen table. It was best if she wasn't here when Dan got back. Otherwise she might call him Dodgy Dan. 'Let's go horse riding,' she told Katie. 'Come on, Oliver, we'll get a lesson for you, too. I don't need to be back for my treatment till after lunchtime.' They were staring at her like she'd just split the atom. 'I bet you can't swing a dead cat without hitting a stable around here. Oh, sweetheart,' she said when she saw Oliver's expression, 'it's just a figure of speech, I'm sorry. I promise there are no dead cats involved.'

Katie couldn't stop looking at her as she rang the number of the first local stables that came up. Sophie loved that look, like she was the cleverest mum on the planet. She'd seen it less and less over the years. Teens were harder to impress than children. Give a six year old a biscuit and she'll think you've just pulled a rabbit out of a hat.

But the doubts started niggling before she'd even finished reading out the long number on the front of her credit card. It had been ages since she'd been on a horse. What if she'd forgotten what to do, or it ran away with her or threw her into the fence and she ended up in traction?

Katie wouldn't be so awestruck then.

She tried not to listen, but the doubts were whining at her in Dan's voice.

Well, you can just piss off! she thought. Right. Back to the stream. She watched as Dan floated off on a leaf (along with a fat pony who wouldn't do what she wanted).

This mindfulness stuff was fantastic.

The stables were down one of those long, winding, barely paved roads. Brambles and summer lilacs scratched at the sides of the car. She hoped Dan had the extra insurance. Then she sort of hoped he didn't.

Once they'd parked, she kept hold of Oliver's collar so he wouldn't run ahead and accidentally end up underhoof. The shine would go right off her little bid for independence if she lost one of the kids. Katie stayed close, though. She was often shy around new people. Sophie grinned at her. 'This will be fun!'

The stables bustled with children who all looked like they knew more about riding than she did. Nearly everyone had jodhpurs and proper boots instead of her family's jeans and trainers. She should have checked Harriet's cupboards. She'd bet there were entire riding outfits there. Labelled and everything.

'Watch the pile!' She pulled Oliver away just in time. 'We're definitely in the country now.'

The woman who ran the stables found velvet helmets for each of them. 'Can you please take a picture of us?' Sophie asked.

Katie pulled her long plait over one shoulder so it shimmered down her front. With an arm around each child, Sophie beamed. If she wasn't careful, she'd float away on this feeling. Despite what she'd just seen in Dan's briefcase, she was on top of the world.

Then she was on top of her horse – a big brown and white one named Blaze. That wasn't quite such a comfortable feeling. Every time Blaze shifted from foot to foot, Sophie got the vertiginous feeling that her saddle was slipping sideways. 'Are you sure it's on tight?' she asked the instructor for the third time. For the third time, the instructor said yes, it was.

What was making her so anxious? Blaze hadn't even taken a step yet. At worst, she'd slide three feet off a standing horse to the ground. Besides, she did know how to ride. She ought to be at least as confident as riders who only came up to her waist.

As soon as the instructor led Oliver's pony towards the ring, Sophie's nerves disappeared. Blaze, and Katie's pretty dun horse, followed without so much as a giddy-up from their riders.

For the next fifty-seven minutes, Sophie Mitchell was reminded of who she used to be. Amid the instructor's gentle guidance, she caught glimpses of a long-lost and dearly loved friend. Every clip-clop of Blaze's hooves drummed up another snippet of her old self, and each time she shared a laugh with her children, a bit of the old Sophie returned.

By the time she climbed down from her saddle, her bum was aching but her heart sang. She remembered, and she liked it.

So maybe she was a little shorter with Dan than she meant to be when she rang him after.

'You just took the children and left,' he said.

'Dan, I didn't kidnap them.' She watched them petting the horses in the stalls. 'You were out running. I took them horse riding. We've finished now. I want to stop in the village on the way back, so sort yourself out for lunch. We'll eat something there.'

The silent treatment loomed large. She could practically hear him seething.

She wrestled down the pandering urge. It was a feisty little so-and-so.

Not this time, she thought. 'I assume you heard me.'

'Loud and clear.' Scorn oozed from Dan's every word.

'Good. I'll see you later this afternoon if you're around.' Click.

She couldn't remember ever hanging up on him before.

She turned her phone off, breathed in the dung-tinged air and felt happy again. She called to the children. 'How about lunch at the tea shop?'

When Bea saw them, she acted as if her grandchildren had come to visit. 'Come 'ere, my lovelies!' She hugged Oliver, then Katie. 'Been riding, have you?'

'How did you know?' Sophie wondered. She hadn't even thought of it till this morning. If the government ever needed a faster mobile phone network, it could always upgrade to the village grapevine.

'You smell of horse,' Bea said.

'Oh, of course, I'm so sorry!' The other customers wouldn't appreciate that. Instinctively, she clamped her arms to her sides.

'No, no, it's fine. Nice clean smell. Now, sit down and tell me how it was. Wait, do you want to order first?'

Sophie was starving, though she wasn't sure quite why. It was the horse who'd done all the work.

The clouds had rolled in while they were taking their lesson, but it didn't make the tea shop any less inviting now. The pastel-painted tables and chairs were just as cheerful, while conversation hummed around them. She wasn't surprised to see a few of the same women as last time. If she had a place like this close by, she'd be their most loyal customer.

She reached for her phone to check the time. Then she remembered it was off. It slid back into her bag. 'I should quickly stop into Delia's after to pick something up for Harriet's birthday,' she told the children as Bea brought their sandwiches.

She owed Harriet an apology.

Bea rolled her eyes. 'Suppose I should get something, too.'

'For Harriet?' She couldn't mean Harriet.

'Aye, she's an odd duck but we're all doing our best for James's sake.'

An odd duck didn't sound so bad. Maybe Harriet wasn't quite as disliked as Sophie had first thought. Except by Delia, the would-be groom snatcher.

'For me?' Dan picked up the gift that Delia had wrapped for Harriet. There was no trace of his earlier irritation. Maybe hanging up on him did him good.

Sophie plucked the little box from his fingers. His hair needed a wash, she noticed, and he hadn't changed out of his running shorts. Someone's standards were slipping.

'Oh, be*have*!' he said, smiling. Sophie's mind flashed back to watching that Austin Powers movie, when she and Dan adopted the phrase. It was their inside joke for years. Only it wasn't a joke, was it? All that time, it had been a command, and she'd laughed over it.

Well, based on what she'd seen in his briefcase, he should be the one behaving. 'It's not for you, unless you're in the market for a pretty new necklace. It's for Harriet's birthday.'

'You've become awfully cosy with someone you hardly know.'

'Because I got a little gift for someone's birthday?' She shrugged. 'Then yes, I suppose so.'

'I don't think I like her influence on you.'

Funny, because as cross as Sophie had been about Harriet dishing the dirt on him, she had no problem with her influence. 'I'm sorry about that.'

'You shouldn't plan to carry on this, this friendship, or whatever you want to call it, once we're back in London. It's fine to talk while we're in their house, but really, Soph, you've got nothing in common.'

'Actually, we have a lot in common. And I'll pick my own friends, thank you.'

'You can do better than some uptight woman who's on the spectrum.'

'Dan! She's not.'

'Come on.'

'She's not.' What a bloody know-it-all.

'She so clearly is. You only have to look around this place. You said it yourself. She labels her pillowslips.'

Sophie felt terrible about that. Who was she to make flippant judgements – medical judgements – like that? 'You don't know what you're talking about.'

'You don't have to attack me,' he said. 'I'm not saying there's anything wrong with it.' His petulance increased with every word. 'I was just stating a fact.'

'Well, it's not a fact, and you're wrong. I asked her and she said she's not.'

'Oh, right. Soph, you don't ask an insane patient if he's insane.'

'Harriet isn't insane!'

'I'm making a point.'

'Dan, you can't go throwing around diagnoses about people. You're not qualified, and even if you were, it's not your place. And actually, she is the person who would know because she knows herself better than anyone else.' Although to be fair, Dan didn't know that he was a bit of an arsehole, so maybe he did have a point.

'Why are you smiling?'

'Just thinking about something,' she said, turning away from him to hide her smirk.

Chapter 25

Thursday

There wasn't a thing left in Sophie's house to sort, stack, label or tidy away. Not so much as one overstuffed drawer. Harriet walked through the house, from the pristine kitchen with its bare worktops, sensibly arranged cabinets and sparkling appliances, to the hallway that had taken her breath away that first day. Now it was free of clutter. She'd even thinned out the coats on the hooks – two adult ones and two for the children. She'd probably picked the wrong ones, but that wasn't the point. It was just to show them how tidy it could be, and how nice it was to be tidy.

Upstairs was just as neat, except for Spot's room. She wasn't about to go near that thing.

So, her work was done. But instead of enjoying the accomplishment like she usually did, she wanted more to do. That way, she wouldn't have to think. Her eyes found her usual go-to places. The kitchen cabinet fronts and all the squares there for counting. The staircase (spindles, spindles and more spindles). The windowpanes in the living room. But her mind wouldn't settle.

What she really wanted was to talk to a friend. She knew she could talk to James, and she had been, but he was so damn reasonable about everything that it just made her feel more out of control than ever.

Her London friends were all working. She'd never ring their offices on a personal phone call. She'd hate having them do that to her.

Even if Sophie was still cross with her, on a mum-to-mum level she had to understand.

She answered! 'Billie is gay,' she said as soon as Sophie said hello.

'Uh-huh, okay, thanks for telling me, I guess.'

'No, I mean we've just found out.'

'Oh. Oh, I see.'

Harriet didn't like the silence that followed on the line. 'Hello?'

'Hello, sorry. I was just thinking of what to say next. What do you want me to say? Is everything okay?'

Yes, that was what she wanted Sophie to say. A simple question to let her thoughts tumble out. And did they ever tumble. Harriet replayed the whole scene from the other day. Her ugly thoughts included. Sophie got everything, warts and all. 'I'm prejudiced, aren't I? I'm a homophobe.'

'No, you're not! You were surprised, that's all, caught off guard. I'd have reacted just as—'

'Badly.'

'I was going to say that I'd have been just as stunned. This is a huge thing to take in. I don't mean that she's gay, because lots of people are gay. It's no big deal.'

'Clearly it is to me.' She couldn't expect Billie to forgive her when she'd probably never forgive herself.

'Oh, I'm sorry, nothing I say is coming out right today. What I mean is that Billie will be fine, and you and she will be, too. You'll see. You've only just found out. You need time to get used to the idea. Anybody would, when it means changing how you thought Billie would live her life. That's not easy. We all imagine how our children's futures will be. I do it all the time. You'll have to adjust some of that now.'

'Like what?' Harriet braced herself. There were probably dozens of things she hadn't yet tortured herself with.

'Well, I guess if Billie gets married then there probably won't be a groom on top of the wedding cake.'

Sophie had hit the nail on the head. Billie's whole future would be different now. Not even James had completely understood that. 'It is an adjustment, isn't it?' she said. 'Of course the most important thing is for Billie to be happy and loved. Of course it is. I just thought I knew what that would look like. Sophie, I think I'm in mourning. Isn't that stupid, when nobody's died. I'm having to change my dreams for her, which probably aren't realistic anyway. Nobody even gets married these days.'

'I understand.' The kindness in Sophie's voice made Harriet want to cry. 'I guess this holiday has thrown up all kinds of adjustments for both of us.'

Selfish Harriet, she hadn't even asked how Sophie was. 'What's your adjustment? Hello? You don't have to tell me if you don't want to.'

She had to strain to hear Sophie's answer. 'I'm not sure I want to say it out loud,' she said. 'It's like Beetlejuice. If I say it then I might conjure it up.'

Like in that old 1980s film with Michael Keaton? What a ridiculous idea. Sophie was smarter than that. Any rational human being knew there was no such thing as fate or influencing the universe by putting sodding wishes on a pinboard to make them come true. 'You don't have to tell me. Not because it tempts fate or any such nonsense, but because you just might not want to.'

But clearly Sophie did want to. 'This isn't what I expected on holiday,' she said. 'I wanted to eat too much pasta and relax, not have a relationship crisis. Harriet, I'm afraid Dan might be an arsehole.'

'Wow, don't hold back. How do you really feel?'

They both laughed, but then what she went on to tell Harriet was no laughing matter.

'I know we've not known each other long,' Harriet said when Sophie had finished cataloguing all the insidious ways Dan controlled her, 'but I'm here for you. Whatever you need.' An ear, a shoulder. Referral to a good divorce lawyer.

'Thank you. Isn't it weird how it feels like we've been friends for longer than two weeks?' Sophie said. 'And I'm really sorry for reacting the way I did before. I know you weren't trying to be mean. You're just direct sometimes.'

Finally, she understood! 'I assumed you knew about Dan,' said Harriet. 'Or at least that you'd want to know.'

'It was a shock, though I guess it shouldn't have been. I looked it up, too. He's been acting strangely about work since we've been here, hiding away in the office and being so cross with his assistant. Something is making him nervous. I'm afraid he's doing it again.'

'What will you do now? I mean about you and Dan, not what's going on with his job.'

'Nothing drastic right this second,' said Sophie. 'There are the children to think about, for one thing. They'd need to be prepared . . . I can't believe I'm really talking about this! Part of me keeps hoping that my wonderful husband will wake me up with kisses and tell me it's all been a terrible dream.'

'Not too many kisses,' Harriet said, 'or one thing might lead to another and the last thing you need is to get pregnant now.'

'Wow, Harriet, now who's telling it like it is?'

'Too direct again?'

Sophie laughed. 'Not from you. I'd expect nothing less. You don't need to worry about that, anyway. Dan had a vasectomy after Oliver was born. He always knew he only wanted two.'

A vasectomy! 'How many did you want?' Harriet wondered.

'I probably would have been a baby machine,' she said. 'I couldn't get enough of being pregnant. I didn't even mind the birth or the lack of sleep or the poo bombs or teething. I loved having babies, the way they're so warm and snuggly. I craved the feeling, the smell.'

'That's just the hormones your body makes so you don't eat your baby,' Harriet said.

'I like the emotional explanation better, thanks. But Dan didn't want another one, and then he went off and had the vasectomy, so there wasn't a decision to make any more.'

'And then he let you have Owen,' she added. 'Like giving a child a puppy.'

Sophie sighed. 'Hmmph. I guess so.'

'Yes, hmmph,' Harriet agreed. It was bad enough that Dan had unilaterally taken the possibility of more children so definitively off the table. But if he'd had a vasectomy, then why would he need those condoms she'd found behind the towels? He wouldn't, was the answer, at least not with his wife. Which meant that Dan was practising safe sex with someone else.

Harriet wasn't about to mention that now. What she'd viewed before as straightforward information-sharing about Dan's activities was, she now realised, probably a little insensitive. Sophie had enough other ammunition against her husband. No need to hurt her with this revelation unless she really needed to.

*

You can do this, Harriet told herself, drawing her eyeliner in a swish that perfectly matched the other eye. Nobody was more expert at what James liked best. She couldn't give him his goats and countryside tonight, but she'd do the next best thing. The *better* thing, in her opinion. The raspberry-red lipstick she smoothed on made her blonde highlights stand out. James might be a farmer at heart, but he was partial to a red lip. Tonight, James would get exactly what he wanted.

He did a double take when she sauntered into the kitchen. She smoothed the front of her best dress – yellow, fitted and flirty – and fiddled with the strap on her wedges. James was possibly the only man in the Western hemisphere who actually liked the way wedge heels looked on women. Possibly they reminded him of hooves. Harriet didn't want to ask. 'We'll need to leave by six. We're having dinner at a farm.' So nonchalant, like they regularly ate with animals.

James's eyes were alight as he gave her a lopsided smile. 'What did you do?'

'Only booked a table for us.'

'In the farmyard?'

'No, James, that would be daft. In the restaurant. In a farmyard.' She was smiling now, too. It was an inspired idea. It had only taken seventy-five minutes of googling to make it happen. 'There's live music, too. Jazz, I think, and maybe we can hang out with the animals first. So you can get your goat fix.'

She meant that to be a joke, but James's eyes glazed over with the anticipation of being reunited with the hairy beasts.

'S'pose we shouldn't be here for Owen's party anyway,' he said.

'It's not a party, it's just a few of his friends coming over.'

James pursed his lips but said nothing more.

The approach to the farm did look rather enchanted, especially after skittering past council estates and wholesale knock-off handbag shops on the way from the Tube.

Summer's deep-green trees arched overhead and a myriad of mismatched plant pots, troughs and trellises bloomed with bright flowers along the cobbled path. Harriet noticed tall glass candle lanterns dotted along the way. The scene would be especially magical in flickering candlelight a few hours from now.

But by then the animals would be tucked up in bed, or hayloft or hutch or whatever they slept in, and they wouldn't be able to go into the farm. Which would be just fine by Harriet – she wasn't keen to navigate droppings in open-toed sandals – but tonight wasn't about her.

They let themselves in through the large weathered wooden gate and spent a pleasant enough half-hour with the animals as they bobbed and scratched, bleated, hopped, wallowed, mooed, quacked and hee-hawed.

James caught her looking at the time. 'How much have you allocated?'

'Thirty minutes.' She scanned the hay-strewn enclosures. Three fluffy-footed rare-breed chickens scratched in one corner. Another chancer loitered by the pay-over-the-odds-for-a-dusty-handful-of-feed machine. There were more white ducks. Did seven make a team? A raft? A paddling? There'd been four brown floppy-eared rabbits and five, no, six guinea pigs. That made eleven feathered and ten furred. The furs have it. No, she mustn't get started down that road. 'You've seen everything, so that's sufficient, isn't it?'

'Sufficient. On to the next activity,' he said. 'Got it.' He sounded good-natured about keeping to her schedule. So far, so good.

She wasn't keeping time for no reason. She'd got them a table for drinks in the cosy open area before their dinner reservation. Starting four minutes ago.

The waitress wasn't bothered by their tardiness, though, so Harriet acted like she wasn't, either. Tonight was all about reminding James how much fun they used to have, not keeping to a strict schedule (at least as far as James knew).

The outside bit where they sipped their sloe gin fizzes was full of trendy twenty-somethings. Not that she wanted to be that age again, but she would like to roll back from the precipice of forty-five. Forty-five years old. She remembered thinking at twenty that she'd get her lifespan all over again before she reached forty. Now she was past that. All of the life expectancy calculators she'd tried did predict that she'd get another lifespan, but who knew? Without seeing the assumptions that went into their models, she wasn't sure she could trust them.

The dinner menu was all velouté this and essence of that. There were at least half a dozen things she wouldn't put money on knowing what they tasted like.

'What are you having?' she asked.

He scanned the entire menu, which he'd just done two minutes ago. 'Steak and chips or sea bass.'

'Order the steak and I'll get the sea bass so we can share,' she said, just to watch his reaction. 'Only kidding. But I am having the sea bass.' James hated sharing his food. You'd never think he was an only child the way he guarded every meal. When they first went out, Harriet made the mistake of suggesting tapas restaurants. She loved eating that way, picking the tastiest morsels instead of having to commit to a single dish that just made her envious of what everyone else had.

That was the sort of thing couples learned about one another early on, she supposed. Sharing plates versus main courses, how they squeezed the toothpaste tube or the way they put the loo paper on the roll. Then there were the million other quirks and habits revealed over a lifetime of living together. Yet, even after so much time, James could still surprise her. She knew that he always put his socks on before his jeans so he didn't have to pull the legs up over his sturdy calves, but now she also knew that he wore his belt one notch looser than he really needed to. That was because his boxers sometimes shifted uncomfortably while he was working, and he didn't want to offend Marion by unbuckling to make adjustments. Although a sneaky reach-in probably wasn't ideal either, it was typically kind of James to want to spare his colleague.

Inside, the restaurant was more canteen than cosy, but with three empty sloe gin fizz glasses before they'd even sniffed the wine, it didn't matter. 'You should hear what Sophie told me today,' she confided as their burrata starters turned up – oozy, creamy, buttery-tasting perfection.

James clasped his big hands to his knees. 'Do tell me!'

'Don't make fun or I won't.' But she did.

The mirth in James's expression drained away. 'That poor woman. What will she do?'

'I hope nothing drastic until she's thought everything through,' Harriet said. Not that she shouldn't leave the bastard once she had a solid plan. 'She's only now real-ised how long it's been happening. Evidently this holiday triggered something.' It was a good thing Harriet wasn't a superstitious person, who might wonder whether relation-ships went to die in their village.

They watched the jazz quartet setting up around the upright piano on the stage area that took up one corner.

'Now she's looking all the way back at their entire marriage,' she added. 'He stopped her from working, you know. Not directly, but the way he undermined her makes it more sinister.'

They were quiet while they finished their starters. Then the singer introduced the quartet to the groovy *tsth-tsth-tsth-tsth-tsth* of the drummer's snare and *bwow wow wow* of the upright bass. 'Do you think anyone ever remembers the musicians' names?' Harriet wondered once they'd begun playing properly and their main courses arrived.

'Nope,' he said, 'they're just those guys we heard that time at that place.' They watched a few couples get up to dance. 'I am sorry about Sophie.'

'Me too, but it's better she knows something's wrong now. There's no sense in living in la-la land.' She swallowed down a thought that was too close to home. 'How's your steak?' *Get back on target, Harriet.*

Instead of answering, James carefully cut another piece and swirled it around in the Béarnaise sauce. Then he held the fork across the table. 'Try.'

'Seriously?' What had got into him tonight? She opened her mouth so he could feed her the steak. 'Mmm.' But it was much more than flavoursome goodness that she was savouring.

Their plates were cleared when James asked her to dance. 'Your toes are tapping,' he said. 'Want to?'

'What's brought all this on?' she teased. 'Sharing your food, volunteering to dance? I feel like I don't even know who you are any more.'

He caught her smile and lobbed it back. 'I know I don't always seem like I appreciate all the effort you go to. Like tonight. You wouldn't eat at a farm in a million years if it weren't for me. Just because it's not always my thing doesn't mean I don't appreciate how hard you try to make everything perfect. I do.' He stood up and held his hand out to her. 'Let's dance.'

They could barely move with all the other couples on the floor, but there, folded into his arms, she never wanted to lose this. Nose whistling, slow talking, filthy rucksack wearing, Waitrose rejecting aside, James was a good egg. She only had to think about the way he'd handled Billie's news to know that. 'This reminds me of when we used to like each other,' she murmured.

'Me too.' His arms tightened around her.

Chapter 26
Thursday / Friday

Harriet and James walked together onto Sophie's road behind three lively teens. The boys' glances darted back at them like they feared being robbed. That must mean she had street cred! But her delight ebbed away as they followed the boys through Sophie's wrought-iron gate, up her steps and into her front hall.

The house was heaving with kids. 'This is bad,' she shouted to James. She could feel the music thumping in her chest.

'Bad as in good?' he shouted back.

'Bad as in liability. It's not even our house!' Then she spotted Owen heading for the kitchen. 'Owen!'

Instead of slinking away from the danger in her voice, he bounded up to her and clasped her in his arms. Then he threw his arms around James. 'Come and join the party!'

'Owen, we thought you were just having a few friends over,' she said.

'I know, it's bangin'! Look how many friends I've got!' he gurned at them.

'It is bangin'!' James said.

'You don't even know what you're saying,' she told James.

'That's very nice, Owen,' she said, 'but what I meant was, we didn't think it was going to be this big.'

Owen shrugged. 'Shit happens.'

'Where's Billie?'

Owen gestured down the hall. 'Hey, you'll love this.' He shook two pills from a little plastic bag and dropped them into James's hand. They had smiley faces on them.

'What is it?' Harriet asked.

'E.'

She looked up just in time to see Billie watching them. 'My parents doing drugs. I never thought I'd see it.'

'We are not, and you'd better not be, either.'

'I don't do drugs, Mum. But Jesus, I wish you would. Please, I beg you. You need them.'

'You'd better not be,' Harriet repeated.

Billie put her face close to Harriet's. 'Look at my eyes. Normal pupils, see? Now look at Owen's.' She pulled a compliant Owen in front of her. Owen's nearly black eyes gazed happily into Harriet's face. 'Huge pupils. That's drugs versus no drugs. You're welcome. But seriously, do it, Mum.' With that she walked back towards the kitchen.

'Should we?' James asked when their daughter was definitely out of earshot.

Harriet scoffed.

'Come on, have you ever?'

He knew she hadn't. That was definitely an early-on couples conversation.

He grasped her hand. 'Let's do it. Nothing will happen. We're safe in the house. What do you say?'

Harriet examined her stance on drugs. She wasn't anti, per se, as long as it wasn't Billie doing them. They'd never held any appeal for her, tripping or toking or snorting or whatever it was called. Harriet didn't need to be out of control to feel good. Quite the opposite, actually.

Although being in control hadn't done her any favours lately, either, had it? 'How do we know it's safe?'

'Look at everyone else. I think they're all on them.'

Harriet glanced into the faces nearby. Huge pupils looked back. 'Maybe a half.' She couldn't believe she was about to take drugs! 'Let's get a drink first.'

'If there's anything left,' James said.

But most of the kids clutched cans or bottles. She didn't see anyone drinking wine. That was, they discovered when they went upstairs, because Owen had stashed their bottles from the kitchen up in their bedroom. Harriet pushed the door closed behind them, muffling the music from below and hopefully keeping their daughter from seeing her parents do drugs.

James broke the smiley-faced pill in two. 'You take the bigger half,' she said. 'You're bigger. Ready, steady, go!' They both swallowed the pills down with grimaces. 'I hope the high is better than the taste,' James said.

'No glasses,' she said as James picked up a bottle of red.

'Ah,' he said, grabbing their toothbrush mugs from the bathroom. 'How's that for ingenuity?'

'Nice one, but give them a wash first.' She wasn't keen on shiraz with notes of minty freshness.

They sat together on Sophie's quacky bed sipping their wine. It was better being upstairs anyway. Nobody wanted parents like them hanging around. And it *was* Owen's birthday. She wondered if anyone had bought him a cake. Hopefully so, although he probably wouldn't be too upset without one tonight. 'They don't seem like bad kids,' she mused. 'Normal.' Then she cringed. What did she mean by normal these days, anyway? 'Are we being irresponsible?' The bass was pounding through the floorboards.

'Why? Just because we're on drugs while kids drink in our house?' James laughed. 'This isn't like us.'

'I kind of like it,' she said.

'Me too.'

'Why don't I run us a bath?' She'd meant to schedule in a sexy bathscapade earlier in the week. Sophie had one of those Jacuzzi jobs with the water jets.

When she came out of the en suite, James asked, 'What's Ecstasy supposed to feel like?'

She bounced back onto the bed beside him. 'Why? Do you feel something? What is it? It's a happy pill, isn't it?'

'Supposed to be,' he said. He didn't look any happier than usual.

She read aloud the information she found on Google – wondering if she could get into trouble for going on websites about illegal drugs – but neither of them could definitively say they were high.

Harriet was starting to feel something, though. Confidence, maybe, that everything would turn out okay. And anticipation tickling her tummy. Whether that was the drug, or just having been on a great night out together, she wasn't sure.

It *had* been a great night, she thought, gazing at James. His eyes were more beautifully blue than usual. They were certainly darker, with only her bedside reading lamp turned on.

The lamp wasn't the only thing that was turned on. Objectively, there wasn't anything sexy about James reclining like that, propped up against the pillows with his long legs stretched out. He had his shoes on the bed, for goodness' sake! Yet he looked so relaxed and happy. Even dirtying the duvet, he was everything she wanted him to be. She could just eat him up. 'Want a bath?' she asked.

Bathing together always looked sexy in films, but it definitely wasn't comfortable for normal-sized adults. Even in Sophie's big tub, getting both their bodies under the water took some effort.

James sat with his chin on his knees. Harriet's bum squeaked on the bottom when she leaned forward to turn on the hot water tap. 'That wasn't me.' She turned the tap off a little. Otherwise the tub would overflow.

All of a sudden, the tickle in her tummy swelled, travelling up her body until it enveloped her entire head. She let out an enormous sigh as euphoria flooded, flooded, flooded her. She giggled. When she looked at James, he was grinning.

'You too?'

It was happening!

The most enormous feeling of calm washed over her, as if she was being cushioned inside a warm loaf of bread. It pressed down on her. She sighed again. 'Wow.'

'This is . . . wow!' James said.

Harriet squeezed some bubble bath into the tub. She could feel James's foot against her shin. The water was beginning to heat up. The bubbles churned as she shifted around so that she could lie with her back against James's chest. When his arms enveloped her, it felt so *good*. His hands caressing her body sent shivers through her.

Then his hand found the Jacuzzi control panel on the side of the tub. The jets were unnervingly well-aimed, but not unpleasant. 'It's like being in a car wash!' They both started to laugh as the bubbles multiplied.

The foam grew. And grew and grew. If she wasn't laughing so much, she might have turned off the jets. Then again, she might not have, because who was she to try to control bubbles?

Something else was growing along with the bubbles. 'James, are you happy to see me?'

'It seems so.' His voice was low behind her ear.

But with the best will in the world, they weren't going to have sex in that position. She squeaked again – her heel, this time – as they got themselves out of the tub.

They didn't even bother drying off. It didn't seem to matter that the sheets would get soaked. They could always wash them tomorrow.

They fell, kissing, into bed, their bodies sliding against one another in the most delicious way, languid, exploring. They had all night. No need to rush. Every touch seemed to ignite nerve endings she'd forgotten she had.

Just as Harriet started to level off, another wave of euphoria hit her. They both found themselves laughing for absolutely no reason other than it was wonderful to be alive at that very moment, and together. It was wonderful to be together.

Harriet did hear people on the stairs, but she didn't pay much attention. It was a party. There were dozens of kids in the house. Of course it was noisy.

'This is above the kitchen!' she heard someone cry. Though the sound was muffled because she was under the covers. James clamped her head with his hands as he bolted upright.

'What the hell, Owen!' James said.

Harriet scrambled up his torso to peep out over the top of the duvet.

Half a dozen kids stood in their bedroom. No, seven, eight, nine. More were crowding in.

She had to agree with James. 'What the hell, Owen!'

But Owen wasn't listening. He went straight into the bathroom with the first of the other kids. 'It's the bath!' he shouted out. 'Shit!'

'What's happened?' Harriet was aware that she was naked under the duvet.

Owen's feet were dripping with suds when he came out with an armload of towels. 'You left the tap on.'

That's when Harriet noticed the water spreading across the bedroom floor. Thank goodness it wasn't carpeted.

Harriet and James creased up with laughter as soon as they looked at each other.

'Nice one, Mum,' Billie said. 'So irresponsible.' But she was smiling.

Harriet smiled back.

Being out of control wasn't nearly as scary as she'd imagined.

Harriet had no right to feel as good as she did when she woke the day after the party. Google had been very clear about that, yet she bounced out of bed. Comedown, shmumdown.

Good thing she hadn't slept the whole day away. They needed to get the emergency builders in to fix Sophie's ceiling. It was the least she could do after leaving the bath running.

She giggled again thinking about last night. They'd been like teenagers! No – even the teens were more responsible. They were the ones who'd mopped up all the water from the bathroom and bedroom. She remembered seeing the towels hanging on the clothesline outside when she went down to the kitchen. The house wasn't Harriet-neat, but it wasn't as bad as it could have been. The cans and bottles were in recycling bags and most of the glasses were in the dishwasher. She added the pod and turned it on. She'd mop – a favourite pastime – then wait to hoover till everyone was up. It could be a while. Owen had still been wide awake at 4 a.m. when she and James had finally gone to bed. She wouldn't see Billie till at least noon.

Most of the sofa cushions were nearly on the floor. She busied herself putting them back where they belonged.

Someone had dropped a mobile phone down the side of one of the reading chairs. When she hit the home button, a view of their barns lit up the screen. James had been sitting there last night (this morning).

She knew the code. Not their wedding, or Billie's birth. It was the date he'd got his first goat as a child. They'd started celebrating it as a joke. Now it was a tradition.

She could unlock his phone. But being able to do something and it being the right thing to do could be vastly different things. Harriet wasn't a snoopy person. She never had been and, until she held that phone, never imagined she would be.

She wasn't keen to become that person now. But she also didn't want to bury her head in the sand when she still had the Persephone question to answer. That wasn't practical.

What if she had only the quickest of scans? She could look but not look, just to satisfy herself. All right: a scan only.

Harriet held her breath. She was really doing this.

She'd never crossed that line before.

Would it be better if she only looked at the most recent text? Not a full invasion of privacy. Just a little one.

She made little 'if, then' adjustments like this until she'd agreed with herself to only look at a text notification of the most recent text, if it came up on the home screen when she unlocked the phone. Anyone could accidentally see those.

She punched in the code.

> The lacy or the red? Can't wait till you're back! P xx

She slumped into the chair that had just offered up the answer she thought she was so keen to know. Everything over the past months, all the little clues, fell neatly into place.

As soon as James came downstairs, she handed him his phone. 'I saw the notification. Of your last text.' She couldn't believe she sounded so calm.

Warily, he looked at the text.

James slowly closed his eyes. 'It's not what you think.'

'What do I think, James? That Persephone can't wait to get you back so she can show you her new pants?'

'It's not that. I knew we couldn't keep anything from you. I'm sorry.' To give him the tiniest smidge of credit, at least he looked it. 'Here, read them all.'

'I don't want to read your texts.'

'I beg to differ, dear heart, or you wouldn't have unlocked my phone.' He held his phone out to her.

How was he making her feel guilty when he was the one choosing another woman's knickers? 'This is how you want to tell me?'

'I promised Persephone I wouldn't tell you, no matter what. This way I'm not telling you.'

'So nice to see you showing such loyalty to Persephone,' she snapped.

'Just read through the texts. Then you'll know.'

She started swiping down quickly, scrolling back through all the texts till she got to the first one, which had been sent more than five years earlier. It took thirty-seven swipes. It seemed like a lot of texts. She tapped on her own name and started swiping back. It only took thirty-one swipes to get to the same period.

So that was one conclusion. They were talking more by text than she and James were. The question was: what else were they doing more?

As she scrolled forward from around Persephone's birthday, at first the relief that sped through her made her giddy.

Then she got to the punchline.

'I should have guessed this was her idea,' she said, handing back his phone. 'You were going to spring this on me with no warning?'

'I'm sorry,' he said. 'I know that was a stupid idea. Persephone – I – we – thought this would be the best way.' He sighed. 'I'm sorry. I wish none of it was happening.'

'Well, you can't undo things now, can you?'

Chapter 27

Friday

Sophie was frightened. There was no way for her to go back now. It was like when she woke in the morning and her mind started turning over. No matter how hard she tried, she couldn't get back to sleep. Once her eyes were open, she couldn't close them again.

She wasn't sure she'd want to, even if she could. She couldn't quite believe that her feelings had changed the way they had, but now she saw Dan for exactly the man he was.

Sophie was woke.

She didn't mean to have a go at her dad when she rang him, but hadn't they noticed the way Dan had treated her over the years? 'We wouldn't have picked him for you, love,' her dad conceded, 'but then, nobody is good enough for my daughter. And you always said you were happy. We did check in to be sure. Remember? Especially your mum.'

Sophie would have loved to talk to her mum right then. Her voice was choked when she answered. 'I know, I do remember. I've always said I was happy.'

But she'd said much more than that, hadn't she? Time and again she'd told her parents, friends, random strangers, how much she loved the way Dan took care of her. She'd gloated over it when other women complained about their partners.

How things had changed.

Miracle of miracles, Dan wasn't in the office this morning. His bare toes wriggled on one of the kitchen chairs as he read the newspaper spread over the table. He glanced up when she came in. 'Perfect timing. Give me a refill, will you, please?' He held up his coffee-stained mug. His eyes were back on the article.

She poured him more coffee from the professional-looking machine, and one for herself. There was only a little milk left. She filled her cup just the way she liked it. Dan's coffee barely changed colour.

'What do you want to do today?' he asked. He sipped his coffee, then looked into his mug with a frown.

'Sorry, we need more milk,' she said, before savouring her own delicious brew.

Dan sighed like he'd just missed one lottery number. 'I thought we'd go to Cheddar caves. The children will love that. I looked it up and we can go caving.'

'It's the children who'll love that?' Dan was the adventure junkie.

His voice got quiet. 'That's what I've just said. They've got space for us this afternoon.'

'Then why bother asking me if you already know you'll do what you want?'

'You don't have to come if you don't want to.' His expression could have been hewn from marble.

'That's a nice thing to say.'

'Well, then, what do you want from me, Soph? I find something interesting for us to do, together like you wanted, and you shit all over the idea. If you want to join us, then do. If you don't, then don't. I'm not going to beg you to spend time with your family.'

That was a low blow. As if her family hadn't always (always!) been her first concern. She listened to her heart

283

thud. 'If you're going to take the children down into caves then I'm coming with you.'

'Just try not to be such a damper on the party, will you? It's getting old.'

That wasn't the only thing getting old.

The orange boiler suit made her look like an Oompa Loompa.

'You'll be glad of it,' said the caving leader, handing out helmets. His suit was stylishly blue and grey, she noted. They must dress the tourists in hi-vis so they didn't lose any. 'It gets a bit dirty underground.'

She liked him; he seemed friendly but didn't make any jokes. She didn't want to rely on a comedian to lead them safely into the bowels of the earth.

'That's all part of the fun,' said Dan. Like he didn't always make a big moany deal over the tiniest spill.

She laughed to herself, thinking back to the airport. It really had been Oliver who'd spilled the iced water into his lap. Now she wished she'd done it instead.

They'd barely uttered a word to each other on the drive here. She wasn't sure she trusted herself to make small talk. *Hey, Dan, nice weather, isn't it? Oh, and about that time you went to court and didn't tell me. Kind of something I'd imagine a husband should share with his wife, don't you think? I just wondered whether you're being dodgy again. Is Laxmi covering for you?*

But the children were excited, and that made Sophie happy. As happy as she could be, knowing she was about to dangle over a gaping hole.

The leader double-checked everyone's safety equipment, and explained again that it was only a twenty-foot drop to the cave below.

That still sounded like a long way. 'Are you sure you're happy doing this?' she asked the children.

'They're excited,' Dan said. 'Stop coddling them, Soph.'

'Actually,' said the leader, 'it's right to check. I was just about to ask. It's important that the whole team feels comfortable, or safety could be compromised.'

Dan winked at the leader as if he'd just praised him, not slapped him down. 'You're comfortable, aren't you, kids?'

'Yeah!' they both said. They did look excited. Sophie tried to relax and they all descended.

As they crept through the luckily-not-too-claustro-phobic-making tunnels, Sophie did start to enjoy herself. Despite Dan.

'How many kilometres is this system?' He'd been shining his torch into every crevice along the way, saying things like, 'I bet I could squeeze through there.'

'I've been through fifteen kilometres,' the leader answered.

'And how much is accessible?'

'Fifteen kilometres. Try to stay together as we go through this next bit.' The leader shone his torch at Dan so he didn't wander off.

'Can't we go that way?' he said. 'It looks more inter-esting. This has been okay for the kids, but kind of tame for the rest of us. Am I right?'

The still air in the cave was perfectly quiet.

Sophie nearly apologised. Then she remembered that she wasn't the one being an arse.

'It's a dead end,' the leader said.

'How do you know?'

'Because I'm the leader and, I'm guessing, you've never been caving before.'

Sophie laughed. Dan had never climbed into anything more complicated than their loft.

'It's not rocket science, mate,' Dan muttered so only Sophie heard him.

The children were full of chatter on the drive back, and Sophie spent most of the journey twisted round in her seat so she could talk to them. Dan was too full of his success as an expert caver to notice that she had hardly spoken to him.

'All right, showers everyone,' she told Katie and Oliver when they got into the house. 'Upstairs now. Then you can go and see the goats.'

She was just about to go upstairs herself when Dan stopped her. 'That was a good day, wasn't it?'

She was wary. 'I think everyone enjoyed it. Thanks for the suggestion.'

'I'm glad you appreciate it, Soph. So, I was right, wasn't I?'

He looked so bloody pleased with himself. 'It's not that I don't appreciate the things you do, Dan. I just don't like feeling that I have to be grateful for every little thing. Just because you do so much doesn't mean that I can't. You don't let me do things for myself, and I want to.' Her voice sounded as off-kilter as her heart felt.

Dan's laugh had no joy. 'Hold on, there, Pinocchio, don't make the mistake of thinking you're a real boy.'

'That doesn't even make sense.'

'You just don't understand it.'

She wanted to wipe that arrogant look off his face. 'Stop talking like you invented me, Dan.'

'But that's exactly what I did, silly bean. I made you. I introduced you to all the good things you have now. All the good things you *are* now. I don't expect you to thank me. I don't need to be praised. But you *are* everything because of me. You'll do well not to forget that.'

Who was she, exactly? Sophie wondered, because she felt like a woman who was tired of paying homage to an overbearing husband who controlled her. A woman with heart palpitations and, until this holiday, no sense of her own worth. 'I'm not so sure I like the transformation,' she said.

'Please. What were you before, huh? Tell me that. No, I'll tell you. You were an average woman in a dead-end job who didn't know the difference between Martin Luther and Martin Luther King.'

Sophie smarted at that memory. She'd been a bit tipsy, to be fair, and Dan was throwing around so many names she didn't know. It was an easy mistake to make. Dan never let her forget it.

'You'd never been further than Spain, or to the ballet, let alone the opera, and you'd never eaten oysters.' Dan was warming to his theme. 'What's your favourite food now?'

'M&S chocolate volcano, actually.'

'Liar. I showed you everything you know.'

Not quite everything, because Sophie felt that she knew quite a lot on her own about what she was going to do. 'I suppose you're taking all the credit for the children, too?' she asked. She might not know her Luther from her Luther King, but at least she was on safe ground with the children. Dan had never so much as sniffed a nappy.

'Our children, Soph. Our children. And that's the least you can do when I'm taking care of everything else. You should be grateful I let you be a full-time mum. Most women would love that luxury.'

'You *let me* have that luxury? Dan, you're deluded if you think that getting up at the crack of dawn seven days a week and being depended on for every single thing in someone's life is a luxury. I put more miles in than an Uber driver, carting everyone where they need to go. And you've got me volunteering for all and sundry, remember? I'd say that amounts to bloody hard work.'

His gaze was sub-zero. 'Don't I know it. Sophie, I do it every day in an office.'

'And you remind me every chance you get. I'm sick of it, to be honest.'

'Well, join the club.' Dan's voice was rising now. Sophie braced herself. 'I'm sick of a lot of things you can't even conceive of with your tiny little mind. You've got typically bad timing, Sophie, because now is really not a good time for me to have to deal with this, too.'

After everything she'd just said, *that's* what he came away with? The inconvenience to him? 'Well, Dan, for once it's not about you. It's about me, and I'm telling you what I need.'

'What, Sophie? Tell me what you need.' He grabbed her arm. 'Never mind, I'll tell you. You need me, that's what you need.'

'I don't need you, Dan, and what's more, I don't want you, not like this.' She jerked away from his grip. 'I don't want to be bossed around by you all the time. I don't think that's too much to ask.'

'Well, I don't want a wife who doesn't let me be a husband.'

'Your idea of a husband is so skewed! It's not the 1940s.' Had she really not known how controlling he was? Was she so delusional? No, not delusional, just lulled by an easy life. She'd willingly walked into that cage and closed the door. Well, she wanted out now. 'And you don't get to dictate what I accept from you,' she went on. 'Not any more. I can do things on my own. I have done. I took over the entire Scouts event, and as much as I'm sure you hoped I'd fall on my arse, it went fine. Better than fine. I

288

did that. It reminded me that I don't need you all the time, Dan, and you shouldn't expect me to. That's not what a marriage is supposed to be. I don't want it to be like this.'

'Don't be ridiculous,' he said. 'What are you saying, that you're going to leave me over a bunch of Boy Scouts? You won't do that.'

Unbelievable. He was still trying to tell her what she could and couldn't do. The problem for him was that she was no longer listening.

'I think you need some time to think about this,' he said. 'So, I'll just go back to London early, shall I? Give you the space you claim you need, now that you're Miss Independence? Good fucking luck with that.'

'You can't go back. Harriet is there till Sunday.'

'Ah, simple Sophie.' He couldn't have sounded more patronising. 'It doesn't occur to you that I can get a hotel? Psh, and you think you don't need me. We'll see how long that little idea of yours lasts.'

'Yes, we will.' With that she climbed the stairs, locked the en suite bathroom door behind her and slid to the cool tiled floor. They'd never had a row like this. There was no way to take back what they'd said. What had she just done? Her hands shook as she tried to catch her breath in the echoey room. With each exhale, more tears seeped out. Then she was crying so much she could barely breathe – over what she was losing and, maybe, what she only thought she'd had in the first place. They hadn't had a relationship at all; at least, not what she thought of as a relationship, built on respect and trust. She'd been in a hostage situation with a lenient captor, as long as she did everything he wanted. Even worse, she'd sung his praises to everyone she knew. She was suffering from Stockholm Syndrome.

She buried her face in a bath towel, hoping that only she could hear her shuddering sobs.

Yet still she wanted Dan to come for her, to knock on the bathroom door and take her into his arms and tell her everything was okay. Even though she knew she was right. Even though she was livid over the way he controlled her and the cruel things he'd said. She still wanted the comfort. She still loved him.

But the only sound she heard was the shower running in the other bathroom. One of the children had listened to her, at least. They did listen, generally. She wasn't nearly as hopeless a mum as Dan would make her out to be. She knew that. She *knew* it! She could not let him work his judgements into her brain. He was a master at playing the tactics, but she knew all his moves.

Within a few minutes she could hear him whistling to himself in their bedroom like he hadn't a care in the world. Like she hadn't threatened their marriage.

It was a bluff. He liked to do that to cover his fury. She would stay strong.

She didn't offer to drive him to the station. If he thought she was such a helpless creature then let him get a taxi. She wasn't a silly bean any more.

When she was sure he'd left, she rang Harriet.

'I'm sorry, there was a bit of an overflow situation in your bathroom last night,' Harriet confessed straight away. 'Not a leak or anything, thank goodness, just a running tap. I've sorted it, though, and they delivered the fans and dehumidifiers today. They're running now. Luckily you haven't got carpet in the bedroom! It only leaked through the kitchen ceiling, though, so there was no water damage to furniture. I've already booked the plasterers to come next week when it's dried out, and I could come back to oversee the work, too, if you'll be out, so there's no inconvenience. That's the least I can do for wrecking your kitchen ceiling. Sorry.'

'That's okay,' Sophie answered. She couldn't care less about the kitchen ceiling. 'I think I may have just wrecked my marriage. Or at least put a serious dent in it.'

'Er, okay. You want to talk about it, I presume, since you rang.'

'Your logic never fails you, Harriet.' She recounted as much of the day as she could remember. Even though the exact details of who said what were already getting fuzzy, the feeling was as strong as ever. She didn't regret anything she'd said.

'Listen,' said Harriet, 'I'm not the right person to give you advice, professionally speaking, but I can ask around and recommend someone good. If you're going down that road.'

'It's too early for decisions. It's complicated with the children, and the fact that I'm not working and he's living in the house with us. Plus, there's the not inconsiderable fact that I might still love him.' That was the real problem. Her head gave her all the evidence she could ever need. It didn't stop her heart from wanting to stay with him despite everything. This didn't feel like the end, although it was the beginning of it.

Later, she glanced through the front window, again letting the tears fill her eyes. Blurry, the scene outside was even more idyllic. Off to one side, bright expanses of grass were dotted with James's prize goats. A wild profusion of blooms and greenery filled the garden nearer the house: tall-stemmed irises, multicoloured gladioli and foxgloves that reached skywards; purple-blooming butterfly bushes and huge-headed lavender hydrangeas. Bright geraniums in shades of pink and red nestled among the merry violas and pansies that tumbled over the sides of their pots. There was absolutely nothing in her line of vision to suggest that it wasn't a hundred years ago . . .

But there should have been, she realised.

Dan had taken the hire car.

Chapter 28

Saturday

'I feel like death warmed up,' Harriet muttered. Yesterday was supposed to be comedown day, according to Google. How could she feel so bad now?

'Can we stay in bed all day?' came the response from James's side.

'You can. I've got to get up.' She went to rise, but James threw an arm over her shoulders.

'Hang on,' he said. He waited, maybe to see if she'd shrug him off. When she didn't, he said, 'I know it doesn't even come close to being enough, but I am sorry we're putting you through this, I really am. I promise I'll make it as painless as possible for you.'

She wondered how he planned to do that, unless he had a way to rewind the last several months.

'It would have been painless if it wasn't happening.' She was right to be suspicious when she'd put two and two together.

'I know,' he said. 'I'll make it up to you. I'm not saying you shouldn't be angry, but can you at least not hate me too much?'

'Oh, James. After all this time, you know me better than that.' Her eyes slid along the curtain rail at the window. Twenty rings exactly on each side. She was glad to see the symmetry. 'I don't hate you. I can't say the same for your actions, though.' It was a distinction they'd always been careful to make with Billie. They always loved her. They just didn't always like her actions.

'Yeah, I see that.' His kindly eyes looked tired. She'd felt him tossing and turning until the early hours. 'For what it's worth, I am truly, heartily sorry.'

'I know you are, but it's too late for that to change anything now.'

With that, she got up. Selecting a cocktail of tablets from her well-stocked medicine bag, she tried not to unbalance her pounding head as she staggered to the bathroom. No sign of the flood remained, except that most of the towels were still drying downstairs.

She was tempted to take a bath, but the memory of the other night was too fresh. It had been so *fun*. As much fun as she and James had ever had together. She pushed the thoughts from her mind. Today, her focus was on Billie. Besides, there was nothing she could do now about James's little plan. It seemed she wasn't as in control as she'd thought.

Maybe she never had been. All those years she'd congratulated herself on her ability to be ready for any situation. It was exhausting. She saw the strain now in the mirror, and for what? For everyone to do whatever they wanted anyway. She'd actually believed that chaos was just for the want of a foolproof plan. Ha! If only.

She showered as usual, then put the finishing touches to her outfit.

As Harriet examined her reflection, she felt butterflies waking up in her tummy. Taking a deep breath, she went downstairs to wait for her daughter to get up.

But clearly, Billie couldn't wait to get to Brighton today. She was already in the kitchen. 'Mum!'

'Before you say anything, please let me say something first. Please. I'm so sorry for the way I've reacted.' The words were strangled in Harriet's throat. 'I'd give anything in the world to do it differently, to get to have that conversation again. Everything came out wrong, or didn't come out at all, which is worse. I do support you, Billie, and I will in whatever decisions you make in your life because I love you more than anything. Sometimes that gets lost in my reaction. I'm sorry for that, too, sweetheart, more than you'll ever know. I hope that one day you'll be able to forgive me, because I was wrong for behaving like I did when you told us.'

'To be fair, you've done loads more wrong than that,' Billie said.

'Thanks.'

'You only get one chance to make a first impression.' Harriet recoiled at her own words. 'I deserve that, too.'

'Yeah, you do, but you probably mean well in your own totally misguided way. You can't help it. You're just . . .' Billie grimaced. 'You.' Then she raised her eyebrows at Harriet's outfit. 'You've been on Mumsnet again. Haven't I told you?'

When Harriet glanced down at the badges on her rainbow t-shirt, the hot pink pompom deely boppers on her head bounced forward. *Pride* was pinned to one side and *Love is Love* to the other. She was glad she'd gone out yesterday to buy everything. She wasn't sure she'd have managed it with the way she felt today. 'Too much?' she asked, turning round so Billie could see the *Proud and Loud* badge on the waistband of her jeans.

'You're always too much, Mum.' Billie flicked her deely bopper. 'I wouldn't expect anything else from you.'

'Good, because I want to go to the parade with you. You don't even have to walk with me if you don't want. I just want to be there to support you. Will you let me?'

'I doubt I could stop you.'

'Yes, Billie, you could. If you don't want me to go then I won't. I think it's time I started listening to you. I won't always get things right, but from now on it won't be for lack of trying, if you'll let me. Can we try, sweetheart? I'd love it if we could.'

In those few seconds before Billie spoke, Harriet felt the weight of everything she wanted hanging in the balance. It was all in Billie's hands. Now Harriet realised that it always had been. As heartbreaking as it would be, she could face losing James. She wouldn't lose her daughter.

Finally, Billie answered. 'I suppose I can't let you wander around Brighton on your own looking like that.'

'I know,' she said. 'I'm cute enough to kiss, aren't I?' She felt like such a fool.

'Hug, anyway, I suppose.' With that she let Harriet put her arms around her. 'You're insane, but you are my mum.'

Harriet's tears made tracks through the glitter on her cheeks.

The Brighton train was mobbed, and a few passengers were even more colourful than Harriet. She wished she'd bought the pink wig, too. 'This is fun!' she told Billie as they squeezed into one of the carriages.

'Let's see how you feel after being packed in for an hour,' she answered.

'And seven minutes. It's an hour and seven minutes.'

Billie patted her shoulder.

It took ages to get out of Brighton station after the train pulled in, but Harriet felt like she was already at Pride. The atmosphere was electric, with music and whistles and drums, more colourful outfits and lots of rainbows.

'How will we ever find your friends?' she wondered as they made their way with the mob towards the city centre.

'WhatsApp,' Billie said. She showed Harriet the map on her phone. 'They're there.'

'But what if the network goes down with all these people? What's your Plan B?'

'We'll meet at Starbucks at noon.'

Harriet's hand went to her heart. Billie was her girl after all.

The crowd swelled along with the noise as they approached the parade route. She had to shout so Billie could hear her. 'So, darling, you're a lesbian. What do I call a gay man?'

'Christ, Mum.'

'Well, I want to get the terminology right for when I meet your friends.'

Billie stared at her. 'You really do, don't you?'

'Yes, that's why I'm asking what the correct singular noun is for a gay man.'

'You'd say a gay man.'

'Then gays are men and lesbians are women. Got it.'

'Not a gay, Mum. A gay man.'

'That's not very efficient. There should be a singular noun.'

'You shouldn't need a singular noun because you're not going to use it, are you?' Billie asked. '*Are you?* Please don't ask my friends any embarrassing questions.'

'Since when have I ever embarrassed you?' She twanged her deely bopper.

'Oh God,' Billie muttered.

But she didn't ask Billie's friends any embarrassing questions. They were all very nice and not creepy at all.

'She's your mum?' said one of the boys. Like Billie, he was dressed simply in jeans and a t-shirt. In fact, they all were. Still, Harriet was having too much fun to regret her outfit. 'That's dope.'

Billie didn't look convinced about the dopeness of Harriet being there.

'Come on,' she cajoled her daughter. 'You've got to admit, it is dope.' She looked around. 'How many other mothers are here with their daughters? I'm right, aren't I?' she said to the woman she happened to notice beside her.

'What?'

'I was saying that not many mothers like us are here with our daughters.' Harriet pointed to the young woman holding her hand.

'She's not my daughter.'

'Really? But—' Actually, now that she examined them carefully, the only resemblance between them was the dirty looks on their faces.

'Sorry,' Billie said, steering Harriet away. 'Smooth, Mum.'

'Well, she was young enough to be her daughter. Anyone could make that mistake.'

'It was so invigorating!' she told Sophie later that night on the phone. It had taken hours before they were able to get on a train back. Normally Harriet would have found half a dozen more efficient options, but she was enjoying herself too much. 'To see everyone there supporting each other was wonderful, and Billie couldn't have been happier. And her friends weren't at all the online psychopaths I was afraid they'd be. They were really nice boys and girls from all over the South East. This social media thing is something, isn't it?' Harriet knew she sounded like her gran marvelling over colour television. 'I still don't want her on it all the time, but I see the attraction. We even took selfies!'

'It sounds like a great day, I'm really happy for you,' Sophie said. 'My day was pretty good, too, even though there's still no sign of Dan. I guess he really has gone back to London.'

'I'm sorry, are you upset?'

'Only because I'm starting to second-guess myself. Harriet, what if I'm overreacting, or twisting things somehow and that's making him seem like an arse when he's really not? What if his motives aren't actually sinister? That would make a difference to how I should see his actions, wouldn't it?'

'I don't know,' said Harriet. 'If his actions have a negative impact on you then does it matter what his motivation is? It's still wrong to make you feel like that, no matter why he's doing it.'

'I know,' Sophie said. She sounded deflated. 'I can't believe I haven't seen this before. Maybe because he's always made our relationship so easy. You know like when you usually go out with someone and there's all that effort to get him to like you? None of that happened with Dan. He's always overwhelmed me with his love. There's a lot of security in that.'

Harriet wondered whether it was love or need that Sophie had been overwhelmed by. They weren't the same thing.

Sophie went on. 'I can't trust anything I'm thinking at the moment.'

Harriet's heart went out to her friend. And she was certain that Dan was exactly as big a knob as Sophie suspected. Hadn't she found ironclad evidence of that behind the Celebrations in Sophie's cupboard? Even though it might mean going back into the deep freeze, she had to tell her now. 'Sophie? I found something when I was putting away a few things. I debated telling you because I hoped I wouldn't have to, but now I think I do.' Harriet steeled herself. 'There was an open pack of condoms in the back of your towel cupboard.'

'I have a towel cupboard?'

'The one in the bathroom. That's your towel cupboard, now I've labelled everything. But that's not the point. The point is that they probably mean Dan has been lying to you.'

When she didn't answer, Harriet soldiered on. 'You told me Dan had a vasectomy, so presumably he doesn't need condoms with you. But Sophie, he's got them, and the pack is open. Which means he must be using them with someone else. I'm so sorry, but you should know this if you're thinking about your options. Besides, you're my friend.' That felt good to say, and scary because Harriet knew she couldn't take their friendship for granted now that she'd rubbished Dan again.

'You're right,' Sophie finally said. 'We're not using them.'

Harriet felt terrible for breaking this news to her friend. Though she had to say, Sophie was taking it awfully well. Maybe she was in shock.

'But they're not Dan's. They're mine,' Sophie said.

Harriet spluttered.

'Why is that so unbelievable? Thanks, Harriet.'

'But what if Dan had found them?'

'Please. He never puts anything away. He doesn't even get his own clean towels. Believe me, there's no risk of Dan going into any cupboards. I could hide anything in there and he'd never find it.'

If Sophie had condoms and she wasn't using them with her husband, then . . . 'You're having an affair?'

Sophie snorted. 'Blimey, no, of course I'm not! It's – I – I should have chucked them out, I know.'

'I don't understand. You're not sleeping with someone, but you want to?'

'No, definitely not, though Carlos would like to. I have said no, but he's still hopeful.'

'Snake Carlos? Your next-door neighbour Carlos?'

'I know, it's a cliché, isn't it? Dan and I spent a lot of time with them before his wife left. She was my friend more than him. Still, I felt sorry for him when she left. He mistook that for interest. I guess I was flattered by the attention – cliché again – but then when he brought over that box . . . I had to tell him it wasn't going to happen. I did tell him.'

'But you kept the box?'

She sighed. 'He left it in the loo. Luckily I found it before Dan got home. I should have chucked them out, but like I said, it was flattering. I suppose it felt good having someone be so nice to me all the time. Hmm. I've never thought about it like that. Part of me must have known that Dan wasn't being nice. But it wasn't fair to let Carlos carry on when I knew I'd never . . .'

Harriet's brain was whirring. 'The box is open, Sophie.'

She giggled. 'Well, I wanted to see what extra-large condoms looked like, didn't I? I couldn't believe he'd brought them over. Talk about cocky.'

'Yes, well, that seems to be his implication,' said Harriet. 'And? Did you see a difference?' She'd never had the occasion to see one herself in the wild.

'Well, they're not elephantine or anything. Just a little bigger than usual, I guess. It's hard to tell without seeing one on.'

'Which you definitely didn't see.'

'Which I *definitely* didn't see. I'd never cheat, as bad as things might be. As bad as things are. Even if Dan and I split, I wouldn't want to be with Carlos. I'll find a nice way to tell him that when I get back. Anyway, it's our last day here and I don't want to waste it thinking about what happens when we all go back to the real world. Will you be happy to come home?'

'No, I'm dreading it!' Harriet said. She wasn't only thinking about the stifling little village now.

'Me too, but at least we both got away, thanks to you. We wouldn't have met each other if it hadn't been for that ash cloud.'

'That bloody ash cloud.'

Sophie laughed. 'Even with everything else, it's still been a win, don't you think? You got to go to Pride with Billie. That couldn't have happened in Rome. And I, well, I probably would have been a well-massaged wife with no more backbone than when she first got on the flight. I wouldn't have realised what Dan is really like if we hadn't met, if I hadn't done the fundraiser or had these two weeks here. Maybe I'd never have stood up for myself at all. And we wouldn't be friends now. My marriage might be over but I still say thank you, you bloody gorgeous ash cloud.'

Harriet set her own doubts aside for a moment. Sophie was right about Billie. She'd probably still get things wrong – in fact she could almost guarantee that she would – but her daughter might be a little more forgiving now. 'Of course, yes, cheers, you bloody gorgeous ash cloud.'

It still seemed strange that Harriet could feel so close to a woman she'd seen exactly once for a few hours. But sometimes that's how friendship worked. At least, that's how she remembered it working, eleven years and seven months ago, the last time she'd made a friend. 'I'd love to stay in touch,' she told Sophie. 'We could schedule periodic calls after work if you like.'

'Or we could just ring each other when we want a chat.'

'Yes, we could do that too. Ring me any time,' Harriet said. 'I can always change my plans to talk.' Strangely, she thought as she hung up, she didn't find that idea too uncomfortable.

Chapter 29

Sunday

How's the journey going? Dan texted. *Tell me when you need me.*

Sophie reread it. A month ago, she would have seen it as a thoughtful offer. Sweet Dan, as concerned and accommodating as ever, always thinking about her, ready to ride in and save the day. She used to think his apologies were sincere, too. Oh, he was good at those. Just when she most feared his anger, he flipped to the loving, contrite husband. She never questioned how out of character those apologies seemed, given the meanness of the moments before. They did their job, always reeling her straight back in.

Now his text definitely didn't read as helpful, not when she knew exactly what kind of bloke she was married to. He'd flounced back to London at the first sign of insurrection. He'd had the cheek to call it that, like he was some kind of army general! Worst of all, he'd taken their hire car, with an empty boot save for his overnight bag. She and the children were saddled with getting back home with all the luggage on the train.

Now she'd pull every muscle in her body before she'd admit she needed his help.

She supposed she'd better get used to problems like that. There could be a lifetime of them ahead.

Instead of giving him the satisfaction of an answer, she turned off her phone.

The leaves had deepened their green in London since they'd been away. The whole road was lush with summer vegetation. Maybe her view had been countrified, but it looked prettier than she remembered.

Sophie winced as she heaved open their front door. Her biceps were screaming, but she'd done it. She'd got them all safely home on the train without Dan's help.

At least, she *thought* it was home. It was definitely her front door, yet something didn't look right. First of all, she didn't remember that border on the tiled floor in the hall. Quite a nice one, too. Second, none of her family's belongings was strewn across it.

'Where is everything?' Katie asked.

Sophie's question exactly. 'Harriet must have tidied.' More like renovated. The only personal items in view were their jackets, and even those had been artfully arranged on their hooks like props at a photo shoot. 'Don't worry, we'll find everything.'

Once the children realised that the rest of the house had received the Harriet treatment too, they dashed through playing Spot the Difference. Sophie followed more slowly, more thoughtfully. Tears pricked her eyes as she realised that Harriet had unknowingly swept away much of what reminded Sophie of her life with Dan. She hadn't thought about that; about how it would feel to step back into a family home without her whole family. Now she didn't have to imagine it, because this didn't feel like their home. Or it did, because everything was familiar. It just felt like *her* home. The kind of home where her best self might live.

But it didn't take long to bump up against reality. They settled back in once they'd lugged their bags into their bedrooms and kicked off their shoes. The evening's television was decided and thoughts turned towards dinner.

Thoughts also turned towards Dan. There'd been no more texts from him when she'd turned her phone back on. Wherever he was staying, it clearly wasn't going to be in their house.

'Is Dad coming home tonight?' Oliver asked. Spot was draped over his arm, her strong coils slowly undulating. She looked happy to be reunited. Or as happy as a snake ever looked.

Sophie kept her head in the fridge for a moment. Harriet had stocked it for them, and left fresh bread and some fruit, too. She was glad she'd thought to do the same at the cottage.

There was no sense in pretending to the children. 'No, sweetheart, he's not.' Even if he did give in (and she was sure he wouldn't), Sophie didn't want to go back to normal. Ha, normal. What was that anyway? She'd thought they were normal for years. No, better than normal. Sophie had been smug. She must have looked ridiculous to everyone. Had they all seen what she hadn't? She found she didn't care one way or the other. 'Your dad is angry with me. We're angry with each other.'

Oliver's solemn eyes stared into hers. 'When we get angry at school, Miss Peters makes us both say we're sorry. No matter whose fault it is.'

Sophie hugged her son, trying not to upset the snake in the process. 'We will say we're sorry, too,' she murmured into his silky hair. 'I don't know if that will make everything the way it was, though.' She reached down to hold him by the shoulders. 'But I can promise you one thing: your dad and I love you and Katie more than anything in the world, and that will never change.'

Katie sat with her legs over the side of her favourite chair, examining her long plait for split ends. 'He's not always nice to you,' she said. 'Is that why?'

Sophie's heart sank. They had noticed when she hadn't. *Children* saw what she didn't. That was humiliating, but, more importantly, she hoped it hadn't scarred them. 'Well, I won't let him be unkind again.' Sophie had a hard time controlling the wobble in her voice. 'I think we all deserve kindness, don't you?'

Katie nodded. 'Are you getting a divorce then?'

'I don't know,' she said, even though she did already know, because as hard as it would be to get over loving Dan, she loved herself more. That was a love affair she could guarantee would last a lifetime.

She wondered where he was now, what he was doing. Whatever it was, he was still brooding.

The house felt strange without him. Not that he hadn't been away before. As she thought back, he'd taken several trips on his own to do adventurous things that she wouldn't enjoy (he'd informed her). Always at the weekends, though. Now she knew he'd had a good reason for not taking off workdays.

His absence felt different now. He wasn't just parasailing in Spain.

Still, she marvelled, their life was carrying on in all the mundane ways. Laundry needed doing, though as usual it wasn't urgent (as long as they still had a few pairs of clean pants). They got hungry, so she made dinner. Not as fancy as Dan would have done, but she hadn't dirtied every pan and bowl in the kitchen, either.

'What do you think about me going back to work?' she asked her children as they slurped their spaghetti. 'Not just volunteering. I mean real, paid work.'

Katie looked at her like she'd just proposed becoming a circus clown. 'Can you do that?'

'What, do you mean legally? I'll check my motherhood contract, but I don't think there's anything in there that says no.'

'I mean *can* you?' Katie asked.

'Of course I can! I used to work, you know, before you were born. I had a full-time job just like your dad.'

'Cool.' Katie went back to her pasta.

Yes, thought Sophie, *it was rather cool*. 'It would mean some changes for us all, though. I wouldn't be here after school, for example.'

Katie waited till she'd finished chewing. 'I wouldn't mind that.'

'Thanks.' Sophie laughed. 'As long as you're sure you wouldn't be too upset about it.'

The children were in their rooms when Sophie opened her wardrobe. All her shoes were there, neatly paired and perfectly aligned on the floor. Harriet had them in colour order, then by heel height. She smiled. Her friend would have weighed up all the organisational options. Maybe grouped by season first, or formality or some other system that only she saw.

She counted eight pairs of work shoes; the ones she'd shoved into the bathroom cupboard. They all needed a good polish. Most of the heels were worn down and a few were completely knackered. She picked up her lucky shoes. She'd loved those, with their stylish heel and soft black leather and low vamp and the way they'd always made her feel so strong. A warrior woman in a kitten heel. Those were the shoes she'd worn in her interview and at every performance review, and whenever she felt like being on top of the world.

She slipped them on. They fitted. Better, even after all these years, they still felt right. She'd wear them for her next job interview. She'd wear them if she ever had to face Dan over a solicitor's table.

Then she sat down, surrounded by shoes and memories, and cried.

Chapter 30

Home

The week after both families went back to their old lives, nothing had changed and everything had changed. Sophie took the children to their summer activities. She did the shopping and got cross with Katie over staying up too late. When the fridge was bare, she made them all pasta from one of Harriet's neat containers. She settled down to finish a box set she'd started before the holiday, absently snacking on the open packet of Shreddies she found in the cabinet, even though she wasn't hungry.

She took baby steps back into the real world, degree by degree, and it began to feel okay. Better than okay. The doubts and second-guessing were making less noise now that she was home. Surrounded by the life she knew, Sophie saw just how stifling it had been with Dan. Most of her wardrobe was an unhappy reminder of what he'd thought she should look like. They were nothing but costumes, personas that Dan wanted her to put on.

She filled a bin bag with most of them. Maybe another woman would like to try them on. She no longer did. Sophie wasn't sure what she did want – that's what her future was for – but it wasn't that. She'd say that to Dan when he eventually did ring.

The feeling of lightness had followed her home because her husband hadn't.

Meanwhile, routine returned for Harriet, too. Her first Monday back at home, she woke as usual a few minutes before her alarm and left for the station at the same time she always did. She stood just where the bicycle lock-up was on the platform so that the doors of the 8.15 opened directly in front of her, and she got into the second-to-last carriage as usual. There was a free seat, but instead of opening her laptop and working for the thirty-five minutes until the conductor announced their arrival in Oxford, Harriet glanced around her. Despite probably sharing the same journey for years, she didn't recognise her fellow commuters. The scenery, too, was unfamiliar in places.

In the office, once the mandatory post-holiday pleasant-ries were finished, Harriet made her first To Do list of the day. But instead of concentrating on her work, she found herself checking her mobile, and not only at the usual scheduled intervals, either. She felt like a new girlfriend waiting to see if he'd rung.

Finally, just before lunchtime, the text chime sent her diving for her phone. She smiled.

> How's your first day back in the office? Sophie xo

> Good so far. How's your first day back in the real world? Hx

> Surprisingly calm considering Dan rang last night.

Harriet waited for more, then realised she was probably meant to ask.

What happened?

It's not really a text
conversation.

Her fingers hovered over her phone. For eleven years and seven months, Harriet had worked through lunch.

I can ring you at lunchtime?
Hx

Then, pausing, she added: *Or any time. x*

Dan turned up at the house midweek. Sophie's heart had seized when she'd heard the key unbolting their front door. She knew it wasn't Carlos. She'd got the keys back from him when she told him, once and for all, that she'd thrown away the extra-roomy condoms.

Her heart began knocking its uneasy rhythm in her chest. It was the first time she'd really noticed it since that day in the village with the children. Her doctor was right. Stress did bring it on. Taking a deep breath, she'd unwound herself from the sofa and gone to meet her husband.

'Hello.' Dan's voice was ice-cool.

She matched it. 'What are you doing here?'

'Well, you keep hanging up on me when I ring, so how else am I supposed to talk to you? Besides, I've got every right to be in my own house. I do own it, in case you've forgotten.' He glanced around the hall at the (relative) neatness.

She didn't have a witty answer like Harriet would have done.

'We need to talk,' he said. 'I've decided that I can forgive you. It's not your fault you're so easily influenced with that woman yapping in your ear the whole time. Now that you're back, I'm sure you can see how silly you've been.'

'I don't want your forgiveness,' she said, walking back to the sofa. As Dan followed, a coughing fit seized her.

'Listen to you. You can't even walk around the house without your heart practically giving out. I've told you, you need to exercise. You're not getting any younger.'

Sophie wheeled round so fast that Dan nearly ran into her. 'What I need, Dan, is for you to stop telling me what I need. Why can't you understand that?' He still assumed he could control her.

Instead of giving her the courtesy of an answer, he made himself comfortable on the sofa. Then he picked up the Shreddies she'd been munching. To her surprise, she'd found she actually liked Harriet's breakfast cereal of choice.

Dan shook the nearly empty packet and raised an eyebrow.

'Yes, so what? I can eat what I like, Dan. I can do what I like, wear what I like and, shock horror, even think what I like.'

'I'm not loving this side of you. It's delusional, Soph. If this is what you're eating, what are you feeding my children? Are they eating dry cereal out of the box, too?'

'Don't you dare imply that I'm not taking care of them. I've done nothing but take care of them their entire lives. Me, not you, so don't you dare.'

Dan sighed. 'I didn't come here to fight. I came to say that this is enough. You've had your little Bridget Jones moment. Congratulations. Now, stop being silly and let's get back to normal.'

She glanced at the clock on the mantelpiece. The children would need picking up soon. Then something occurred to her. 'What are you doing here now? Shouldn't you be at work?'

'Yes, I should be, but this is how important my family is to me. I'm being the bigger person. I've taken time off, which I don't have because you had to have your two-week holiday. Though what you needed a holiday from I can't imagine, because you're not even working,' he sneered.

Dan wasn't wearing a suit and, she noticed, he hadn't shaved that morning. 'You're lying, Dan.'

He barely whispered. 'What did you say?'

Sophie wobbled hearing the threat in his voice. Then she took a deep breath. 'I said, you're lying. It seems you've been doing that quite a lot. What a shame it took me so long to notice.'

'You don't know what you're talking about. As usual,' he said.

'No? Then why don't you answer this? What was your bonus last year?'

'What has that got to do with anything? And that's not your fucking business.'

'Isn't it? We celebrated it, as I recall. Very nice champagne. Except that Jeremy apologised to me for not giving you a bonus last year. So, what were we celebrating, actually? A lie. Like this. You aren't at work, because something's happened there. Like something happened three years ago. I know all about that.'

'Oh really. And what is it that you think you know?' He was still lounging back against the sofa cushions with his legs crossed, but his foot had started bobbing up and down.

'I know that you were messing with your clients' files and you were found out. It was reported in the papers, so don't try to deny it.'

314

'Well, if you'd read carefully, you'd have seen that I wasn't found guilty of anything.'

'Maybe not technically, but what I don't get is why you'd mess with files in the first place. For all your faults, Dan, I didn't have you down as dodgy.'

'I wouldn't expect you to understand how the legal process works. You've never been anything but an admin assistant and a stay-at-home mother. There's nothing wrong with expediting administrative paperwork when it freed me up to concentrate on the real fee-earners. That's what Jeremy pays me for, to get things done. Though I don't expect you to have any idea what kind of pressure there is out there in the real world – what I'm expected to do, the hours I should be putting in. But I couldn't work eighty-hour weeks like everyone else, could I, not when I had to take care of you too. Remember? You fell apart when your mother died. So while you're accusing me of being dodgy, why don't you admit that it's your fault if I had to cut corners.'

'And what's your excuse this time, Dan?'

'As usual, I have no idea what you're talking about.'

'But you do. The Khan file? Mason, was it? And one other, it'll come to me in a minute. Something Italian. You're in deep shit again, Dan, aren't you? That's why you were hidden away in that office the whole time we were at Harriet's. You were trying to keep control of things. But you couldn't, could you, even though you tried to get Laxmi to do your dirty work. Did she do what you wanted? Are those files still in your briefcase where your boss can't find them? I bet he'll be worried they're lost. Maybe I should give him a ring.'

That made Dan sit up. 'Don't threaten me, Sophie. This is my career and you know nothing about it.'

'Then don't think you can play me for a fool. You've missed the whole point. Don't you get it? I don't need your forgiveness for standing up for myself. And I don't want you controlling me any more.'

'Even though you need it.'

She laughed. 'I'll be deciding what I need from now on. Right now I need you to leave. Goodbye, Dan.'

'Have it your way. You'll come round. Do you know why? Because you can't do it yourself.'

'Goodbye, Dan.'

She watched him through the front window, stomping towards the Tube station. He didn't look back.

Sophie rang one of the other mothers to ask her to pick up the children. Then she drove herself to A&E, coughing most of the way, to check that she wasn't having a heart attack.

They brought her straight into a treatment room and hooked her up to an ECG monitor. She did have to wait for the results, though. Eventually, the doctor invited her into a little office.

'Your ECG is normal,' the doctor said.

'Even though it's skipping?'

'We caught one of the beats, and it's the regular ectopic that we saw last time. It can be uncomfortable but it's not dangerous. And looking at your notes, your blood pressure is better. It's nearly normal now. Did you go on the medication?'

'No, I wanted to see if I could get it down naturally.'

The doctor flashed Sophie a smile. 'Well, whatever you've been doing, keep doing it. It's working.'

'I will,' said Sophie. 'Thank you.'

★

The following Sunday, Harriet sat in Bea's tea shop sipping another strong coffee. She would need it for later. Her calves ached from exertion, much more than if she'd done her normal weekend Zumba at the village church. She wasn't used to walking on the rambling paths, but she hadn't disliked it. In fact, she wasn't sure why she'd chosen to do Zumba for the past three years when she could have been outside doing, well, whatever she liked. There was something to be said for sometimes living life unscripted. Within the bounds of common sense. She didn't see herself ever turning up to a train station without checking the timetable first or not bringing an umbrella when there was rain in the forecast.

Maybe she'd risk it now for a fifty-fifty chance, though.

'Finished?' Bea didn't wait for an answer before slapping down Harriet's bill. Charm personified, as always.

'Yes, thanks.' She didn't reach for her purse.

'Closing soon.'

'How soon?'

'Soon.'

It was time to go home anyway and face the music.

The cottage was completely silent, as she knew it would be. She tried to ignore her thudding heart but it was no use. She had to face the facts. James and Persephone's plans were in motion.

She stood with her key in the lock.

Stop being dramatic, she chided herself, *or you'll be up for James's drama queen crown*. Nobody had died, for goodness' sake. People managed these situations all the time. It might not even be all bad. One never knew.

As she reached the darkened living room – the curtains had all been pulled – the floor lamp in the corner flicked on.

Surprise!!!

And she honestly was, because the room was absolutely heaving. Her work colleagues were all there, her London friends, and Billie and James and Persephone, of course.

Plus, it seemed, the entire village. She'd have expected them to turn up for James's birthday, but not for hers. Yet the smiles reflected back at her weren't obviously fake.

It was possible they didn't dislike her quite as much as she'd thought. Or at least, they were making the effort for James. They were such a close-knit community and, she supposed, that had its advantages.

Perhaps she'd been applying the wrong assumptions to the problem all along, and the results she'd observed weren't down to the villagers. If the outcomes were the same no matter which neighbour was in the equation, then common sense said to look at the other variable.

Harriet needed to update the inputs on her side. Maybe a little more effort from her (and fewer direct questions). She found she looked forward to testing her hypothesis.

James waited for her beside Bea, who was shaking her head. 'Someone wouldn't leave my shop in good time. Had to run all the way 'ere to get ahead of you!'

Perfect. Her first test. 'I'm sorry you had to run,' she told Bea, 'but I'm glad you're here.'

At first, Bea hesitated. 'So am I,' she said. Her smile looked genuine.

It was too small a sample to be conclusive, but Harriet was encouraged by the result.

Strings of red and white balloons floated overhead from the dark beams and a huge Happy 45th Birthday banner hung over the windows. She cringed seeing it written out in all its huge curly-font glory. So much for slipping quietly into middle age.

Persephone was among the first to reach her. It felt

good to hug her now that she knew she wasn't getting off with James.

How wrong could she have been about that? It just went to show what happened when logic got chucked aside. And she knew all about confirmation bias, too. It took only one tiny suspicion to spark things off, and then every interaction after that was coloured by it.

'Were you surprised?' Persephone asked.

'Totally. I would never have guessed this was what you had planned.' She reached for the red and lacy alternating serviettes fanned out on the long table, which was laden with food. 'I love these. They're exactly right. Everything's perfect.'

She caught James's eye. Nobody but her would have seen the tiny wink he gave. After all the trouble everyone had gone to, they'd never tell a soul that she'd found out beforehand. Not even their nearest and dearest.

'Well, it's done now, so we can all go back to normal.' Persephone handed her a glass of champagne. 'Pub next week? Just us. Let's leave James at home.'

They almost always went out as a threesome. 'I'd like that,' Harriet said. She pulled out her phone. 'When? Which day?' Then she paused. 'You know what? Let's decide next week. You can text me.' She put her phone away again.

Persephone raised her eyebrows. Then she nodded towards the cluster of people waiting. 'Everyone wants to wish you happy birthday.'

That sent Harriet's anxiety skyrocketing. As they filed past to offer their congratulations, Harriet realised that she didn't even know all their names. Jim Simmons, the Scout leader, of course she remembered, but only because he'd so formally shaken her hand when he'd introduced himself. She was glad to see that he wasn't wearing his badges tonight.

When Mrs Miller introduced herself, shaking her hand as formally as Jim had, Harriet tried not to stare at her hair, since keen observational skills didn't seem to be the best route to friendship. Still, she doubted that a hurricane could blow a strand of that hairdo out of place.

She was only able to calm down when everyone had filed past her. People stood or sat in groups all around the crowded room. Her colleagues huddled together, naturally, since they didn't know anyone else. The same went for her friends from London. But it was the villagers who were the most interesting. Seeing them chatting easily with each other, Harriet realised that she wouldn't mind being included. Occasionally, just a few people at a time.

'Happy Birthday again,' James said as his lips met hers. 'It's as bad as you feared, isn't it?'

'I'll forgive you eventually. I do appreciate the effort. Just promise you'll never try anything like this again.'

James smiled. 'I promise. Never. Those were the most stressful months of my life.' His warm lips met hers again. 'For you too. I'm sorry.'

Calls for a speech sparked up around the room. 'Don't make me,' she murmured.

Even though he hated talking in front of people, James stepped up. He was doing more stepping up now, and she was trying not to control everything. They were both works in progress.

James made that noise in his throat. 'Ahh, thank you for coming tonight to celebrate Harriet's birthday, and for keeping it quiet while we planned it. It's hugely appreciated. Some of you will know that Harriet wouldn't let anyone make a fuss over her fortieth. Or any birthday since

I've known her, actually.' He raised his thick eyebrows. 'But so many people love you and wish you well, that we wanted you to know that. So I guess I'd just like to raise a glass to Harriet.'

Then he began to talk just to her. 'You drive me mad, but I know not as mad as I drive you, so I'm grateful every day that you still love me as much as I love you. I love you, Harriet. I admire you, I respect you and, frankly, after two decades I'm still in awe of you. I'm sure nobody would look at us and think "made for each other", but we've rubbed along pretty well, haven't we?' Harriet nodded. 'I think so, too. So, before everyone gets too bored, the reason we're here: to Harriet!'

'To Harriet!' everyone said, holding their glasses aloft.

'To the Snarkersons!' shouted Billie.

'To the Snarkersons,' Harriet said, tipping her glass to James. 'Not everyone's cup of tea, but for us, for some reason, it works.'

Harriet was swept up in another whirlwind of good wishes. There was Marion, laughing with the young butcher. Harriet couldn't be sure, but he seemed impressed that she'd swapped her dungarees for a dress, and mucky boots for little heels. And either the lighting in the room was funny, or Marion was wearing make-up.

Then she spotted Sophie, talking to Molly the masseuse and the Bumblebee Bakery woman. 'You're here!' She threw her arms around her friend. Then she remembered her working hypothesis and smiled warmly at the other women, too. 'Thank you for coming. The cake looks delicious, and . . .' She searched for an equivalent compliment for Molly. 'I look forward to my next massage.' Small talk wasn't so hard after all.

'Were you surprised?' Sophie asked.

'Given how much we've talked this week, I'm surprised you kept it a secret,' she said. Though she hadn't admitted to knowing about the party to Sophie, either, so that made them even.

Somehow, the women seemed to know to leave them to their discussion.

Sophie suddenly smiled at someone over Harriet's shoulder as she sipped her champagne.

'I see you finally got your bubbly,' the woman behind Harriet said. An old man in a three-piece suit stood next to her. Sophie raised her glass to them both.

Then to Harriet, she quietly explained, 'That's the barmaid at the pub. And the man next to her? He's got a girlfriend. And a wife; can you believe it?'

'You know more people here than I do,' Harriet said.

'You might get to know them better.'

'I think I will. How are you doing?'

'Okay, considering.' Sophie took a deep breath. 'Dan's still livid that I'm standing up for myself, though he's being true to form. He sent another a text apologising. Not that it means anything. I know him. He's just trying to get his own way. But he's got bigger problems than me right now. His boss is accusing him of shady stuff again with his clients.'

'He told you that?'

Sophie nodded. 'While he was ranting. According to him it's the world's biggest stitch-up, of course, but you know it's probably not. Poor Dan's not having a very good summer.' She didn't look at all unhappy about that. In fact, she looked rather radiant.

'At least he got a holiday out of it,' Harriet said.

'Here's to holidays.' They touched glasses. 'May they always be this illuminating.'

Harriet watched her friend. 'You seem like a different person now.'

'I feel a million miles away from that woman in the airport who didn't even pack her own suitcase, let alone carry it.'

'Or know where her fake tan came from,' Harriet reminded her.

Sophie pulled a face. 'I'll be buying my own fake tan from now on.'

'And keeping your spices in date, I hope.'

'I'm sorry, Harriet, but that will never be a big deal to me.'

Harriet looked at Sophie, then out across the room at Billie, at James, at her friends and colleagues. Everyone in her world. 'You know what? You're right. Life's too short to worry about little things like that.'

Acknowledgements

I owe so much to my agent, Caroline Hardman, for her superb guidance and always-honest feedback. Thank you. I don't know what I'd do without you. Many thanks, too, to Sam Eades, who brought me into the Orion family, and to my editor, Katie Ellis-Brown, who has been with me every step of the way on this book. Katie, your insight into the story and character development has been tremendous, and so much appreciated.

Project editor extraordinaire, Rosie Pearce, and Jenny Page, my copy-editor, made sure the manuscript was whipped into shape. The behind-the-scenes heroes of the publishing world, your attention to detail ensures a beautiful reading experience for booklovers, and is so valuable.

Thanks to Krystyna Kujawinska and the rights team, who are championing the book around the world, to Charlotte Abrams-Simpson for designing the fantastic, eye-catching cover for it, and to the publicity and marketing teams for getting it in front of readers.

To all the amazing authors who have taken the time to read early copies, share your thoughts and support the launch, I am deeply indebted. I do believe we have the most supportive community imaginable.

I'd also like to pay tribute to the UK's wonderous libraries and enthusiastic, overworked and underpaid librarians. Thanks to you, everyone has the chance to read my books for free. I would encourage booklovers to use them as much as they can. Thanks to the UK's Public Lending Right, we authors get a payment every time you borrow one of our books.

Most of all, thank you to everyone who borrows or buys my books. I wouldn't be an author without you.

And finally, Andrew. Through the publication of every one of my seventeen books, you've given me an ear for bending, a shoulder to lean on and a heart that could not be more perfect.

Credits

Trapeze would like to thank everyone at Orion who worked on the publication of *The Staycation*.

Agent
Caroline Hardman

Editor
Katie Ellis-Brown

Copy-editor
Jenny Page

Proofreader
Donna Hillyer

Editorial Management
Sam Eades
Rosie Pearce
Charlie Panayiotou
Jane Hughes
Alice Davis
Claire Boyle

Audio
Paul Stark
Amber Bates

Contracts
Anne Goddard
Paul Bulos
Jake Alderson

Design
Loulou Clark
Lucie Stericker
Joanna Ridley
Nick May
Clare Sivell
Helen Ewing

Finance
Jennifer Muchan
Jasdip Nandra
Rabale Mustafa

Elizabeth Beaumont
Sue Baker
Tom Costello

Marketing
Jen McMenemy

Production
Claire Keep
Fiona McIntosh

Publicity
Alex Layt

Sales
Laura Fletcher
Victoria Laws
Esther Waters
Lucy Brem
Frances Doyle
Ben Goddard
Georgina Cutler
Jack Hallam
Ellie Kyrke-Smith
Inês Figuiera
Barbara Ronan
Andrew Hally
Dominic Smith
Deborah Deyong

Lauren Buck
Maggy Park
Linda McGregor
Sinead White
Jemimah James
Rachel Jones
Jack Dennison
Nigel Andrews
Ian Williamson
Julia Benson
Declan Kyle
Robert Mackenzie
Imogen Clarke
Megan Smith
Charlotte Clay
Rebecca Cobbold

Operations
Jo Jacobs
Sharon Willis
Lisa Pryde

Rights
Susan Howe
Richard King
Krystyna Kujawinska
Jessica Purdue
Louise Henderson

Help us make the next generation of readers

We – both author and publisher – hope you enjoyed this book. We believe that you can become a reader at any time in your life, but we'd love your help to give the next generation a head start.

Did you know that 9 per cent of children don't have a book of their own in their home, rising to 13 per cent in disadvantaged families*? We'd like to try to change that by asking you to consider the role you could play in helping to build readers of the future.

We'd love you to think of sharing, borrowing, reading, buying or talking about a book with a child in your life and spreading the love of reading. We want to make sure the next generation continue to have access to books, wherever they come from.

And if you would like to consider donating to charities that help fund literacy projects, find out more at **www.literacytrust.org.uk** and **www.booktrust.org.uk**.

THANK YOU

*As reported by the National Literacy Trust